The COLLECTED SHORT STORIES
of HARRIETTE SIMPSON ARNOW

T0288254

The COLLECTED SHORT STORIES *of* HARRIETTE SIMPSON ARNOW

Sandra L. Ballard *&* Haeja K. Chung, *editors*

Michigan State University Press • *East Lansing*

Michigan State University Press is a member of the Green Press Initiative and is committed to developing and encouraging ecologically responsible publishing practices. For
more information about the Green Press Initiative and the use of recycled paper in
book publishing, please visit *www.greenpressinitiative.com*.

♾ The paper used in this publication meets the minimum requirements
of ANSI/NISO Z39.48-1992 (R 1997) (Permanence of Paper).

Michigan State University Press
East Lansing, Michigan 48823-5245

Printed and bound in the United States of America.

11   10   09   08   07   06   05   1   2   3   4   5   6   7   8   9   10

LIBRARY OF CONGRESS CATALOGING-IN-PUBLICATION DATA
Arnow, Harriette Louisa Simpson, 1908–
[Short stories]
The collected short stories of Harriette Simpson Arnow / Sandra L. Ballard and Haeja K. Chung, editors.
p. cm.
Includes bibliographical references.
ISBN 0-87013-756-5 (pbk. : alk. paper)
1. United States—Social life and customs—Fiction. 2. Kentucky—Social life and customs—Fiction.
3. Michigan—Social life and customs—Fiction. 4. Ohio—Social life and customs—Fiction.
I. Ballard, Sandra L. II. Chung, Haeja K. III. Title.
PS3501.R64A6 2005
813'.52—dc22
2005014237

Cover design by Heather Truelove Aiston
Book design/composition by Sharp Des!gns, Lansing, Michigan

Visit Michigan State University Press on the World Wide Web at *www.msupress.msu.edu*

Contents

vii   Introduction

KENTUCKY: THE 1920S

 3   Winky Creek's New Song
10   Dreams Come True
19   The Goat Who Was a Cow

OHIO & KENTUCKY: THE 1930S

33   Marigolds and Mules
40   A Mess of Pork
50   Ketchup-Making Saturday
60   The Washerwoman's Day
66   Zekie, The Hill-billy Mouse
72   An Episode in the Life of Ezekial Whitmore
78   The Two Hunters
88   No Lady
92   Tin Cup
100   Home Coming
105   Blessed—Blessed

115   The First Ride

121   Almost Two Thousand Years

131   Fra Lippi and Me

140   White Collar Woman

150   Failure

159   Sugar Tree Holler

MICHIGAN: THE 1940S & AFTER

185   King Devil's Bargain

196   The Hunter

209   The Un-American Activities of Miss Prink

226   Love?

237   Interruptions to School at Home

251   Notes

257   Works Cited

259   Acknowledgments

Introduction

HARRIETTE SIMPSON ARNOW's short stories have been on library shelves for years. To locate them, readers would have to search through university archives and dusty back issues of magazines and journals ranging from *Southern Review, Esquire,* and *The Atlantic Monthly* to little literary magazines that are now out of print. Written early in her career for the most part, these stories remain among her less-examined writings because most of them are unpublished and they have never been collected together. Yet readers will find flashes of brilliance in Arnow's short stories, clearly revealing her artistic vision and narrative skill; they serve as the harbinger for her later fiction. These stories show her long-standing interest in both agrarian and urban communities, the sharpening of her social conscience, and her strong commitment to creating credible and complex characters. These stories lead readers from gravel roads to city pavement and open layers of Arnow's development as a novelist to expose the full range of her contributions to American literature.

The twenty-five stories in this collection are presented roughly in the order in which they were written, interspersing the ten previously published stories with the fifteen unpublished ones. Not all of Arnow's stories achieve the same level of narrative success, but in reading them readers may trace her evolving artistry and sociopolitical consciousness. As editors, we have corrected Arnow's misspellings and created uniform spellings of characters' names and other words, adding notes wherever we believed explanations to be necessary or useful. Being careful not to alter her meaning, we have standardized Arnow's punctuation to some extent; most changes involve deleting or inserting commas to ease readability. To highlight the significance of Arnow's journey to maturity as a fiction writer, we have organized this collection of short stories into three sections: Kentucky: The 1920s; Ohio and Kentucky: The 1930s; and Michigan: The 1940s and After.

For consistency, we refer to the author as Arnow throughout, regardless of her age and marital status, even though several of the stories were published under the name Harriette L. Simpson or H. L. Simpson.

KENTUCKY: THE 1920S

In the first section, we present three unpublished stories Arnow wrote in her teens while living in Kentucky. Born in 1908, she grew up in south central Kentucky, in Burnside, a small town located on the Big South Fork of the Cumberland River, where she first tried her hand at writing fiction.

Because of her age, she was perhaps oblivious to the "literary America" of the 1920s, when the short story lingered in the shadow of the novel despite the proliferation of diverse short stories ranging from Henry James's "art" stories to O. Henry's formulaic magazine stories. According to Thomas A. Gullason, "An impressive renaissance was also clearly taking place in the short story; it seemed hardly noticeable because of the attention being given to the novelist, poets, and playwrights. Short story writers were considered a lesser breed."[1]

Arnow created at least two fairy tales or fantasy stories before she graduated from high school at the age of sixteen in 1924. She remembered her first was in response to a fourth-grade assignment:

At the time I wanted a desk, a place that I could fill with whatever—all my scribblings and everything that I wanted to put in it—and nobody would touch it. But instead of writing about a desk I might have, I imagined I was an old desk and told of various people who'd written on me and used me . . . and the teacher praised it. . . . I was tickled to death, so proud.[2]

When she was in high school, she wrote the fairy tale, "Little Winky's Creek," the first she ever offered for publication. Although the editors of *Child Life* did not accept the story, they liked her wildflower characters enough to encourage her to submit other stories to them.[3] A version of that story, "Winky Creek's New Song," written around 1922, opens this collection. Another unpublished story, "Dreams Come True," written around 1924 when she lived in Burnside, is an adolescent work, but we have included it here because it demonstrates that at a very young age Arnow had developed empathy with the poor. "The Goat Who Was a Cow," also written in Burnside, perhaps a few years later, after she had begun teaching, is a comedy of errors—a tomboy's tale of mistaken identity and moonshine whiskey, set in the back hills of Kentucky.

After high school, Arnow packed up her writing tablets and attended Berea College, where she spent two years and earned a teaching certificate. She often told interviewers that she met no one at Berea who was interested in writing. She complained of having no peers who enjoyed writing and admitted that she had occasionally written essays for other students. Years later, in *What Berea Meant to Me*, she described some encouragement she had received from one of her English professors, Dr. Weeks, who helped her to have the "courage to try to write, not of long ago far off things but of the world I knew."[4]

Arnow's first teaching experience was in a one-room school in Pulaski County, Kentucky, where she boarded with the family of one of her pupils and became acquainted with the community, an experience that inspired her writing career more than her teaching. However, teaching, not writing, was a family tradition. Arnow's mother, Mollie Jane Denney Simpson, thought teaching was one of the few "respectable" occupations for women. Mollie Simpson had herself been a teacher before her marriage, as had Harriette's father, Elias Thomas Simpson, who eventually had to find more financially lucrative work to support his family.

After two years as a teacher, Harriette again became a student, attending the University of Louisville from 1928 to 1931. While a member of a literary sorority there, she began writing stories that were, according to a classmate, different from those of other students. While others wrote "in a terse, cynical style" and imitated or parodied well-known writers, "Harriette wrote of her experiences in her hill-country: of riding muleback on mountain trails, her love of vegetation and animals of her Eastern Kentucky land." Her writing was full of "blooming plum-trees" and hill people.[5] She graduated with a B.S. in education in 1931.

Between 1931 and 1934, primarily to please her mother, Harriette taught again in rural Kentucky schools and then in Louisville. But the job took its toll on her. She wasn't happy with the contrast between city schools and rural ones. In Louisville classrooms, she had to cope with the new practice of dividing children into groups by their IQs. She was assigned to teach the new subject of "social studies," and she had to deal with unruly children who broke her glasses.[6] Never entirely at home in the classroom, Arnow grew impatient with teaching because she longed to spend more time writing.

Having spent five years as a teacher, she was ready to devote herself full time to being a writer. Arnow said, "I would rather starve as a writer than a teacher."[7]

OHIO AND KENTUCKY: THE 1930S

The second section introduces Arnow's most prolific period as a short story writer, when the cultural and literary renaissance that began in the 1920s ushered in the "golden age" of the American short story. James G. Watson says, "The years 1930–1945, from the start of the Great Depression through the end of World War II, mark the most prolific outpouring of American short fiction in the history of our national literature. It is a climactic period, representing the high point of an era that H. E. Bates, in his 1941 book *The Modern Short Story,* described as a modern American renaissance begun by Sherwood Anderson, taken up by Ernest Hemingway, and carried into the 1930s by William Faulkner, Erskine Caldwell, Katherine Anne Porter, and William Saroyan" (and Zora Neale Hurston).[8] Harriette Arnow set a time limit on her experiment in short story writing: she would give herself five years to write. She also promised herself that she would not write more than five pages of a story without finishing it: "I let myself try numberless pages or so of this and that, but if I do five I will have to finish it."[9]

All of the stories in this section were written in the 1930s, when she lived in Cincinnati, Ohio, and in Covington, Kentucky. According to letters in the Arnow Special Collection at the University of Kentucky Libraries, Galena Hopkins, Arnow's agent in 1936–37, encouraged the author to write short stories while the manuscript of her second novel, *Between the Flowers,* was circulating. Although most of these stories are set in Kentucky hill communities and explore an agrarian theme, in at least three stories she introduces urban settings and a new theme of the struggles of alienated urban people.[10] Clearly, living in Cincinnati during the Depression helped sharpen her already keen social conscience. To a certain extent, Arnow joined other writers at that time in expressing "the unique social realities of the Depression," drawing resources both from rural Kentucky and the city.[11]

In particular, women suffering under patriarchal hill culture and organized religion receive Arnow's special attention. While delineating the stifling and restrictive feminine space, she depicted not only victimized women but also their private, often inarticulate, and futile war to control their own destinies. By writing about women's cultural subjugation as well as their independent thoughts, Arnow makes a unique contribution to American feminist literature. According to Watson, the predominant subject matter during this period is what R. W. B. Lewis calls "the central figure in 'an emergent American myth,' . . . the American Adam."[12] It is unfortunate that Lewis did not look further to investigate the descendents of Eve in many writings done by women, including Arnow, who did not "appropriate Adamic materials as naturally available, traditional matter of American literary expression."[13]

While none of the story manuscripts are dated, the return addresses on the stories offer some clues about their chronology. Upon arriving in Cincinnati in the fall of 1934, she rented a room, where she remained for almost a year, until relocating across the Ohio River to Covington, Kentucky. She moved back and forth until February of 1939, when she began receiving mail at a Cincinnati post office.

When she began her "five-year plan" in Cincinnati, Arnow, like many writers at the time, took advantage of the proliferating little magazines. Watson says, "the number of new little magazines published . . . rose from eighteen in 1931 and fifteen in 1932 to forty-three in 1933 and a remarkable forty-nine in 1934."[14] She had some immediate success, placing her first story, "Marigolds and Mules" (1935), in a short-lived little literary magazine, *Kosmos: Dynamic Stories of Today*. Then followed several rejections for stories such as "Crazy Blanket" before another little literary magazine, *The New Talent*, accepted "A Mess of Pork" (1935). Critic Glenda Hobbs reports, "*The New Talent* received more appreciative letters for this story in a fortnight than it had for any other piece of fiction to appear in that publication."[15] *The New Talent* editor, David Bernstein, wrote to Arnow that, judging from the letters he had received, her story was "making literary history"; readers were praising it and predicting its writer would go far.[16]

Apparently anticipating criticism for her story's grim reality, Harriette Simpson defended her work by writing to the editor, "I cannot preach, . . . and I will not go two blocks out of the way to put a belch or a bedbug in a story."[17] While she wanted to write realistic and powerful fiction, she steadfastly refused to degrade or demean her characters in order to make them more "marketable" to Depression-era editors who were looking for stereotypes they recognized or "proletarian" fiction about impoverished mountain people.

In December 1935, she received a notice that the renowned *Southern Review* wanted her story "The Washerwoman's Day" (1936). Though the editors, Cleanth Brooks and Robert Penn Warren, had rejected "Ketchup-Making Saturday," which features a strong woman like Gertie in *The Dollmaker*, Brooks assured her: "we congratulate ourselves" on acquiring "Washerwoman's Day."[18] It is the first story for which Arnow was paid. She received a check for $25 and felt "on top of the world." Dealing with hypocrisy in a small town, this story has become her most frequently anthologized one.[19]

Softening the disappointment of rejection letters and returned stories, her first novel *Mountain Path* was released in August 1936 and received a number of favorable reviews. Despite its success, she continued to write short fiction. In fact, her agent, Galina Hopkins, wanted Arnow to publish as many stories as possible so that the reading public would be familiar with her name when her second novel appeared.

Arnow wrote a number of stories for young readers in 1937. A personal notebook in the Arnow Special Collections at the University of Kentucky Libraries dates several stories in 1937: "Dog Story," "The Last Snow," "Pie Supper" (in parentheses she added "Juvenile" beside this title), and "Mouse Story." The Arnow archives contain no stories with these titles, though "Mouse Story" could be an early version of one of the two stories in this volume about a "hillbilly" mouse named Zekie—"Zekie, The Hill-billy Mouse," written in 1938, and "An Episode in the Life of Ezekial Whitmore," probably written in 1939. The latter was written before Arnow married, likely while she worked for the Federal Writer's Bureau on WPA guidebooks.

Arnow's stories became increasingly ironic. In 1938, *Esquire* purchased "The Hunters," which was eventually published as "The Two Hunters," a chilling story of a seventeen-year-old boy's confrontation with a deputy sheriff. At the time, *Esquire* did not accept submissions from women, and its editors had no idea that writer H. L. Simpson was not a man. Years later, she admitted in an interview, "it worried me a little, that big lie, but I thought if they wanted a story, let them have it."[20] Like other magazines whose editors complained of a glut of "rural" stories, *Esquire* must have accepted more than it could use, for editors held the story in backlog until it was published in July 1942. *Esquire* paid her $125 for this story. The contributor's notes at the back of the magazine include a photo of "H. L. Simpson," actually a photo of one of her brothers-in-law. It was her little joke on a publisher that discriminated against women.

She wrote at least four other stories in 1938. Two of them, published posthumously in the *Appalachian Heritage,* continue with agrarian settings and focus on entrapped female characters' vague internal stirrings for freedom. "Blessed—Blessed" was published in 1988 and "The First Ride" in 1989. Two other stories introduce Arnow's new urban proletarian subject; despite its masterful narrative technique, "Almost Two Thousand Years" remained unpublished until now, but "Fra Lippi and Me" was published in the *Georgia Review* (1979).

All of these stories introduce themes that recur in Arnow's novels. Regardless of the genre, as Glenda Hobbs says, "Arnow has been particularly drawn to stories involving a character's struggle against social pressures or political, economic, and religious forces that threaten one's integrity or freedom, even one's life."[21] Despite her social conscience, however, Arnow did not blindly subscribe to proletarian naturalism of the period; she said to an interviewer, "I wanted to write of life in America without the ugly realism of Mr. [Erskine] Caldwell."[22] She often proclaimed herself a realist, and various critics noted her "rare gift of realism." She was a regionalist in the best sense of the word, "placing regionalism in the realistic mode."[23] Katherine Anne Porter claimed that "all true art is provincial in the most realistic sense," and Flannery O'Connor stated, "The best American fiction has always been regional."[24] These writers no doubt would have admired Arnow's rendering of the Kentucky hills. Depicting the hardships endured by men and women in rural Kentucky, she also challenged the image of the Edenic pastoral South advanced by the Southern Renaissance, a literary movement lasting from the 1920s to the 1940s.

After meeting Harold Arnow while working for the Federal Writer's Project in Cincinnati, Harriette Simpson began to long to live close to the land herself. Harold, a former Chicago newspaperman and WPA co-worker, shared her dream. The story "Sugar Tree Holler" is a fictionalized account of their courtship. Like the character Abel, Harold Arnow had lived in Alaska during the early 1930s. One of Harold's favorite relatives was Mike (Myer) Abel, a Cincinnati artist. The story was probably written in Cincinnati in 1939, shortly before or after the couple's marriage. "Sugar Tree Holler" is "extremely autobiographical," according to their daughter Marcella Arnow. It focuses on the meeting and courtship of Abel and Susie, two young WPA workers whose lives closely resemble those of the Arnows, who worked for the WPA during 1938–39 and married on 23 March 1939. In Arnow's only epistolary story, the courtship unfolds as her narrator, Susie Hardwick, surreptitiously types personal letters at work, shifting suddenly to her assigned project whenever her supervisor might be looking over her shoulder.

When the Arnows moved to 150 acres joining the Cumberland National Forest and began living as subsistence farmers and writers, Harriette Arnow began another five-year experiment, though she did not consciously set a time limit from the outset. In later years, she often remarked on her time "subsisting," commenting that little time remained for writing in the early 1940s. They also faced tragedy in their home in the hills. They lost two children. Thus Harriette Arnow shared firsthand the experience of many hill women who knew the pain of walking by tiny graves in the family cemetery.

As World War II heated up, Harold left Kentucky to find work. He moved to Detroit, where he secured wartime housing for his young family. Harriette, their daughter Marcella, and soon their son Thomas lived in the cramped quarters that Arnow imagined as the home for her character Gertie Nevels. She finished her novel *Hunter's Horn* there in Detroit and worked on *The Dollmaker.*

MICHIGAN: THE 1940S AND AFTER

In the third section of this collection, we have gathered a small group of short stories Arnow wrote and published while she lived in Michigan, from

1944 until her death in 1986. As scholar Ray B. West Jr. comments, Southern writers of short fiction, notably Eudora Welty, "continued their dominance into the 1940s," but during this period the short story declined in popularity. West calls attention to "the low total output and the apparent inability of the best writers of this generation to develop. And the market for short stories was not favorable for beginning writers."[25]

Arnow was not one of the frustrated short story writers. By this time the agrarian and urban themes she experimented with in her short stories had come to fruition in her novels, including *Hunter's Horn* (1949), *The Doll-maker* (1954), and *The Weedkiller's Daughter* (1970). Obviously, the novel was her passion, and that partially explains why Arnow rarely wrote short stories later in her career. She preferred the medium that allowed for fuller characterization, and she once said:

> I wish I could turn out short books. I don't seem able to. It gets longer and longer. I start out with a character and there's a family or friends, and a community, and they all talk, and this happens . . . and oh God, I'd have to write about a person living alone in a cave, I think, to get a short book.[26]

William Faulkner, who competed successfully against Arnow for the National Book Award in 1955, shared the same passion for the novel. Despite writing more than one hundred short stories between 1930 and 1950, Faulkner preferred the novel to the short story that "demands a nearer absolute exactitude."[27] Although he wrote stories not related to the novel, "Sometimes Faulkner used short stories as preliminary sketches for ideas, characters, and techniques he later appropriated for his novels. . . . At other times he used stories as separate episodes as chapters in extended fictions."[28] The same can be said about Arnow's writing strategies. She attempted to publish three chapters of *Hunter's Horn* as short stories. Of those, "The Hunter," a variation of Chapter Four, appeared in the *Atlantic Monthly* in 1944.[29]

Throughout her career, Arnow sustained her interest in history, and living in Michigan's industrial city of Detroit during World War II helped sharpen Arnow's focus on social and political issues. Her protagonist in the "Un-American Activities of Miss Prink" faces the dilemma of a conscientious history teacher who suffers from the prejudice of her pupils (and their parents) during the McCarthy-era "red scare," prejudices Arnow explores more fully in her novel *The Weedkiller's Daughter* (1970). Written in Ann Arbor, Michigan, where the author lived from 1950 until her death in 1986, the story remains a working draft with blank spaces where some characters' names were to be added, though Arnow's liberal left-wing political orientation during this period is clear. In a 1962 letter to Michigan activist Jo Gomon, Arnow deplores the eroded civil liberties in this country. Her letters in the 1960s indicate that she was an active American Civil Liberties Union member who voted enthusiastically for Eugene McCarthy for president in 1968. Arnow's political ideals as well as her earlier experiences as a teacher undoubtedly gave her empathy for Miss Prink.

Not surprisingly, as a writer with a strong sense of place, Arnow reclaims her kinship with Kentucky in her later writing, as demonstrated in her last published novel, *The Kentucky Trace* (1974). In the final short story published during her lifetime, "Interruptions to School at Home" in *Adena: A Journal of the History and Culture of the Ohio Valley* (1980), Arnow offers readers a glimpse into her final novel-in-progress, *Belle*. Set in the same region of Kentucky as her first three novels, the story focuses on a family during the Civil War. The matriarch, Belle Barstow, reminiscent of Gertie Nevels, faces a range of challenges through which she creatively tries to hold her family together.

The stories in this collection reveal the range of Arnow's short fiction, her dedication to creating characters that she obviously cared about, and her commitment to exploring themes of personal freedom and social justice—all of which combine to make her short stories important to the body of her work. While the stories themselves are somewhat uneven, some rendering a character or a conflict in more memorable terms than others, they ultimately reveal her central concerns as a writer. As Haeja Chung explains, "these short stories are crucial to Arnow scholarship: they serve as the barometer of Arnow's full range of artistic achievements, illustrating the central thematic and artistic concerns that would come to fruition in her later novels."[30]

Harriette Arnow once admitted, "I have encountered many characters, scenes, and episodes that elude[d] me when I tried to get them on paper." In an article she wrote to offer encouragement to struggling writers, she

told the story of one dark rainy summer evening when she was a child sent
to bring the cows in; she "found a beautiful hunk of red-green fox fire":

> I ran with it into the kitchen, but under the lamplight, there was nothing
> but a soggy chunk of wood.
>
> A lot of my writing is like that: fox fire in my head, but soggy wood on
> paper; but I am learning; mostly now I know that fox fire is fox fire and
> never waste time trying to make it shine in the light. But maybe somebody
> with even less time than I, has that magic it takes to make fox fire shine in
> all lights and weathers.[31]

We hope that this collection will please readers and scholars alike and
contribute to a new and renewed appreciation of Harriette Simpson
Arnow's fiction.

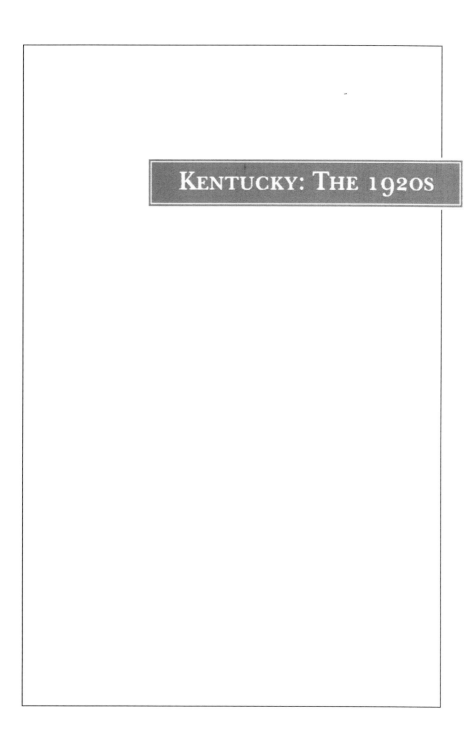

KENTUCKY: THE 1920S

Winky Creek's New Song

Arnow's typewritten note accompanying the manuscript of this story explains,

> There was a tin trunk at my mother's in which for many years I kept among other 'precious' things my first story and later the manuscript of *Mountain Path* but now can not even locate the trunk; there has been much moving on my part, and some on hers. I thought I had seen the manuscript some years ago; the story was written when I was in the fourth grade as I recall,[1] but it along with all my early manuscripts has disappeared. This fairy tale is the earliest I could find; written sometime while I was in high school; I remember I sent it to *Child Life,* and they retyped it for me, and I think corrected most mistakes in spelling.

Arnow later remarked that she had written it during her junior year in high school and surreptitiously typed it single-spaced on her mother's stationery before mailing it to the only magazine for children to which her mother subscribed. When it was returned, typed double-spaced on standard typing paper, a letter from *Child Life* editors explained that it had been re-typed because it had been torn in handling. The editors had liked the story and asked to see more of her work. Years later, Arnow realized that the editors had tried not only to send her encouragement (though she hadn't yet learned that a letter was much better than a rejection slip), but they also had shown her the way to prepare a story for submission to a publisher.

This story, published here for the first time, is the earliest example we have of Arnow's initial efforts to write fiction.

*T*he little valley where Winky Creek begins its long race to the river is usually one of the quietest places on earth, quieter than an empty church, even. But on a certain breezy, blowsy afternoon in mid-April you should have heard it: that is, if you have fairy ears, and can understand flower talk. The Hepaticas and Anemones simply made the early butterflies' ears ache with their loud and breathless conversation. Jack-in-the-Pulpit was preaching uncommonly loud in order to be heard above the din. Even the tiny, blue-eyed Forget-me-nots were forgetting their shyness, and screaming across a fallen twig to Dogtooth Violet.

But I'm sure you will want to know about whom they were talking, so I won't waste any more time in naming the gossips. The subject of conversation was Lady Larkspur, that dignified forest cousin of tall blue Delphinium that grows in your grandmother's garden. The other flower people in Winky Creek's Cove, even though they are famed for their sweet dispositions, often made eyes at my Ladies Larkspur, and called them conceited and unneighborly. But I don't much wonder at this because these pretty flower ladies are just a little stiff and unbending. Perhaps they are a bit too proud of their grand cousins, blooming in so many fair gardens: just as you sometimes like to put on a few airs when talking of some wonderful aunt of yours, who sends those thrilling presents at Christmas time. But this isn't telling you what the flowers were saying about Lady Larkspur, which was very important indeed.

"I have always said," Double Anemone was saying, "that the Larkspur Ladies had a touch of royal blood, and now," nodding its head like a wise old uncle, "this proves it."

Jack-in-the-Pulpit gave a squeaky, "Humph," and announced that big names didn't always mean big people.

"But such a wonderful name," a pale Hepatica enviously sighed.

"Have the Lady Larkspurs' names been changed, or why all this hubbub?" a puzzled Breeze Boy, who had just blown in, wanted to know.

"Oh, you've never heard all about the great to-do the big man creatures made over her Ladyship this morning?" Lavender Hepatica asked in a shocked voice; for she, being a simple thing, supposed it had traveled over the whole world.

"One hears nothing when smothered in a cloud prison, as I have been this blessed morning," grumbled the Breeze Boy.

"If you'll promise not to make us jig, or whisk away just when I get to the most important part, I'll tell you the whole thing," Dogtooth volunteered.

But without waiting for an answer he began: "Well, this morning very early before Father Sun had chased the Dew children home, there came two great man creatures. One was young; but the other, the one who did all the talking, seemed nigh unto half as old as our Guardian Oak. He had a gray beard, and carried a book of a thing, which he wrote in every once in awhile. But the strangest thing was the way they behaved. Would you believe it? Those creatures walked right past the Hepaticas and the Anemones and the Reverend Jack and the Bluets and myself, and never even seemed to see us."

At these words all the flower people mentioned, looked very aggrieved, and nearly nodded their heads off to show that Dogtooth was telling facts.

"But the worst part, the most unbelievable thing," Dogtooth continued sadly, "was the way they walked right up to the Larkspur Ladies, and then acted as if they were the only flower people in this valley."

"Hateful old things," a Hepatica said so spitefully that the Reverend Jack was forced to give her a reproving squeak.

"Don't interrupt the speaker please," said the Breeze Boy, now greatly interested, and with no thought of skipping away.

"But it is just as Miss Hepatica said. It does seem as if those man creatures might have given us just a bit of notice; for I am sure we deserve it as much as those conceited ladies. But what do you think! The man creature with the great beard sat down by them, and after looking at them very closely for a long time, wrote in a book of a thing he had. The younger one drew Lady White Larkspur's picture. Yes, really and truly drew her picture. I know, because Dogwood looked over his shoulder, and then told us all about it."

"No wonder their Ladyships stand so stiff and straight this afternoon," observed the Breeze Boy.

"Hurry up, Dogtooth, and tell about what the bearded man said," cried Lavender Larkspur.

"I'm getting to that part," said Dogtooth, getting impatient with so much interruption. "The bearded man said something about a book. Yes, they are going to put my Lady Larkspur's picture in a book, with things in it about the Larkspur family. Did you ever hear of such a thing? And would you believe it, he said that White Larkspur's name wasn't Larkspur at all but—say it, Reverend Jack, your tongue is more limber than mine."

"Ranunculaceae Delphinium tricorne," said Jack all in one breath, and with a great air.

"Wonderful! Wonderful!" the flowers all exclaimed together. Though they had already heard it many times in the course of the day, they still delighted in its tongue-twisting syllables. Even the Breeze Boy was greatly impressed, and quickly found himself grumbling because of his own short name. Having heard the gossip, he flew away, whispering Lady Larkspur's name as he went, though he made a sorry mess of it.

The afternoon lengthened until the Shadow Giants touched the feet of the Guardian Oak with their gray fingers. Still the flower people, excepting the Larkspurs of course, talked of nothing but the wonderful name, and the fame that had come to its owners. Each felt just the teeniest bit jealous of the Larkspurs, but was too proud to say so.

Two whole days passed, a very long time in the life of a flower, and still the flowers tried to whisper the great name to each other, and thought constantly of their famous neighbor. And oh my! You should have seen the behavior of the Larkspurs. They stood stiff and straight as off-with-your-head queens, scorning to speak to anyone less important than Dogwood; and actually sniffing when the Master Breezes begged the favor of a dance. The Reverend Jack was greatly troubled by such unflowerlike behavior, and warned the rest of his flock of the evils of false pride.

The third day came, but scarcely had Father Sun touched Winky Creek's bottom, before the two strange man creatures were seen coming. But wonder of wonders, instead of going to the Larkspurs as everybody expected them to do, they stopped by the Hepaticas. Everybody in Winky Creek fairly held his breath while the two man creatures talked about Lavender Hepatica. Then the gray beard began writing, and the young one [began] to draw her. She held herself very straight and still, so that the picture might be a good one.

"And what is the name of this pretty thing?" Hepatica heard the artist ask.

But instead of answering "Hepatica" as expected, the gray beard mumbled, "Ranunculaceae Hepatica acutiloba," through his beard.

When Lady White Larkspur heard this, she nearly fainted and would have fallen had not a husky Breeze Boy stood at her back. Poor conceited thing, she had supposed that hers was the grandest name in the whole world; and now here was one of her common neighbors with one much like it, only longer.

But Lavender Hepatica, sensible little thing that she was, did not feel at all proud; but secretly decided that she would still be just plain 'Hepatica' to her friends.

When the gray beard and the artist had finished with Hepatica, they did not leave, but went to Double Anemone. He, too, had his picture drawn, and was given a great name. I won't tell you what it was, because I don't want you to risk a sprained tongue by trying to say it.

All day the man creatures worked. By the time the Shadow Giants came, each of the flowers I have mentioned in this tale had been given a great three-piece name; and each was trying to say his, and sometimes getting fearfully mixed up. None of the flowers were half so proud as Lady Larkspur had been. In fact, some of them looked downright troubled.

"What ails you, brother?" Reverend Jack asked Double Anemone.

"I have just been wondering what David and Baby Joe will do when they learn what my real name is. They can't possibly ever say it."

Now Baby Joe and David were the two children who came so often to see the flowers, and now and then gently pick a few to carry to their mother.

"I have thought of that, too," Lavender Hepatica spoke up. "They can't say mine either. Besides, I like to hear Baby Joe call me 'Patica.'"

"We'll just keep our long names a secret, and not use them except on formal—"

At that moment a Shadow Giant gently touched the speaker and his listeners, and they were forced to go to bed. However, some of them did not sleep very well, but tried to say their new names in their sleep.

Next morning Double Anemone was awakened by something he

thought sounded strangely like a groan. Surprised at such a sound, he listened again. This time he heard Tiniest Forget-me-not actually give a great big groan. Such a terrible groan it was that it awakened Dogtooth also; both asked in the same breath what the matter was.

"My head, oh my poor head, it aches," gasped the sufferer.

"You mean to say you have a headache!" exclaimed Double Anemone. "How awful! I never knew of anyone in our valley to have such a thing before."

"It's all because of that horrid new name of mine. Last night I forgot part of it, and kept trying and trying to remember what it was. I've tried so hard my brains are sick," and here poor Forget-me-not was forced to groan some more.

"Oh you poor thing. Don't ever think of that hateful name any more. Bluet is much nicer. My, but you're looking frightfully pale. Double Anemone, what does one do for a headache? I never saw such a thing before."

But Double Anemone knew as little about headaches as Dogtooth; for aches and pains of any kind were almost unknown in Winky Creek's valley. I don't know what they would have done, had not the Guardian Oak heard Bluet's groans. He, being very old, was wise in such matters, and sent a white butterfly to fan her poor head. A Breeze Boy brought a bit of star dust for the patient to take. Tiniest Forget-me-not quickly began to feel better; but still she sobbed now and then because she had forgotten her name. A kind-hearted Breeze Boy ran to ask the Reverend Jack what Bluet's name was. "Good morning, Jack," he called out cheerily. "Little Bluet has forgotten her name. She has made herself sick trying to remember it, and wants you to tell her. You know all their names, don't you?"

Then the Breeze Boy got the shock of his life: Jack did not answer. "Are you deaf, or just stuck up like the Lady Larkspurs?" At this Jack looked pained and acted very queerly. The Breeze Boy, now greatly alarmed, stepped up to him and gently shook him.

"I can't talk," Jack faintly whispered in the hoarsest, weakest voice imaginable. Then little by little, and in a very strange low voice, he told the sad story: "Last night I tried to say all the new names three times, so that I could remember them. At the end of the second time, my voice just left me, and my tongue was so twisted it wouldn't move. Oh those names.

Those hateful, hateful names." And here poor Jack looked ready to cry, but didn't because he couldn't.

In no time at all, the terrible news of what the new names had caused was over all the valley. The flowers decided to hold a council, and see what was to be done. Things were getting worse all the time: Double Anemone was complaining of a slight dizziness, and Lavender Hepatica said her great name was weighing her down.

You may be surprised when you learn what the Flower people did with all those names they had thought they wanted so badly. However, the Guardian Oak said they did a very wise thing when they had the Breeze Boys gather up all those grand names, and put them under a flat stone at the bottom of Winky Creek's deepest pool. Yes, they really did that, and when it was all finished they were so happy they danced for two hours.

You may think the new names were forgotten by everyone in the valley, but you are mistaken. Sometimes of a winter's day, when the flowers are safely asleep and Winky is a great rushing yellow stream with many voices, he says the names over and over: Ranunculaceae Delphinium tricorne, Araceae Arisaema triphyllum, Boraginaceae Myosotis laxa, Ranunculaceae Hepatica acutibola, and so on and on.

Dreams Come True

This story was written while Harriette Simpson lived in Burnside, Kentucky. It has never before been published.

———⊶⊷———

"Ann, have you heard the latest?" Jeanette sang out, as Ann and her younger sister Willie entered the kitchen. Not giving her sister time to answer, Jeanette continued: "You know those awful Godbys. Well, Mrs. Godby sent her little boy up here to know if you wouldn't be so kind as to come down and cook her children something to eat. Her husband is still in bed with pneumonia, and she got up too soon after this two-weeks-old baby was born and has taken a relapse."

"What did you tell the child?" Ann asked.

"Naturally, we told him to tell his mama you were busy and couldn't come."

"That woman certainly has her nerve," said Sue indignantly. "The very idea of asking people like us to come down and work for those trashy Godbys."

"It would be terrible to cook in such a filthy place, but still I can't help but feel sorry for that family. They have had sickness all winter." Ann was always more sympathetic with people in distress than her more sophisticated sisters.

"Oh, Ann, don't be silly and think this is just one more form of social service. What would the neighbors think if you were to go down there?" Jeanette remonstrated.

Ann said nothing to this and the subject was dropped; the talk [changed] into other channels: high school basketball, a certain story in a favorite magazine, doings at the office where Jeanette worked, and comments of Sue's latest beau. The Bertram girls lived with their widowed mother in a small town, in the northeastern part of Kentucky, called Rothington. The Bertram family was very much like any of the other millions of decent, up right, church going families scattered over the world. They were rather poor, but as Mrs. Bertram was so fond of saying, came of one of the South's proudest and most aristocratic families. Of the four daughters, Sue and Willie were still in high school; Jeanette, the oldest of the four, did stenographic and secretarial work, while Ann had chosen teaching for her career. After two years of college study, Ann had decided to teach a year before finishing her studies. Her school being a rural school, and consequently of a shorter term than those in town, she was for the time unemployed save as a helper to her mother in the house work.

The other members of the family often spoke of Ann as being peculiar and full of queer notions. On more than one occasion she had been scolded by her mother and laughingly ridiculed by her sisters, because of some contribution made or work done for certain of the many destitute families around her home. While still in high school she had all but created a family scene by helping some older, public spirited women clean and fumigate the home of the shiftless Brays, while the whole family was down with typhoid. In spite of the severe rebuke called forth by this act, during the remainder of the epidemic she spent her spare time in visiting various sources of water supply in the outlying districts of Rothington. From these different places she collected samples of the water and sent it to the state board of health to be examined. Sometimes it was heartbreaking to have the results show a high count of the germs, and in many cases, see the owners of such a water supply listen stupidly to reports, and stubbornly continue to use the water. The local doctors, the only two within a radius of more than ten miles, did not greatly encourage vaccination of any kind to those ignorant and superstitious families. The doctors themselves were too nearly worked to death to preach vaccinations and sanitation.

However, Ann never became discouraged; not even when Mrs. Newcomb, mother of nine children, persisted in ignoring her plea that little Jimmy with his crooked feet be sent to an institution where his feet could be straightened at no cost to his mother. In spite of everything Ann had her dream, a dream of a time when things should be different. In college, while studying sociology and rural hygiene, the dream had grown brighter and assumed a more tangible form. A sympathetic instructor in college was the only person who knew of her hopes and plans; her mother would have laughed at them, while the minister of her church was too busy with other matters to have time to talk of sore eyed children and tubercular milch cows.

When the dinner dishes were washed, the younger girls studying, Jeanette gossiping at the home of a girlfriend, Ann found herself thinking of the Godby family instead of reading the book she held in her lap. It wouldn't hurt anything, she decided, for her to run down there tomorrow, take them some cooked food and maybe cook the children some dinner. She glanced apprehensively at her mother; it would take much explaining and persuasion to win her half-hearted approval. Ann was the sort of girl who did nothing in direct opposition to her parent's will.

"Mother, is there anything special you want me to do tomorrow?" she at length asked.

"Nothing that I know of, why?" her mother asked suspiciously.

"I thought that if you didn't need me, I would cook something and take it down to the Godby family."

"Ann, are you never going to get over these fool notions. Let that woman's relatives, if she has any, take care of her. You know that I believe in being charitable as much as anyone," Mrs. Bertram hastily added, seeing the expression on Ann's face. "But I don't believe in a young girl like yourself degrading herself by doing menial work for people like the Godbys. There is nothing in my religion to teach it."

"But, mother," Ann quietly remonstrated, "someone has to do it. They have no relatives near here, and there is scarcely a girl in this whole neighborhood who makes a business of caring for the sick or doing housework for other people. I do wish the people in this community would wake up to conditions and get a public health nurse or someone to see after such cases."

"Public health nurse! Fiddlesticks! There are more charities now than one can comfortably contribute to. But in any case, why should you worry about it? You will have to give up this sort of thing sooner or later, anyway. It looked rather cute while you were still a child, but now that you are a grown woman it looks perfectly ridiculous. Besides, you can't possibly go tomorrow. Have you forgotten all about the reception the Crawfords are giving for that Mrs. Haden?

"No, I hadn't forgotten. I don't much care whether I go or not, though. I would like to see Mrs. Haden; they say she is worth millions. Some of her people used to live here, didn't they?"

"Yes, and I've heard (it may just be gossip of course) that in memory of some relative, a grandmother I think it was, she is going to give this town some kind of community thing or other. I hope it's a library for we certainly need one. There is no good up-to-date fiction in this town."

"I wonder if Mrs. Haden is interested in social service?" Ann mused.

"Ann, I sometimes lose patience with you. Social service is all you think of. Mrs. Haden is hardly the type of person who would be. She's frightfully prominent in New York society I've been told."

Her mother, evidently finding the new serial in the magazine she was reading of more interest than the Godbys and Mrs. Haden, conversation ceased.

Yet the following morning found Ann, armed with a basket of food and bottle of disinfectant, on her way to the Godbys. Her sisters had good-naturedly chided her for her "silliness"; Jeanette had said her name should be "little Eva" instead of Ann. Her mother bemoaned the fact that she would not get home in time to dress for the reception. When Ann reached her destination she found the oldest child, Oval, a boy of ten years, cutting firewood, standing ankle deep in the filthy muck that surrounded the house. Two pigs and some dozen or so hens fought for bits of garbage recently thrown from the kitchen window. Ann shuddered a bit but bravely plowed through the mud and knocked at the kitchen door. She was admitted by eight-year-old Lucy, who seemed to be making a bad job of minding her eighteen-months-old brother and washing the dishes at the same time.

Two more very sticky and dirty children, both under six years of age, sat in one corner noisily playing with the cat.

"I'm awful glad you've come," said the little girl. "Mom's worse, and gone to bed agin. Pop ain't no better, and the new baby cries all the time. I've been tryin' to cook but Pop won't eat it."

"I've come to stay awhile," Ann answered, feeling guilty that she had not planned to stay longer. She left her basket in the kitchen, and went into the sick room. This was a small, low ceilinged, dark room, containing two beds, a broken down rocker, a red hot stove, a dilapidated sewing machine, now covered with a profusion of dirty cups and spoons, half empty bottles of medicine, and various articles of clothing. The air was stale, and full of a nauseating odor of feverish bodies and soiled bedding. The one window was tightly closed, and darkened by a flannel petticoat. From her place in the doorway, Ann could hear the labored breathing of Mr. Godby, and dimly discern the passive bulk of his wife, lying with her face to the wall. At the sound of Ann's voice she turned over, and invited her visitor to take a seat in the rocking chair.

"It 'pers like," she answered in regard to Ann's question concerning the family health, "I jist don't git a bit stronger. Jim thar don't seem to git much better neither. The doctor said the pneumonia fever was all gone and that if he would jist eat the right kind of food he would be well in time, but I cain't git him to eat hardly a thing. The baby, too, ain't gittin along like it ought to. I've tried catnip and watermelon tea, but it don't seem to do it much good. I think I'll send the kids to git some walink and try that."

Ann wondered how any of this mother's children could have survived, if she had given them all the miscellaneous concoctions she was forcing down this one. However, she was too wise to speak her thoughts, and instead explained that she had come to be generally useful for a time. Her first task was to persuade the convalescents to sit up while she made their beds. She straightened the sick room as best she could, and then went into the kitchen.

With hands on hips she surveyed the place. The idea of cooking food in such a kitchen filled her with a sickening disgust. At best Mrs. Godby was an indifferent, untidy housekeeper. During her illness the kitchen especially had suffered. In summer it swarmed with flies; in winter there were still the great hordes of cockroaches and scurrying mice. As Ann lifted the greasy dishpan from its nail behind the stove, she watched with horror the scuttling swarm of dark brown insects. For an instant she had half a notion to leave the sordid place of misery and think no more about it; at most she could do such a very little. It was discouraging to think that no matter what she did for the place today, things would be much the same in a week. However, she summoned her weakening resolution, donned the large denim apron she had brought, and fell to work.

Her first act was to open the doors and windows as wide as possible.

"Ain't you afraid this 'ull make Pop worse? The damp air ain't good fer him." Little Lucy objected when she saw what had been done.

"I don't think so." Ann wished devoutly that she could persuade Mrs. Godby to take the black rag from the window in the other room, open it and let in some air and sunshine. From past experiences Ann knew such a thing was hopeless.

With Oval acting as fireman, the cook stove reached a passable degree of warmth; Ann then filled as many pots and pans as could be crowded on the stove with water. While the water was heating she gathered up the dirty pots, pans, and dishes. This task required no great selective powers for there was not a clean dish in the house. She found every available bucket half full of milk in various stages of sourness and disintegration. Lucy advised her to give most of it to the pig as there was another churning waiting to be done. Ann was only too glad to do this, though she felt she was doing the pig an injustice. With her sleeves rolled above her elbows and a great pan of hot soapy dish water, she next attacked the dishes. Lucy, thinking to be helpful, started drying them with a greasy rag.

"Don't you rinse your dishes?" Ann asked with a show of surprise. "I think," she tactfully added, when she saw the look of astonishment on the child's face, "that we'll just pour boiling water over the dishes and let them dry themselves. If you want to do something you may gather up all these dishcloths, and wash them in good hot water with plenty of soap; then we'll scald them."

Lucy was rather aghast at such proceedings, but obediently scrubbed the offending cloths until Ann pronounced them clean. Oval, through with his wood cutting, begged for something to do. To him she gave the job of scrubbing the ill smelling wood and tin contraption that served for a cupboard. Ann noted with interest the willingness of the children to work, and their surprising intelligence concerning common everyday matters. "They might do and be most anything, if given any encouragement and half a chance," she thought with a sigh.

It seemed no time at all until time to prepare the noon meal. She found plenty to cook, for it was commonly said of the Godbys that they ate up anything Mr. Godby, who was a hard working man, made. But when one looked at bowls and pans and plates of left over food, waiting for nothing but to be thrown away, it was no hard matter to see where a large part of the family earnings went. Ann wondered why Mrs. Godby was so wasteful, then thought that more than likely no one had ever tried to teach the poor woman how to save. Ann's dinner, though simple, was pronounced good by the whole family. Mr. Godby even asked for a second helping of baked potato and cup custard.

"Ain't it funny," one of the children remarked. "Mom couldn't git Pop to eat hardly nothin,' an' he eat your cookin' right along."

Ann said nothing, but she rather thought that the way the food was served, and the cleanliness of the service might have something to do with the matter.

After dinner Ann was in the kitchen, baking gingerbread and making Mr. Godby a supply of chicken broth when Oval and Lucy, who had been out laying down boards for a walk from the kitchen to the barnyard, came scurrying in with the announcement that somebody was coming. Ann looked out the kitchen window, and saw her mother, Mrs. Crawford, and a large, imposing, well dressed woman whom she had never seen before; all carefully picking their way through the mud and coming toward the house. Seeing her in the window, the three came around to the kitchen. She noted the interest with which the unknown woman observed the things about her; nothing escaped her zealous inspection.

"Mrs. Haden," said Mrs. Bertram, addressing the stranger when Ann stood before them in the door, "this is my daughter Ann. I'm sorry she's in such an unpresentable condition, but——"

"That is perfectly excusable," interrupted Mrs. Haden, who seemed not at [all] like the terrifying society matron Ann's mother had pictured. "Ann," she continued, "it's a shame to call on anyone as busy as you seem to be. But since hearing of you and your interests I just had to see you. Since I am going to be here for only one day this is the only opportunity."

Ann, puzzled and mystified by this little speech, expressed her regret for not having been home, and invited her visitors to be seated.

"It is only a short time until the reception so I must be brief. Mrs. Bertram, and Mrs. Crawford, tell the sick woman that I shall be in presently but can't come just now."

The two ladies took this as it was intended, a gentle hint to withdraw.

"I'm afraid I am being a trifle abrupt and upsetting," said Ann's visitor when the others had gone, "but I have come to you to discuss welfare work. You seem to be the only person here who is interested in such matters. From what I see I know that you are deeply interested. Such work as you are doing now requires not a little grit and determination."

"Oh, are you interested in such things, too?" cried Ann with a gasp of pure joy.

"Yes, very much indeed. For years I have spent a large amount of time and money in various forms of charity. I have been thinking of the need in this place for some time, but this is my first opportunity to visit Rothington since I was a child, and I am sorry to say that there seems to be about as much suffering and ignorance now as there was then."

"There isn't very much real poverty," said Ann, letting her overwhelming interest run away with her. "But there is much useless suffering. A great many of these mountain people are heartbreakingly ignorant and superstitious. They haven't the faintest conception of thrift or germs or sanitation. You would think their children would learn such things at school, but they don't. Then there are so many crippled children. Nothing can be done for them here, and their parents refuse to send them to institutions where their deformaties could be cured free of charge. But worst of all is the suffering and sickness and death among mothers and very young babies. This country needs above all things a hospital that could take care of maternity cases among the poorer families."

"I have been thinking of such an institution," said Mrs. Haden quietly.

"You mean—you mean you're thinking of endowing one?"

"Yes, but it must be more than a hospital. I want a public health nurse; we will hold free clinics; I am planning to have a home demonstration agency and free classes in practical nursing, home making, and such things as the care and preservation of food."

"Oh, Mrs. Haden, that is what I have been dreaming of and hoping for,

for years and years. And now you're going to make it come true. It's like a fairy tale."

"There, there, child, don't get so excited. Perhaps if I had never seen you and your work, your dream would never have come true. It will take lots of hard work, and even then you may be disappointed. You must not expect to banish all the suffering and ignorance from this small corner of the world in a single life time."

"It will at least be a big step forward. We can at least give them a chance," said Ann who now saw herself as a happy worker in the hospital and institution of her dreams.

The Goat Who Was a Cow

An early effort at short fiction, published here for the first time, this story could have been written as early as 1924. She signed the manuscript "Harriette L. Simpson, Burnside, Kentucky."

———⟫◦◦◦⟪———

With a great yawn Jezebel Denny tossed the dog-eared geometry from her, shifted her sprawling position on the floor, and then as she thoughtfully masticated the rubber tip of her pencil, she leveled her searching, pensive gaze upon me. I, too, closed my textbook, thinking it worse than useless to try to cram a pupil for the approaching geometry exam when she was already hopelessly full of something else. It was only early May, yet the day was filled with the deadening stifling heat that May can bring to southern Kentucky. I concluded that Jezebel, like myself, found day dreaming of the approaching vacation more pleasant than studying angles, lines and triangles. Jezebel did not live in the little backwoods town in which I was teaching, but came from some vague, out of the way place farther up the Cumberland.

"Do you know," she at length observed, "I sort of like you."

"I thought you hated everybody from the bluegrass and the states as far north and east as the one I come from," I said by way of showing my appreciation for this unlooked for affection.

"Yes, but you're different from all the other Northerners that come down here to teach school or do social service work. You don't seem to expect us to be such a bunch of half civilized, blood thirsty people. Why half the people who come up home, and even around here, expect to see a lot of blood and thunder people, wearing coon skin caps and carrying old fashioned rifles and powder horns. Why they nearly faint when they learn that such a little half breed as I am is actually in school. Now you don't seem surprised at anything, not even me."

I nodded thoughtfully, but made no comment. The truth was that the place was a great deal worse than I had expected. Yet certain stray remarks of Jezebel had given me an idea that, compared with her own home, the dull little town in which she now stayed was the epitome of civilization. In spite of this Jezebel bitterly resented anything said or written of the mountains that was not absolutely true.

Seeing that I had no intention of imperiling myself in a conversation that might cause her volatile temper to burst into sudden flame, Jezebel sighed, and wriggled into her favorite position: flat of her stomach on the floor, with her slim legs waving over her back, and her chin in a cupped hand. For a time she lay silent: like the rest of her kin, she was no great talker except on rare occasions. "Well, I have the satisfaction of knowing that one old codger left this place with what he came after."

"Didn't expect much?" I asked.

"Lots."

"Your community isn't as bad as all that, I hope."

"I turned bootlegger for awhile, and supplied the good man his moonshine with all the thrills possible."

"Jezebel, you are teasing. How could you bootleg without any moonshine? Besides your mother would never let you do such a thing; your grandfather a preacher, too."

"I'm tellin' you the honest-to-goodness truth. A ripping good time it was, too. I had as much excitement as my customer."

"Tell me about it," I coaxed.

After much persuasion on my part, Jezebel consented, and presently the room was filled with the slow music of her words.

Last year when we ran out of sweet potato slips, David (that's my brother just a year older than I am, you know) went 'way over to Tub Tudor's after some. As we were jogging back in the heat along a hot sandy road, David remembered a bird's nest he knew of just over the ridge. Of course, nothing would do David but go and look at it, and see if the eggs had hatched. It was so hot, and I felt so lazy that I didn't go with him, but sat there on my pokey old mule instead. Suddenly old Kit pricked up her ears and looked up the road. A stranger rode, or rather perched, on a horse and came toward me. You think it queer that I should know he was a stranger to our country the minute I saw him? Well, there isn't a man in our whole neighborhood who is clean shaven on a Thursday morning; neither is there one who could be dragged into a pair of riding britches with two mules and a log chain, but for all that our men are no fools. Moreover, fat men do not live in our neck of the woods; red nosed they may be, but never fat. I jumped at the conclusion that this man was some Northerner spending his vacation at the 'falls,' and finding things a trifle dull and dry, had, with the aid of a guide, come over into our neighborhood in search of amusement and liquid fire.

"Good morning, son," said he in one of those sharp hateful voices.

"Howdy yerself," I replied. I don't know why I addressed him thus, for I am not in the habit of speaking to people in any such fashion. I was not surprised that he should call me "boy." I was bare legged, and dressed in a pair of David's old overalls, a blue shirt, and a dilapidated old straw hat. I know I just looked terrible, but in the summer time I run wild to make up for having to go to school all the rest of the time.

The stranger eyed me thoughtfully, while I tried to stare just as little mountaineers are supposed to do, with mouth and eyes wide open.

"Excuse me, mister," said I after a minute, "fer starin' so, but them fancy pants ye got on made me think ye might be a sheriff or somethin,' and I wuz plum scairt to death."

I couldn't for the life of me tell why I talked in that awful fashion, but I had a hunch that he was on the hunt for liquor, and that would be a good way of finding out. Oh please don't think I'm in the habit of finding out such things, but something got into me that day. Grandpa would have said that it was the devil, and I guess that would be right. I just felt good, care free sort of. Then I knew that I looked like some ragged moonshiner's son, and this tempted me to live up to my looks for just a little while.

The thirsty man, I never knew his real name, regarded me with hopeful eyes. "Why wouldn't you want to see an officer of the law?" he asked.

"Why don't the people back in here usually want to see a raiding officer?" I asked, instead of answering.

"Well, but you look to be too young to be engaged in the business I am thinking of."

"That's all ye know about it, mister. We do quair things in these yer hills," I answered in my best possible dialect.

I realized that I did not fill the bill when it came to looking like a moonshiner. These much discussed personages are supposed to be great gruff-voiced individuals, who disfigure the landscape with tobacco juice; who are never heard to utter a sentence without swearing; and who are always encumbered with about a ton of firearms. I soon thought of a way to remedy the situation. "Well, ye see," said I, "I don't have anything to do with makin' the stuff. I jist look around and hunt up customers, and stand guard."

"I suppose," he said cautiously, "you would not sell to a perfect stranger." His very life seemed to hang on these words.

"Well now, ye look like ye wouldn't tell, an' I guess we would sell ye some; I'm most sartin ye could git it."

"When could I see the manager?" he asked more eagerly than most of these crusty Northerners usually do.

I did not answer him immediately, but sat there thinking. The thing had gone farther than I had expected. Here I had a poor thirsty creature, thinking he would soon get what he was after, and me meaning never a word of it. I wanted to dig my heels into old Kit's sides and beat it, but somehow I thought to play a good joke on this man.

"Well, 'bout the only time ye can see the head o' the works is down at the still, long about eight o'clock tonight."

The thirsty man frowned. It was evident that he did not like the notion of going to a still in these wild Kentucky hills at night. But in the end, thirst conquered fear, and I promised to meet him that night at the place where we then were, and from there go to the still. Romantic and creepy I call that. After that he jogged off down the road, without even asking my name; but I was glad of that, for I hated to tell any more lies.

While I was talking to him, I had been so busy trying to keep from laughing or making a mistake in my dialect, that my conscience didn't have a chance to bother me. But when David hopped out of the bushes it struck me full force; and hit me even harder when I learned that he had heard most of the conversation. David isn't a bit like me, or at least mama says he isn't. He began telling me what a wicked thing I'd done. He is unfortunate enough to have an awful conscience which is always pestering him. He fussed a lot for a little while, then said nothing more until we were 'most home. "It's too bad for that man to be disappointed," he told me with a great tender-hearted sigh.

I nodded, thinking not so much of the man's disappointment, as of how much money I could get out of him if I were a moonshiner. Don't raise your eyebrows so. I know it doesn't sound respectable, but a person can't help thinking of such things. Suddenly I thought of the most wonderful plan, and told it to David, but he didn't think much of it.

"Why, crazy, if we carried that out we'd get turned out of church."

"Hypocrite," I retorted, "you'd get turned out of heaven any way, but the church needn't find it out."

It was a wonderful plan. I had thought of the bottle of whisky Papa always keeps, and the one that the hired man keeps hidden in the hay. "For snake bites," they are always careful to explain. Though there has not been any one in our family snake bitten in years, Papa's whisky decreases just the same. I watch it closely; hidden in the left end of the bottom drawer of the bureau in the spare room. I had suggested to David that we hunt up this whisky, and sell it to thirsty man; but David insisted on listening to his conscience instead of me. However, his conscience must have been a bit out of order that day, for finally he said:

"That cave we discovered 'way up on Redeye creek, last summer, would make a dandy place for a still. If you weren't afraid, you could bring the man up there, and I could pretend I was taking care of the still in the absence of the owner. I could sell the man the stolen liquor without ever letting him see the inside of the rock house, and he'd never know the difference."

"David, you wouldn't do that. Why not just take the whisky to the man when I meet him in the road?" I asked, for I wasn't any too keen on this wild plan of David's.

But David would agree to nothing of the kind. "It would take all the fun and thrills out of it," he said. I had never known before that he liked thrills.

Well, the long and the short of it is that we did carry out his plan, or rather we tried to: everything didn't go just as we expected. I was so busy working 'round the house all the rest of the day that I didn't get to think much about it until night. David collected the whisky, getting about a gallon in all: I think that even religious old Grandpa kept some. Mama, who had gone to help those no 'count Lovelaces with their sick baby, sent word that she would stay all night there. This was good news, because Mama usually sits up late. Although we were so excited we could scarcely eat, we managed to get our work done and everything fixed. Eight o'clock found Papa and Grandpa snoring like sixty, and after such a day's work as they had done that day, it takes nothing less than a cannon to awaken them. Since it was only three or four miles to our "still," we thought we could go and get back by midnight.

Isn't it funny how much noise everything makes when you are trying to be still? Until that night I never knew that the kitchen screen door needed oiling, or that the back porch creaked piercingly under the lightest of foot steps.

"We'll sure give that human the thrill of his life," David chattered excitedly, when we were clear of the house. "We couldn't have picked a better night for moonshining in a thousand years."

And sure enough, that night would have made an iron horse poetical, after he had taken the trouble to look at it. The moon was like a big golden dishpan, all swathed about with filmy, snowy dish towels. It was beautiful, but kind of creepy. The south wind blew very, very softly, making the pines on the ridges whisper in mournful little voices. The ridges were sweeps of silver, with mysterious rivers of shadow between. The whip-poor-wills kept up a constant serenade, with now and then a few notes from a screech owl or frog. I could have written a poem there on the spot, and me never having studied poetry. But for the magic of the thing I would have been afraid. I did shiver a bit when we came to the place of parting. David was going by a different road, [so that he would] get there sooner, and have everything just right when I got there with our customer.

I found a somewhat impatient, creepy, thirsty man awaiting me at the appointed spot. I think that there was a part of the time during the trip that he forgot his thirst, and heartily regretted ever having seen me. I didn't try to make him any gladder, either. Oh, but I led that frightened man a merry chase over huckleberry ridges, through ferny marshes prickly with black-berry briars, and him a cussin' all the way. That night I did not envy that man, for all his riches. There he was, cringing at the sound of a screech owl, and constantly fearing a rattlesnake, while I walked on, staring at the moon and thinking of romance and poetry. Every little night noise, that is when he could hear them between the mighty thumps of his own heart, sent him into panic. To his frightened fancy, every rock in the moonlight was a rob-ber, crouching ready to spring forth.

After walking seemingly numberless miles through scratchy underbrush, or in will-o-the-wispy paths, we came in sight of our destination. During the last thirty minutes, my frightened companion had sworn between each puff that no man alive could make head or tail in such a jungle. But, never letting him know the true state of my thoughts, I had pushed on, with wild panic threatening to overwhelm me at every step. Moonlight is such a strange thing, making crazy mysterious mazes out of respectable cow paths. So it was with no little feeling of relief that I saw the inky splotch of shadow on the yel-low walls of the sandstone cliff, which marked the site of the rock house.

As we came closer, a shadow disentangled itself from blacker shadows, and stood waiting. "David," I thought, and was happy. With the thirsty man puffing close behind, I stepped into that shadowy hole. The long shadow shambled forward. "I didn't know that David was so tall," thought I, cock-sure little fool that I was.

I thought quickly of my opening lines. Yes, David and I had planned it all out, just like a play. "Wal, Mister, here's another customer fer ye."

I used the best dialect I could summon, with all the swagger possible.

Now in better spirits, the thirsty man eagerly awaited the reply. It came in due time, rumbling and tumbling out of the shadows. "Deed hit's a quair time to be bringin' a customer, an' how in the heck d'ye know I want one uv any kind, let alone a teetotal stranger."

The cocksureness left me, just as stiffness deserts a wet hat, making it all floppy. My heart got weak and wobbly, and I guess my knees did, too. I was too scared to notice anything except that that gangling shadow and growly voice didn't belong to David. Happily, the thirsty man was too busy listening to the growly voice to notice my sudden loss of composure.

As the shadow approached, it took on the form of a very lengthy but not shadowy sort of man; a wild looking person, all boots and brushy beard, who looked very businesslike and foreboding as he stood regarding us suspiciously.

After subjecting me to a long and careful scrutiny, he swapped his tobacco from one lantern jaw to the other, spat twice, then spoke. "You're shore some punkins to be traipsin' 'round this time o'night, little as ye air."

I gave him to understand that I was much older than I looked, and knew the country perfectly. I felt relieved when I realized that I was as much a stranger to this moonshiner as he was to me. David and I had not been about the cave since the summer we found it, and most anything may happen within a year. Since the people on the other side of Redeye creek used a different post office, went to a different church and school from the one at home, we knew little of them, and they of us. This fact saved me from complete disgrace, and once more I thanked my lucky stars for having a boyish bob, and no figure at all.

I managed to act fairly natural, and muttered something about the still having changed hands. In answer to this the moonshiner grunted something to the effect that a body could never tell about stills. At length I summoned what remnant of courage I possessed, and asked him point blank if we could get any liquor. We waited impatiently for the answer, while he manufactured and disposed of a perfect river of tobacco juice.

"Wal, ye see hit's this a way. I hain't th' owner o' these works, only guardin' them while th' boss sleeps a little. An' bein' as I don't know who ye air, I jedge hit a little onsafe to sell. There's another party here," he continued by way of consolation, "that has come to see 'bout buyin' some fer some people at th' falls. He's jist a kid, too."

I certainly was glad to hear that: I knew that David was alive at any rate. He certainly was smart that time to change his plans so quickly, and invent such a nice little tale. But the thirsty man shared none of my feeling of relief. He heaved a great and audible sigh when he heard that it would be unsafe to sell. He was no longer afraid of anything, except the idea of returning empty handed. "Wouldn't you sell me even a quart?" he begged.

That was only the beginning. For hours, so it seemed to my restless spirit, that man entreated for liquor. He offered staggering sums for it, and made great promises that never a word of the matter should cross his lips. But all to no avail: as the books say, "the heart of the man was as flint."

When the would-be customer finally became convinced that this man would sell him nothing, he suggested that we be going. Needless to say, I was glad to hear this for the whole business was getting on my nerves. However, leave we could not. Just as we turned to go, the moonshiner calmly gave us to understand that, "Hit would be mighty ondesirable fer you'ens to leave jist now."

"But why?" asked the thirsty man.

"Plenty uv reasons," that terrible man answered. "Fer one thing I hain't a wantin' no man to leave this place mad as a hornet 'cause I won't sell 'em no liquor. More'n likely, you'd go an' rake up ever sheriff in th' county, an' have 'em out here 'fore mornin.' Hit's tough on th' pore youngen, but I don't think he'll mind, an' he kin talk to this other youngen in here. Th' chances are," he continued, "thet if ye behave till early mornin,' th' big boss 'ull come an' sell ye some."

The thirsty man didn't seem to mind this sudden turn of events so much as I expected. A new chance of getting what he came after cheered him wonderfully. But believe me, 'th pore kid' didn't feel cheerful. I kept wondering what would happen to us when we strolled in home about eight o'clock the next day. Just the thought of it almost turned my hair gray.

There was nothing to do but sit and wait as patiently as possible. Of course, David had to wait, too, for he couldn't have gone home without me; and if he were to leave without seeing the "big boss," it would look most too suspicious. David and I pretended that we were only slightly acquainted, and talked but little. Most of the time I just sat near the mouth of the rock house, staring at the moon. In spite of my conscience-stricken and remorse-eaten soul, I felt a bit proud of David and myself: from the looks of things, we evidently knew how to pick a place for a still; but then that is a very wicked thing to be proud of. Sometimes I would think of Mama, and what she would say and do when we had to tell her the truth, and then I felt like jumping into the shadows and going away forever. Grandpa would preach a sermon on the sins of bootlegging, telling a curious throng of church goers all about what we had done. Mama's part in our punishment would consist of her praying a public prayer of hell fire and the demon alcohol. But such thoughts would soon kill a wooden man, so I put them away, and let my mind dwell on pleasanter things.

The night passed somehow; and about three-thirty or there abouts, the entrance of a red-nosed individual set things to humming. Having been introduced in true mountaineer fashion, and the nature of our business made known, he proceeded to look us over. Fortunately, he did not seem so formidable or squeamish as his guard, but he did look surprised and disconcerted when he saw that strangers knew of his still. But I explained to him that I had not visited the place for some time, and during my absence the still had changed hands. This soothed him some, and after a little parlying in a dark corner with his colleague, he announced that he would sell all that anybody wanted to buy.

You should have seen the thirsty man when he learned that he could get all he wanted. He fairly jumped out of his skin, so great was the joy in him. He bought five gallons, paid; and we left that hateful place with its smell of whisky and dirty feet. David soon followed. The man believed him quickly enough when David told him he didn't want to buy any that night, but just wanted to find out if a man down at the falls could get ten gallons. He explained to the men that he had heard of the still in some round about fashion, and then promised to bring his man about a week later. Of course, he never went back again.

My companion, now no longer thirsty, thought it a most pleasant coincidence that David's way led the same as ours. Such a little 'shine can do wonders. Forgotten were the briar scratches, the holly prickles, and the heart jumping scares that had been his on the way out. He was very jolly, and did not seem to care at all for my mistake, and the long wait in the rock house. I was glad that his "little partner," as he called me, had given him no idea of the true state of affairs; that instead of a carefree moonshiner's accomplice, I was a religious young lady, walking home to a surprised and horrified family. I thought bitterly of how in a week's time, the news would be over the entire country that Jezebel and David Denny had been sent to reform schools for trying to bootleg. It would be six o'clock before we would get home, and Papa always gets up at four.

About half way home we ran into Ole Bones, one of our cows, who had strayed off, and hadn't been milked for two days. She was a sorry looking sight. I claimed no relationship to the ball of mud, briar scratches, and cockle burrs, but David explained to our companion that she was his father's cow. She walked in front of us willingly enough: we didn't much care what became of her, we felt so blue and woe-begone.

David and Bones walked on, while the thirsty man and I stopped to straighten out our business affairs. Needless to say, I did not leave that gay gentleman empty handed. The thought of what he gave me made David and me, too, dizzy.

"If we had only got home sooner, I was going to tell Mama in a day or two that we had won the prize for that word puzzle we were working on last night. But that's all off now," he added miserably.

I know we must have been a sorry sight, the three of us: first the mud covered cow, tail drooping, and emitting ear splitting and heart rendering sounds at every step; next came me, a very pitiable object I must have been, ragged, weeping, and grimy as I was; last came David, not crying but ready to.

Mama and Papa were milking when we reached the barnyard. Mama turned toward the sorry looking group angrily and disgustedly. "Yes bawl, bawl, you reprobate you; it's a pretty looking time to be getting in home, all covered with mud and cockle burrs, and looking like I don't know what. Stay out all night this a way: you won't give any more milk for a week."

It was then that I realized that Mother was talking to the cow, and not to me.

"This cow will be the death of you children," she continued, while I only blinked. "Out running around in the dew before you've had a bite to eat will ruin your digestion. Jezebel," she added briskly, "you're such a baby to cry every time a piece of stock doesn't do to suit you."

Greeted only with blank stares, she rambled on: "I didn't think you children would have gumption enough to go hunt this cow, if she didn't come up last night. It's a good thing you went after her early before she wandered clear out of the country. Chin Lovelace told me last night that he saw her 'way up towards Redeye creek. I guess you children have walked every bit of six miles, for you've been gone a mortal long time: it was just around four when I came in, and you were gone then."

"The next time a cow gets up on Redeye, I'll do the goin' after. I've been hearin' some pretty rough tales on moonshining up there. I'd a gone this morning, but you were gone when I got up." Papa is always very careful that we never get our reputations sullied.

"Unrespectable brute," said Grandfather, who had just come from breakfast. "She looks like some ungodly man, who has been out bootlegging and moonshining all night."

"Disgrace to a decent family," said Mama. "Run along now and eat. I cooked an extra large chicken, knowin' how hungry you'd be."

"That is all," said Jezebel after a long pause. "I never saw the thirsty man or the moonshiner again; but sometimes my conscience gives me awful twinges, especially when the bootlegging cow looks at me so reproachful like."

OHIO & KENTUCKY: THE 1930S

Marigolds and Mules

In 1918, when Harriette Arnow was a fifth grader, her father, Elias Simpson, worked in the oil fields in Lee County and Wolfe County, Kentucky, where his family lived with him and learned about some of the inherent dangers that oil workers faced.

"Marigolds and Mules" was her first published story, appearing in the third volume of a now defunct little literary magazine, *Kosmos: Dynamic Stories of Today* (Feb/ March 1935): 3–6. She said she was paid in "free copies" and "the glory" of seeing her name in print. The editor unfortunately misspelled her first name: at the end of her story, her name appears as Harriet L. Simpson.

I stopped at Mrs. Joe Madigan's. I liked talking to her. She was young. Not so old as my mother. She was cooking black bean soup with cheese and onion. She gave me a taste. I remember wishing it were a bowlful.

"I made it special for Joe," she said.

"Will he be home for supper?" I said.

"Sure," she said.

"Don't you get worried?" I said.

"No," she said. "Joe knows how to handle the stuff. He hauled it in Texas before he came here."

We talked about the weather then. October in Wolf County, Kentucky, is a pretty month. There are poplars there. They make the ridge sides yellow, but the maples are red like blood. I liked the poplars best. It had rained a lot the day before. In spite of the oil and salt water and gas the world, if you didn't look at it too close, looked clean. Mrs. Madigan came with me into the yard. We looked at the marigolds. She gave me a handful. "Joe planted them," she said. "I'll pick a bunch for him. He likes the smell of them after the oil. He doesn't like the oil. But a man must live."

"Is he afraid?" I said.

"No," she said. "He is never afraid. Sometimes when the mud is deep in the valleys he doesn't eat so well."

"The mud is deep by Big Sinking," I said.

"Yes, it is deep," she said. "But tonight he will eat. He likes my bean soup."

I went home. I put the marigolds in my father's empty supper pail. My mother found them there. My father was a driller. He worked from twelve to twelve. Every night I took his supper.

"Who sent the marigolds?" my mother said.

"Nitro Joe's wife. She picked a bouquet for him," I said.

My mother looked at them. She touched one with her little finger. She shook her head. "Fool," she said.

"Joe likes flowers," I said.

"There is no place for flowers. Not here," she said.

I didn't say anything. She didn't either. It was still there in the kitchen. We could hear the squeak of the pumping rods by the window. We'd been in that shack three years. Those rods had never stopped. Not once.[1] They were like my father's boiler fires. It took six weeks to drill a well. The fires were never out. We had no Sundays. Every day he worked from twelve to twelve. I hated those rods. They were like long black snakes. Moving, eternally moving in long black lines. They never stopped. One night I dreamed they'd stopped. I dreamed the snakes had died.

My mother listened to the rods. I know she hated them. They brought oil and gas. The smell of it choked you on a day with no wind. The oil was always in my father's clothes and hair and eyebrows. The oil was green scum on the creeks. In the valleys the wild pansies died from it. There was no grass in our yard. Nothing will grow where salt water has run. The water we drank tasted of oil. We knew there was oil in it. Sometimes when it stood in the bucket for a time lights would shine on top. That is oil.

"It will frost tonight," my mother said.

The black snakes by the window went with a long hiss and a rasping growl.

"We'll have a fire," she said.

"Mother," I said, "does Joe bring his load by Big Sinking?"

"Yes," she said. " He has sixty quarts. One horse was lamed. He had to borrow mules. Pete Crowder told me."

She looked at the marigolds. She listened to the rods squeak. "It is good," she said, "there are no children."

"He is not dead," I said.

"No," she said. "He is not dead. But his wife gathers flowers for him before he is home. He drives rough mules. The mud is deep."

"We will saw wood," she said.

I had found an oak log in the valley. Pig Eye Norton pulled it to the yard with his mule. We sawed that. The cross cut saw made a buzzing sound. It drowned the slither of the black snakes through the ridge grass. The wood was clean wood, with no oil about it. When the saw bit deep a fine trickle of saw dust came from each end of the cut. It made a clean oak smell in the air.

I liked to saw. I drew my arms back and forth. I did not think about the work. The sun had set. There was no wind. There were no clouds. Just light. Overhead the light was blue green. Lower it was clear yellow. That shaded into orange. Below that there was a clear rim of red where the sun had been. One star came out. I looked at it.

It looked so high. Away up there above the gas and the oil and the dirt. It was a big star, orange red. It made me think of the marigolds. It looked the way they smelled.

The wood was all sawed. I carried it into the house. I made a lot of trips to the woodpile. I wanted to look at the star. If you looked long enough while you stood in the wood smell you could forget the pumping rods, and the gas smell, and the feel of oil in your hair. I looked[2] a long time. The red faded, then the orange. The lemon yellow and the blue green were left. I carried in the last stick of wood.

My mother was in the kitchen. She stood by the window. She looked at the star. "It's pretty," I said.

"Pretty," she said. "You don't belong to talk about the stars."

I did not feel my head hit the floor. I did not feel anything. I opened my eyes. The star was still there. It was big and clean and beautiful. The window glass was shattered. It fell with a little tinkle on the floor by my hair. The water bucket lay on its side. Water trickled everywhere. The cupboard door had banged open. The dishes still fell. Slowly as if they didn't want to fall.

I did not think of anything. I had no time to think. It was less than a second before the sounds came. It was as if all the sounds of the world had become one sound. It was too big for my ears. I felt it in my head and breast and spine. The floor quivered with it. The stove played a rattly tune. Soot came in black clouds from the stove pipe joinings. The sound shook itself through the house and was gone. I thought it had deafened me. I could hear nothing. The rods by the window were still. I got on my hands and knees.

The kitchen was almost dark. I looked around. I saw my mother by the table. She had not fallen. She held the pine boards of the table with one hand. I could not see her face. I saw her hands in the starlight and the sunset. She held the table so her fingers and knuckles were blue like sick gas flame.

"Marigolds," my mother said. "She picked him marigolds."

She laughed. She sat in the fallen glass and laughed. Her body went back and forth the way the pumping rods had moved. She laughed like that once in Texas. The time a storage tank not so far from our house exploded. My little sister had her play house there. My mother laughed when one of the lease hands brought her a teddy bear. He'd found it half a mile away. It had been my little sister's.

Big Sinking Valley was just over the ridge side. I left my mother laughing there, and went down the path. I took a flash light. A hundred yards from the road I stubbed my toe on a piece of buggy wheel. I fell over the wheel. My face struck something warm and sticky. I rubbed my hands over it. When I drew my hands into the light they were red like the sunset. I saw that I had fallen on a piece of mule. I knew it was mule. There was a bit of brown hair there. It was too short for a man's hair. Nitro Joe had yellow hair. The lease men called him "that yellow headed Frenchie."

I sat on my heels looking at it. I raised my head. I saw the star. It was bright and clean and beautiful. I went on. I saw a foreleg in a bush. I tried to get it down. I shook the bush. Blood made a little pattering on my nose. Blood does not feel like rain.

I went on. I got there first. The road had been deep with mud. It was spattered on the trees and rocks. The mud was red clay mud. Sometimes on the rocks and ground were stains redder than red clay. I couldn't find anything. The place where the nitroglycerine cart had been was a clean pit scooped from the mud. Mud oozed back into it. Soon it would be full again. The platform that had carried the pumping rods above the road was gone. I flashed my light up the pumping track a ways.[3] I saw dead lengths of steel warped and twisted and bent upon themselves.

Men came then. Lease hands and drillers and tool dressers off shift. Their lights made a weaving and a flickering over the place. Slow Jim was the oldest driller. "Find anything, son," he said.

"Mules," I said.

"Build a fire," he said to Bandy Cock Eye.

Bandy built a fire by the road. Buck Thomas helped him. They brought pine logs from the ridge side. Slow Jim and the other men hunted for pieces of the mules. They put them on the fire. It was a big fire. It roared. It didn't roar loud enough to kill the hiss of the mule flesh when the flames touched it. It smelled too.

The men found more pieces of mule. It was mostly like jellied blood mixed with bone and pieces of skin. Slow Jim scooped it up on a piece of tin from the pumping platform. In a yellow beech tree a piece of intestine made a slimy red garland. Over one piece the men argued. "It ain't right," Slow Jim said.

"You ain't fer shore," Bandy Cock Eye said. "Who wants to sing hymns over a bloody bit of blasted mule."

They threw the piece on the fire. I saw the flames lick over it. They died to coals. I saw an overall buckle glow red in the heat. It lost itself in the fire.

We looked a long time. Fifty feet from the hole I saw the end of a black snake whip. I pulled it up. It was very heavy. I pulled the handle into the light. A hand and a piece of forearm were on the handle. The fingers of the hand were tight about the whip. I could not get them away. I took it to Slow Jim.

The men gathered around and looked at it. They didn't say anything. Buck Thomas took his jack knife and trimmed the red rags of flesh away.[4] Slow Jim took it to the creek and washed it. He cut away all the whip except the part between the fingers. He cleaned the thumb nail. It was black. The whole hand was black. The little hairs were still red gold. Drill Stem Cook had the cleanest handkerchief. They wrapped it in that.

The lease boss came then. He swore some. "You've looked enough," he said. "Bandy, get two more roustabouts and fix the pumping rods. Buck, you got any kids?"

"No," said Buck.

"Take my buckboard and the two gentlest lease mules. Go to Torrent for sixty quarts of nitroglycerine. Leave about midnight. Get started out of Torrent by daylight. Number twenty will be ruined if she's not shot by tomorrow noon."

"Yes," said Buck.

The superintendent left. He took the hand. He was going to give it to my mother. She was to give it to Mrs. Madigan. The lease hands went for tools to fix the pumping platform. Buck and Slow Jim did not go away. I stayed with them. We squatted by the fire. It was almost out.

"It ain't right," Slow Jim said.

"No," Buck said, "The most of Nitro Joe's in them coals."

They sat and watched the fire for a long time. They didn't speak. I looked at the fire, too. Sometimes I'd raise my head. I'd see the star. It was big now. Bright like a light on a Christmas tree. Slow Jim chewed his moustache. "Can you pray, son?"

"No," I said.

"Can't you, Buck?"

"Hell, no. I wisht I could.—What about yourself?"

"Be durned if I know how."

"You begin with 'God our Father' or 'Blessed Jesus.'"

"Them Spanish in the Argentine prayed to the blessed Virgin."

"'Mother of God' is a pretty word. I think I'd ruther say my says to her."

"'Mother of God' is swearin'."

"The Hell it is. Remember that Spanish woman in Mexico when her man got burned alive. She rocked on the floor all night. She said 'Mother of God' a million times."

"Suit yourself."

They sat for another time without speaking. Then Slow Jim took off his hat. Buck did the same. Slow Jim brushed away pebbles and dead coals, and made a place for his knees. Buck and I knelt, too. Slow Jim began:

"Mother of God," he said. "Nitro Joe was an oil man. He went quick. He wasn't bad. Not fer an oil man. So, Mother of God, pity him. All blowed to death and burned to death with these yer mules. He sweared a lot. He drunk, too. He was a devil with the ladies. But, Mother of God, he was born in a drilling rig. He couldn't help it. So, Mother of God, unmix him if ye can from these mules. Amen."

The coals died. Still we sat there. "I hope he didn't go to Hell," Buck said.

"Hell will be an oil field," Slow Jim said.

"Hell won't be so bad," I said.

"Why son?"

I couldn't tell them. I couldn't make them understand. I looked at the star. It was big and clean and beautiful. "There won't be any God damned stars there," I said. "Pretty stars to shine on bloody mules and dirty, bloody men."

A Mess of Pork

This story appeared in the first issue of the small literary journal *The New Talent* (October–December 1935): 4–11.

On the first page of "A Mess of Pork," an editorial note promised "a story filled with latent power, rising to a tremendous and fascinating sweep of horror. A story you will remember." Apparently anticipating criticism for her story's grim reality, Arnow defended her work by writing to the editor, "'I cannot preach,' she tells us, 'and I will not go two blocks out of the way to put a belch or a bedbug in a story. . . .'" The editor's note also explained "Harriette L. Simpson was born twenty-six years ago in Kentucky, 'thirty-two miles from a railroad, and second from the top of six children.' She was graduated from college, and has been teaching in the public schools. 'A Mess of Pork' is her second published story."

<hr />

*I*got off the bus at a town called Somerset, in Kentucky, and went to the post office. I wanted to see if my picture was there. It was. A tall man looked at me with his dead blue eyes, and I was afraid. I went outside, but he did not follow me. I stood still in the street, and I heard a man say, "He didn't have a gun. He fell on his face."

"Six children, they say," another man said.

"They run after the other one. They left him for the hogs."

"Did they mess him up?"

"Some. His wife come with the dog before they'd done much damage."

I walked over to the men. They were throwing bags of mail into a truck with Mount Victory written on the door. "Howdy," the taller man said. "Aim to go out?"

"Yes," I said.

"You're new," he said.

"Yes," I said.

"That store is locoed. The same travelin' man never comes twice," he said.

I sat in the cab with the mail-carrier and the other man. They didn't talk much. "Know him well?" the other passenger said after a time.

"Knowed of him," the mail-carrier said. "Tred Fairchild was a good man. Steady goin'. Made good liquor."

"The law's the law," the other man said.

"Hell," the mail-carrier answered, and spat between his teeth.

November dark comes early in the hills. Ten miles out the lights were turned on. Mount Victory was twenty-seven miles away. Down there twenty-seven miles is a long way. The roads are full of ruts and holes and rocks bigger than a man. I couldn't tell much about the country. I saw little stunted cedars and limestone rocks, then sandstone and pine. We crossed a creek. "Buck Creek," the driver said. Then we went up a twisted, rocky road. Twice we stalled. I guess it was ten o'clock when we got to Mount Victory: a store and a school house and a church on a high windy ridge.

"Store's closed," the mail man said. "Ye'd better stay the night with me. Hardgrove lives two miles away."

I stayed the night with him. I slept without undressing on a tick filled with shucks. They were up by daylight next day. "I'll be going," I said after breakfast. "By the way," I said, "where does this Tred Fairchild's widow live?"

He walked to the door, and pointed across three hills. "Over yonder. Clean over Rockcastle. The revenuers crossed at Shad Keeney's place. Ye know the way to the store?"

"Not exactly," I said.

"I'll take you to the forks, and point it out," he said.

He did. "Aim to walk over to Dykes and see the store keeper there?"

"Yes."

When he was gone away I went toward the river. I followed a wide yellow road. It stopped, and I followed a path to a log cabin. A hound dog barked and a woman came to the door. "Where is Shad Keeney's?" I said. "I want to go over Rockcastle."

The woman did not answer me. She said to someone behind her, "A stranger man wants to go over. Run fetch your paw."

I waited. Soon a loose-jointed man with his overalls tucked into muddy boots came. "Be you the tax 'sessor?" he said.

"Yes," I said.

We went across a field and down a bluff to the river and his boat. When he had rowed me over he showed me the path to the Fairchild place. It was a long way, and once I thought I was lost. When it was nearly dark I came to a log house. I knocked and a woman came to the door. She was not an old woman, but she made me feel young. I guess because I'd never had any trouble like she had. She wore a shawl over head, and had a baby in her arms. The baby was nursing. When she saw me she pushed her breast out of sight. "I killed a copper," I said.

"What's that?" she said.

"It's a man. A man like the ones that killed your husband. It was in a city. He wore a uniform."

She stared at me.

"My picture's in the post office,[1]" I said.

"They would pay money for me," I said.

"Come in," she said.

I went in, and sat down by the fire. It was almost out. Two small children played in the ashes. The woman laid the baby on the bed. She went into another room. She called me soon. She gave me overalls, and a shirt, and a pair of brogan shoes. The clothes were not a bad fit. "Can you cut wood for the fire?" she asked. "It is hard to cut wood in the rain."

"Yes," I said.

"You are my cousin come from Shearer Valley by the falls of Cumberland. He is called Dick Hansford, and has never been here. His hair is black. Tomorrow you and the boys go to Feldew Ridge for black walnuts. Then your hair will be dark, too."

"The mail carrier and a Keeney man saw me."

"They are from the other side," she said. "They never come here. Nobody comes here but Julie Meece."

"The children?"

"They are not ones to talk."

She made me a bed in the loft. I went with her to the barn next morning to help with the work. I'd never been about a barn, but she taught me what to do. On the crib door was nailed the skull of some animal. The teeth were in the skull, two of them tushes three or four inches long. "What is that?" I said.

"'A hog's skull," she said. She touched a long tooth. "The hogs they left Tred with had teeth like that."

"Your dog fought them," I said.

"It got them to chase him," she said. "Nothing can fight the hogs of Rockcastle. They were mean things—the hogs. Near as mean as the men."

I got the corn and went to feed the hogs she was fattening. Most of them were young male hogs. They had been castrated and did not seem fierce. They were not like the hogs I saw at the World's Fair. These were big boned and flat sided, with long legs. They did not make a lot of noise. "Feed him fifteen ears," the woman said, and led me to a pen behind the barn.

In the pen was a boar hog with teeth like the teeth of the skull. The woman looked at the black hog, and I thought she smiled. "He will make a fine mess of pork," she said.

"He looks old and tough," I said.

"He is. He is a cannibal hog. Last spring he got out and ate seven young pigs."

I looked at his teeth. "He could eat a child," I said.

"More like him could kill a man—two men," the woman said. She looked at the hog. She looked at me. "I think God sent you," she said.

After the work was done at the barn, the biggest boy (he was twelve years old) took me to Feldew Ridge for black walnuts. The ridge was a narrow neck of land twisted into a high horseshoe. The walnut trees were on an inside slope of the bend, and beyond the trees were yellow sandstone bluffs. Below the bluffs I could see beech trees, and holly with red berries growing there. I thought it would be nice to go down and pick some holly right off a tree. I looked about the bluff for a place to go down. They were not high bluffs. No higher than a two story building, but steep. Les, the boy, was hunting wintergreen berries higher up the ridge side. I called to him, "Les, is there a path down the cliff here?" He did not answer me, but ran quick down the hill side.

"I want to pick holly down there," I said.

He walked to the bluff edge, and looked over. "You couldn't go down there. Nobody goes down there."

"Why?"

"They stay there. When my granma was a girl a neighbor woman got lost with her baby. She went in there. They found the buckles on her shoes, and pieces of the baby's dress. It was red lindsey-woolsey. Hogs—them hogs will eat anything. They're hard to kill, too. If you do shoot one there's a dozen others."

He stood there and looked down the cliffs into the holly trees, and I thought of the black boar in his pen. I thought of the teeth in the skull on the crib door, and I quit wanting the holly berries. I wanted to take the walnuts and go away.

"I wish I could see one," the boy said, and he talked in a whisper now. "Them hogs are the stillest things. They're all in their holes under the sand rocks, asleep."

"We'd better get home," I said.

"They never come up here," he said. "They stay in the valleys, and eat beechnuts, or go over to Cumberland and eat pig nuts and acorns. There they don't bother much unless you have a dog. They hate dogs."

I looked down the cliffs again. It was like a room down there. A man might climb down but not up. I was glad I'd asked about the path.

When we were started home Les pointed over the ridge toward Rockcastle. "See that old chimney?" he said. "That's in the mouth of Holy Creek. People lived there maybe a hundred years ago. They raised hogs to send to Georgia, so my granma said."

"What is Holy Creek?" I asked.

"That's where the hogs live. Only it's not a real creek. Just a valley where you can go in but can't come out."

We hulled the walnuts, and the woman took the hulls for my hair. That night she carried the walnuts to the black hog. She stood a long time and watched him eat them. I watched too. He would get a walnut between his back teeth, throw back his head, and close his little eyes. Then there would come the crunching sound, and I would remember how Les had used two stones up there on the ridge side to crack a walnut. Somehow I did not like watching that hog. It made me think of things. I could not see how the woman could watch him either. Her man had been left dead in a field with hogs like that.

The next day I cut wood. Les helped me. When we were carrying it in, Julie Meece came. I hid in the loft. She and the woman sat in the big house by the fire. Through the thin boards I could hear their talk. "How's the baby?" Julie Meece asked.

"Poorly."

"He'll be a puny one. Your milk is poisoned with hate for the two that killed your man."

"I know it," the woman said.

"If you would cry like a sensible woman."

"I can't cry 'till them that killed him are in their graves."

"Pray to Jesus."

"I can't pray—not yet."

"Such talk," the neighbor woman said, and spoke of other things. "It'll soon be fine hog killing weather. You'll have plenty of meat. I would kill that boar hog first. He is not safe."

"I will kill him when the time comes. His pen is strong."

"He will be fit only for lard. The meat will be strong."

"Yes, it will make a fine smell."

I helped with the hog killing the first cold days in December. We did not kill the black boar. Every day I gave him corn, and every evening the woman went to stand and watch him eat.

It was a cold winter that year. The woman's children had no shoes. She made them moccasins from the skin of a calf we had killed. There was no flour or sugar in the house. We ate pork and molasses and fodder beans and cornbread. Sometimes the lesser children cried with the cold, but the mother and the older ones never complained.

It was a cold night late in January, and the woman and I sat by the fire. She had sent the children away to bed. "How much money is it they would pay for you?" she said, and looked into the coals.

"A thousand dollars," I said.

"Do you trust me?" she said, and turned and looked at me.

"Yes," I said.

She took a stubby pencil from the mantel, and a piece of brown paper bag. She smoothed the paper slowly on her knee. She wet the pencil with her tongue. She looked into the fire. She talked. She did not talk to me. "They'll come alone—the greedy devils—they'll tell none. They don't know me. I'll be Julie Meece."

She wet the pencil again. This time she talked to me. "I can't spell all the words. Can you spell?"

"Yes," I said.

I spelled Rockcastle, and February, and chimney, and secret, and Ransom Ledbetter, and sunrise. Then I addressed the letter. I wrote "Andrew Combs, Somerset, Kentucky" on a crumpled envelope. The next day Les took four eggs for a stamp, and went over Rockcastle to the post office and mailed it.

One morning, I guess it was three weeks later, the woman woke me early. It was dark. I couldn't see her there in the loft. I could feel her shaking me, and hear her say, "It's time to kill him. Come help me."

"Kill who?" I said, and sat up and felt the cold.

"The black hog. I'll have to shoot him. I need you to hold the light."

Outside the stars had not paled. It was a cold time. I could hear the timber on Fellow Ridge crackle with the frost, and when I laid my fingers on the door latch they stuck there. "A fine day," the woman said, and looked at the stars, and sucked up lungfuls of the cold.

The black boar was not asleep. He stood and blinked at us in the smoky red light of the pine knot. I could see the coarse hairs raised across his shoulders, and the bits of frozen mud and ice on his feet. "He hates the cold," the woman said. "The others will hate it too. They cannot root in the frozen ground, and empty bellies make them mean."

She shot the hog between the eyes. It ran a little with the bullet in its head. It died, I think, standing up. Its forefeet slid over the frozen ground, and the black snout came down between them. Then its eyes stopped blinking and I knew that it was dead. The woman climbed into the pen, and stabbed it between the forelegs with a butcher knife. The blood froze about it in a ragged pool, and then she said, "We will scrape him now."

Together we half dragged and half carried it to the iron kettle of water hissing above a fire of fat pine. The woman took gunny sacks, and spread them over the hog's bristles. I dipped bucketsful of the boiling water and poured it over the hog. Together we scraped off the stiff black hairs.

The woman hurried. It was as if she had to have him cleaned and cut up by a certain time. I hurried too. I don't know why. She kept looking over her shoulder toward Kender's Mountain. Behind it the stars were thinning out, and the sky blue-gray instead of black. She was watching for the sunrise. I watched and worked against it too. When the hog was scraped and cleaned she had me wrap it in sacks and pour hot water over it. "To keep him warm," she said.

She left me and went to the house. She came back soon with two suits of ragged overalls. They had belonged to Tred. She did not say anything. She took bits of hair and parts of the hog, the boar parts you know, and laid them in the pockets. Then she took a threaded needle from her bosom, and sewed the pockets up. She put more around the bottoms of the trousers, and folded and sewed it smooth away. I never asked her what she was doing. I don't know what I thought about while I stood there and watched her hide pieces of the bloody, stinking meat in the ragged overalls. I do not remember thinking that she was crazy. I know that I kept watching for the sunrise. I seemed to know that her work must be done before sunrise. I know that I forgot the cold. The pine knot burned low and I lit another.

All the stars paled, and on Kender's Mountain the pines stood black against a pale wash of pink. The woman finished with the clothes. She took a clean cloth (there was no paper in the house) and put bits of the still warm liver and heart and kidneys in it. She tied the bundle, and wrapped it in the overalls. She wiped her hands on a gunny sack. "I'm going now," she said. "Come behind if you want to. Not too close."

I walked behind her toward Feldew Ridge. The thin layer of snow crunched into powder under our feet, and all about us trees cracked in the cold. It was so still. I wished a little wind would blow. I thought it might take away the boar smell on my hands and clothes. Even under the pines the air was drenched with it. We came to the spot where Les had pointed out the old chimney by Rockcastle in Holy Valley. The woman walked down the ridge side toward the chimney. "Don't come much nearer," she said.

I went as far as a thick low growing clump of ivy, and hid there. The woman went on until I could see her standing by the chimney. She held the overalls and bundle of warm meat close in her two arms. You'd thought it was a child she held. The sun came and touched the top of the chimney. It came lower, just above her head. Then I saw two men come up from the river. The woman walked a little way and met them. I could not hear much they said. I saw them take the overalls. They laughed and put them on. I heard one, the bigger of the two, say, "You'd make a smart sheriff, sister." I saw them take the bundle of meat, and heard them laugh some more.

The woman pointed up the valley, and said something. Then she walked away. When she was gone a little piece the shorter man called to her, "No danger of gettin' lost?"

"No," she said, "just keep up the valley 'till you see the cliffs. He'll be there in his rock house. Say, 'Mrs. Meece sent you some meat by us.' He will come out, and the rest will be easy."

When she was gone a little farther she stopped and called to them again, "In case you see a hog just make like to call a dog. The hogs here are afraid of dogs."

They laughed and waved to her. She came straight away then, and did not look at them again. She walked past the ivy bushes where I was. I think she had forgotten me. When the men were out of sight I ran up the ridge side. I wanted to go to the place where Les and I had gathered walnuts. I was almost there when I heard men in the valley below me whistle for a dog. I ran a few steps, and heard revolver shots, a whole lot of them coming fast. I heard a pig squeal. I reached the patch of winter green above the bluff, and saw the woman sitting still on a gray sandrock. I don't think she saw me. I was below her near the bluff edge. I could hear hogs now down in the beeches and holly. They made soft, "Woofs, woofs," and I could hear their feet on the frozen ground.

I wanted to look over the edge without being seen. I lay down on the sand rock, and stretched out to look down. I never looked. I heard a man scream. I put my hands over my ears, and pulled my head hard against the rock. Once when I was a boy I saw the brewery stables burn. I remember a big horse screamed and ran back into the fire. Then it screamed again. This scream was like that, and like a woman's. Sometimes I can still hear it.

I lay that way a little while, and then everything was still, and I took my hands from my ears and stood up. I listened and I heard them. Their teeth made crunching sounds. The black boar's teeth when he ate the walnuts had sounded that way. I knew there were no walnuts down there.

Ketchup-Making Saturday

Robert Penn Warren at *Southern Review* read this story in 1936 and returned it to Harriette Simpson along with an invitation to send others.

———◦◦◦◦———

*D*aisy shoved her buttocks hard against my stomach again, and I heard eggs sizzle in the little skillet with the broken handle. Delphie's elbows raked my spine, and I wiggled a little and thought that coffee and cornbread and bacon would taste good in this half way time between midnight and morning. I couldn't sleep anyway. I couldn't do anything but remember yesterday and wonder about today.

I got up and lighted the lamp and saw a pile of uncorrected fourth grade arithmetic papers. Thoughts of anything that had to do with numbers filled me with a great unhappiness. When Monday came I might no longer be the teacher of Sawbriar School. "Teacher, it ain't mornin'," High Pockets[1] called from the front room where he doubtless lay and looked at the shine of my lamp through the cracks in the door.

"I know," I answered, "but I'm hungry."

"Ellie's might nigh got her ready. I been a layin' a waitin' to hear her set th' table. I've got a big mornin' a squirrel huntin' ahead."

Dishes rattled in the end of the lean-to away from the kitchen, and while they rattled, High Pockets rolled out of bed and into his shirt and overalls. When he had gone into the kitchen to put on his shoes, I followed with the lamp and set it on the eating table between a jar of watermelon rind preserves and the noseless cream pitcher filled with tin teaspoons. In the kitchen Ellie stood by one of High Pockets' long bare feet and carefully poured gravy into the rusty bowl with the yellow flowers. High Pockets looked up, saw me in the door, smoothed lank black hair away from his forehead, and said, "Rollin' out early, Teacher."

"Yes," I said, and made way for Ellie and the gravy.

When High Pockets had put on his shoes and washed his face, and I had washed my face and we were sitting at the table, I remembered yesterday's trouble with a sharper pang, and Ellie's good breakfast grew tasteless and stale.

"Ye're not eatin', Teacher. Trouble at school?" High Pockets asked.

I nodded.

Ellie sighed as she ladled gravy onto a hunk of cornbread. "I reckin' it's that Lurie Haines' Zorie. She's spiled too much to ever larn. Many's th' time I've wished we'd have a teacher that'ud risk givin' her a genuwine good spankin'."

I wept suddenly into my overdone egg. "You have such a teacher now."

High Pockets stared at me, pity in his smoked pearl eyes, "Ye mean we did have. Lurie Haines'ull run you off this ridge come daylight."

Ellie's wispy dun-colored hair framed a face sick with woe, "An ye wuz sich a good teacher. I'd hoped ye'd stay till Reuben an' Bertie wuz big enough tu start. Peared like th' big uns wuz a larnin' so."

High Pockets chewed bacon and frowned. "Long ez Caleb Haines is trustee an' thet Lurie's his wife an' runs him an' th' school, an' ez thet youngen a their'n won't so much as larn tu count her fingers, we ain't goin' tu have no teacher two yer straight."

Ellie nodded. "Thet youngen's too mean tu larn. She's got sense. Didn't last yer pore Mr. Walls send away fer ever'thing calculated tu make a youngen larn tu count—an allus no good."

"But she's seven years old, and this is her third year in school and—."

"She's Lurie's least'un—spiled rotten," Ellie said. "Her a comin' so long atter th' others an' all, like a second fam'ly you might say. An' Lurie allus bragged thet she's naiver laid a hand on her, an' she'd like tu see th' color a th' teacher's eyes thet would—right 'fore th' youngen too."

"Teacher shore laid a hand, though." It was eleven-year-old Delphie, wide awake with her dress on backwards and her shoes in her hand. She stood in the doorway and blinked at us.

"Shet up, Delphie," High Pockets said. "Me an' yer Mom hev told ye youngens 'bout tattlin' ever'thing frum school when we're boardin' th' teacher."

"I lowed ye'd know last night when she couldn't eat," Delphine apologized and sat on the doorsill and put on her shoes. She knotted a shoe string and sighed. "I'm afeared this'ull be th' finish a teacher, but us youngens hev done all we kin do. We follered thet Zorie down th' road a good piece an' double double dared her not tu tell her maw on Teacher fer givin' her thet paddlin'."

"Don't be a tattlin' now," Ellie warned.

"There's not much to tattle," I said. "Zorie got four fingers on one hand, seven on the other, and the stove with three legs—then she giggled and looked at me and said the way she always does, "Teacher, I'm gettin' nervous. Mom, she don' want nobody to make me nervous."

"Then Teacher she upt an' paddled Zorie with thet cedar paddle ye whittled fer her. An her naiver a paddlin' none before this schooi."

"I wisht tu God I'd naiver a made thet paddle," High Pockets mourned.

"Zorie she shore needed hit, but," and Delphie's braids moved slowly as she sighed and rocked her head, "pore Teacher."

"Pore Teacher is right. Thet Lurie Haines'ull be here come daylight," Ellie prophesied.

High Pockets pushed his plate away and took a chew of tobacco. "I'd best be gittin' on. I ain't a goin' to mix in no woman fracas." He got up and stood staring down at me with eyes as mournful as his hound dogs.' "Teacher, ye're welcome to airy gun I've got. Better take yer pick an' set in th' door."

"If I did that, I'd be without a job," I said.

"Better tu be alive an' a livin' on rabbit an' poke shoots than daid an' kilt by Lurie Haines. Why she could knock ye clean acrost th' ridge an'—."

"Don't be a skeerin' her so, High Pockets," Ellie begged.

"Women, women," he mourned, and spat through a crack on the floor and then went away with a last solemn, "Take keer a yersef, Teacher—if ye can."

I helped Ellie break a mess of cornfield beans for dinner while she waited for breakfast and milking time to come. "Ye kin hep in th' ketchup[2] makin' today, Teacher," she told me. "Hit'll take yer mind off'n yer troubles, an' I want to use up ever'thing left in th' garden."

Delphie bestirred herself from her drowsing back of the stove. "Kin I be th one to go an' borrie Willie's sassage grinder, Mom?"

"Soon's daylight comes. I'll haf tu send Daisy an' Rhodie tu Peter's fer more red peppers an' cucumbers. I ain't hardly got enough."

Daylight and the children drifted in, and Ellie fried more bacon and eggs, made another skillet of gravy, baked a pan of unsalted cornpone for the hounds, milked the cow, and fed the hounds and hogs and chickens. I helped Delphie wash the dishes, and when they were done she went for the sausage grinder, and Daisy and Rhodie went to another neighbor's for cucumbers and red peppers. I took Jerry and the younger children to the garden back of the house on the ridge and gathered the last of the green tomatoes. They grew on a level with the pine tops in the hollow below so that we could look out and away and see the sun like a red-enameled pie pan hung neatly against a gold and purple wall. It would be another day of glory with the poplar leaves blowing in and out the windows, and the sun shining hot and yellow into the white sandy yard, and the crows caw-cawing over the corn, and the chickens cackling in the barn. And with all that promise of a windy day, I wished for low clouds and rain and wind and sleet and snow—anything that would keep Lurie Haines and her Zorie away.

When we had gathered in the kitchen to wash and cut the ketchup vegetables, Ellie glanced through the window at the rising sun and then at me. "Teacher, why don't you go off huntin' hick'ry nuts or somethin'?"

"She'd find me," I said, and looked down at the cucumber I held and wondered if I ought to lay it down for a Smith Wesson.

Ellie sighed. "I wisht she warn't so big, er else one a us wuz bigger." She pushed Queenie's brown nose away from the cabbage she held. "I recollect th' time—Delphie, don't let th' tumater juice git all over th' floor. Ketch th' leak in a skillet." Bertie the baby whimpered, and she threw down a shining cabbage leaf for him to play with, and patiently pushed the hound dog's nose away again. She looked at the pan of onions and Jerry's red weeping eyes. "That'll do, Jerry. Go fetch in some stove wood. I reckin we got stove wood."

Jerry returned soon with a few pine chips in his hand. "Pop fergot tu cut wood yisterday," he said, "an' last night we'uns picked up all th' chips fer supper."

Ellie blinked her lashless eyes, sighed a little. "I recollect now. I fergot tu remind him." She untied her apron full of cabbage and laid it on a chair, reminding Jerry to come sit on the poles as she went out the door.

When they had gone, Delphie stuffed green tomatoes into the sausage mill and looked at me. "Hit's th' onliest time I ever wish you was a man, Teacher. Last yer when Pop 'ud fergit th' wood Mr. Walls he'd cut hit while he's a boardin here."

I slit a cucumber. "I wish I were a man," I said, "or at least a woman— a great big woman that could cut wood and—."

Delphie watched green tomato juice spread over the kitchen floor. "Ye naiver could cut wood. Ye're like Mom. Ye need tu be heftier. Miz Haines, thet Zorie's mama now," she went on with an ominous shake of her head, "she kin shore cut wood. Good ez eny man. Why, las winter she hepped her man split rails.—Ye had ought tu a gone tu town with th' Pings, Teacher.— Miz Haines she's awful foolish over thet Zorie."

"I wish," I began, and Jerry's frightened scream rose suddenly above the blub and squeak of the sausage mill. I rolled cucumbers out of my lap, stepped over Reuben and Bertie, plowed through the dogs, Queenie, Lumber, and Drum, reached the door, and Jerry raced into my arms. "Mom she's kilt hersef. She let a stick a wood fly up an' hit her on th' haid. Now she's a settin' daid by th' wood log, blood runnin' all over."

"Don't skeer Teacher no worse," Delphie ordered, and stopped the sausage mill, and opened the cupboard door. "Mom ain't daid er she wouldn't be a settin'. Whar's th' linimint?"

I picked up Bertie and ran after Jerry to the wood log while Delphie came at a slower pace with the other children, the dogs, and the liniment. "I'll naiver larn tu cut wood," Ellie said when we came up to her. She sat on the ground and rocked her head a little, and looked at us out of one pale blue eye while blood from a gash in her forehead flowed in a red curtain over the other.

I set Bertie on the chopping log, pushed Queenie and Lumber out of the way, and tried to examine the cut, but Ellie only pushed away my hand. "I'm all right," she moaned, "but I cain't cut no more wood."

"Pop had ought tu a cut hit," Delphie said.

"I fergot tu remind him," Ellie answered, and got up and tried to walk.

"You'd better lie down," I said.

She fainted then, but came to in time to tell the children not to scream their heads off. Delphie and I got her into the house, and washed the ragged tear and poured in liniment at which she winced a little. We wanted to use a clean flour sack for a bandage, but she was saving flour sacks for petticoats for Daisy so that we had to use only a little salt sack and fasten it to her head with one of High Pockets' blue bandanas. She lay still in the bed with Bertie at her breast and whimpered a little. "I've jist got tu have some wood. I kin let th' ketchup go, but pretty soon High Pockets he'll be a comin' in hungry."

The children and Queenie and Lumber and Drum all looked at me. "Don't you fret," I said. "I'll get some wood. I can cut wood."

Ellie sighed—half with relief, I thought. "I hate fer ye tu do sich, Teacher, but High Pockets he'll be comin' in hungry."

Queenie and Lumber and Drum and all the children followed me to the chopping log. "Kin ye cut wood, Teacher?" Daisy asked.

"I never tried," I said, "but—I have split kindling."

A long green pine pole lay by the chopping log. I looked at it. Pine was soft wood, so I had heard. I laid the pole on the log. I told the children to get out of the way. Delphie tittered. "Go grind your tomatoes, Delphie," I said. I picked up the ax. I had never known that an ax could be so heavy. High Pockets had made it. He'd made it to fit his size he had always said. It was double bladed so that when I raised it a little, the blade on top seemed ready to graze my hair, and I could not get my fingers all the way around the handle. "I'll hold th' pole," Jerry offered.

I raised the ax and brought it down. It came sharp against the seasoned maple of the chopping log, and jarred my head and my shoulders and my heels. "Whack at th' pole, Teacher," Jerry advised.

"Mom could naiver cut wood uth thet ax neither," Daisy comforted me.

I raised the ax high and brought it down hard. It struck the slippery pine pole, glanced off and out of my hand and came to rest not far from my foot and Queenie's nose. Queenie moved.

Jerry sat on the pole and looked at me. "Thet'll naiver do, Teacher. Ye're a goin' tu kill Queenie."

"An' mebbe slice off her own yer an' hack up her toes," Daisy said. She pushed Rhodie and Reuben behind her. "Ye youngens git back. Tain't safe—pore Teacher."

I stood and studied the pole. I forgot to look toward the ridge road as I had been doing all morning. I picked up the ax. "Now, Teacher, jist cut straight intu th' pole," Jerry said and glanced toward the road. "Oh Lordy God," he cried in the manner of High Pockets.

I saw the road, too. But I couldn't say anything. Could only remember that I had an ax in my hand while Lurie Haines and her Zorie walked up the road and across the yard toward me. Lurie drew closer and I laid down the ax. I knew it was no good. If I couldn't make a dent in a pine pole, I couldn't graze her. She was of a size to fit the ax, and the sun glinted on her long straight brown nose and her straight tight black hair and her straight black eyebrows. She carried a bushel basket of eggs over one big arm, and when she passed the porch, she set it down. "She's gittin' ready, oh my Lordy," Daisy squeaked, and hurled herself toward the kitchen door followed by Rhodie and Reuben and the hound dogs.

Jerry sat still and clenched the pine pole and moaned, "Oh Lordy God. I wisht Pop was home. Pore Teacher."

Lurie stepped quickly and firmly over the white sand of the yard. I was afraid to look at her. I stared past her. The first hills were green islands of pine in a sea of yellow poplar and red oak and maple leaves. The farther hills were purple—my help cometh from the hills. I will lift up mine eyes— I wondered if I prayed. I wished the hills would swallow me. I wished I could fly. I wished I could squinch my eyes and wait without looking at her. Ellie's head had bled. Maybe mine would too—all over the pine pole and the chopping log. She came nearer, and I looked through her to the hills.

Her hand came hard down on my shoulder, and her voice came with a louder boom than Queenie's on a moonlit night, "I jist couldn't hardly wait, Teacher. Naiver wuz I so happy."

Jerry fell off the pine pole. She reached down and heaved him to his feet. "When Zorie came home last night an set around so quiet-like, like she was a thinkin' hard on somethin', I thought she's sick." Her laughter came in a great trumpeting. "An' pretty soon she come up tu th' barn whar I was a tryin' tu break up a settin' hen, an' she says tu me she says, 'Mom, I've larned tu count things.'"

"'Well, count them aigs,' I says. An' she went slow an' tuck her time an' counted th' aigs—six a them. Still, I wasn't so tickled as you'd think I might be. Zorie's sich a nervis little thing, she's been countin' things at home fer more than a yer now, but she never could do no good in school. So when she'd counted th' aigs so nice I says to her, 'Zorie, it's a pity we can't find a teacher that'll teach you to count in school.'

"She studied a while an' looked at th' aigs till pretty soon she says, 'I think you've got a teacher what can teach me to count in school.' 'Honest?' I says. 'Fer certain,' she says, 'Counted today.'"

Lurie whacked my other shoulder. "Jist think, Teacher, I've been a hopin' fer over two yer thet some fool teacher 'ud larn thet youngen tu count things in school. She ain't no fool, but I'd about give up, her a bein' so nervis an' all."

Zorie pulled her mother's skirt. She looked at me with her round black eyes. She rubbed her buttocks, tenderly, reflectively. "I ain't so nervis—no more, Mom," she said.

"Mebbe Teacher 'ull cure ye a that, too, Zorie," Lurie said.

Jerry sat down on the pole again. "I reckin she will," he said.

Lurie looked at the pine pole and then at me. She glared at Jerry. "Ye'uns shorely ain't got th' best teacher we've ever had out a cuttin' wood."

"Mom, she hurt her haid."

"Whar's High Pockets Casteller—fox huntin'?"

"No—No Ma'm, squirrel huntin'."

Lurie spat on her hands. She grabbed the ax. "Ellie bad hurt?"

"Bleedin'," Jerry answered, and got up from the pine pole.

"Git back ye'uns," Lurie commanded. "I'm a goin' tu cut some wood—fer Teacher. But it'll gripe me some if'n thet squirrel huntin', fox horn tootin', fiddle playin' High Pockets eats airy a bite a bread baked with it."

She swung the ax eleven times, and eleven sticks of pine wood lay by the chopping log. She kicked one of the soft pine sticks disdainfully with her toe, while her brow contracted with some acute displeasure. "Thet wood won't heat th' stove enough tu fry spit. Hit's fit fer nothin' but sappin' an' sobbin'. What ye need," she continued when her brows had straightened themselves a little, "is somethin' good an' seasoned fer a hot stiddy fire—an' I don't see nothin'." Her eye happened upon the maple chopping log, thick and seasoned and hard as iron. "Th' very thing," she said. "Git back, Zorie." Her ax fell and the chips flew before Jerry could find words for protest.

"But thet's Pop's sugar-tree choppin' log," he cried, and ducked a flying chip. "He borried Willie's mules an' snaked it clean frum Redeye Holler. Thar ain't no sich good wood fer choppin' logs up here. Pop he—."

"Don't Pop he me," Lurie threatened, and stopped and wiped sweat from her forehead with the back of one leathery wrist. "I want jist onct," she went on, "fer yer maw tu have good dry wood tu cook with—ye an' Zorie git frum under my feet. Go stay with th' rest a th' youngens."

When the sugar tree chopping log lay as a pile of sticks along with the pine, Lurie looked about for a pine stump. Found one suited to her purpose, and with one ox-felling blow sank the ax deep into the soft wood. "Teacher, ye an' nobody else 'bout this place 'ull be a cuttin' wood till a man-sized man comes tu git thet ax out."

I tried to imagine the language of High Pockets while he heaved at the ax, but I only said, "Won't you come in and stay awhile."

She squinted at the sun through one black eyebrow. "I ain't got th' time. I've got tu git on to th' store, but I'd like to speak to Ellie—pore soul. Where is that Zorie now? I want her here ready tu start when I git through a seein' Ellie."

"I'll find her," I said, and went to the young ketchup makers in the kitchen while Lurie stood in the porch door and scolded Ellie.

The green tomato and onion juice was a great lake by the stove now, but Delphie and Daisy and Jerry were taken up with more important things than a leak in the sausage mill. They and the other children were deep in a serious conversation with button-eyed Zorie. She had backed defensively against the cold stove and was saying in a tremulous lisp, "Cross yer hearts?"

Delphie nodded solemnly over the spluttering sausage mill. "We won't do nothin'," she promised.

"Ye won't be a puttin' a lizard down my neck an' a toad in my dinner bucket an' pizen in my apples?"

Delphie stopped the sausage mill and crossed her heart. Jerry, Daisy, Rhodie and Reuben did the same, while little Bertie sat on the floor in the green tomato juice and pounded with a broken monkey wrench and crowed. "Thet is," Delphie said when the heart crossing business was finished, "if'n ye behave."

Zorie crossed her heart. "I ain't nervis no more, an' I'll count my toes like fightin' fire," she promised.

I stepped through the door. She saw me and dashed wordless into the other room.

When she had gone, Delphie smiled at me. "With ye tu learn her, an' we'uns tu make her behave we'll hev thet youngen doin' long division come cold weather."

Jerry stood in the door and looked toward the spot where the wood log had been. "I'm shore glad Miz Haines she didn't kill you, Teacher, but what'll Pop say 'bout his choppin' log. Sich a good hard choppin' log he had," and he sighed and shook his head.

The Washerwoman's Day

Written in 1934 or 1935, this story was first published in the prestigious *Southern Review* 1 (Winter 1936): 522–527, when its editors were Cleanth Brooks and Robert Penn Warren. "The Washerwoman's Day" is the first story for which Harriette L. Simpson was paid. She received a check for $25 and felt "on top of the world."

It is her most frequently reprinted story, having appeared in a number of collections including Cleanth Brooks, John Purser, and Robert Penn Warren's textbook, *Approaches to Literature* (1939, 1952); Brooks and Warren's *Anthology of Stories from the Southern Review* (1953); Albert Stewart's *Kentucky Writing. No. 4. Deep Summer* (1963); and Robert J. Higgs, Ambrose Manning, and Jim Wayne Miller's *Appalachia Inside Out* (1995).

"*I*t was pneumonia all right, but the lye maybe had something to do with it," Granma said.

Mama shifted Joie to her other breast. "Ollie Rankin ought to have had more sense," she said.

"She didn't know the old fool would take off her shoes and scrub the kitchen barefooted."

"Can I go to the funeral," I said.

"Be quiet," Mama said. "Her shoes were new, and she maybe thought to save them. The poor fool, her legs were swollen purple to her waist, Molly Hardwick said."

"If that Laurie Mae were fit to go into a decent house. They say that baby is exactly like Perce . . ."

Mama looked at me. Granma hushed. "Can I go to the funeral?" I said.

"No," Mama said. "It does make it unhandy. I guess we'll have to get a nigger from Canetown, but I don't like niggers about."

"I always said I'd rather have black trash than white trash any day . . ."

"Did she walk home without her shoes? Susie Chrisman said she did, and there was snow and . . ."

"Hush, Jane," Mama said. "You'll be late to school."

"Spell *vegetation*," Granma said.

"V-e-g-e-t-a-t-i-o-n," I spelled.

"Wear your overshoes," Mama said.

"Don't go about the funeral," Granma said.

"The Ladies Aid are burying her. Susie Chrisman said her father . . ."

"Don't argue," Mama said, and Granma tapped her cane.

I ran all the way to school. I thought all morning, and at noon I said, "Miss Rankin, my little brother Joie was croupy this morning and Mama forgot."

"What?"

"To write a note of excuse for me to go to the funeral. Susie Chrisman is going."

"Are you sure your mother wanted you to go?"

"Yes, mam. Clarie Bolin has always done our washing. Mama said I should go out of respect for the dead and the Ladies Aid . . . if she was poor white trash. I know my spelling."

"You may go at one-thirty," she said.

Susie and I held hands and ran fast down the sidewalk from the school. We laughed as we ran, for it was good to be out of school and there was a snow promise in the air and Christmas was only two weeks away. At the foot of the hill we stopped. "It's not proper to run all the way to a funeral," Susie said.

"No," I said. "Did they undertake her?"

"No. My father said it was a waste of good money to undertake poor people in cold weather. He sold the Ladies Aid the coffin, though."

"Is it true about the roses?"

Susie skipped twice before she remembered and was proper again. "Yes. The Ladies Aid sent all the way to Lexington. Two dozen white roses, and it the dead of winter. They cost three dollars . . . and her the washer-woman, Papa said."

Inside the church Mrs. Hyden was singing a solo. Her mouth was very wide open, and while we tiptoed to the second row from the back she held the word *dew* until it seemed she would not let it go until we sat down. I was embarrassed and in my haste stumbled over Susie. Susie tittered. When we were seated, Mrs. Hyden sang on about the dew on the roses and the voice she heard.

Susie nudged me. "Laurie Mae don't look so nice. That coat Mrs. Har-vey gave her don't fit so good."

I craned my head down the aisle to see. Laurie Mae sat alone in the front row before her mother's coffin. Beside her was a long bundle wrapped in a piece of dirty brown blanket. "Mama said, 'She'll have her nerve to bring that baby.' The Ladies Aid'll be mad," Susie whispered.

"Mama said the baby looked like Mr. Perce Burton," I said.

"On account of Laurie Mae was a hired girl there last year."

Something jerked my pigtail. I looked around. Mrs. John Crabtree set her lips tight together and looked hard at me. She was president of The Ladies Aid, and Mrs. Ollie Rankin sat with her. I nudged Susie, and we were still. Reverend Lipscomb read The Beatitudes and prayed. While he prayed Susie and I raised our heads and looked at all the people. Susie pinched me. Laurie Mae didn't have her head bowed at her own mother's funeral. "Isn't she awful," Susie whispered.

Then the choir sang "Lord, I'm coming home." Then Reverend Lip-scomb preached the funeral. I was glad he made it so short. He talked about what the Bible meant when it said things like the poor and the meek shall inherit the earth. He explained that the poor must be hard working and patient and righteous. He said that righteousness had this day been shown by the ladies of the church in their beautiful putting away of the dead. I thought his words were so wonderful that I would remember them.

He said that man was made to err, and that the dead woman had been no different from the world of men, but he hoped that God in His divine mercy and goodness and infinite wisdom would look down on her and forgive her sins and take her to His bosom. He hoped that the one of the living nearest and dearest to the dead would profit by the affliction that God in His almighty wisdom had seen fit to lay upon her, and change the path of her ways and walk henceforth with uprightness and decency. "He means Laurie Mae," Susie whispered.

"She's not even crying," I said.

He finished and the choir sang. Then Miss Virginia played the piano, and we all walked around and looked at Clarie Bolin and the white roses and Laurie Mae. "Didn't she look ugly," Susie whispered when we were back in our seats.

"She looked mad," I said, and didn't want to whisper any more. It was no longer fun. I wondered why the dead woman looked the way she did with her teeth clamped tight together and her thin blue lips drawn back a little ways. She looked, I thought, as if she had just come back from a long fight, and had lost in the fight. I wished in a dim sort of way that she could know The Ladies Aid had spent three dollars for white roses. I thought it would have made her feel better.

Susie's father wheeled the coffin down the aisle. The rollers made a little squeaking as they rolled over the carpet, and the white roses quivered until one pale petal slipped loose and fell behind the coffin. Laurie Mae sat and looked straight in front of her until the coffin was going through the door into the vestibule. She got up then, and took the ragged bundle from the seat and laid it carefully on her arm, and walked slowly down the aisle. All the ladies looked at her and the bundle, but she did not look at anything.

When the coffin was in the vestibule Mrs. Crabtree and Mrs. Rankin started whispering. We turned around to listen. "Not so much as a thank-you for all we've done," Mrs. Crabtree said.

"As soon as I heard that she was dead I went right up there into that hut," Mrs. Rankin said.

Mrs. Hyden and some other ladies left their places in the choir and joined them. Mrs. Hyden leaned over me to talk to Mrs. Crabtree and I could feel her fat breasts on my shoulder. "What about the roses?" she said. "You're not going to send them to the cemetery?"

"No," Mrs. Crabtree said. "I had thought we might give Laurie Mae some and keep the others for the sewing circle tomorrow afternoon."

"What would Laurie Mae do with roses?" Susie's mother said.

"We could give her just a few . . . I think maybe we ought to."

"I'll go see to it," Mrs. Crabtree said, and got up.

We followed her to the church door, where men were carrying the coffin down the high steps. Susie's father had taken away the roses and stood holding them all bundled in his hands. Mrs. Crabtree took them. She looked at the flowers and arranged them in a neat bouquet. When she had finished arranging them, she turned the bouquet round and round and looked at it. She saw the rose with the petal missing and took it out. Then she took out five others.

Laurie Mae stood on the top step watching the men carry down the coffin. For a moment it looked as if they were going to drop it and Susie and I held our breaths. Mrs. Crabtree tapped Laurie Mae on the shoulder. "Here are some roses," she said, and handed her the six roses. "Reverend Lipscomb will drive you to the cemetery in his buggy."

Laurie Mae took the roses and did not say anything. She waited until the coffin was down and in the hearse, and then went to the buggy. Susie and I watched to see how she would manage. Reverend Lipscomb hadn't come out of the church, and no one offered to help her into the buggy. She tried first to step in it with the roses and the baby almost fell over into the muddy road. Then she laid the baby and the roses on the seat and climbed in.

Susie and I followed the hearse and buggy. The grave was on the far side of the cemetery away from the road where there were no fine big tombstones, and the weeds and grass from the summer stood high and brown. We walked up to the edge of the grave and stood while the coffin was lowered, and Reverend Lipscomb said a short prayer.

The others went away then, and left us to watch the men throw the yellow dirt in. Laurie Mae stood behind us a few feet away and watched the men, too. "She means to put the roses on the grave," Susie whispered.

Laurie Mae didn't do that. When the men were finished she turned and started home. "Let's go after her and ask to see the baby," Susie said.

"Mama wouldn't want me to be seen talking with her," I said, and hung back until Susie ran past me calling, "We want to see the baby, Laurie Mae."

The girl stopped and laid the roses on the ground and with her free hand unwrapped the bundle. We stood without saying anything and looked at the baby. I didn't think it was a pretty baby. Its head was too big with the veins showing in its face. "Doesn't it ever cry?" Susie asked.

"No," Laurie Mae said. "He hardly ever cries." Her voice sounded hoarse and rusty as if she had not used it in a long time. She wrapped the baby up again, and picked up the roses.

"Don't you think they're pretty roses," I said.

"They cost three dollars," Susie said.

"Three dollars," Laurie Mae said, and stopped and looked at the flowers.

We thought she would be pleased to know The Ladies Aid had spent so much. Her voice sounded full of something else. We didn't know what it was. "Three dollars is a lot of money," Susie said.

"I know," Laurie Mae said. "It's a lot of money."

We left her then, for she could walk but slowly with the baby and the roses. Susie left me at the cemetery gate for she went one way and I another. I slipped behind the concrete pillars of the gate and waited. I wanted to see Laurie Mae. I thought that now she was alone she might cry. I wanted to see her cry.

She came out of the gate and looked all around; up and down the road, and at the nearest houses, and up into the snowy sky. When she saw no one she laid the baby on the ground, and took the white roses one by one and threw them in the yellow mud of the road. She pushed them out of sight with her foot and raked the mud over them, and then she picked up the baby.

Zekie, The Hill-billy Mouse

Before her first novel was published in 1936, Harriette Simpson wrote a story called "Fiddle Music," which may be an early version of this story. It no longer exists in her papers, though this story apparently has gone through several revisions.

By May of 1937, she had written a "Mouse Story," probably an early draft of "Zekie" which she re-titled and completed in 1938. She wrote a satiric sequel about this mouse, Ezekial Whitmore, later that year or early in 1939, while she lived in and near downtown Cincinnati.

This story has been unpublished until now.

---

*T*he city mouse and the country mouse had another cousin. His name was Zekie. He was a hill-billy mouse. He lived with his wife and children in the high hills. They lived in a log cabin. It was a little house with only two rooms, but it was always clean. There were many trees by Zekie's cabin. The hickory trees dropped nuts upon the ground for Zekie's children. The beech trees gave nuts, too; and in the fall their leaves made Zekie think of flakes of gold. The oak trees gave acorns for the squirrels, and in the fall their leaves were red. The tall pine trees dropped their needles on the ground, and sang soft sad songs in the wind.

Zekie loved the trees, but best of all he loved the cedar trees. Their needles were green, and in winter they held blue berries for the birds. When the wind blew, the cedar trees whispered little songs. Zekie liked to hear the soft south wind say h-u-u-sh-sh through the cedar trees. He liked to hear the north wind cry w-o-o-o through the branches of the cedar trees. He liked the west wind that sang so-ooo-so-oo, and east wind that laughed ee-ee-ee.

But no matter what the wind it never sang so sadly in the cedar trees as in the pines. Zekie did not like sad songs. Zekie, himself, was often sad. He was sad because he was so poor. Sometimes he could not buy all his children shoes. He could never buy oranges or candy or ice cream cones for them to eat. He could never buy them toys or pretty dresses for his wife. Zekie was a farmer. The hill land was thin and poor. On it he could not grow fine crops of corn and molasses cane.

Sometimes Zekie's cousin would come. He would bring the children oranges and candy and a pink apron for Zekie's wife. He would say to Zekie, "You must come away from the hills. Come to the city. I will get you a job. You can make money and buy all your children shoes. In the city your children can go to picture shows and have an ice cream cone every day and you can have a fine new suit and your wife a bright blue dress."

And Zekie would say, "I do not want to go to the city. I love the high hills. I do not want to leave the high hills and the trees."

And Zekie's children would say and almost cry, "We do not want to go away. We love the high hills. In the city there is no wind to sing us lullabies. We could not watch the sun go down between the poplar trees. We could not listen to the laughter of the creek. In the city there would be no squirrels to talk to us."

And Zekie's wife would say, "I do not want to go away. I love my children. I love Zekie. If they love the high hills I love them, too."

The city cousin would be angry. "You are all very foolish," he would say, and then he would go away.

The country cousin would come and visit Zekie. He would bring presents of potatoes and corn and apples and pumpkins. "Come down and help me farm the flat land, Zekie," he would say. "My land is rich black land. It is by a broad quiet river where the steamboats pass. On my land the corn grows fine and green and tall. The potatoes are big beyond all believing, and the clover hay smells sweeter than a fresh wild rose."

"I would rather smell the cedar trees than your fine clover hay," Zekie would say. "I would rather farm my thin rocky hill land than your rich black land by the river. I do not want to go away. The beech trees and the cedar trees do not grow down there by the river."

And Zekie's children would say, "We do not want to live in a valley low down. We'd rather live in the high hills than on your rich flat land."

And Zekie's wife would say, "Aye, it would be fine to have so much to eat, but I could never love that flat black land."

And Zekie lived in the high hills and grew poorer every year. A summer came then there was little rain. The corn grew thin and pale and the potatoes were small like marbles. Fall came and Zekie's wife said, "There is not food enough to take us through the winter."

Zekie thought of his country cousin with his barns filled with corn. "I will borrow from my cousin," Zekie said.

"How will you pay him back?" Zekie's wife asked.

"When spring comes we will all go down to the flat land. There we will live and work for him and grow fine corn of our own."

The children heard him and they began to cry. "We do not want to go away," they said.

"You cannot go hungry through a winter," Zekie said. "When spring comes and we go away that is time enough to cry."

Zekie wrote a letter to his country cousin. Soon the cousin came. He brought wagon loads of corn and potatoes and beans. Zekie thanked his cousin. "When spring comes we will go down and farm for you in the fine flat land," Zekie said, and his cousin went away.

Now there was plenty of food. The children obeyed their father and did not cry. They never spoke of spring when they would go away. The leaves fell and the wind blew. It sang in the cedar trees and laughed and cried in the high hills. Zekie's children were not afraid of the wind. The wind was their friend. It sang them to sleep with lullabies, and sometimes it whistled tunes in the chimney. Often the wind grew very strong. Then there was a storm, but the children were not afraid. Zekie's cabin was low and strong and sheltered from the wind.

Once a great storm came. The pines bowed their heads and shivered and moaned and cried. The oak trees rattled their branches and fought with the wind. The wind was strong that day. It caught the little cedar trees in its great strong hands. When the sun went down and the storm died Zekie went to look at his cedar trees. The finest tree of all lay on the ground. The fallen tree made Zekie sad. He would miss the wind through its branches. He would miss the birds that had gathered its berries. The little cedar tree would never feel the snow or the fog or the dew. The spiders would not hang lace from its branches.

Zekie sat and watched the stars come out. He sat by the fallen cedar tree and thought and thought. He thought of going away from the high hills in the spring. He knew that his children would cry when they went away, and that his wife would look at the hills and wipe her eyes on her apron.

He heard the night wind in the hills. The wind was far away, but it laughed and spoke to Zekie. "Take up the little cedar tree, Zekie," the wind said. "The cedar tree is for you."

And the wind sent a stray breeze down to the fallen cedar tree. The breeze moved softly through the little tree's branches, and the tree whispered, "Take me up, Zekie, and carry me home. I am for you, but first you must lop off all my branches. Then you must take your sharp knife and whittle on me. If you whittle long enough and carefully you will find something. What you find will keep your children from crying when they go to the rich flat land."

Zekie gathered up the cedar tree. He lopped off its branches, then he carried the trunk home. The bark was gray and soft, but under the bark there was sweet smelling wood. The wood was fine and red. Many nights Zekie sat by his fire and whittled the fine red wood. He whittled and smoothed and polished. Winter came and the nights were cold. Snow covered Zekie's cabin, but Zekie and his wife and children did not care. They were safe and warm and fed.

Sometimes Zekie's wife would say, "What do you whittle on so long, Zekie?"

And Zekie would answer, "It's a secret until spring."

One day a robin came to say that spring was on the way, and then soon a blue bird brought it. The soft south wind blew. The arbutus and the wind flowers bloomed above the fallen leaves. The lamb's tongue was yellow by the creek. The dogwood bloom blew white in the hills. But Zekie did not come out to look at the dogwood flowers. He did not help his wife and children pick wild greens or gather mushrooms. He sat on his door step and whittled on the bright red cedar wood.

One day while the paw-paws bloomed their dark red flowers Zekie finished his whittling. That night the whip-poor-wills cried from the pine trees on the hill. Zekie's wife stood on the porch and listened. "When the whip-poor-wills call it is time to plant the corn," she said.

"Yes," Zekie said. "Tomorrow we must go down to the rich flat land by the river. There I will work and grow fine corn and you and the children will have a garden."

Zekie's wife wiped her eyes on her apron and the children gathered round. "We do not want to go away," they said, and they began to cry.

"Hush your crying," Zekie said. "When we leave the high hills that is time enough to cry."

Morning came and they went away. They walked down the hill and across the foot bridge over the creek. Zekie's wife and his children looked back at their little cabin. "It looks lonesome," Zekie's wife said, and she wiped her eyes on her apron.

"We will miss the wind in the high hills," the children said, and they looked up at the pine trees. But the children couldn't see so well. Their eyes were filled with tears.

"We will not live always away from the hills," Zekie said. "Hush your crying. When we come to the flat land by the river that is time enough to cry."

They walked all day. The sun went down and the stars came out. Then the moon rose, and in the moonlight they came to the flat land by the river. Zekie's cousin showed them their new home in the flat land. Zekie's cousin's wife had a fine hot supper ready for them to eat.

"We are not hungry," Zekie's children said. "It is too quiet here. The river never makes a sound."

Zekie's wife sighed and shook her head. "It is so low like down here," she said. "I wish I could see out across some hills," and she and the children began to cry.

"Hush your crying," Zekie said. "When the hills go away that is time enough to cry. I brought the hills with me."

He sat down on his new door step. He took the fiddle he had whittled from the red cedar tree. He tucked it under his chin, and he drew the bow across the strings. Zekie's wife and his children listened and they forgot to cry. They heard the wind in the cedar trees. They heard the laughter of the creek and the chatter of the squirrels. The wind whistled tunes and sang them lullabies. Sometimes the fiddle music cried low like the late night wind, sometimes it rang high like the west wind in the hickory trees at noon, sometimes it whispered like the south wind through the dogwood bloom, sometimes it laughed and sometimes it moaned but always it was the wind.

Zekie stopped and wiped his face on his red bandana handkerchief. He heard his children laughing and he saw that his wife was smiling. "There's time enough to cry for the high hills when this sweet singing fiddle goes away from me," Zekie said.

An Episode in the Life of Ezekial Whitmore

Unpublished during her lifetime, this fairy tale was written before Harriette Simpson married, likely while she worked for the Federal Writer's Bureau on a WPA Guidebook to Cincinnati.

In a similar version of this story, she added a subtitle: "A Person of Small Learning but Great Wisdom."

———————

Once there was a little mouse. His name was Zekie. He had long black whiskers like a pirate. But he wasn't a pirate. He was a hill-billy mouse. He was a pure-blooded Anglo-Saxon hill-billy mouse. Literary ladies said he was. That made it true in spite of his long black whiskers.

Zekie had a tail longer than his whiskers. He carried a gun longer than his tail. He used swear words longer than his gun. He lived up a holler longer than his swear words. He chewed tobacco. He had a jack-knife. It was sharp, and less long than his whiskers.

Zekie was a bachelor. He spent much time with his friends. Some of his best friends were the cedar trees. Their needles were green and their berries were blue. Zekie loved the soft gay tunes the trees sang in the wind.

Once a great storm came. The thunder roared about the little cedar trees. The rain swept through their needles. The wind caught them in its strong hands. When the sun went down, the storm died. Zekie went to look at his friends the cedar trees. The finest of all lay on the ground. The fallen tree made Zekie sad. It could never sing in the wind again.

Zekie sat and watched the stars come out. He sat by the fallen cedar tree and thought and thought. He remembered his jack-knife. He looked at the broken tree. The bark was gray and soft, and under the bark there was sweet smelling wood. The wood was red and soft and fine.

Zekie trimmed the cedar's trunk. He carried it home. Many nights he sat by his fire and whittled the fine red wood. He whittled and smoothed and polished. Autumn came and the red maple leaves and the yellow poplar leaves came down. Winter came and the nights were cold. Snow covered Zekie's cabin, but Zekie did not care. He sat and whittled by the fire.

One day spring came. A robin came to say that it was on the way, and then one dawn a blue bird brought it. The soft south wind blew. The arbutus and the wind flowers bloomed above the fallen leaves. The lamb's tongue was yellow by the creek. The dogwoods were white in the hills. But Zekie did not come out to look at the dogwoods. He did not pick wild greens or gather flowers. He did not watch the white clouds race in the high blue windy sky. He sat on his doorstep and whittled on the cedar wood.

One day while the paw-paws bloomed their dark red flowers, Zekie finished his whittling. That night the whip-poor-wills did not cry from the pine trees on the hill. The little frogs by the spring were still, and the great owls forgot to hoot. They listened to sweet music. The music came from Zekie's cabin. Sometimes it was the patter of rain and the twitter of birds. Sometimes it cried the way the north wind cried. It was still like the snow, and then again full of silver tinkles like the drops of dew.

Zekie made the music. He made it with the fiddle he had cut from the cedar tree.

All of his neighbors in the holler came to hear his fiddle sing. Then others heard about it from the other side of the ridge. They came. Many nights and many lazy summer afternoons, there were great crowds in front of Zekie's door. His cabin would not hold them all. They heard about him in the county seat town. They asked him to play for the Fair. He played and the whole country heard. They wrote a piece about him in the paper. The paper said he would win the fiddlers' contest that fall.

One day while Zekie whittled with his jack-knife in the shade, he had a visitor. His visitor was a lady city mouse. She was a literary lady mouse. She had read about Zekie in the piece in the paper. She lived north of the hills and lectured to people about other people.

She stayed in Zekie's country a week or so. She listened to Zekie play his fiddle. She watched him a great deal. She asked him many questions. She wrote about him to her friends. She did not call him Zekie in her letters. She called him Material.

The lady mouse went back to her city in the North. She told all the literary ladies about Zekie. The more she talked, the more she knew. Soon she knew enough to write a book. She wrote about Zekie's great sharp knife and his long gun. She wrote about the way he loved tobacco. She wrote that Zekie did not work.

Other literary ladies liked the book. They said that it was real and true. The critics said it mirrored life. It went through one hundred and forty-nine editions. It was a Book-of-the-Moon. The lady mouse earned three great cheeses full of enormous holes. The publishers declared extra dividends when they had earned twenty great cheeses full of enormous holes. The book became famous. All the mice in the country squeaked about its worth. The New York mice said that a great realist was born. Even Zekie heard about the book. He did not squeak. He worked three days in a neighbor's cane patch. He took his pay and sent away for the book. It came.

Sweet music no longer sounded from Zekie's cabin. Zekie sat by his hearth and read the book. He pointed at each word with a long black whisker. That caused him to have to hold his head sideways. This gave him a crick in his neck. Still, he read. He had paid his money for the book. He wanted to read it through. He read and learned a great deal.

He learned that he did not live in a holler in the hills. He lived on sub-marginal land in the Great Economic Problem. He learned too that he was lazy. He did nothing but whittle in the shade, swear, and chew tobacco. He learned that his fiddle was clumsy. The tone of it was poor, and his elbows were awkward when he played. He learned that he was poor and pitiful. His diet was all wrong, and he was dirty because he had no bath-tub. He was ignorant and lived without any of the Finer Things of Life.

He learned many other things. The more he learned, the sadder he became. His fiddle hung on the wall, and when his friends came, he never played for them. He did not take his fiddle to the fiddlers' contest that fall. There was no heart in his fiddle for playing.

One day when the sweet gum leaves were red and the poplar leaves were yellow, the literary lady mouse came again. She had a new car and a new mink coat. "You are a famous man now, Zekie," she said. "I have made you famous with my book. In all the great cities of the North, mice have read my book about you. Now they want to hear your fiddle."

"What is it like in the cities of the North?" Zekie asked.

"Wonderful," the literary lady said. She told him of her country.

Zekie listened. Soon, he understood why she had found his country ugly. The literary lady's country was fine and beautiful. When she talked, he could shut his eyes and see the fine high buildings made of marble and granite and trimmed with silver and gold. He saw their tall towers higher than the pine trees. He wondered how an orchestra would sound. He thought of the fine mice who lived in her country. They were strong to have built a country where there was no ugliness nor hunger nor pain. Mice there had conquered the rain and the cold and the snow, and all were safe and warm and fed. He heard of mighty rivers and beautiful parks and forest reservations. He saw the country like a vision in a cloud, and there the Finer Things of Life grew, and were plentiful as the rocks in his hills.

"I will come," Zekie said. "And when I have journeyed up and down the country a bit, I will play such music on my fiddle as has never been heard. The music here is of the hills. There, it shall be of your country."

The literary lady mouse was pleased. "You shall make much money, Zekie. Soon, you will have a car and a mink coat like mine. Travel through the country this fall—that's long enough—and then at the beginning of winter, you shall give concerts."

Zekie journeyed north. He visited the great cities. He found all the things of which the literary lady had told him.

Winter came and Zekie went to the home of the literary lady. "You will have a great season, Zekie," she said. "I have rented great halls for you. You will have much money. You can take off your raw hide shoes and overalls—not now, for I have advertised you as a hill mouse—but soon you can go about in a limousine and wear a mink coat and a sable neck piece like mine. Is your music ready?"

Zekie nodded. "It is all in the fiddle here," he said.

"Play some of it for me, Zekie," the literary lady begged. She smiled and came so near she tickled Zekie's chin with her whiskers. "Oh, but you will be a rich and famous man some day, Zekie," she said. "If you can make beautiful music of your poor hills, I know that music of me and my country will be wonderful."

"It is," Zekie said. He tuned his fiddle and rosined up the bow. "First, I will play city music for you," he said.

The literary lady clasped her hands and smiled.

Zekie put the fiddle under his chin. Soon the music of the city filled the room. And soon the literary lady's eyes grew round with horror. At last she raised her hand for silence. "But that is not the music of the city," she said, and shook her head. "In it I cannot hear the joy of busy mice or see the great buildings flashing in the sun. I hear nothing of the culture—the symphony, art, literature—none of the Finer Things of Life." She clasped her hands to her bosom. "That music—I cannot describe it—but it is ugly like a shrill mouse, a fish peddler say, demanding that all mice buy her fish. And again, it makes me think of drunken mice or of angry hungry mice crying for bread—not clearly for something always muffles their cry." She knit her brows and pondered. "Sometimes I thought I heard mice groaning, moaning like they moan when they get caught in a trap, and sometimes they seemed crushed to death by a great weight, or caught in a wire cage." She shook her head. "You will have to leave that off your program. It is more like the music of a prison than a city. Maybe you are mixed in your tunes."

Zekie shook his head. "That is the music of the cities," he said. "Would you now like to hear the music of the children mice?"

The literary lady smiled and clasped her hands to listen. "I know that will be sweet," she said, "gay and carefree like our children."

Zekie played again. The music was sad and thin, cold sometimes as moonlight on snow, or troubled like the cry of a fledgling bird lost on its first flight. Sometimes it was hungry like wolves crying at night, and again it was dreary and ugly as rain dripping out of a smoky sky. The literary lady lifted her hand for silence. "That cannot be the music of the children," she said, "not the children of our cities," she said. "The children of my friends are not like that."

Zekie nodded. "That is the music of the children—but they are not the children of your friends," he said.

The literary lady frowned. "This music is not the kind I have advertised. I said you would interpret the country." She pondered a time, and then she smiled. "Play me the music of the country itself, the parks and rivers and playgrounds. That should be gay."

Zekie played. The literary lady listened. The longer she listened, the more she frowned. She saw rivers that were still and sad. They were ugly, yellow, foul-smelling scars. The parks had their grass worn away by hordes of earth-hungry feet; they were ugly like mangy mice when their hair falls off in the spring. Soon, the literary lady asked for silence. She arose and looked at Zekie. The whiskers on her chin quivered with anger. "Zekie, you must get better music. We cannot give concerts of that. You will be hissed and booed. The mice will want to hear of their country."

"It is of their country," Zekie said. "My fiddle is my friend, and so will speak only the truth."

"Bah," the literary lady said, and stamped about the room. She clenched her hands. "Zekie," she hissed when she could get her breath, "you must have seen something of my country. Can't you see its fineness and its wonder? What of the music for me? I am neither shrill nor hungry nor ugly nor sad. The mice who have bought tickets for your concerts would like to hear the music of me and of themselves. Let me hear that on your fiddle. It is not too late to save the situation, though I cannot refrain from remarking that your way of looking at things is most peculiar."

Zekie shook his head. "My fiddle is not enough to make the music of you," he said.

The literary lady smiled. "Try it, Zekie," she said. "On the stage you may have a whole orchestra."

Zekie shook his head. "For such music I would need only a few pebbles such as are found in my country and an empty tin can such as is found in yours." Zekie said goodbye. He went back to his own country.

The Two Hunters

This story was published in *Esquire,* under the name H. L. Simpson (Harriette Louisa Simpson), Arnow's maiden name. She wrote it late in 1937 or early in 1938, before she married Harold Arnow in 1939.

When she offered the story to this "men's magazine," which did not at the time accept writing by women, Arnow did not mention her gender. Years later, she admitted in an interview, "it worried me a little, that big lie, but I thought if they wanted a story, let them have it." *Esquire* paid her $125 in February of 1938 for this story and did not publish it until 1942. The contributor's notes at the back of the magazine include a photo of "H. L. Simpson," who is actually one of her brothers-in-law. It was her little joke on a publisher that discriminated against women.

He was a tall boy, slender, with small hands and small feet, a narrow thin-cheeked face, and hair the color of weather-bleached sandstone. His eyes were blue, now dark, now light; quiet, bottomless eyes that, like deep quiet water, covered and revealed and reflected many things. In one hand he carried a rifle, and carefully cradled in the crook of his other arm was his old felt hat, lined with moss and half filled with flowers.

Now and then he looked below him toward the bottom of the narrow valley where a faint thread of pale blue smoke wavered up above the spruce trees, and from some hidden place behind the trees there came the thin sour smell of boiling mash. But most often he looked at the ground, and when he saw a sign of the thing he hunted, he would drop to his knees and search under the dead damp leaves, carefully, with slow gentle movements of his hands. The clay bank hound dog that followed at his heels would pause to watch, and then come to sniff the flowers the boy drew from under the leaves. He showed a sympathy each time the boy shook his head and said in his slow soft voice, "They're little, Mose. I wanted bigger ones— pinker like Millie likes."

Many times he stopped for no reason at all, but was still, looking at the flowers in his hat, caressed them with his eyes, and there was a gentle dreaming in his glance that went to something past the flowers.

He was dreaming so with a half smile on his mouth when the dog pricked his ears, looked up the ridge side, and growled low in his chest. The boy listened, too, and the listening concerned look on his face killed the wandering lights in his eyes, and they were cold and dark and quiet. He glanced toward the smoke. "It's somebody comin' where they've no business to come," he whispered to Mose, and turned up the hill.

He walked more quickly now, the hat filled with flowers carried gently as before, the gun held high and clear of the laurel bush. He walked soundlessly, careful to twist his shoulders and slide through the brush, his eyes on the ground as if he would pick a place for his feet, and when the feet came down they never snapped a twig or ground against a stone, but rested lightly and silently against the dead leaves and the damp earth, then lifted again and swung away in the long unhurried stride of the born hill man.

He went up the steep moss covered ground, through clusters of dark green ivy and laurel bush until he came to the open growth of the ridge top. There the pines were straight and dark and tall with little undergrowth between except the coarse ridge grass, greening at its roots in sign of the coming spring.

He stood by a tree and listened again, then looked at the listening Mose and nodded slowly. He looked toward the white sand of the ridge road that lay pale and straight and dead between the black pine trunks, and he and the dog drew nearer the road, not walking openly through the grass, but flitting quickly from tree to tree. There was a curious oneness about the boy and dog as if they were no longer two things, separate and different, but one, some strange, machine-like thing, planned for watching and listening and slipping through the trees.

They came at last to a tree by the road, and the boy placed the flowers in a cup-like hollow formed by the roots of the tree, and stood with both hands on his gun and watched the road. The road had the old, never-used look of something lost and forgotten so long ago that it was less a place for people to pass over than the memory of a road. On it there were no wagon tracks or signs of the feet of men or of animals. Dead grass like a carpet was brown in the center and in a puddle the shimmering gelatinous life of young tadpoles trembled under still water.

Now and then fitful gusts of wind made a strong singing in the pines, then gradually ebbed and died into hoarse broken mutterings and whispered sighs that seemed more a plea for silence than a beginning of sound. Somewhere a creek, swollen with late winter rain, roared in a muffled thunder, and still farther away the troubled fretting of river water torn on the rocky shoals of the Cumberland came fitfully on the wind.

The sound of a mule's feet came first at intervals and then more steadily while the boy waited motionless by the tree. Only his eyes moved in slow careful glances as the mule and rider came into view. The man who rode the mule had the air of a hunter, giving little attention to the road, but turning in his saddle and peering among the pine trees as if some game might be lurking there. The gun he carried seemed a thing made for hunting, longer and heavier than the boy's, though the steel of the barrel did not shine so blue and the brightly varnished wood of the stock was less worn with use. He carried it awkwardly in the manner of a man unaccustomed to riding a mule and carrying a gun, such a heavy gun at that; an automatic rifle mounted with a telescope sight.

He was looking away through the trees when the boy stepped noiselessly into the road. He turned and gave a nod more of surprise than of greeting, and the boy smiled, a slow grave smile that drew his curling upper lip away from his teeth and did not brighten his eyes. The man drew his bridle rein and grinned and asked, "Huntin'?" The boy nodded and studied his face, a large face, hard and heavy with something of the pig and of the fox crawling across the bottoms of his narrow slate-colored eyes. He examined the boy with an unconcealed air of appraisal as he asked, "What's your name?"

"Lacey."

"Lacey? Sounds like a girl's name," he said, and stared critically at the boy's thin beardless cheeks. "How old are you?"

"Goin' on seventeen."

"You're tall but youngish lookin' for your age," he commented critically.

"Pap, he was slow gettin' his growth, he says."

"Who is your dad, anyhow?"

"Big Jake Bledsoe," the boy answered, and did not look at his questioner but watched the sunlight play on the copper mountings of the telescope.

The man's eyes narrowed suddenly and the expression of his face changed as if the boy were a person different now from what he had been. "I've heard of your dad but never seen him. I've not been in this country so long," he continued, and his voice was more cordial than it had been.

"I lowed ye wuz a stranger when I seed ye on this road."

The man studied the boy a time longer, and in a moment said in a low voice, "This road takes me where I want to go."

The boy's eyes widened and darkened, but his voice showed neither fear nor anger as he said, "Th' road down in th' valley is better."

"Not for me. I can see more from this when the leaves are off like now."

"You want to see Pop, I reckin."

"No."

"Pap an' Buck Huffacre's fam'ly they're th' only people livin' in this bend."

"I know that."

"You want to see th' Huffacres I take it."

"Not exactly see them—somethin' they have—more like," the man answered and glanced swiftly at the boy from the corners of his sliding eyes.

The boy's eyes were flat now and quiet, swinging slowly in their sockets from the man's face to the telescope mounted gun, then back to the heavy chin or forehead, never into his eyes. The man craned his head and twisted his neck as if some soundless, forever elusive winged creature flitted about his face. He made a vain effort to catch the boy's glance then asked abruptly, "What's your game, Son?" And the boy answered with a rolling glance toward the telescope, "Huntin'."

"How'd you like to have a gun like this?"

"This here's just as good."

"But with this telescope now you could kill a squirrel more'n half a mile away."

"My bullets carry that piece."

"But you can't see to take good aim."

"I can beat Pap an' all my bigger brothers in shooting without one a them things."

"You must be a pretty good shot."

"Pap says I am."

"You've fooled with guns a lot I guess."

"Since I can first recollect."

"You ought to have a telescope, though. They're handy things to hunt with."

"I reckin they cost a sight. More'n Pap 'ud give me in six months."

"Maybe you wouldn't have to wait on your dad's money."

"Mom says I'm too spindlin' to work. Anyhow Pap keeps me busy— huntin'."

"Maybe you wouldn't have to work for the money you'd need to buy one a these."

"How else?" the boy asked, and his glance struck coldly against the man's forehead, then slipped away to the gun and the telescope.

"There's ways."

"Like what?"

"You know your Kentucky law I guess. Rewards for finding certain things."

"What ways?" the boy insisted, and the man was silent, fidgeting under the glance he could never catch. He reined his mule nearer and leaned from the saddle and asked softly after a careful glance up and down the road, "What you guess I'm in this God awful country for anyhow?"

"I don't reckin. I know."

"You know, eh. You're thinking maybe I've come to have a look at your dad's still."

"You're welcome to a look," the boy answered, and shifted the butt of his rifle from the toe of one shoe to the toe of the other shoe.

The man smiled. "I'm no fool. Ever'body knows what the Bledsoes do for a livin', but me I'm not botherin' them. Don't be afraid now."

"I ain't afeard."

"There's plenty more in this stillin' business—the Huffacres say?"

The boy was silent staring at his forehead. He tried again. "You know 'em. The Bledsoes and the Huffacres had trouble once, so I've heard."

"Pap, he killed Miz Huffacre's man."

"And they caused your dad to be sent to the pen," the man added.

The boy looked faintly troubled. "Pap he's out—stayed almost a year—but Buck Huffacre he's still daid."

"Some a them Huffacres will come killin' him one a these days."

"I don't reckin so. They're mostly girls, an' th' boys they double an' twist an' make good liquor, but they're not much on shootin', couldn't kill a cow. An' anyhow they naiver got along with their pap. He was a bad man—better daid."

"But the girls when they get married they'll have their men come killin' your dad."

"All th' girls an' their men have moved away, but Millie, th' least 'un. She's still at home."

"Well, she'll up and get married and her man, she'll make him do your old man dirt."

"I don't reckin so. Millie's littler an' spindlier than me an' hatin nothin."

"Listen, Boy, I know you—hill billies—you can't tell me. Somebody do you dirt you'll hate 'em all your lives. Why, I bet your old man he'd jump at th' chance to turn up th' Huffacres still and get a little something for it."

The boy smoothed his gun barrel. "Pap he ain't so hard run as all that," he said.

The man drew still nearer until the boy stood like a thing trapped, his back to the tree, the stirrup leathers almost touching his body. He held his gun more tightly, more carefully, and his eyes were still, fixed on the other's gun. "Listen, Son, your old man won't ever know, but recollect this, he and—well—maybe the high sheriff, they might know you same as said your people was stillin and the Huffacres too. You might get called into town for knowin' too much. You might be asked questions and indicted by the grand jury. I could see to that." He bent over and tried to look into the boy's eyes. "Know who I am?"

"You're a special deputy sheriff sent out to make a little money turnin' up stills. You'll git some a th' reward th' state gives."

"You know two an' two when you see it, Son. I can collect th' reward money and never show myself in the breakin' up posse."

The boy looked at the deputy's heavy gun and asked tonelessly, "Ain't you afeard?"

"What do I have to worry about? You can't tell your old man. As for the Huffacres they'll never know. From all you say they couldn't hurt a flea. Anyhow they'll all go to jail. People in jail can't ask questions." He waited, and when the boy gave him no answer, he continued, "You've said too much already. When I rode back this way I wasn't certain. Now thanks to you, I am. I'll find 'em with no more help from you. Now all I'm wantin' to do is to give you a chance to make a little somethin'.'"

The boy studied him a time before asking, "You're certain you could find th' Huffacre still, then?"

"Yes, but with a little more help from you it would be easier."

The boy straightened his shoulders, and for the first time looked into the deputy's eyes. "Supposin' I help. What do I git?"

"Now you're talkin'. But supposin' you tell me the wrong holler, then you don't get anything."

"My people don't lie, but I ain't so certain about you. Maybe I'll tell you where they still, an' then you'll fergit me."

"I won't do that. You can trust me."

"Naiver trust th' law, Pap allus said."

"Your pap's got no hand in this. If I give you money now you'd have it spent. I couldn't get it back."

"I ain't a wantin' money. I ain't a needin' money," the boy said, and his eyes fondled the brass telescope.

The deputy saw his glance "You could buy a contraption like this with money."

The boy looked at it a time longer and when he took his eyes away his face seemed thinner, the skin about his teeth and eyes drawn and pale, until his teeth and eyes stood sharp and bright like those of one sick or afraid.

The deputy said, "Don't get cold feet, boy."

"I don't reckin I will." He ran the tip of his tongue lightly against his upper lip and studied the telescope as if it were some puzzle he could not touch but must solve in his mind. "Will that thing work on any gun?"

"On any single barreled gun."

The puzzle in the boy's mind seemed mostly finished. His eyes grew brighter, were like hands reaching for the bits of metal and glass, "Give it to me—I'll tell."

"Supposin' you don't tell me right."

"Then you can write to Pap. You'd get that back, an' me—I reckin I'd git killed."

The deputy pondered. "Son, you've got a head now," he at last said, and bent to the unscrewing of the telescope sight.

The boy's hands trembled a bit, and the man took his gun and mounted the telescope for him, and when it was finished he returned the gun and said, "Now, see how that works."

The boy lifted the gun to his shoulder, stared at a distant bunch of mistletoe on a black gum tree. "Fine," he said.

"It's a bargain then?"

"Y-e-e-s," he said.

"Let's get goin' then," the deputy said, and turned his mule about.

The boy hesitated, but his face held less a look of indecision than of listening. The man listened, too, and said when the wind-driven murmur of sound had somewhat receded, "Creeks about here must be pretty wild."

"Not too deep for fordin'," the boy answered, and added slowly, "That is in spots. I reckin around this way will be th' best ford."

The deputy turned his mule in the direction indicated. They were silent then until they came to a narrow path dropping over the ridge side, and the boy said, "I dasn't go no further. You foller this path till you come tu th' creek. Cross th' creek an' keep on a follerin' this path. You'll go up a hill. When you're on top look down in a little holler tu th' right an' you'll see smoke."

The man looked down the steep, pine needled path. "It's a lonesome road," he said.

The boy nodded. "Fer you it's better that th' road be lonesome."

"Who knows my business? If th' Huffacres saw me they'd take me for a hunter."

"I reckin they would," the boy said. He studied the man a moment, and his eyes were no longer hard but gentle, touched with the quiet acceptance of some sorrow.

"Don't look so sober, Son," the deputy said. "If you've told me th' truth an' by God it had better be, there's not many men but what would do what you're doin'."

"I'd swear it on a Bible it's th' truth I've told you," the boy answered, and watched the man as he turned down the path. "Recollect tu take yer feet out a th' stirrups when you ford th' creek," he said.

"I've sense enough to keep my feet dry, Son."

The boy stood in the road and when the deputy had gone a little way called in a ringing whisper, "Recollect tu take yer feet clean out a th' stirrups."

The man rode away with no answering, and the boy stood motionless until the trees swallowed him. He turned quickly then and walked a distance up the road. The dog followed at his heels. The road climbed a shoulder of ridge, and at the highest spot the boy turned and slipped between the trees until he came to flat table-like masses of sandstone. Past the stones there was a gorge-like wooded valley, split by a creek and crossed by a path.

He dropped to his stomach and crawled over the bare yellow rocks, screening his movements as best he could in the masses of ivy and twisted huckleberry bush and stunted pine. He shielded the gun with his body so that the brass work of the telescope and the steel of the barrel made no flashing in the sun. He whispered to Mose, and the dog dropped to his belly and was still, following him only with his eyes. He came at last to the bluff edge. Below him were the tops of tall growing spruce and poplar trees and past them was the narrow valley with the creek and the path.

He crawled behind a screen of ivy bush and lay with the gun butt resting against his shoulder, and only his head and his hands moved as he looked through the telescope sight. When he saw what he wanted to see, his hands and his head were still. He waited while sometimes his slow glance swung away to the soaring flight of a hawk, a ground squirrel peering at him from a crevice in the stone, or to his hands that were still like frozen hands.

Sometimes the wind trumpeted in the stunted pine trees and last year's red huckleberry leaves swirled over him or a few pine needles sifted onto his hair, but he took no notice of such things. When a mule's feet clicked over the rocks in the path below he gave no sign that he had heard. His eyes were still, fixed on a bit of creek water as if that disc of yellow swirling water were the world, and apart from it there was nothing to hear or feel or see. Something dark came into the circle of yellow and for a split second his glance lifted and he saw the tiny figure of a man on a mule belly deep in the swift water, and the man's feet seemed lifted from the stirrup leathers.

Then there came a sound and a bit of smoke and the boy dropped his head on his outstretched arm. When he looked again he saw a mule struggling riderless up the path on the other side of the creek while some dark object that might have been a man's hat bobbed down the water.

He sat up then and unscrewed the telescope sight with slow fumbling motions as if his mind were hidden from his hands. He held the bright thing and looked at it a moment, then searched with his eyes until he found a deep crevice in the stone. He went there and dropped the telescope in. He listened intently to the muffled clinking sound that came faintly up from the stone, and when there were no more sounds he walked away. His face was pale, and he shivered at times as if he felt the coldness of the wind.

No Lady

According to one of Arnow's personal notebooks, she wrote this story in 1938. She submitted it to the literary magazine *New Masses*, though it remained unpublished until now.

———⟨∞⟩———

I've heard it said that a lot of men fell in love with her that night, my great-great Aunt Kate, the time she wore the blue satin dress with the wide foaming skirts below her narrow waist and a red rose between her breasts. The blue silk, no baby blue it was, nor dark, but bright with shadows, matched her eyes, and the red rose matched her mouth.

They say she bowed and smiled that night and played with her fan and held her skirts daintily as she tripped to the music of the violins. Her hair they said was red-shot[1] in the candle light, but pure black in the gloom, and the lashes on her eyes were even black as were her brows, and gave her glance a look of frost above the warmth of her mouth.

She was regal in her corsets, a lady she was that night they said, with every inch of the lady showing through until nobody saw the woman at all, not even the dancing beaux or the grinning black slave men with silver trays in their hands.

She stayed till the last, they said, and watched the last guest go. Some widower they said it was, with the smell of saddle leather and the talk of hunting and hounds always about him. She smiled and let him hold her hand and bow above it as it was proper that he do, and she made polite talk of the newest gossip and the late hunting weather as she smiled him through the door.

She said good-night to the Negro slave men, and she said good-night to her father, a straight backed man with a white goatee. She went up the long winding stair, trailing her hands on the carved cherry banister, up past the stained glass by the landing where nymphs danced always in a field of flowers.

I've heard it said that up past the landing, her steps were slow with her hands sometimes clutching the bright cherry banister wood. Some say she staggered in the hall, but that was only slave girls' talk. She reached her room and opened the door. Her Negro body slave waited there, nodding as she sat bolt upright in a high backed chair.

My great-great Aunt Kate forgot to smile and her fingers fluttered over the gown. "Get a knife. Cut my laces. Jerk my petticoats away. Undress me quick, quicker than you've ever done before."

"Lawd, God a'mighty," Nannie Mae shrieked, and sprang tearing at the satin gown. "Lawd, God a'might what'll we do? Oh please, Miz Kate, jus' lemme——."

My Aunt Kate's hand came hard on the black woman's cheek. "Remember what I said, you fool. Lose your head and I'll sell you off to the cotton fields." She fainted then, and a trickle of blood stained the blue satin gown before Nannie Mae could lift her up and tear it away.

She lost her head then, the black slave woman. She was no lady, only a black serving mammy with children of her own. She went running and crying down the hall, right up to her master's door. Twice she knocked with a loud calling, until he came, angered by her interruption.

He stood straight by the door and listened. And when she had finished he didn't smile and he didn't frown, but he walked like a wooden soldier straight to his daughter's room. Hour after hour he watched her writhe and he heard her moan, faintly for she bit her lips and clenched her hands against the pain instead of making a sound.

The morning light lay blue in the valleys and red-gold on the hills, before my great-great Aunt Kate was still, and Nannie Mae held a child, a little thing it was, weazened by corsets and starved by its mother's own will, but shapely it was with red-bright hair, a short snub nose and eyes that might have been gray—it was too little to use its eyes.

Nannie Mae looked at the child, and so did that ancestor of mine, but my aunt lay staring at the wall. "Take it away—to my dressing room—now," she said. "And you, Nannie Mae, you'll go this night. I've managed, you see. Ring for the house girl. Say I have a slight cold. Do not leave this room."

The child squirmed and cried in the black woman's hands, a troubled cry I've heard it said . . . they heard it cry below, you see . . . as if it maybe knew that in all of Fauquair County there was no man of blue-blooded birth to match such hair and nose as it had.

I know no more than what they said, the black ones down below who listened and watched and waited for Nannie Mae. She stayed all day in my Aunt Kate's dressing room, and nursed the baby as if it had been her own. Some say they slipped to the back veranda and saw her by a window, peeping through the dead wisteria vines down to where her cabin was. Some said they heard her sob—she might have sobbed, she was no lady—and some said they heard her pray, but no one heard a sob or a prayer from my Aunt Kate on the bed.

And that night my ancestor ate alone in the wide, still dining room where candle flames like bright trapped moths fluttered all about his head. He began with port and finished with brandy, and then he said to a black slave man, "Have Andy bring the closed carriage around to the side. Tell Andy that tonight he'll drive alone."

It was late at night when they drove away, my grandsire and Nannie Mae. There were peeping faces down the dusky halls, and from behind the dead wisteria vines, but little they saw and less they heard as the black woman got into the carriage and went away. Some say she had a bundle in her arms, some say a baby cried, but Andy was away, cracking his whip as he had been told to do, before there was time to know.

He and his master returned in two days' time, but the black man had nothing to say. All he had heard was, "Hold the horses and look sharp ahead and wait for me."

Upstairs my great-great aunt Kate lay in her wide, sweet-scented bed. A young slave girl waited on her now, fetched her food and drink and wine—and mirrors too. People came to call. And to the men below, her father said, as he offered the guests a bit of bourbon, or maybe sherry straight from Spain, "Katherine danced too much at the ball the other night, or maybe got into a draft. Nothin' serious, I'll have no fuss with a doctor."

And when the ladies fluttered into my great-great aunt's room, she smiled up from the lace-covered bed, "Nothin' serious, a cold," she said.

She was up and about in six days' time, singing light dancing songs down the wide shadowy halls, tinkling her hands on the piano keys. And all the dusky listening faces and the white rolling eyes, they never heard her sigh and they always saw her smile.

It was all a long while ago, that business of my Aunt Kate. She was a white-headed woman walking on her gold-headed cane, then dead in a silver-mounted coffin, pale under black brocade before the darkies leaked the news away. They were afraid of the down South cotton fields, you see.

I've heard it said that when at last some of our people learned of the come-by-chance child, they smiled on the memory of my great-great aunt Kate, and said with a bit of fondness and a lot of pride, "Aye, she was a lady through and through," and forgave and forgot the come-by-chance child.

It was all so long ago, and she was such distant kin, and that is why I guess her blood was hardly a bit like mine. For me, I'm no lady, I've had my tears and I'll have my pain and it can take its will of me. They'll hand no stories down about a lady that was I. If they recollect me at all, it'll be for my come-by-chance child.

I'll strut with him proudly, bear him in glory with a nurse all in white right over the foot of my bed. For me, I'm no lady; I'll have and I'll keep my come-by-chance child.

Tin Cup

Around 1938, Harriette Simpson wrote this unpublished story while she lived in Cincinnati.

———————

I knew it was childish of me to beg. But the room was so quiet, and all over an even grey whiteness with neither shadows nor sunshine. I'd look for hours in the hope of finding one crack, just a little one in the plaster that I might have missed, but there were no cracks there. Every day I wished one of the nurses would yell once, or drop something, or come in with her cap askew, or that Dr. Waters would forget to come, or come too soon, or forget to order a glass of half and half for me at ten and four. Of course, none of those things happened.

Then, too, it was spring, and I wanted to go to the flower market, or climb up to Eden Park and sit on a bench and watch men cut dandelions from the grass. I liked the dandelions. I always hoped the men would never get them all, but leave just one. Most often though they didn't, but cut them all.

"I'm plenty well enough to leave," I'd say every morning to Dr. Waters.

"That new brace is doing you good," he would answer.

"It's me," I would say. "When can I go home?"

Sometimes he would answer nothing at all; just stare at me with his red-dish brown eyes, or make some professional witticism, the kind, I suspected, he ordinarily reserved for paying patients. Other times, he would say doctorish things about eating everything on my tray and lying flat on my back as much as possible.

Peg helped a lot by coming three evenings a week. Visiting hours were in the afternoon, but Peg worked a kitchen goods counter in the basement of Freidmann's Department Store every weekday and couldn't come at the regular time. I thought a lot of Peg. We had lived together in one furnished room two years and never had a quarrel, unless one [would] call what she used to say when I spent money for "foolish things" quarreling. It was a good thing for me, I guess, that I lived with her, because she had enough sensible sense for the two of us. She couldn't abide useless, impractical things. She once told me of how eight years ago when she came first to Frei-dmann's they tried her for a week on the counter of cheap tin ware.

"I was an out and out failure," she said. "I couldn't put my mind to it. It's so silly to buy a tin sauce pan for fifteen cents and have it spring a leak in six weeks, when for fifty cents you can have cast aluminum for a lifetime."

"Tin sauce pans are nice and shiny," I remember I said, "and what if you needed a sauce pan in a hurry and had only fifteen cents."

"No sensible person would buy a sauce pan when she had nothing but fifteen cents," she answered, "or come home with some fool book when she needed the money for galoshes."

"You mean me," I said, and laughed to think that she was so sensible she was stupid. My galosh money had gone for a book, but a second-hand copy of *Thais* bound in red leather, and illustrated with sketches of funny fat little devils and long, thin-faced, knobby-kneed hermits with lots of bushy hair and beard.

I knew that it was nice of her to pay car fare and come way out there to see me, but sometimes I'd wish she'd bring me flowers, though I knew she never would. Once she did ask me if I wouldn't like a cactus in a pot. "It would keep well," she said, but I shook my head. I wanted the silly kind of flowers, the ones that are not good bargains but wilt in one day like snap dragons or yellow roses.

It was Peg who finally persuaded Dr. Waters to let me come home. One evening while she was there, a spring thunder storm came, and I wanted to see it, but could not because my window opened on the court. I could smell the rain a little, and see some flashes of lightning, and hear thunder, but it was all muffled. We sat there in the dark (I had turned out the light because the lightning was prettier in the dark) and I said a lot of things—silly things. I wondered that Peg did not laugh at me. But she didn't. In the flashes of light I could see her moon face looking at me while I rambled on about the rain and how I hated the room. I don't know exactly what I said—my thoughts, I guess.

I thought of the streets all full of the spring rain, and the electric lights shining through it, their hard, bright glitter blurred and soft in the rain, and Mabley Tower holding its glow high in the mist, with little jags of lightning playing from its highest pointed roof. I wanted to get out there and walk in it, and feel it and smell it the way I used to. I thought about back home, that is, down on the hill in Kentucky where I lived until I was fifteen—seven years ago. The hill faced west across [the] Cumberland [River], and I could stand in the front door and watch the curtain of the rain blot out the other hills until it came to our own, and then come creeping right across the tree tops to the front door. Or on summer nights, [I could] see the lightning low toward the south, and watch it grow higher and brighter until I could hear the thunder, and the rain would come hard and heavy on our tin roof, and my mother would wonder if the cow would have sense enough to come to the barn and if the chickens were in the dry, but on the whole be pleased and say the warm rain would sprout the peas and potatoes and bring out the apple bloom, and that tomorrow we could all go to the old new-ground for a mess of wild greens.

I didn't wish for all that, because I knew I couldn't have it, but I did wish to be in our furnished room where I could hear the rain outside in the street, and smell the wet earth in the little strip of parkway below our window. I suppose I talked a lot about such fool things for when the storm was over and I turned the light on, Peg did not finish her story of how she had that day sold a woman a cast aluminum double boiler and two skillets when the woman had at first thought that all she wanted was a wire tea strainer, but got up and said she would go and talk with Dr. Waters.

After what seemed a long time, I heard her coming back down the hall with him. They were talking, but I couldn't hear much they said. Outside the door they stopped and I heard her say, "It's six of one and half-dozen of the other. It's the only sensible thing."

"Sh-h-h," he said, and went on down the hall. I wondered why he did not come in.

Peg came over to my bed. "Don't get excited," she said. "You are leaving Saturday."

I was excited, but I didn't show it. Glad, too. I couldn't help but show that—a little, but I tried to be sensible and think of practical things. "It's not too early to wear my blue suit, is it?" I asked Peg, for in spite of the suit being two years old, I was anxious to wear it. It was a nice suit, the nicest thing I ever had. I bought it before I knew Peg, or else I guess I'd never [have] spent so much money for it, but she admitted that it was, in spite of being pretty, a sensible thing, because I could wear it forever. It was plain tailored with a three-quarter length semi-swaggerish coat. The cloth was a soft all wool and the prettiest shade of a darkish blue.

Peg thought a time and said she guessed I could wear it when she changed it a little. "It won't matter about the coat. It's loose fitting anyway," I told her, "but the skirt ought to fit snug over the hips."

"I'll take it up," she said.

"Be sure and fix it the way you did last fall," I said. "Just tuck the belt and take big seams over the hips."

Peg had been the first to think of that. Through the summer I grew thin, and when September and time to wear my suit came, I would have cut it down if it hadn't been for Peg. She said it would be a shame to spoil it for most likely I would be weighing a hundred and fifteen again in no time. So she was careful just to tuck the belt and take up the seams without cutting the cloth. "Just fix it the way you did the other time, only more so," I said. "I won't have this movie figure always."

"I'll measure you," she said, and took the belt from her dress and passed it around my waist, and put a pin where the end met the side.

"Don't ruin my one and only suit," I called after her when she was leaving. More to tease than anything else, because Peg never ruined anything.

Saturday was two days away, and Dr. Waters made me stay in bed all of both days; to save my strength, he said, but the time didn't seem so long. I was busy thinking of all the things I was going to do. I would pawn my wrist watch again and spend the money. Maybe I could get more if I took it to another place. I would spend the little extra for jonquils—they would be cheap now. I would put an ad in the paper "Manuscripts typed" or "College graduate desires position as tutor." When I got a job, I would write home. Maybe send some money to show how well off I was.

Peg got the day off and came for me early Saturday morning, though I told her that for once she was the foolish one because I was plenty able to come home by myself. When Dr. Waters came to tell me good-bye, he made me feel well all at once. He didn't say a word about not starting to smoke again, or eating the right kind of food or resting a lot. I could hardly believe that I was hearing him right when he laid his hand on my shoulder and said, "Have a good time."

"She will," Peg said. "Leave it to Denny and the Irish to have a good time."

In spite of my feeling so well, I was glad that we lived on the third instead of the fourth floor. But once in the room, and looking out the window, I soon felt rested again. Peg had put some boiling beef to cook before she left and had a cup of the broth ready for me. She could do more with twenty cents worth of boiling beef. She would make broth or soup, and then cook the meat with noodles, and when we had eaten the noodles, she would make stew or hash. She was smart that way.

I drank one cup and she gave me another. "I want you to drink this and rest, for we are going places this afternoon," she told me.

"Where?" I said, and thought she intended to take me to a movie.

She fidgeted a little. "I have tickets for a symphony matinee."

It was hard to believe that it was Peg who said that. The cheapest matinee tickets would be fifty cents, and more than once she had fussed at me for spending money for concerts. "It's all foolishness," she would say. "You can get two hours foolishness at the movie down the street for a dime, so why not go there." Thinking of all that, I felt a little guilty. I knew she wouldn't like the music and had bought the tickets just for me. I even thought of suggesting that she return the tickets while she could get a refund. I think she saw how I was feeling for she went over to the cupboard where we kept our dishes and opened the door and bent over for something. "You'll have to go now," she said, talking with her back to me. "I have something here you'll like."

She handed me a peanut butter jar with a corsage of the prettiest violets—the big hot house kind—stuck in it. I couldn't help but hug her. I laughed to see how sheepish she looked. "You think you've sinned," I said, "to spend money for violets for me, but some day I'll buy you a pair of those expensive sensible shoes with the big toes like you've been wanting."

I was laughing until I looked at Peg, and then I stopped laughing. She did not look gay as I was. I had not felt that way in so long I'd almost forgotten how good it was to be able to go some place, and have flowers to wear, and a pretty spring day in which to wear my suit. I felt so gay that not even Peg's glumness could do more than make me stop laughing aloud. I was still laughing inside. "What is the matter, Prudence Sensible (I called her that when she lectured me), sorry you spent the money?"

"No," she said. "I'm not sorry. I was just thinking—hadn't you better sit down and not tire yourself—about one day last spring when you went to market for butter and came back with a pound of oleo and a bunch of daffodils that wilted before the day was over. I was remembering all the things I said to you."

"I deserved them," I said, laughing again. "I think I'll try on my suit now. I want to strut around and look at myself."

"Wait a bit," she said.

"I can't wait," I said, and went over to the dresser. "I want to see how the violets are going to look on it." I held the flowers to my face. Peg was watching me. I could see her broad face back of mine, and I remember thinking that I looked almost pretty beside her. She must have had the same thought too, for she said, "The violets match your eyes."

"You know," I told her, still looking at myself, "I think my winter under cover has improved my face."

"I've noticed it," she said. "Your eyes are so bright they fairly shine."

"I'll be a beauty queen yet," I said, "but where's my suit?"

"I had it cleaned and pressed," she said, and took her time about getting it from the closet, and made a little business of taking it out of the crackly paper the cleaners had put it in. I gave a little gasp when I saw it because I had forgotten how pretty it was. I took the skirt first and held it up to my waist to see if it were the right size. It was. I wondered how much she'd had to tuck the belt and turned it down and looked at it.

There was no tuck at all. She had taken off the belt, shortened it, and sewed it on smooth again. I looked at the hip seams. They were small seams with the cloth freshly cut away. For a moment, I thought I wasn't seeing right, and looked at them again, and felt them with my hand to see if they were really narrow. I looked at Peg. She was staring at me, and still holding the wire hanger with a long ribbon of the rustling paper hanging from it. "But—you cut it," I said.

"Yes," she said. "I cut it."

I didn't say anything. I couldn't. I kept remembering that Peg was sensible and never made a mistake. I turned around and walked to the window and stood there and looked into the street. I looked at the sycamores in the parkway and thought of a million things at one time. My mind felt the way it used to when I was going to school and would take strychnine to keep awake at night, only now it was a thousand times clearer. Each sense was keen as if I'd strained it alone and closed all the others. I heard the ticking of the clock, the beef boiling over the fire, the hiss of the gass flame, people walking about in the room above, and others talking below, and the rustling of the paper that Peg still held in her hand. I heard noises of traffic on our own street and other streets. Somewhere a fire engine was going by, and the traffic signal on the corner began its clanging. I smelled the cooking meat, the dye and cleaning fluid and wool smell of the skirt in my hand, and the sweetness of the violets.

I saw in the park the benches were freshly painted a bright apple green and that on one a big man in rusty brown seemed to be asleep. It was a bright day with clouds and a pale blue sky and a little wind shaking through the sycamore trees. Mabley Tower was a brown finger poked into the blue sky, and the copper scrolls on the new telephone building made me think of gold. Under my window two women were going by, and one said something so that the other laughed until the red quill in her hat trembled.

I heard and saw those things without really thinking of them. My thoughts were very clear, not confused at all. It was only that there were so many of them; the dogwood at home, and the smell of the plum trees—I must burn my letters; some of Julian's were pretty terrible. I wouldn't need to spend money and have my winter coat cleaned—I wouldn't see the rough brown sycamore balls next fall—or Mabley Tower in a snow storm with its lights shining like a Christmas tree. I wouldn't need to have my wisdom tooth filled, or buy a new typewriter ribbon, or put an ad in the paper.

Peg would move to a back room now. She'd always thought me silly because I wanted to spend fifty cents a week for a few trees that didn't belong to me. Peg could sell the typewriter—too bad she couldn't wear my shoes. She could sell my books, but they wouldn't bring much—the forsythia on the campus—why had I ever gone to college—it would be blooming now. That silly poem I wrote to the forsythia—golding bubbles shifting in the sunshine. Bubbles disappeared when something touched them.

I wasn't afraid or sorry or sad. I was only angry. I wanted to beat against something with my hands until the palms bled. So many things I had wanted to do. I'd never be in Ireland, or have a job on a newspaper, or go home a Success, or own a first edition. I wished I had done more. Lots more of both the good and the bad, so long as it was doing. I remembered how glibly and how often I had said, "We only regret the things we never do." Now I could not say it, could know only how terribly true it was. It made me want to laugh.

Then I was laughing, and Peg was shaking me. Then we were sitting above the blue oilcloth of our table, and I was drinking broth. The broth was very hot, and I burned my tongue. For a moment, I thought that was why I was so angry. Then I remembered. I knew that it was senseless—useless, but I wanted to argue. "But, Peg, I hardly ever cough," I said.

She made the figure eight three times on the oilcloth with a fork handle. She looked hard at the fork handle. "You can't cough in your backbone, kid."

* * *

Yesterday a nurse told me I had been back a week. It seems much longer than that. It's like waiting days for a streetcar on a dark, deserted corner. But I can still think of Peg. It is funny to have lived two years with someone, and not know them at all. You see, I thought she was dumb. But she wasn't. When nobody else would tell me a thing she could and never say a word.

Home Coming

Arnow's personal notebook in the archives at the University of Kentucky dates this story in 1938. It was submitted to *Scribner's* and *Esquire*, but remained unpublished until now.

·······

*N*ow, you oughtn't to be a settin a cryin by the fire. Here yer ole pappy comes in wet an cold an finds th big house dark an th fire low. Ain't ye shamed, Son, snubbin like a two year old?

But, Pop, what's a keepin Mom so?

Aye, Lord, son. You know how women talk. I can see yer Mom now a settin' up at Becky Meece's, a laughin with her head throwed back an her hair a curlin down into her eyes. She's got no notion uv th time.

I'm gittin hongry. I wisht we could eat.

Not fore yer Mom gits in. She'll give us some cornbread hot frum th pan, an mebbe bake us a lasses cake. Wouldn't ye like a little cake?

There is a cake. Mom, she left supper ready an cooked when she went away. She baked a cake an made a high stack a fried dried-apple pies. 'You be good,' she says to me, 'an stay in th big house by th fire til yer pappy comes home.'

She must not a knowed th roads wuz bad an I'd be late. Th mules couldn't hardly make it up through Fiddle Neck Holler an on Elk Spring Hill th mud wuz turrible deep.

She knowed th roads wuz bad. Thet timber measurin man he couldn't git in today. We heared his truck on Black Gum Ridge a blowin an a blowin away.

No car could git down into th holler when th mud's like th devil's own. He must a had a pressin need to drive out in all this winter's weather.— There's yer Mom on th porch now. Run let her in.

Thet's not Mom. Thet's ole Zollie a beggin to set by th fire.

Let him in anyhow. I wouldn't leave a houn dawg out in thet cold black rain. Lord, it's good to git in an git off them soppin muddy shoes an stretch my feet to the fire.—Yer Mom'ull be soaked to th skin, an her feet all wet an muddy an cold. Let's have her Sunday shoes a warmin on th hearth when she gits in. They'd be in th corner there.

They wouldn't be there. She went away a carryin her good shoes in her hand.

Aye, I guess she wanted her feet nice an clean an dry while she sets by Beckie Meece's fire—yer Mom's got pretty little feet.

—Listen.—Sounds like her a walkin now.

Thet's no woman a walkin. It's th fire a trampin snow.

Ye needn't whisper, Son. Yer eye're like a sick sheep's eyes. Whut ails ye anyhow?

—Play me a fiddle tune, Pop, so's we won't hear th fire tramp snow. Mom, she never liked it neither. Nights when we wuz by ourselves like this, she's set an hear it. 'Like haints a walkin in their sleep,' she'd say.

Come set in my lap, Son. You're not too big to set on yer ole dad's knee. Yer hair it needs a combin an there's lasses on yer chin, but we'ull fix all thet when yer Mom gits in. In th winter time like this she gits lonesome lots a times, I know, an has to go off an have a little woman talk. But spring'ull be here soon, an I'll quit my loggin an stay home. She'll not be so lonesome then.

But in th spring she didn't allus laugh. Nights when she was a cookin supper about th time a dusty dark she'd stand in th kitchen door an listen up th holler. Now an agin she'd say to me, 'Benjie, them whip-poor-wills, they make me want to cry,' she'd say.

But, Son, she'ull like th wahoo an th ivy bloom, an there'ull be little new lambs a comin on, an wild strawberries tu hunt in th ole pasture field.

Oh, she'll like all thet. Many's th time I've seen her look at a ivy or a laurel bloom an say, 'Aye, Benjie, how wouldn't it be to have a dress pretty as a ivy bloom.'

I'll tell you a secrut, Son. I've—listen—there, thet wuz th gate creaked. She's a comin now. Run tu th winder; you'ull see her light.

It's th gate a bangin in th wind. I've heared it since dark, an anyhow I wouldn't see no light. Mom, she didn't take th lantern.

She never meant tu stay this long an be so late an dark a gittin in.

Heavy dark wuz a comin down an th rain wuz a fallin freezin like an slow when she went away.

Now don't be afeard. She'ull borrie a light. Hit's pitch black outside.

Is thet why th shadders in th corner is black like coal? Look in th corner. A body cain't see th bed.

Jump down an I'll build ye a brighter fire, Son. Some flames ull take them shadders away.

An then they'ull be like people a dancin?

An how would you be a knowin how people looked a dancin?

Mom, she tole me stories—th timber measurin man tole her—men an women a dancin in th town where th lights is red an blue an green, an crowds a people an music gayer than a fiddle tune.

Thet timber measurin man is a might one fer tellin tales, but we've got music gay a plenty. Yer Mom can sing an me with my fiddle tunes.

Fiddle me a tune, Pop. Lorena, or th Two Little Girls in Blue.

Wait til yer Mom gits in. She'ull sing while I fiddle you a tune. Th fiddle itself cain't beat yer Mom fer singin.—Thet sounds like her a singin a way off there.

You're th one's a whisperin now, Pop.—Thet's th wind in th white pines by th spring. Play me a fiddle tune so's I won't hear th wind. Listen to it cry in them high back hills.

You're a talkin in whispers yourself, Son. Now don't be skeered.

I wisht th wind, it wouldn't blow so lonesome like an cold.

But who's afeard uv th wind?

Mom wuz afeard uv th wind. Nights when you'd be out late a loggin like this she'd make me set on her lap. She'd hold me tight like an say, 'Aye, Benjie, I'm sick a hearin th wind a cryin an a cryin away.'

She's foolish in her notions like a little child, allus laughin or a cryin. I didn't tell my secrut, Son. Now don't you let on. I've got eyes. I've been a savin. Ever day when I stop at Joe Dick's store to warm a spell I see th prettiest piece a cloth. White sprigged with blue. Jist matches yer Mom's eyes.

Silk?

N-o-o. Cotton, but hit's finer than any she's ever had.

Th other day I heared th timber measurin man tell her about th women in Lexington. They dressed in silk, he said. An then he looked at her, an then he said, 'Some a thet silk ud be mighty becomin to you,' he said.

Lord, I'd love to see yer Maw in a pink silk dress an patent leather shoes. They would become her to a fare ye well.—Sounds like her a talkin low like now.

Thet's th rain a drippin frum th eaves. Play me a fiddle tune an I won't hear th rain.

Aye, th rain's gone to my fiddle's throat. It'll have no heart fer happy singin til yer Mom gits in. You don't want a sad song.

Play down in th valley, th valley so low; late in th evenin I heared th train blow.

Now wait til yer Mom gits in. She likes thet song.

It's not th song she likes so much, but th train a blowin away. Recollect how last summer when we worked in th high ridge corn field, how Mom, she ud stand a leanin on her hoe an listen to th train blow.

She wuz jist tired an a restin herself.

But she used to say, 'It's a talkin,' she'd say. 'Whut's it a sayin?' I'd ask her. An she'd answer me with her voice low an soft like a train a blowin acrost th hills, 'I'm a goin away. I'm a go-o-o-in aw-a-a-ay,' she'd say to me.

Her voice'ull be hoarse frum this cold wet rain, an people like th timber measurin man won't be a sayin they'd come ten mile to hear her sing.—Run to th corner in back a th door. We'ull put one a her dresses here by th fire an have it warm when she gits in.—

Here's yer other pair a overalls fresh patched an clean, but none a her dresses.

She's moved their place I guess.—Mebbe they're a hangin in th kitchen. We'ull go hunt one an git you a bite to eat.

Pop, you'd better light th lamp. The fire's out in th cook-stove an th kitchen's cold an dark.

Benjie, whyn't you tell me th mailman stopped? Looks like a letter here by th lamp.

There cain't be no letter. Th mailman, he didn't stop.

Le'me git down closter to the fire. Thet writin—

Whut ails yer hands, Pop?

—N-o-o-thin, Son. You an Zollie git away. Le'me read.—

Cain't you make hit out, Pop? Teacher up at school ud never let th big'uns thet kin read go along like you, a pokin their finger at ever word.— Them words must be awful long an hard.—You're a whisperin like a baby with th croup.—Look, Pop, at yer shadder on th wall. You cover all th room when you hunker clost to th fire like thet.—Did you fin'ly make hit out?— Hit must ha been hard words. Pop, yer eyes they shine like Zollie's in th dark.—What're you a puttin on yer shoes fer, Pop? Th wood's in an th night work's done.—What ye a lookin fer, Pop, over there behind th door? Nothin but th shotgun there.—Pop, ye ain't a goin a huntin off in thet rain, an th wind an th dark?—Pop, le'me an Zollie foller ye. He's a whimperin so.—Please, Pop, please.—Please.

Blessed–Blessed

Published posthumously in *Appalachian Heritage*, 2 & 3 (Spring/Summer, 1988): 7–12, this story was probably written in 1938.

Early manuscripts show that the character Katy was originally named "Sissie." Arnow's correspondence dating back to 1936 suggests that she wrote other "Sissie stories." This story is the only one extant, though a character nicknamed Sissy does appear in *Belle,* the unpublished Civil War novel that Arnow was revising when she died.

———

"**B**lessed are the peacemakers for . . . for . . ."[1] The words would come no further. Katy's mind was winging away to the cry of the bloodhounds, no longer faint but suddenly loud, eager, sweeping in hot quick waves of sound down the wagon road that ran below the farm.

"Go on, Katy," old Mrs. Fairchild said, and counted three and purled.

Katy squirmed on the low hard footstool, pushed back her brown forelock with sticky restless hands. "For . . . for . . ."

Her grandmother exploded with a "Study some more," and handed the Bible back to her. Katy cradled the big book on her knees and wished it were sundown. It would be harder to find a black man in the dark, and by then maybe her grandmother would have forgotten her anger over her mother's gray mare.

Lurie, the hired girl, rested on her iron. "They'll git him, th' blood thirsty nigger," she said, and listened, head tipped above the ironing board to the bloodhounds and the shouts of men, sweeping now below the farm.

Young Mrs. Fairchild bit off the thread from a sock she was darning. "Makes me think of a fox hunt."

Katy peeped up at her mother, remembered her grandmother, and let her head fall lower, so low that only with her lashes lifted could she see her mother's hands. They were little thin brown hands, with the knuckles blue-white against the black socks. And now while the bloodhounds boomed out in a full-throated triumphant cry, the hands did no darning, only clutched the socks and the sock darner. Katy marveled at the voice coming out above the hands, cool and uncaring as her mother's always was, laughing almost, not matching the hands. "I reckon Fiddlin' Turpin's fox-hunted so much in his time he'll take to th' lower creek like a fox an'. . . ."

"Fox huntin'," old Mrs. Fairchild snorted. "That nigger was never any good for anythin' but fiddlin' an' fox huntin' an'. . . ." She stopped to listen as the bloodhounds cried their confusion at the spot where the creek crossed the road.

Lurie took a fresh iron from the stove, tried its heat with spit from the tip of her finger. And to Katy, waiting, listening, arms clenched about her knees, the sound of the spit sounded loud above the bafflement of the hounds, loud like gunfire. "They're a losin' the scent," Lurie said in a hoarse whisper. "He's took tu th' lower creek jist like a fox."

Then one hound gave a joyous eager cry, and in an instant the pack of four took it up, moving straight across the creek and on up the road. "Scent must be gettin' stronger," old Mrs. Fairchild said with satisfaction, and added as she resumed her knitting, "Just let him try any of his fox tricks, goin' off down th' creek toward th' river. . . . They'll find him, hid like a fox somewhere down on th' river bluff or in th' lower creek."

Lurie rolled her eyes, and glanced uneasily out the window. "I don't reckon he'd take hit into his head an' come up th' creek into Mr. Fairchild's pasture."

"Not less'n he's a plum fool," old Mrs. Fairchild said. "He couldn't go in water any further than th' spring in th' west pasture where Little Sinkin'

Creek begins, an' th' hounds could pick up th' scent soon's he tried tu go above th' spring. An' anyhow what nigger would be a hidin' out on a white man's land, an' th' man a helpin' hunt him?"

"Maybe Fiddlin' Turpin doesn't know Papa's after him, an' that they're goin' to hang him with our plowline. I saw 'em take it out of th' barn an' Mr. Crabtree, I heard him tell papa that. . . ."

"Shut up, Katy, an' get on with your studyin'," old Mrs. Fairchild commanded. "When I was a little girl like you I never spoke out before my elders." She gave a sharp angry sigh above the gray knitted socks. "Th' old people would turn over in their graves to see how th' world's goin'. Here a white storekeeper can't total up his store books without runnin' th' risk a bein' cut up by a nigger." She glanced sharply over her spectacles at her daughter-in-law. "An' when he breaks out a jail there's white people to hold out for such goin's on an' won't lift one finger to see that law an' order's kept."

Young Mrs. Fairchild studied the half darned heel of a sock. "Law, Mother, I never meant it to sound like I was holdin' up for him. I just said that I guessed he broke out of jail . . . maybe with help . . . because he was afraid th' McChesneys would get a mob an' storm th' jail. Ever'body knows that that young Judge Montgomery would never ha passed a heavy sentence on him. Sam hit him first an' Fiddlin' Turpin lost his temper, an' cut him a little. An' ever'body knows that Sam McChesney does overcharge th' darkies."

Old Mrs. Fairchild forgot both her knitting and Katy. Katy raised her head, and studied her with intent round blue eyes, while she sputtered. "There you go, Mollie, talkin' on so before your child. She'll be holdin' up for trash an' no good fiddle-playin' niggers an' white people wastin' their time on fox hunts an' God knows what else. She'll be like kin of some I could name, but out of respect to you I won't." Her voice rose while she twitched at the unfinished sock, "You know you didn't do right about not lettin' Mat take Chariot. Her eatin' her head off in th' stable an' sayin' she's not strong enough for a long hard ride, an' her able to out jump any horse in th' country."

Lurie who had been leaning heavily on her iron relaxed and peeped around at young Mrs. Fairchild. Katy remembered she was studying the Beatitudes and bent quickly over the Bible. Young Mrs. Fairchild turned the sock over and considered it with tilted head. "It didn't seem to me they needed th' mare—looks like twenty men with some a th' best horses an' bloodhounds in th' country ought to be enough without takin' out a mare with a colt that's hardly weaned. Mrs. Fairchild, you heard me tell Mat when he wanted her that I'd leave her in th' stable, so they could come an' get her."

"You might ha knowed that after they'd started they couldn't take time to come back. Why you didn't even know that Fiddlin' Turpin would run up this way at all," old Mrs. Fairchild said, and knit with short jabs of her needles as if the thread were a something she would like to break. Her gray eyes from behind their steel rimmed spectacles sent Lurie bouncing to the stove for a hot iron, but her young granddaughter studied her unblinkingly. Katy asked, "How many children does Fiddlin' Turpin have?"

"Six, not countin' th' baby," young Mrs. Fairchild said, and the older woman's rocking chair gave an impatient angry squeak, as she said, "Katy, you're not studyin'. You'll disgrace th' family in th' quotation contest. When I was your age I knew th' Ten Commandments, th' Beatitudes, th' Sermon on th' Mount, an' twenty-seven Psalms."

"Long ones?"

"Go on with your studyin'."

And Katy went on. The bloodhounds' call came faintly now, though steadily. They had gone up the road below the pasture and down the other side of the hill. Katy closed her eyes and prayed for a thunderstorm, then remembered that in September thunderstorms with rain enough to wash away the scent of a man's feet were rare. She opened her eyes, and studied her mother's hands. They darned the socks slowly, clumsily, as if they were stiff with cold. Her grandmother's rocking chair gave a warning creak, and Katy's eyes skipped to the cramped black print of the Bible, hunted until they found the words in red—all the red was said by Jesus.

"Blessed are the pure in heart for they shall see God." Katy knew that she would never see God. She was wicked. Less than two weeks ago she had run away and played with Fiddlin' Turpin's youngens, and learned to dance like the two middle-sized girls, and patted her feet and whirled her petticoat and skirt in sin while Fiddlin' Turpin fiddled fit to kill. Maybe it was better to have danced so, than to come face to face with God. She was like her mother's people, old Mrs. Fairchild said, a hillbilly with loose wild ways.

She shuddered with wickedness as she remembered that she had decided she didn't want to see God, not her grandmother's God. She stopped, forefinger on one red word, listening, her eyes on her mother's hands. The room was so still, too still for any sound to break through—maybe the noise she thought she heard was the wind in the white pines by the gate.

"The meek shall inherit the earth." Her mother would have the Fairchild farm and all the farms in Somerset County and the whole world. She would live in a brick house with white shutters, older than Fairchild Place, built a thousand years before the battle of Bunker Hill instead of less than fifty. She would—but Fiddlin' Turpin would have nothing. He was not meek like most darkies. Sam McChesney, the storekeeper, laughed about the meekness of darkies. The ones who paid whatever he said, they would, along with Mama, inherit the earth, but Fiddlin' Turpin, he would never have even a blade of grass or one of his cold-nosed hounds. "Blessed are the merciful for they shall obtain mercy." Granma would not get mercy, not one little drop. Disappointment hurt. Katy remembered that her grandmother would not need it. She was Elijah Fairchild's widow with Fairchild children and a lifetime right to Fairchild Place. The preachers and the old county judges all came to see her. Katy tried to find a blessing for Fiddlin' Turpin. Blessed . . . blessed . . . He was not weak, nor did he mourn, and he nor his children ever looked hungry. His heart could not be pure for he had knifed a white man.

The shadow of the box elder tree was almost touching the paling fence by the garden, and still no more sound from the bloodhounds. Lurie banged more wood into the stove, and rattled down the ashes. Old Mrs. Fairchild was toeing off,[2] and could not talk. Young Mrs. Fairchild almost never talked. "Blessed are they that hunger and thirst," Katy whispered, and peeped at her mother. She would be blessed in that one too, maybe. She always looked hungry—not like she wanted to eat—but hungry at night when they stood sometimes on the hill together and her mother looked west toward the hills, rising up against the sunset. Her own blood kin was there in the hills, and maybe she was hungry for her fox-huntin' hillbilly kin, that had in the old days never owned slaves or fought under Lee.

Katy puzzled over hunger and mercy—and thought of the plowline, the long brown snakelike length of it dragging out of the barn. She shivered and hugged her knees, squeezed her eyes tight to shut out the plowline, opened them and saw the red words. Blessed . . . blessed . . . blessed . . . somewhere there must be a blessing for Fiddlin' Turpin. Maybe God would give him some since he didn't have much time left to make his own. Maybe they'd found him already, and that was why it was so still. She ran her finger over her throat, held it at the soft curve above her dress, pressed harder. She felt sick, as if she might be going to throw up all over the Bible; Granma would get her then for sure.

Lurie folded the last of the shirts. "Must be gettin' nigh supper time. I think I'll leave off ironin,'" she said with a cautious glance at old Mrs. Fairchild.

Old Mrs. Fairchild considered, then twisted about in her chair and frowned at the shadow of the box elder tree. "Better iron on a while longer. Th' men'ull maybe not be in 'fore a good spell. Maybe be gone all night." She glanced angrily at her daughter-in-law. "Mollie, you oughtn't to let that mare stay in th' barn all day—a standin' there when she's better in th' pasture."

Young Mrs. Fairchild pulled two socks together, dropped them into the willow work basket. "I was thinkin' that myself, that maybe I ought to turn her out now."

"An' who'll be takin' her I'd like to know? You can't in your condition. An' you know Lurie can't do a thing with her."

"Lord, yes," Lurie agreed, "she fairly hates th' sight of me."

Katy gave her mother's anxious face one quick glance, then bent over the Bible, whispering with tightly shut eyes, "Please Jesus, let me get away an' turn out th' gray mare."

"I could put a halter on her in th' barn, an' Katy could lead her to th' pasture," young Mrs. Fairchild said.

Katy opened her eyes and lifted her head with careful slowness, and said in careful disconcern with a finger on a red word, "What did you say, Mama? I was studyin' so."

When her mother had repeated her plans for the gray mare, Katy said, "I wouldn't mind," and was careful to be slow about getting up from the stool and marking her place in the Bible. Old Mrs. Fairchild fumed and fretted, told her daughter-in-law to be careful in the barn, and told Katy to be careful of the gray mare's heels, and ended by flouncing up from the rocker and declaring that they'd better wait until the men got home.

Katy glanced nervously at her mother's face, saw her chin lifted and her eyes blandly blue and not caring, the way they were sometimes, and then no longer concerned with her grandmother's wishes she skipped out the door.

She was by the stable door, stroking the gray mare's nose when her mother came, walking rapidly for her mother. She said nothing but took a halter from a peg on the wall and slipped it over the gray mare's neck. She never seemed to hear when Katy jumped up and down and begged to ride, but hurried the gray mare through the barnyard and up the pasture hill toward the bars that led to the west pasture. They were rushing up under the yellow leafed apple trees when old Mrs. Fairchild's long drawn scream of "Mo-l-l-ie," followed them up from the kitchen door.

They both turned and listened to Lurie's explanation: "Miz Fairchild says ye know ye cain't put that mare in th' west pasture. She'll jump th' fence an' git out, or break her leg in one of them sinks in th' creek."

"She's too hungry to bother," young Mrs. Fairchild said as if she didn't much care whether they heard her or not, then turned sharply up the hill again with no looking back at old Mrs. Fairchild babbling in the kitchen door.

"Won't Chariot get out a th' west pasture like Granma says?" Katy asked.

But her mother only walked a little faster, pulling on the gray mare's rein, until the three of them were almost running up the hill. Young Mrs. Fairchild's breath came short and her cheeks were red when they reached the pasture bars at the top of the hill. They stopped a moment to lay down the bars. As they worked both listened and looked below the west pasture to where the wagon road ran until it lost itself in the woodland that crowned the hill. "It's awful still," Katy whispered.

Young Mrs. Fairchild nodded and laid down the last bar, then straightened her shoulders and looked toward the bottom of the west pasture where Little Sinking Creek began. But though bars of the late red sunlight touched them there on the hill, below the cows grazed in shadow heavy like golden purple smoke. "I thought maybe he'd learned somethin' from th' foxes he's hunted all his days," young Mrs. Fairchild said, and continued to hunt over the bottom of the pasture with her eyes.

Katy studied her, uncertain of whether her mother spoke to her or the gray mare or maybe only to the air. "Can I take off th' gray mare's halter now?" she asked. "She's in a hurry to graze."

Her mother considered without taking her eyes from the field. "Maybe Chariot ought to have a little drink first. Maybe you ought to ride her down over th' hill . . . to th' spring at th' head of th' creek . . . an' leave her there to drink."

Katy climbed the rail fence, while the gray mare side stepped and minced and seemed to dance with a rolling of her eyes when she saw what Katy was about. Young Mrs. Fairchild quieted her with gentle strokes on one shoulder. "She'd love a long good run," she said.

"Reckon she'd jump th' fence?" Katy asked, and sat waiting on the top rail.

"Not if she grazes down by the bottom of the pasture and fills herself with a good long drink." She listened, head bent above the bars. "I guess it was only th' cowbells . . . if she did run away she'd go straight to Brother Joe's in McLeary County."

"I guess Uncle Joe could use a good mare," Katy said.

Her mother shook her head. "Brother Joe has plenty of mules an' horses, but he could use a good strong man about th' place . . . none of his boys are big enough to help."

Katy stood on the fence, watching for a chance to spring on the gray mare. "Fiddlin' Turpin is a good strong man an' a good worker spite a what Granma says."

"I've thought of that but now—"

"It's the bloodhounds—they're coming back," Katy cried, and stood balanced on tiptoe on the top rail to see if they were coming down the road.

"He did have some sense," young Mrs. Fairchild said, and jerked the gray mare's halter. The gray mare shied and plunged, then was suddenly docile drawing nearer the fence.

Katy leaped and caught her mane, as the hounds cried louder from the stretch of road behind the hill. "You've got to hurry," Mrs. Fairchild said, and Katy heard the trembling in her voice, and a lot of other things behind the words. "Ride her down to th' spring and leave her," she said, "but hurry . . . an' then come straight back home."

She let loose of the halter and the gray mare, mettlesome from her long stay in the stable, plunged down through the deep yellowing clover. Katy dug her heels into her side and clung, and never looked back and hardly nodded when her mother called after her, in a voice loud and excited for her mother. "You might think on th' Beatitudes, Katy. Recollect blessed are they that are merciful for. . . ."

But Katy was halfway down the hill, and the thud of the gray mare's hoofs and the wind in her ears drowned out her mother's words. She was doing what she had always wanted to do, giving the gray mare her head and letting her go at her will. She wondered if the gray mare would stop at the spring; maybe she'd race right by, lunge up the hill, leap the fence and go crashing and crackling through the wood on the other side. They'd swim Elk Spring Branch and go galloping into the hills to Uncle Joe's where. . . . She was flying, rising right up to meet the sky, then her feet were hard in the grass and clover, and she was falling belly downward with clover pushing hard into her face and her hands. Nearby someone was calling in a soft undertone, "Whoa, you gray devil, whoa. Oh, my Lordy," and feet were slithering over the grass to her.

She lifted her head and saw Fiddlin' Turpin with the gray mare's halter rein over his arm, and his eyes wide white and rolling in his black face. "Oh, my Lordy, I've kilt ye for shore," he said, and bent over her. "I heared a horse comin' sudden like an' lickety-split right on top a me here by th' spring. I thought hit was them, an' I started tu run, an' skeered yer—"

"S-h-h," Katy whispered, and listened with her ear near the ground.

"It's them bloodhounds," Fiddlin' Turpin whispered, as if he were too tired to care. "I figgered they'd not git back 'fore dark an' I'd have time tu rest a spell, an' try tu git a head start on 'em through th' woods. I've doubled like a fox till I'm clean winded." He squatted on his heels and stared down the valley to the edge of the pasture where the road ran, hidden now by a screen of persimmon bush.

Katy got up and smoothed her skirt and studied the black man. He looked tired, tireder than one of his fox hounds after a three days' run; there was blood on his face and hands from all the saw briars and barbed wire fence he'd come through, but now while he sat and stared at the road, unmoving as a stone man, he looked somehow as if he wouldn't be running much more, as if all the caring had gone out of him, and he would sit and wait with Chariot's halter over his arm till the bloodhounds came. He never even turned his head when the gray mare jerked on her reins and tried to nibble a mouthful of clover.

"You'd better hold on to that horse," Katy said. "She can jump any fence in th' country. Mama said if she broke out she'd never stop till she got to Uncle Joe's in McLeary County."

Fiddlin' Turpin turned and looked at her, his cracked, puffy lips wide open, as if maybe a thought had come into his mind past the bellowing hounds. "Hit'll not take them hounds long tu foller down th' creek an' then. . . ." He stopped, and for the first time really looked at Chariot, and then he looked at Katy. His mouth was still open, but he didn't look so tired anymore.

Katy pulled a dried clover blossom from her hair. "We'd both better get goin'. Mama said Uncle Joe could use a good strong man," she said, and nodded toward the gray mare.

Afterwards she liked to think that Fiddlin' Turpin had thanked her or said, "God bless you, Katy," or some such thing, but he was gone so quickly—like Elijah in his chariot of fire—that she never knew exactly what it was he said. She stood a moment and watched the gray mare surge up the pasture hill, felt a moment's envy of Fiddlin' Turpin when the two of them cleared the fence with a full foot to spare, and then remembering her mother she ran up the hill and home.

Nothing was changed in the kitchen; old Mrs. Fairchild sat knitting and muttering in her chair, fuming because the gray mare would be certain to jump the west pasture fence and the men would be three weeks getting her home. Katy's mother worked in silence, a look of listening on her face as the bloodhounds cried up from the lower creek. Katy tiptoed to her footstool and picked up the Bible, conscious of her mother's eyes, tight somehow and as troubled as her hands twisting over the socks. Old Mrs. Fairchild laid her knitting on her knee. "Well, I hope after takin' th' gray mare to that pasture where she's bound to get out, you can do a little better learnin' your Bible quotations."

Katy folded her hands over the Bible and looked at her mother and said, "Blessed are the merciful for they shall obtain mercy." She hardly heard her grandmother's angry command to recite the first blessing first, for watching her mother's face and hands.

The First Ride

Written before Arnow married, probably in 1937 or 1938, "The First Ride" was posthumously published in *Appalachian Heritage* 17: 4 (Fall 1989): 12–19.

———◦◦◦———

*S*he heard her mother's voice, hoarse with fright pressing it into a flat stream of sound, "You'll have to hurry." And then her husband's call, "I've fin'ly got him saddled," while Rebel the big gray stallion neighed and pawed by the porch steps as if he too knew the joy of the long, wild ride that lay ahead. Her husband came to the door, and her father turned slowly away and then back to her so that she saw his old face, puckered into pale lines of fright and sorrow. She smiled at him and saw thoughts written into his eyes plain like words He was loath to have her go and feared for her the long ride. She laughed to show him that she was not afraid, but her tongue seemed heavy and useless for words so that she made them no answer as she galloped away.

Behind her she heard their calling and the crying of the child. She did not turn her head or hesitate. Her name on their tongues was enough; they wished to advise her thus and so and warn her of this and that and maybe tell her again of the need for haste. Soon the wind had blown their cries away, and the road, white sand on the ridge crest now, ran smooth and straight between the black trunks of the high pine trees whose deep moon shadows lay like black bars across the silver of the sand.

She raised one hand and half rose in the stirrups and pretended to snatch at a twig on a black gum tree as they flew past, and dropped again to the saddle and laughed to herself as the wind quickened about her ears and raised her hair like the horse's mane. That was the way to make Rebel fly, Luke her brother had once said. She too had wanted to make Rebel fly, but her mother would never let her ride as she had always wanted to ride; her mother lived for the neighbors and God. The neighbors and God, but tonight she could laugh at the neighbors and God. This night was not like other nights, there was the road and the moon and the wind and the ever-quickening need for haste. She thanked the woman sick and about to die who gave the reason for this ride, and sorrow for the woman lay vague and weightless in the back of her mind behind the half-believing wonder that it was she who rode so, riding as she had always wanted to ride, with trust for her body in the horse's feet, and her soul flung to the moon or maybe to the wind. Tonight the wind came neither west nor south, but out of the neverland that lay between and held the freedom and strength of the west and the lazy whispering laughter of the south. The wind was the smell of spring with larkspur and wild roses by the creek and the clover in the hill field and the pine scent sharp through the sweetness, and over it all was the sound of the great trees on Fiddle Bow Mountain and the willows by Laurel Run and the simple wail of hills against the beating, rushing waves of air.

The big horse went like a brother of the wind and seemed to know the need that made her drive him so. He went like a horse undriven, like a horse of God with wings and a dragon for his heart. He did not pause when the road curved and swooped down a hill, black in the shadow with white rocks glimmering and sparks from his iron shoes rising and dying like hasty fireflies. She laughed as they went sliding down into deeper darkness, and knew that she could go there and home again in time. The woman would not die, and she would have this ride, wild and heedless and free as she had always wanted.

She laughed to think she was a woman now with heedless ways and causeless, senseless laughter gone behind her. In the last spring, early when the first wild iris came and she was sixteen, she had married Rufe, and her mother had said, "He'll keep you straight," and her father had said, "It's better that you marry now and never give the neighbors cause to talk," and Rufe had said, "You'll never go hungry."

Rebel was by the creek now, and did not pause to sniff the water, but plunged right in and where his feet struck, the water rose in a flowering spray that stood for a moment clear of the shadow until it seemed that when it fell silver had touched her hair. The creek was deep but clear and the gray horse swam and she trailed her fingers by his side and watched the fan-shaped ripples grow and fade. They crossed the creek and Rebel arched his neck and tossed his head and neighed and snorted with a great trumpeting and flung the water from his sides, and leaped away up the hill and under the beech trees and past the place where the sweet williams grew. Their odor rose and mingled with the wind and she thought that sometime she might return this way and walk all day on the hill and see the flowers and maybe pick a few to carry home; no, not home; Rufe did not like flowers. Better that a woman spend her time in the garden than with the foolishness of flowers.

They came to a level rutted road with a zigzag rail fence on one side and a rolling pasture field beyond. She saw the field open and wide and inviting with the high grass bowing and whispering in the wind. It would be the shorter way, and she wanted to ride across the field and see Rebel race against his black shadow as it flew over the grass. She drew on the bridle rein and the great horse swerved and she felt his body rise in a flying lunge, and for an instant the rail fence in its mat of persimmon bush and red thorn lay below her, and then they were over and Rebel's front feet were striking the ground and he had fallen to his knees, but he was up again and away, and she was laughing and never looking back, her body one with the horse's body that skimmed over the field lightly as foam on swirling creek water.

She dropped the rein across the saddle and gave the horse his head and looked up at the moon that seemed to ride across the cloud-flecked sky in the same glory of reckless joy with which she rode the field. She remembered the woman sick and like to die, and sorrow for the woman sharpened her own joy in the world. Tonight she thought that she loved the moon and the wind-torn feathers of cloud more than yesterday or any of the days before yesterday; though always she had loved light and darkness and rain and sun and snow and the red leaf-whispering dawns of autumn and the half-sad, half-sweet twilights of spring when the whippoorwills began their plaintive callings and the short gray days of winter with the hills secret and shut into themselves against the shrieking, clawing wild beast of the wind. But tonight the world seemed even better and more worthy of her love.

On one side of the hill pasture lay a field of knee-high corn, the freshly plowed dark earth glistening with drops of dew, fine like seed pearls she had read about in school. She smelled the earth and the sweetish smell of the growing corn and loved that too, even as she remembered that sometime, once a long while ago in some vague, formless past when she was heavy and tired from the work she did in the corn rows and some great weight that had pulled against her back and pressed against her heart, the smell of the corn had sickened her nigh unto death it seemed and she had hated the corn and the earth and cried out against them. She bent low over Rebel's flying shoulders and felt a shame and a wonder at the memory, and joy in the lightness of her body and the goodness of the world made her wish to ask forgiveness of something for that faint memory of hatred and pain.

They crossed the pasture and she saw the dark woodland sloping away over the hill down into a narrow valley and up another hill, and past that hill she could see nothing, for it was higher than all the other hills, so high it was like a mountain with its crest hidden in shifting shimmering fog. That, she knew, was where she must go, and by the length of Rebel's flying shadow she knew that she had not been long on the road and would be there on time.

They leaped another fence and plunged into a wood where the wind sang loud in the leafing trees with no sobbing as in the pines, and drops of dew, heavy as rain, fell from the leaves onto her face and hair. Rebel leaped a moss-grown log and leaped through a moonlit glade, cleared a low limestone crag, and plunged again into the deeper darkness of close growing trees. He went less swiftly now and above the slower beat of his heavy hoofs she heard the roar of a creek and trembled with hungry eagerness for the battle with swift white water coiling in darkness and moonlight.

Heavier drops of dew fell on her face and she impatiently flung them back and glanced up to search out the mountain, for it was dark here and she feared she had lost her way. But it was there, higher and brighter and more beautiful, like the Big Rock Candy Mountain it was a sin to sing about because the singing made you want to dance. She sent Rebel crackling through a prickly grove of holly bush. The ground was soft and the horse's feet sank deep and made no sound, and it was then she heard their calling, louder and more insistent. She checked the horse and paused to think. Their call puzzled her, and she wondered that they could have followed all this way and carried the crying child. She saw them then by scarcely turning.

There was her mother with a glass of water in her hand as she stood and looked down at something that seemed to be just behind her own eyes. There was her father, and Rufe too, with his muddy shoes and the overalls she had forgotten to mend. His face looked pale under the sunburn, tight and hard as if he were afraid to come farther than the door where he stood with one foot on the sill. She did not want to look at him. He seemed a man in trouble, and with the joy of the good ride still upon her she had no wish for trouble.

She looked down and saw a hand, small and thin and brown, cupped like a fallen leaf, and as she stared at the hand she wondered at the dew. There was dew on the hand just as on the corn, great drops of it shining yellow in some light that did not come from the moon. She wondered if the dew had fallen on all things and moved her eyes slowly and saw a little mound of patchwork quilt like a hill made small by distance. Her glance which seemed heavy and tired came slowly away from the hill, drew nearer and fell upon a strip of white cotton nightgown with pearl buttons winking in the light. The buttons troubled her—they were so much like some she had once had with four eyes and sewn with coarse white thread. She puzzled over the buttons and heard rain roar on the roof boards, and thought that the next creek would be yellow instead of white.

She heard Rebel's impatient, angry neigh and the thud of his pawing feet against the ground. She heard the planks of the floor creak with the weight of heavy hesitating feet, but she did not lift her eyes. It was such a deal of trouble. She heard her mother cry in a thin hoarse croak, "Don't go away, Paw. It's we've waited too long," and then her father's voice, flat and unlike his own, "Yes. No man could ever a made it over th' creek anyhow." She knew he was wrong about the creek, and hated herself for this waste of time when now they seemed so troubled by the time that had gone. Her thoughts churned in a panic of thinking that she might have lost her way and would maybe be too late. She looked again and smiled to herself for it was still there, high and wreathed in a white fire of moonlit fog. She heard the child crying in another room and Rufe's calling of her name, and there was pity in his call, something more than pity—like terror almost. She saw tears falling on the cupped leaflike hand, and then Rufe's head bent over the buttons on the nightgown. Maybe he had taken her buttons and put them on the nightgown and now was sorry and ashamed. She wanted to tell him that he could have the buttons; there were so many things out there in the night for her to love. It was all so good—she remembered the need for haste and knew that she must wait until another time. Rufe called again, and as she rode away she wondered at the pity in his call.

Almost Two Thousand Years

Arnow offered this story for publication under the name Harriette Simpson. At the time, she lived in Covington, Kentucky, just across the Ohio River from Cincinnati. This unpublished story was probably written in 1938 or early in 1939.

———————

*T*ime was muskmelon seeds on a dusty pavement; the lights on Mabley Tower, twinkling yellow oranges in a deep smoky sky, or one still [quiet] glow in gray rain; strawberries in the market stalls; cherry stain on dirty hands; and the smell of pineapples hanging rich and heavy in a silent sunlit street. Time was cries that went beating up and down the marketplace: "New cabbage, five cents a pound. Lilies of the valley, lilies, lilies of the val-e-e-ey. Tender broilers, thirty cents, tender broilers——." There were so many cries.

They were like the feet, for the feet were time. Not the time of the watermelon rinds, or long and far and cold like the pigeons' wings when they were gray with no flashing in the sunlight. The feet were always the same, yet always changing. Sometimes many feet, angry, quick, impatient, kicking, going away, coming again, big feet in ugly broken shoes, fine feet in thin-heeled slippers.

Lupe, the child who knew time, knew feet well. While he sat under Tony's booth and sorted out the rotten berries or washed the dirty vegetables, he had only to raise his head a little and there would be the feet. The feet were like the church bells, and the steamboat whistles blowing up from the river, and other whistles from farther away, and the blind man with his gospels, and the shopping bag boys, and his own granny who every day walked up and down the marketplace wheezing and sighing over her cry of "Pretzels. Fresh pretzels, five cents."

Such things were always there, except on the day when the church bells rang and rang and all the whistles were dead, and there were no feet in the street. Tony's booth was empty, and the pretzel woman's grandson sat on the steps above his basement and looked at the tower, or sat in the alley back of the corner saloon and listened to the music and the laughter, though he never smiled at the laughter or cried with the music. Sometimes he walked out past the marketplace and down past the warehouses where there were almost never feet at all and on down to the river where he sat and watched the water. He never played. He had never learned.

Time was like the sky above Mabley Tower, far and full of something, yet empty when you looked into it. All his life past seemed cries and feet and rotten berries, and Tony waving his arms and pushing him with his foot, and at night his grandmother sleeping her dead unnatural sleep if the day had been a good one, or silent and full of hard quick slaps if she had sold no pretzels. Time did not go behind his grandmother, no more than the sky went past the tower, but the feet and Tony stopped at something like the far side of the river that he could hardly see, and the hills were far away and back of it, just as something was away and back of Tony and the feet. He had sat so long in the basement room, just sat and watched the light fall, always even and gray from the windows above him, and now and then heard a few feet clap-clapping and tap-tapping down the alley. That was so long. So long ago, and so long he sat there, never seeing the feet and listening mostly to an empty alley. That was there but far—farther even than the hills across the river.

Time grew upon him as he watched the feet and listened to the cries and heard the bells. First, Tony would come kicking by his basement window, shouting and crying down the steps that it was time to set up the booth or that there was a crate of rotten berries to be culled. Lupe would go out into the street then where the lights looked tired and pale in the fog from the river, and all the streets were very still, save in the market-place where men and women were setting up their booths in readiness for the feet that would come when the fog was gone and the yellow lights had paled into white.

Early, when the whistles first blew in the warm still mornings, there were few feet, but later there would be many. Tony would be busy then, and Tony's girl and Tony's wife, and they would cry at him for more clean lettuce, or freshly scrubbed potatoes, and the wet broken-off tops of the radishes and carrots and turnips would fall over him in a cool green flood. Then the feet would be still again, and he would walk about the marketplace and smell the flowers, or watch the pigeons at the head of the square by the grain merchants, or sit and stare into the sky and clouds past Mabley Tower until Tony called for him to come unwrap oranges or sort a barrel of rotten apples. The whistles would blow again and the bells ring and the lights come on, white still as in the morning, and it would be time to go home to his basement in the alley.

The lights were time, too. Now that the watermelon seeds lay black on the hot pavement, the picture of the lights shining yellow on crowds of hurrying muddy feet was dim and faint like the last ripple from a pebble he might throw into the river, but it was there: a picture of dark streets and Tony crying out "Cranberries, cranberries," and many, many feet, and something about his hands—something like pain, and his legs, but it was all so dim, so long ago, but somehow like the church bells. They rang today, and tomorrow they would ring again, and once the streets had been dark save for the tall lights and little fires burning near the market stalls. And now it was bright and hot with the pigeons' wings flashing many colored in the sunlight, and then it would all change, and the pigeons' wings would be gray and they would sit very still, but it was far away. So far, he couldn't see.

One day when Tony handed him baskets of dark grapes and told him to pick the rotten ones away, their warm sweet smell and the purple sticky juice on his fingers filled him with a wordless uneasiness and a kind of fear, though he had no words for the fear and could not have named what he feared. He looked toward the strip of pavement in front of Tony's booth, and it was still with no feet moving, and on it a few green feathers of the carrot tops lay limp and pale in the hot sun. But the grape stain on his fingers told of other things, cruel cold things to come—some cruelty harder and sharper than the cold of the empty street in a snowy dawn. It seemed it was a cry or a word, and he was still a moment, listening, but all he could hear was, "Crab apples, crab apples," and that was not the word. He was still too long, so that Tony glancing down, saw and shoved him a little with his foot, and said, "Fixa da grapes, yu leetle bastard half-a-brain." Two feet came then, fine lady's feet in shining shoes, and Tony caught up the nicest bunch of grapes.

The uneasiness grew upon him [Lupe], this remembering of some terror and the voiceless knowing that it would come again. The mornings darkened, and the lights flared with a longer brightness in their flare, and nowhere were there watermelons or muskmelons, but only grapes and nuts and oranges and cranberries. So many cranberries. He picked over and washed them all, and they, more than the grapes, made him think of the word. New cries came into the street: turkeys, holly wreaths and mistletoe, citron and dates and lemon peel, poinsettias and coconut. They cried them all, and it seemed that the cries brought feet, grinding, crushing hordes of feet surging about the market stalls. The pavement was cold now, and the pigeons' wings did not shine, and the bastard boy's hours were slow hours, filled with the work of going over wet cold cranberries or washing kale and lettuce in tubs where bits of ice made a faint jingling.

Always he listened and heard the feet and the cries and the church bells and angry women voices and the steamboats wailing down the river. There was one word, he knew, that told it all: the mad, pushing, angry feet, the cold, the blood on his hands, the rotten cranberries, the red flower of the stiff poinsettias, and the dead gray of the pigeons' wings. Every day he listened, and as the feet thickened, and the cold and the madness and the noise grew with Tony's cries and kicks, he knew that the time of the word was near. He heard it then one day while leaden rain like liquid ice fell heavily into the street, and the feet were still a little time. It rose clear and high from the corner back of the flower house, "Christmas Trees, Christmas Trees."

The other time was far away and gone, somewhere past the bright bird wings and the greening of the grass by the river, but it had been like this, long and cold and hard with that word of Christmas, and now it was come again. It was the word for the madness of the world and the blood on his hands and the long days that began in yellow street light and ended in that light, and the nights, so short they seemed, that Tony's cries and kicks by the basement window were sounds of the night and not of the morning.

As the feet tramped every day a little thicker, and more impatient, the word continued in the street cries until it seemed that he had never heard the street without it, and that the cold and the blood on his hands and the ice in the water would always be about him. He heard it from the blind gospel man, seller of Mark and Luke and John, the words of Paul and the songs of Solomon. The gospel man rumbled and grumbled behind his big dark glasses, "Remember a pore blind man. A pore blind man on Christmas, the birthday of our Christ."

And Lupe would hear the gospel man and mumble to himself as he cut away rotten cabbage leaves, "Christmas? Christ? Christ? Birthday?"

Above him Tony spoke of Christmas, too. "Maka da beesness good. Da people da buy anyting. Anyting at Christmas. We make da money. Mooch money dis Christmas."

And Lupe would repeat, "Mooch money. Christ? Beesnes? Christmas? Christ?" Once, when Tony bent down for bunches of celery, the boy raised his head and asked his question, "Christ?" and Tony laughed and said, "Make da beesnes good."

Snow fell into the streets and rain, and the yellow lights above the market stalls burned all day long, and back of the stalls were many little fires, where the child might have warmed himself had there been time. But the feet left no time. They began early, before the booth was hardly ready, and ended long after the last whistle had blown, though now with all the feet the whistles came but faintly, and the chimes and church bells seemed far away and muffled like the steamboat whistles crying up from the last bend in the river. The feet were never still, never the same, yet always there, grinding and pounding and surging about the boy as he squatted under Tony's booth and cleaned the things the hands above him reached for.

At night, the feet and the cold and the bloody water on his hands were with him still. The feet walked over him in a bruising flood and ground him down and flattened him against the floor, just as they flattened stray cranberries and loose grapes and every other thing that came before them in the street. Sometimes he would cry out and waken the old woman. She would raise her hand and put on the one light that hung from the ceiling, and then lie there staring at him a moment with her yellow gray eyes, all squinted against the light, and mutter and ask questions that he never answered. "Yu cold? Tony workin' yu too hard, yu pore leetle half-wit bastard. When yu're bigger yu'll git money. Tony feedin' yu?"

He would grow quiet then, and the old woman would sigh and raise her hand and let the room fall once more into darkness. The feet would return, tap-tapping by the window and striding down the broken stair, and over him and up the wall and away, walking across the river and to the hills that he could never see. Tony's feet and voice would sound then, and he would get up and go and work and watch the other feet and hear the Christmas cries walk with the feet up and down the marketplace. He never ran about. There was no time now.

Every day Tony would say, "Da beesnes, she is good," and the boxes and barrels and bales of fruit and vegetables stacked behind the booth early in the morning would be empty when night came. The feet took everything away. The feet and the words that made the feet come for things. Sometimes the child would stop work a moment and, still squatting, turn and stare at the feet, frowning, asking his questions that no one heard, "Christ? Christmas? Birthday? Mooch money?"

The days grew colder so that rain no longer fell, only snow. One night when Tony came calling by his window, the snow lay still and deep in the streets and made a wavering, falling curtain over the lights. Now and then a little wind skipped down from between the houses, and it was very cold. There were many fires in the marketplace and many people. Tony's wife and girl were there with a strange man that Tony called his helper. Trucks came, more trucks than he had ever seen, came unloading boxes and barrels and crates until fruit and vegetables were piled like a hill behind the booth. Tony looked at the snow falling past the lights, and rubbed his hands, and talked of Christmas Eve and the money the snow would bring. A fat truck driver set a crate of rotten looking celery by the boy's feet and grinned and said, "Don't take off too many leaves, Sonny. They'll buy anything on Christmas Eve. They'll eat ever'thing on Christmas Day."

"That's a fact," Tony's helper said, and knelt in the snow and unwrapped oranges. The boy unwrapped oranges too and looked at the helper and asked, "Christmas?" The helper stared at him, until Tony laughed and tapped his forehead. The helper looked at him and shook his head a little, then glanced at Tony. "But he ain't old enough tu hardly tell."

"He is though," Tony said. "He never say nothing. My boy that size, he talka all day."

Lupe crawled under the booth and began washing dirt and snow from the kale. He worked slowly, and Tony hurried him with words and cries and, now and then, his foot. Though after a time, he hardly felt the foot. It pushed him and he moved a little, and that was all. The feet came early, and that day it seemed as if all the other feet of all the other days and nights he had known came into the marketplace brought by this word of "Christmas" and the blind man's grumble of "Christ." He heard his granny go up and down and up and down, stamping her feet to keep them warm, while she sighed over her cry of "Fresh pretzels, five cents."

From the corner back of the flower house, the Christmas trees and holly wreaths and mistletoe were cried more loudly than before. It seemed the cries came forever, like the feet, and would not go away. Once Tony's wife threw him down a bit of bologna and a piece of bread, but he pushed it away and went on cutting away the frozen, rotten celery stalks. He was not hungry. Gray light wavered about him, darkened, grew yellow with the street lamps, while Tony's shadow and other shadows moved and pitched across his broken shoes. He couldn't feel the shadows on his shoes. He couldn't feel his feet. Sometimes he would stop his work and glance at them, then touch first one foot and then the other with one raw swollen finger. He had to do that. Sometimes he was afraid. Once he thought his feet had gone away and were now walking up and down across the dirty snow with all the other feet.

The yellow light deepened and he heard the whistles blow, but the feet in dirty frozen shoes still came. He hardly heard them now and never raised his head. He heard the word of Christmas, the word he hated, and it was everywhere, louder and shriller and stronger than all the other sounds in the street. The word was stronger than the cold. He could not feel the cold—not now when the lights were deep and yellow. He could not feel the frozen cabbage leaves or the celery stalks or the bright oranges when he took their wrappings away. He hardly noticed when the ranks of the feet thinned, came more slowly, or hurried quickly past, and that above the Christmas cries the bells rang and rang. Tony had called for nothing in a long while, but he worked on and unwrapped oranges. He heard first the stillness and raised his head, and saw the street empty with snow falling by the lights. There were no feet now and Tony would be going home, but first he would pack his things away in Benny's basement across the street. He began to wrap the oranges he had unwrapped and was not finished when Tony pulled the crate away and said, "Most ever'ting gone but da orange."

The boy did not move, but only sat and watched the snow fall into the street. Tony's girl put her head under the booth and called to him, "Come on out. Ain't cha goin' home? Me, I'm froze."

He turned and looked at her. "I—me—legs."

"Yu legs have gone sleepin'," she said, and reached and caught him by the shoulder and pulled him over the frozen, cast-off vegetables. She stood him against the booth, but he would have fallen had she not stayed and held him pushed against the boards. "I think you're froze," she said, and raised her voice, "Oh, Poppy, come take the half-wit. He cain't walk, an' I'm froze a holdin' him."

Tony and his helper came from across the street where they had gone to store the unsold fruit. "He set too long in da cold, da leetle fool," Tony said. He stood a moment and rubbed Lupe's back.

"It's in his legs," the girl said, and rubbed his leg. He saw her hands move up and down, but he couldn't feel her hands.

"He need da fire," Tony said. "I'll take him to Benny's. He aims to gitta da trade from da people when da come from da meednight church. Benny never go to church."

"Come on," Rosa said, and took her hands away.

He tried to walk, and fell with his face in the dirty slushy snow. Tony picked him up and carried him over his shoulder. Benny's food shop was warm with the smell of cheese and something sweet. Tony laid him on the floor by the stove, and he moved a little and tried to wipe the gray melting snow away from his mouth and nose. Benny's wife came and looked at him. "You've let him freeze," she said, and knelt and wiped his face, then got up and went for something in the back of the room. She came again and poured a burning drink down his throat that made him gasp and cry, and when he cried and struggled against her hand she nodded and said, "That is good," and got up and went to the back of the room for something else.

The boy sat up and looked about him, saw Tony and Rosa warming themselves by the stove and glancing at him, and Benny, by the showcase, counting money from his cash register. The woman came again, this time with a bowl in her hand. Tony glanced at the bowl. "He'll be O.K. Ju leave him by da stove. Me an' Rosa an' da wife, we want tu go church. At Chreestmas church eet ees beeutiful—beeutiful. We never miss da Chreestmas."

"Christmas?" the boy said, and remembered. He looked at his hands. Blood oozed out in a thousand little cracks. The blood and the feet and the pain that the warmth brought to his body. "I—me—Christmas. Christ? I hate," he said, and looked at the fat woman with the bowl in her hand.

Tony broke into a loud guffaw and slapped his knee. "Da half weet, he's been a listenin' to yu, Benny. He hates Christ. Yu a infeedel, half weet?"

The boy blinked his eyes. "I hate Christ—Christmas—birthday—shoes—make da people eat."

Tony laughed again. "Nobody hates da Christ today, half-weet. Not this day's beesnes, I bet," he said, and turned toward Benny who still stood with lowered head and counted money. "Nobody won't hate Christ this day. Yu calla him da bastard, but he brought yu beesnes, mooch beesnes. Da people da was wild, crazee wild with da buyin'. Best Chreestmas ever."

"It has been a good day," Benny said, and added without raising his head. "You'll be late for church."

Tony and Rosa went out into the snow. Benny finished counting the money and came and stood by the stove, and watched his wife try to feed the boy. He frowned when Lupe pushed the bowl away. "It's good soup," he said. "It'll make you walk." He glanced at the purple legs and added, "Maybe."

The child looked up at him. "Christ? Bastard?"

Benny kicked one of the stove's bright feet. "Eat your soup," he said.

"He don't know what is a bastard," the woman said, pushing a spoon of soup toward him.

The boy frowned and shoved the spoon away without taking his glance from Benny. "But Christ—mooch money—bastard?"

Benny and his wife looked at each other, and then at the child. He smiled. "Christ bastard. Me—I—bastard. Mooch money—good beeznes."

"I'll carry you home," Benny said.

"He ought to eat his soup," the woman said.

"Try him with some little cakes."

The boy pushed the cakes away. "I go," he said, and got up, but could only stand on one foot. The other did not seem a foot at all.

Benny carried him to the basement door in the alley. "Can you go down the steps?" he asked.

"I go."

Benny walked away, and the child crawled down the steps. His grandmother lay snoring under the light. He sniffed and knew she would not waken, but he wanted to talk. He had never wanted to talk until now. He crawled to the bed and pulled himself onto it, and sat and looked down into the yellow, flabby face with the loose, cracked lips of its wide open mouth, fallen away from dirty broken teeth and blood red purple gums. The child touched her rough hairy chin and smiled. "Christ," he said, "Granny, mooch money. Christ—bastard—me—bastard—mooch money— I make. He make da people eat—buy—eat—anyting—anyting, like me— bastard—like Christ—mooch money." He patted her cheek, and she moved her head and stared at him with sleepy drunken eyes. "Christ," he said again, and heard the church bells.

The old woman lay a moment and listened to the bells. "Christmas Eve," she mumbled, "Christ he was—he come—." She was asleep again with the yellow whites of her half-closed eyes shining in the light.

The boy listened to the church bells. "Me—like Christ—mooch money —make da people buy. Wholesaler? Make da people eat—buy," he cried, and laughed and waved his arms like Tony. Gaiety like a bird soared out of him, past his frozen foot and bleeding hands and his grandmother's drunken eyes and the dirt and the stench of the damp walled room, above everything, the feet and the cries and the cold, it rose and rose and mingled with the church bells until he, Lupe, the little one, the witless one, was but a voice only crying with the church bells his gladness born of understanding.

Fra Lippi and Me

Written in 1937 or 1938, this story remained unpublished until it appeared in the *Georgia Review* 33 (Winter 1979): 867–75, accompanied by a brief introduction by Glenda Hobbs, author of a 1975 Harvard dissertation about Harriette Arnow. As Hobbs explains, this story is "one of a dozen distinguished stories she wrote in the late thirties. 'Fra Lippi and Me' was inspired by Browning's poem 'Fra Lippo Lippi.'" Prior to writing this story, the author had supported herself by working as a waitress in the Women's Exchange in Cincinnati.

⟶※⟵

I didn't know she was mad. A minute before she looked at the man and smiled. That was when I heard it first. That name, Fra Lippi, I mean. She was saying something about it when I brought her tea. She looked at the cup. She looked at me. "But I wanted cream," she said. She didn't look at me the way she looked at the man.

I smiled my all mouth and no eyes smile. "I'm sorry," I said. "I didn't know you wanted cream instead of lemon."

"You could have asked," she said. Another woman called across the aisle, "You brought me rolls when I wanted corn muffins."

I smiled again. I turned and said, "I'm sorry. I didn't know." I picked up the plate of rolls and the cup and saucer with the lemon. I hurried. But

I wasn't quick enough. The blue chinned man by the post glared at me. I knew he would. He had ordered a steak well done. He was in a hurry. "My wife could have skinned and cooked a whole cow while I've been waiting here," he said.

I smiled. "I'm sorry, but—"

I couldn't say any more. He slapped the table. "Sorry. You waitresses are always sorry. Sorry." His last loud, "Sorry," brought Ridgeways on the run. She was the hostess. She followed me into the kitchen. "That man's been waiting half an hour," she said, and made her voice loud. I heard it above the dish washers and the order caller and the long curses of the black meat cooks and the sizzling sound of broiling meat. I started to tell her the man had lied. I changed my mind. I knew it was no good. She would believe him. That was her job—believing them. "Don't come back without that steak," she yelled, and rushed into the dining room.

It didn't matter. Nothing much would matter if I . . . [1] I would have to get a manicure. But I wouldn't. I knew I wouldn't. It made me sick to think about it. I told myself I thought I might because I was tired. The people seemed so hard that day, all in a hurry. My feet hurt and my back ached and something inside me ached from just knowing—that tomorrow was today. I was tired of people's chewing mouths and their hands, reaching and beckoning and fumbling with gloves and purses and napkins—and sometimes silver. But I knew I wouldn't do it. I knew I wouldn't.

I pried hot corn muffins from a greasy sticky iron, and then I pulled the order caller's sleeve. "What about a small sirloin well for number twelve?"

I waited while he called, "Lamb chops on two, T-bone well, sirloin rare, chicken on three, roast beef, dry, medium, filet two, tenderloin . . ."

I pulled his sleeve again. "What about—"

He did not look at me. "Get the hell outa my way. Get back on the floor. Tenderloin . . ."

"But," I began, and felt Ridgeways' hand shaking my shoulder. "Patsy, do you know, do you realize—" she gulped her words so fast they choked her—"that you walked off and left Mrs. George Henry Wakefield without so much as a cup for her tea. Not even a cup—and here you stand arguing with Shadoan."

"I couldn't pick up the lemon in my fingers. It's against the rules. And you said for me not to—"

"None of your back talk."

I grabbed a cup and saucer and a creamer. I hurried. Ridgeways kept right behind me. She talked—loud so I could hear. "Do you know who that woman is? She said you were impertinent. Same as told her that it was her place to tell you she wanted cream. And then you must run off. You ought to lose your job for this. You ought to know better. Remember you've been reported twice for not smiling." I was glad when we got into the dining room. There we both had to smile. She followed me to this Mrs. George Henry Wakefield. "I found her," she said.

I set down the cup and saucer. The woman talked to Ridgeways. She did not look at me. "You'd think that with all this fuss about unemployment that those who are fortunate enough to have jobs would try to do their work properly. I would not tolerate dining-room service such as this for one moment, not for a single moment." I can't remember all she said. She didn't talk loud and fast like Ridgeways. I guess she was well bred. She took her time.

I had to stand and listen. I saw the woman who wanted muffins instead of rolls. She was getting mad. I had her muffins but I couldn't go. I couldn't move while this Mrs. George Henry Wakefield complained. That would have been impertinence. The four women at the corner table were ready for dessert. A fat woman by the wall was waving her cup for more coffee. I knew the man's steak was done. It would be cold. I would get bawled out. But I couldn't move. I had to listen to the woman. She said that while she waited for the cup her lunch had grown cold. She talked about courtesy. She said she liked to be served by a pleasant waitress. People must learn to smile, she said.

I stood by her elbow, but I didn't look at her. I looked at the man with her. He wasn't half as old as the woman. But he wasn't a boy. Some men are always boys. This one looked as if he had been a boy just a little while— maybe never at all. He drew pictures on the table cloth with the handle of a spoon. I couldn't see the pictures. The way he looked at the table cloth was how I knew. Sometimes he would look at the woman. Once he looked at me. I smiled the way I've learned. He did not look at me again. I hated him. Not because the woman seemed to like him so. I hated him for his shoulders. They were not so big, but they looked strong. I've wished for shoulders like that. Strong shoulders and big shoulders like the ones some of the women I waited on had. Their strong shoulders and long arms and big hands seemed mostly wasted. With me they wouldn't have been. I always thought that maybe big shoulders wouldn't ache so, get so tired. But I don't know. The man looked as if he might have thought about things like that. Not about shoulders, I mean, but things like rent money. They are all the same.

The woman finished. She listened then while Ridgeways explained and apologized. "I know your food is cold by now," Ridgeways said. "The waitress will take it away, and I will see to it that she brings back everything fresh and hot from the kitchen. You won't have to wait a moment."

The woman smiled. "If it doesn't take too long. We can't sit here all day, you know."

"My lunch is quite all right," the man said.

The woman wanted him to have me take it away. They argued about it. I had to stand and listen. Then the woman had me get her another pot of tea, and more hot cheese rolls for her chicken salad, and put more ice in their drinking water, and bring her a slice of lemon for the salad, and bring the man another pat of butter. He didn't have enough, she said. He didn't say anything.

I hurried. But after that I knew it was no use. I wouldn't make any money. I was behind from spending so much time with her. I never got caught up until the rush was over. Ridgeways followed me around. That didn't help. The man with the steak raised a row. He waited a long while. When his meat came it was cold. That was my fault.

The rush was over. I had thirty cents. This Mrs. George Henry Wakefield and the man were still there. It was after two o'clock. I couldn't leave while I had customers. They had been talking a long while. Mostly she talked. He listened. I listened, too. I had nothing else to do while I stood against the wall and waited. I tried to stand up straight and not fidget. "An appearance of haste or restlessness creates an unpleasant atmosphere for guests." That was what our rule book said. My feet hurt and my shoulders had that two o'clock feeling. I guess I must have fidgeted. The man looked at me—more than once.

I could see he wasn't used to servants. Good servants, I mean. The kind that are like pieces of furniture. I could see he didn't want me to stand and listen. I was glad she talked. I wanted to listen to something. I kept thinking about how easy it would be—in a way. It wasn't like I had never been married. It wasn't like I was young and not knowing. I was almost twenty years old. It would be so easy. But I wouldn't do it. I knew I wouldn't. I didn't want to think about it, so I listened to this woman. She was talking about this Fra Lippi, and another man Browning. The man Browning had said things about Fra Lippi. A painter I made him out. "I read that," she said, "when I was only sixteen, and terribly, terribly impressionable. The effect of Fra Lippi on me was tremendous, just tremendous." She lit another cigarette and looked sad like she wanted to cry. I took her a clean ashtray. I hoped she would notice she was keeping me and go. She didn't though. She talked some more. "I vowed then," she moved the ashtray a little and looked at it, "that if it ever lay within my power to save a struggling young artist from the fate that strangled that genius I would do it."

She looked at the man. He didn't say anything. She went on. "That was so cruel, to smother him so, to stifle him. They made him paint as they wished, and shut out all beauty, all realism, all life one might say." She raised her head and looked full in his face. She leaned towards him. Her big breasts seemed ready to fall on the table. "Can't you see? . . . Your little petty job . . . this—this horrible commercial work will deaden you, blunt you. . . . I will not expect that—"

"Want me to stand a minute, Patsy? If you don't grab a bite now you'll get nothin'. Them cooks are shuttin' down the steam table."

I didn't look around. I knew it was Thelma. She worked the station next to mine. I looked straight ahead. I talked low and hardly moved my lips. That way a hostess wouldn't notice. "I'm not hungry," I said.

"Don't let Ridgeways get you down. She'll ride me tomorrow and leave you alone."

"Ridgeways don't worry me."

"Thinkin' on your boy friend."

"Not so much. Since he got that job in Detroit he hardly ever gets a chance to write."

"You know I don't mean the one you're married to. That oldish guy that eats on your station ever' night."

"I feed a lot a oldish guys."

"The one gettin' thick in the belly and thin in the hair that likes you so."

"He's lonesome as ever," I said.

"There's a heap a ways a man has a bein' lonesome."

"He's just plain lonesome."

"Lonesome like Adam and a boar hog in December?"

"Yes," I said. I wished she would hush. I didn't want to think about that old man. He had so much money. I wanted to listen to the woman. "Don't be silly," I heard that. "I am the one who will be grateful." I heard that, too.

"Still a tryin' to get you to lighten his lonesomeness?" Thelma asked.

"Yes."

"You aimin' to?"

"I'll have to get a manicure and maybe get my eyebrows fixed first."

"Your hair'll do as it is, though."

"Yes. Lucky, it curls in dampish weather like this."

"And when are you aimin' to begin this lonesome work."

"And if you are so squeamish about . . . a loan . . . there are always portraits. I could get some of my friends—"

"I was thinking maybe tonight," I said.

"Does he know it?"

"No, he said call him any afternoon at the hotel where he stays, or let him know at dinner."

"They'd love it. I always find my sittings disappointingly short. You are so . . . so—"

"Don't tell the old fool at dinner. Excite him so he'd maybe choke to death."

"I'll telephone."

"I would ask nothing, expect nothing . . . only now and then perhaps . . . a view of your work . . . and of you. I am so interested."

"You'll come in here to eat, and throw me a quarter tip, pretty as you please, I bet."

"I'd make it fifty cents. He tips that much. Sometimes more."

"I wish I had a few customers like that. He's not hard to wait on either, is he?"

"No. Most generally takes the same thing. Says once he likes a thing he always likes it."

"I would save you from that. When I first saw your work—and you—I came home and read that poem again."

"If he's by his women like he is by his grub you're settin' pretty."

"I saw that child Fra Lippi, hungry . . . watching people's faces to see who would fling a crust of bread. I thought of you . . . and wondered . . ."

"I figure I will be . . . easy with the world."

"Forgive me. I'm only a sentimental old fool. No, not old . . . Henry is good . . . and kind; he just doesn't understand, doesn't realize that I need . . . that I am not old, too old to be interested in . . . art. That child, hungry, watching, haunted me when—"

"Well, Patsy, I'll be lookin' for you any day now. I'll see you come strollin' in—in a mink coat."

"I think I'll take a beaver," I said. I knew Thelma was joking. I wondered if I was. I was glad when she went away. I wanted to get the hang of this man Fra Lippi. I wondered what it was he did to keep from starving. I never did find out—exactly. The man never did talk loud enough for me to hear.

The woman began to get ready to go. She was smiling now. Glad about something. I couldn't tell about the man. I didn't watch him so much. I kept looking at the woman. She was going to pay the check herself. Still, I hoped a little. Maybe she'd leave me anyhow a quarter. She was in a good humor—now. I watched her. The man watched me. I didn't care. I made three dollars a week in wages. I had to make tips.

She fumbled in her purse. She took out a five-dollar bill. She shut the purse. She picked up her lorgnette, twirled it a moment on its silver chain. She unsnapped it, set it on her nose, and squinted at the check. She frowned. She opened the purse again. Fumbled awhile, and brought out a penny. "This tax is such a nuisance," she said. "Eleven cents on this. I hate pennies, don't you." She looked at him, smiled a moment, and then she got up.

The man rushed around and helped her with her coat. She looked down the dining room. "Why if there isn't Florence Sangster. She's one of the kind you must meet. She's an old friend of mine."

The man looked like he wanted to frown. But he didn't. He did look at his wrist watch, a cheap one. "I really ought to hurry on to that—"

She cut him off. "Don't be silly," she laughed. She shook her finger at him. "Remember now I'm saving you from dashing away to see people you don't want to see. Florence might like you to do her portrait when I tell her you're doing mine."

She took his arm. They walked away. I went over to the table. I looked under her finger bowl and under his finger bowl. Nothing was there. I knew there wouldn't be. I didn't care. It wouldn't matter. With yesterday and today I had enough for what I needed. I picked up the crumpled napkin the man had used. Under it was his cigarette lighter. I saw him then, coming back alone.

"You forgot your cigarette lighter," I said.

He smiled. He looked nice when he smiled. "On purpose," he said and laid two quarters on the table. "I'm sorry my companion was so—"

I didn't want his quarters. I wouldn't let him finish. "Keep 'em, Fra Lippi," I said.

All the smile went out of his eyes. His face looked hard and red. "Don't call me that," he said.

I felt giddy and not caring. That name had popped first into my head. "You oughtn't to mind," I said. "The man with that name must have been pretty smart to have people writing and talking about him."

His face didn't change.

"He must have done something bad then," I said.

"He didn't want to starve, so he worked to please. When he was sorry he couldn't change."

"Didn't he please himself?"

"No."

"He didn't starve and had an easy time."

"Yes."

I looked him in the eye. "Is that a sin?"

"It is—for some."

I picked up a finger bowl. I didn't look at him. "I see," I said. "I guess I owe you an apology for calling you that name."

"No, no apology—for me. Fra Lippi would be the one . . . he was a child, and I'm not, but it's all . . . you wouldn't understand."

I picked up the other finger bowl. "I do understand," I said.

He looked me over. "You are studying to be an artist, too—perhaps. I thought your face was—"

"I'm not an artist—exactly," I cut in, "but, well . . . if you're Fra Lippi, I guess I'd be Sister Lippi."

"I'm afraid I don't understand."

I put both finger bowls in one hand and picked up the water glasses. "I'm not an artist, but it's all the same—in some ways," I said.

By the swinging door I turned and looked at him. He was walking away toward the woman. He didn't hurry. I thought about him again that day when I went to the telephone. I walked slow, too.

White Collar Woman

Written 1938–39 and signed H. L. Simpson of Cincinnati, this story focuses on social activism in which the author had a strong interest: the rise and demise of a newspaper union, or press guild. Her husband, Harold Arnow, a Chicago reporter before they met, had first-hand experience with guild membership.

This story has never been published.

———✦———

She didn't look it. Poetic type, some love sick school boy might have called her. Thin she was, with thin hands, and a look of brownness in her hair and eyes that seemed sometimes pure brown and then again nothing more than lights glinting. It was the lights that gave her away. Under the unshaded wire enmeshed bulbs along the alley, her hair had a red look with the brown, and her eyes had green sparks in the brown. She smiled and her teeth were small and even, set close together and tooth tip touched tooth tip, strange matching they made with their even whiteness under the shadows of her lashes like fringe on her thin cheeks.

Her blouse was ripped a little in the fight, but she was quiet now, smiling with the green lights in her eyes, and tooth tip touched tooth tip. One of the policemen glanced at her, but her smile wasn't the smile of a woman for a man . . . nothing asking or begging, just smiling. Maybe it was the smile that made them polite to her, gentler with their sticks and heavy hands than with the others, but then I really couldn't tell. There were a lot of strikers, and a lot of scabs, and a lot of noise; cries of Scab, Fink, and Rat, and answering cries of Reds, Screwballs, Communists. There was some blood, too, but it wasn't so much mixed as the noise; it was mostly on the strikers.

I suspect it started in the patrol wagon, or maybe they only smiled there. I never knew. She and Kerney and the rest of us Guilders who had struck were out of jail and back on the job . . . for a while.

* * *

I remember the girl and Kerney had gone and hit deadline before I ever saw anything. It was at a gypsy joint on Clark Street I saw them one night, not hearing the gypsy music, not drinking the gypsy wine, not seeing me or any of the other night shift men . . . we'd come in late . . . just seeing each other, and Flannigan pointed them out to me. "Look at the way they are," he said and smiled.

I remember I smiled too. I was proud of that smile, but I couldn't brag about it to anybody, though next night I bragged around the office about drinking two quarts of needled red wine and never feeling it more than milk.

I remember how big Kerney looked hunched over the little table, lots bigger than I. A red blooded, gutty man he was, big fisted as a copper, but with a head on him and a good reporter and Guilder. He was quick talking, wise cracking, and his sharp tongue and his chesty way of tossing words about had helped us plenty when we organized. He was handy with his fists, too; more than one fink had felt them. To us little men, the puny ones with soft hands and heads hunched from reading and writing copy, he was something of a hero. That night I saw him a hero; that is, I could see him as that girl saw him, look at him reflected in her mouth and eyes and the tilt of her head. It did not feel so good at first. But she deserved something good.

* * *

"I've thought your case over, and tried to figure out what's wrong with you," he said. He was Mullane, the managing editor, nice guy. He talked with bitter sadness; his nice heart was hurt. "I'm disappointed in you. After all I've done for you. I don't know what's wrong with you. Your copy is flat; you're slow; you make mistakes. You almost got us in a libel suit when you wrote that story about the mayor . . ."

"But that was a year ago," I said. "Besides whoever heard of a politician suing for libel?"

"I saved you from being fired then," he said. "And I'd still like to keep you on. You're a nice fellow . . ." He shrugged, and looked past my shoulder. "But I only work here. It's orders from the top."

"Personally, I think you ought to get out of newspaper work . . . for your own good," he went on. "We'll give you a good recommendation. Actually, I think this will be the making of you; you'll do far better outside. You can write. You've been around. Your training here is invaluable to anybody . . . eight years on the Tribune Press." He sighed.

"Here's eight weeks salary," he said. "You know the Press takes care of its men. It's a good piece of money." He smiled. "Don't spend it all in one place," he said.

I said goodbye. I knew that some day I might need that recommendation. I didn't say anything about the dismissal pay clause in the Guild contract, or anything else. Just goodbye.

Out in the hall, I met Kerney. I was sweating, expecting to drop dead any moment, expecting the world to end. But Kerney did not ask me any questions with his eyes. He just nodded; and I was glad he looked the way he did, strong and not afraid of Hell or high water. With that girl behind him, I knew he could do anything. It wouldn't matter if I wasn't there to get out the Guild bulletin, and to try to do something with words on paper, mimeographed words. I knew that with men like him around, the Guild would hang together and make a go of it.

"You lasted longer than I thought," he said. "You . . . well, hell. Those cracks you made about Johnson's firing got them sorer than hell. I saw Mullane walking up and down in his office, waving the bulletin in the air like a red flag."

"It was the truth," I said. "He was as sick as their advertising revenue, and they're making more dough than they ever did. They fired him, like they're firing me, for Guild activity."

"I know." He lit a cigarette and waved it, a habit of his when he talked. He was a handsome man. His cheeks were filled with a deep ruddiness like the color of a tin of tobacco. "I wish I could do something," he said. "But you know what this business is now. They bring in the little green college kids, willing to work for nothing so they can be *newspapermen* like in the movies, and when the kids begin to get wise there's something wrong, they fire them and get some more. I wish . . ." He hesitated. "If you need any money . . . ," he began again.

That made me mad; old picture, strong man sorry for the puny unfortunate devil. I had been sorry for myself, but I didn't like that. "You'd better spend your money and your wishes on those that're left," I interrupted. "Thanks, just the same. Me, I'll get along. I can get another job, or turn bum, or write a novel, or return to the soil." There had been a window box on the room where I was born.

"How's the Missus?" I asked, not easily even yet. I'd never asked about her before; it wasn't expected of me. Nor in the last few weeks had I thought of her much, just now and then. I'd been too busy.

"Coming along fine," he said. "It's only a couple of months now."

I guess I looked surprised, because he sort of explained with his eyes, a surprised explaining as though he expected me to know. His chest seemed to swell under his shirt and his voice sounded deeper than ever. "We're putting out an extra . . . an extra edition," he said.

"You lucky bastard," I said and whacked him on his shoulder.

"I got to be lucky . . . now," he said. "It's funny," he went on giving me a long glance, "how things work out. This . . . well, this trouble makes a man sort of jittery. I mean when there's responsibilities at home."

I thought of her and I know she wasn't jittery. She wouldn't be.

"Well, you'll help get the bulletin out regular?" I asked off-handedly. I wanted to change the subject. "Flannigan said he'll take over, but he'll need help."

Kerney shifted his glance to my shoe. "I'm pretty well tied up, but you know I've always done what I could."

* * *

I left town then. It wasn't that I was ashamed of being without a job. I think I was a little proud of having been fired and of what I had done . . . or what I had thought I had done. When I left, the Press Guild had been one of the strongest, boiling with militancy and enthusiasm. There was Kerney; and Flannigan, never any better at fists and talk than I, could string words on paper. It seemed to me I had helped form something, just as Kerney and the girl had helped. And when a job's well done, you don't mind leaving. I was sick of the big city anyway and its stink and filth and noise. I went to a hick town where I never saw a big daily and there was nothing to remind me I'd been a hot shot once . . . and had been edged out, branded as no good because I'd told the truth and been a union man.

Now and then I heard from Flannigan. The Guild was strong; he was getting out the bulletin; he was getting pushed around some, not too much. Mullane was afraid of trouble.

It took Mullane about six months to get going good. He worked slowly.

First they pushed Flannigan some more; then they took him off the top copy seat. They put him to reporting, then shifted him to night watch. They put him at the other end of town where they wouldn't miss him. But he didn't care. He'd been there fourteen years. They couldn't touch him, not with an NLRB board sitting in town. His case was different from mine; he was beyond questioning.

So they worked him over slowly. They beefed about this story, and squealed about that. They didn't dare cut his wages though.

I knew what he was going through. Stories aren't ditches, with sides so high and so long and so straight. Mullane would beef about a Pulitzer Prize, if his breakfast disagreed with him, or if the man who wrote it was a good Guildsman; and he'd do it with all the air of an unwilling father forced to chastise an unruly child.

That wasn't all. There were assistant editors, bosses. It's easy for editors to give a guy little assignments when he's always had the big ones, and say it's because the guy can't handle the big ones. It's easy, they got the power. They can rag a man and nag him, say his work's no good until he begins to wonder, or throws up his job to keep from going nuts.

I knew. After two months of it, when I went to bed, Mullane's beefings and the nasty cracks of the rest of them would ride through my brain like horses all night long; the beefings, and the story, names, places, who, why, how, what, when, where . . . until I gave up sleep. But Flannigan, pale and wizened, had no nerves; just guts. The fight in him was different from Kerney's, but was just as good. He kept the bulletins coming, and long before the finish came, he saw it coming, and planned to take it to the NLRB. Behind him he had the Guild, honest men to testify, and the paper's record of firings.

* * *

Somehow, after a while, Flannigan's letters didn't seem to be coming so often. I didn't see anything in them anyway. It was in the bulletin. I got it regularly every two weeks, and it made me wonder. Sometimes he sounded like a football coach talking to a yellow team. The Guild I left hadn't been yellow. Funny? I remembered Kerney with his big hands and big voice and his way of flinging words around. He could manage men, even newspaper Tomcats, and make them believe him. I remembered, too, the woman behind him.

So I was surprised when Flannigan's letter came saying he'd been canned, let out for poor work, fired for not taking enough interest in the paper. He didn't say any more; he just thought I'd be interested in knowing. I should not mail letters to him at the office anymore. He didn't say anything about the NLRB, not a word about a fight.

I borrowed some extra dough and caught a train.

* * *

Flannigan was drunk when I found him. "You'd never believe me," he said. "Talk to Kerney and find out." He looked tired and disgusted; he acted worse than disgusted, like a man ashamed, a man sick of something until he'd like to crawl off and die. "Go talk to Kerney," he said. "But don't tell him I sent you."

Next day at noon I went to the Press Tavern. I sat near the door and drank coffee. I meant to hail Kerney when he came in to lunch. But I didn't. I heard what he was saying to the young fellow with him.

Kerney was chesty still, beefier than ever, and he talked in the same old ringing way. I couldn't miss his words. He was waving a cigarette in that quick way of his, and he led the young fellow to a booth back of me.

"I'm telling you," he said. "The thing to do is sit tight. Times are damn bad. A young fellow like you, just starting in, is a fool to wreck his chances before he even gets started. Look at me. I organized the Guild. But I got a wife and a child. I'm not getting edged out to save a screwball who's just been looking for trouble. Besides Flannigan hasn't been so hot lately." He opened the menu, then slammed it down. "Of course," he went on in that breezy tone he'd used so well to help the Guild. "If you've got no responsibilities you can afford to be a Boy Scout. Me, I can't afford to testify before any NLRB; I've got a wife and child to feed. Besides I told that fool Flannigan to lay off."

"To lay off or lay down?" asked the young fellow. He had a weasel chin, and a funny mustache; a Journalism-school honor boy if there ever was one.

Kerney turned a heavy red. He doubled up one of his big hands, then opened it again. "I can't understand what's wrong with you," he said. "What are you looking for trouble for? Why can't you pay your dues and be satisfied like everybody else. We got everything we wanted when we won the strike, pay raises, shorter hours . . . everything."

"Yeah, everything but the thing we want most . . ." The young fellow turned down his lips and talked out of the side of his mouth like I had used to sometimes when I was a cub, and found an ordinary tone inadequate to express disgust.

"No Guild, no NLRB, can tell Mullane he can't fire a man when he doesn't like his work," Kerney interrupted. He almost seemed to plead. "But that made no difference. Mullane doesn't want to push anybody out; he will tell you that himself. He's a good guy . . . but he's got his job to do. He was a friend of Flannigan's; he told me that himself. Flannigan was one of his best men. But he's a trouble maker, always stirring things up. Men can't work where there's trouble all the time. That bulletin of Flannigan's was full of inciting stuff, nasty, just asking for trouble; and now that he's got trouble he's trying to involve me and everyone else."

"Did the bulletin tell any lies?" asked the little man. He stood up slowly. Kerney opened his mouth to say something, but the young fellow spoke. "That's an old story," he said. "I'm not hungry." And he walked away to the bar.

The waitress came to Kerney then, but he just looked at her, then got up and walked out of the place.

I went up to the little man and told him who I was. Did he know me? He did. Flannigan had told him about me. Was he glad to see me? Flannigan said I was the guy who could and had taken it.

"Can that stuff," I said feeling almost good. "What's happened?"

"It's that son of a bitch, Mullane, and some of our own boys who're yellow. Kerney there. He's yellow, scared of his job, afraid of this and that and his wife and kid."

I thought of the woman Kerney had married. What happened to her?

"Kerney got that crap of his from Mullane," went on the little man. He was no bigger than me. "You know what Mullane's been doing? He corners the men, especially the married ones, to talk to them about hard times and the Depression. He's so nice and fatherly. It's swell to belong to the Guild, he says. After all, he only works there too; he's for it . . . he says. But the publisher will be making cuts and you know . . . blah, blah. Kerney is his chief sucker. Kerney was always showing pictures of his kid around and bragging about his wife. Damn the woman. She's egged him on to lay down too. Know her? They say she used to work for the Press."

"Yes," I said. I remembered the girl in the alley; it seemed so long ago. I thought of the woman now. It made me sick. "Does she ever come around the office?" I asked.

"Hell, no. She couldn't be bothered. Kerney's moved out to the suburbs, and he even quits early to get home to his wife. Christ. What a woman can do!"

"Yeah," I said. I said goodbye to him then, but I'd be around to see him later.

* * *

I didn't sleep that night. It wasn't the hotel mattress, or the smell of the city, or the street cars; it wasn't even worry. It was feeling the way a man can when he learns a dollar can't buy anything or that the sun is shining but isn't warm.

Next morning, I had some coffee and went to see Flannigan. He was drunk. He said something about becoming a press agent and living like a human being, buying newspapermen for a quart of whiskey and an ad. He was just feeling bad. Nothing I could do with him.

I wondered what had happened to the green lights in her eyes; it was no use, with Kerney, the king-pin, down, and work on the others was a waste of time. I looked up Kerney's address in the telephone book; I thought maybe I'd call up and talk to her. It was so far out in the country, a man'd have to take a train.

So I took a train.

* * *

Kerney must have had some big raises to afford a place like that, a whole house and yard and flowers in the yard. "The wages of sin," I thought. I was jittery ringing her door bell, but then it was all right because there's nothing about a pretty young dame in a pink apron and a baby on the arm to make a man jittery. She looked to see what I was selling, and then she remembered. She gave me her other hand.

"I was just passing by," I said as she took me into a living room with baby's rattles and rubber mice and things scattered over the floor. "I didn't know whether you'd remember me," I said.

"As if I could forget you," she said and smiled and patted her baby's back. It was a boy, with his father's ruddy color.

We talked about her house and her baby. He'd licked half the paint off the bathroom wall and liked it. I said he'd make a good newspaperman. She laughed. I told her about my hack writing and my hick town. She knew about hick towns, she was a farmer's daughter, but Kerney'd come from the back of a city like me.

"I think that's why he worries about the baby's getting enough sunshine," she said. "I keep him out in the air at least four hours a day."

I sighed at that, I guess. "Kids aren't what they used to be," I said. "The first time I got out of town into sunshine, I thought the sky was afire."

She laughed. She enjoyed my company. She talked a little about Kerney; her face lit up when she said his name and how proud she was that he was doing so well. We talked, too, about old times, and about the strike.

I told her about seeing her there. She said she'd seen me too.

"I never knew you much," she said. "But after you left Kerney used to talk about you a lot . . . and so did Flannigan. He used to come out every Sunday for dinner. What's happened to him anyway," she burst out in that sudden impatient way she had. "He's not been around in months. Kerney says he never sees him anymore."

"I'll look him up," I said. "I've just come to town you know."

"I like it for the baby out here," she said. "But we don't get around much. And it's hard for Kerney to get to the Guild meetings. Something always seems to be coming up. You don't know how the Guild is doing?" Her voice sounded doubtful. "Lately Kerney's forgotten to bring home the Bulletin."

I tried to look surprised. "Why I thought Kerney was right in the middle of things."

She tilted her head and frowned a little. "Kerney says the big job is over . . . organization, getting it formed . . . and now it will run itself. But I never trusted that Mullane. The Guild'd better be careful. I've been thinking lately . . . the baby's getting old enough so I can leave him for a little while . . . Kerney's afraid to leave him with just anybody . . . that I would like to drop in on one of the meetings."

"Fine," I said and got up. "Make Kerney take you, and bring the baby along. It won't hurt him."

"Kerney's so afraid he'll get germs." She followed me into the hall. "But germs never killed either one of us."

I think I grunted. "A few germs won't hurt *him*. Why when he grows up he'll be proud to know he went to Guild meetings at such an early age."

"He'd certainly be proud to hear his dad talk," she said, and then I saw the old green lights in her eyes. "I'll never forget how he used to talk to you all. I'd like to hear him again . . . but maybe there'll never be any need."

"Maybe not," I said.

"Why don't you have lunch with Kerney," she said on the porch steps. "He'd be awful glad to see you."

"That's where I'm headed for now," I told her. "A little lunch and a lot of blackmail," but I said that so low she couldn't hear, and it would have been a pity if she had, loving Kerney like she did, and just before she was going to see him in action at a Guild meeting . . . like the old days.

ℐailure

In this unpublished story, written around 1939, the author explores a character's mixed emotions about a move similar to one she herself made in 1934.

———◦◦◦———

I had always known the taste of it, that is since I was big enough to feel the wind and smell dead leaves on a wet still night in fall. There were falls when it was bad, like a hunger eating through your insides. But mostly that was when I was young, less than sixteen, I guess, almost too young to dream, but plenty big enough to watch the wild geese go flying south, and watch them till there was nothing in the south but sky. I would feel an ache in my throat, and that wild lifting hunger that made me want to run in circles like the black shepherd dog I had.

I would maybe run then, go up the sage grass hills and between the little cedars and over the limestone rocks, just running. My mother, she was little and weazened and brown with no thoughts past her family and her farm, would watch me from the kitchen door and think I was hunting the cows. But I was running away. In the twilight when I stood still at the top of the pasture and looked into the west, both my mother and Caesar the dog thought I was listening for cow bells, but I was looking past the hills.

Sometimes I saw the hills, I think. There were a lot of them to see, blue-black against the sunset sky, fold on fold of them marching away like men walking out into the world. Sometimes I saw my mother's land, rolling out over the nearer hills. There was a lot of that—no-good, Kentucky hill land—but land. My family had always had land, back in England and France and Ireland—I'm a mixture, you see—they had land five hundred years ago. It was in our blood, the land—land poor we were born to be, and horse poor, and dog poor, my father used to say, for he was a Kentuckian, too. He was dead and I could scarcely remember him, but contented he had been with no heart for going out into the world, a lover of fiddle and hound dog music, and a man who liked to ride his own horses on his own land.

I thought of him sometimes when I stood still until the hills were one dark wall, and then I would see myself, what I would be and where I would go. I would never be one to live bound like a slave to the land. And I would go running home through the dark then, with Caesar rushing the cows before me, hearing the wild geese cry, and the train whistles blow, and never feeling the ground or the limestone rocks or the roots and leaves across the path.

It seemed a thousand years that I lived and heard the wild geese call, saw the lesser birds go south, felt the west wind at dusk when it came whispering and rustling through the holly bush by the front porch steps. I heard the steamboats go blowing down the twisting bends of the Cumberland, heard trains blow down the mountains and the panting rush of the double headers as they twisted up grade. And always the wild geese, and the trains, and the steamboats, and the hills marching until they were flat in the west were like so many promises. I knew that I would go away. When I worked in the steep corn fields, or milked the cows, or sawed the winter's firewood, or ran down the hill to the village high school, I knew that these things were not for me always.

The year I won a scholarship in college, a prized opportunity taking me to a great northern university, I knew that slowly I was pushing past the hills, away from the narrow world of my father. Still, it was a long time counted in dreams and hopes and wonderings, conclusions to be broken and new ones set in their place like store windows freshly dressed for display, new faces, facts, and memories, a few cities, another university or so, jobs, work and more work, tired eyes and a heavy head, long days and short nights, hunger sometimes, cheap clothes and lumpy mattresses, clothing pawned for coffee. The years were hard, but I never minded. I felt the dream merge slowly into reality.

Men said of me that with time and strength, freedom from most things except my work, I could do what I wanted to do. I had positions now instead of jobs. I was a part of the outside world. I felt a sort of lusty knowing, less pride than certainty. I knew that I was free. Nothing could hold me back, no woman nor creed to tie my hands. I could reach the top. I would travel and see the further world; there would be more money for all the things I had never had; I would meet the wise and the great and the strong, learn their ways, for I would be one of them. I felt my freedom to go on and on, strong in my blood like the sharp smell of oak wood in the wind.

Maybe I worked too hard, or maybe it was only that things in a man's blood will come out like the grain of black walnut when a paint rubs away. Whatever it was, I never willed it, no more than a swallow wills the sweep of its circle. At first I was too strong—too sure to let it trouble me. So it came at night, not as dreams, but more as the awakening to something faint as the remembered memory of a dead friend's dream. There was a puzzle while I brushed my hair, and maybe while walking briskly down the street, heels clicking pavement, the soles of my feet seemed to have lately touched something, softer, kinder, and more alive than concrete pavement.

Once at work—it was a good office, clean and air-conditioned with no smell of smoke or sound of wind or rain—I lifted my head from a sheaf of copy and smelled wet pine, fresh it was the way it had used to be on a still day under a light snow. I looked about the room. There was no snow and no pine, only my secretary looking faintly troubled, and murmuring her wonders of what I smelled. The smell was gone in an instant, a hallucination I said, and forgot it in a welter of work.

A few days later, I awakened one night to the earthy smell of snow melting on south limestone ground in the spring, and with the smell there was a something in my hands, not a memory for hands cannot remember, but they were hands that had just come from working in the soil. I felt it on my fingernails. Then I was lifting on one elbow, snapping on the light, and my hands were clean, neat with smooth palms and trim fingernails, odorless as my bedroom.

I lay awake a moment until the earth smell was gone, and I could think of my work and of other things. But I remember that as I lay there in the soft bright light there was something just past the shadows or maybe past the door, something I had touched and felt in my sleep, but on waking would not touch or feel because while I was awake I was strong enough to force it away.

Such things began in an autumn and as the days shortened into winter, they pushed slowly through my consciousness and penetrated it during moments of work that should have been free of everything except the work. I was afraid to sleep for dreams, afraid of wakefulness for fear of smells and sounds and the remembering of my feet and hands. There were the nights when I would awaken tired with a pull at my thighs and the backs of my legs, and know that I had been walking, mile upon mile, all up and down the countless paths. I could not close my eyes for seeing them: the path up the sage grass pasture, the one twisting through the orchard where the high-growing, red-seeded timothy[1] had used to drench my knees with dew; a sandy road down a pine ridge I had followed to hunt huckleberries; the path down the limestone ledges where the dogwood and the mock orange had flowered in spring; the road by the creek—but I cannot tell of all the paths.

I can only say that I walked them all. I saw each least thing, clearly, things I had never noticed but had known were there with my feet and my nose and my eyes: red-washed root of a cedar stump pressing against my shoe, a low hanging briar scraping my coat sleeve, feel of soft shredding cedar bark when I leaned against a tree for rest, feel of green walnuts in my hands, smell of persimmons on a sunny, frosty day, smell of the sweet-leafed wild fern in a low shaded spot where the thick black earth smell was close and heavy and made a tickling in my nose.

Oh, it was a ghostly, weird life I lived through a fall and a winter and a spring, and into a hot ugly summer where on stifling days I could smell the rain on hot limestone rocks, smell clover leaves rotting under the rain, and the rank smell of the hot wet earth, and the cool leafy smell of white fog up from the Cumberland—and the city was shrouded in smoke and noise, a jungle of brick and stone and steel in a flat land with no fogs and no deeply cut rivers.

Fight is a weak word to describe what I did. The years of struggle I had used to gain the world I had and wanted were like the efforts of a half-grown child compared to the fight I made to push away the one I did not want. My superiors talked to me sometimes. "You work too hard," they said. That was all they said. There was no praise for my work—now. I knew it was no good. I went to doctors. Some said it was my nerves; some said it was nostalgia. I knew they were wrong. I had never had nerves, could not afford them; and I did not want to go home.

I hadn't been home in years. My mother came to visit me now and then, but during the last few years she had come but seldom. My younger brothers were gone now, and she disliked to leave the farm and her woodlands. I had never wanted to go home. I knew there was nothing about the pile of rocks, tilted fields and forests that was our land, to teach me, broaden me, make me more useful in my work. And always I had done only those things that would further my career. It was late summer before I realized that in spite of other plans, I would go home. I reasoned, I knew why I went; I would make the ghost a reality, and it would lose its power over me. I reasoned—and I counted the days until October, marked each off on a square of calendar like a homesick school girl or a prisoner slated for release.

I knew October when it came, even in that flat smoky city. I scuffed my shoes down the leafless streets, so that passersby looked at me in wonder. They didn't know I heard leaves rustle and felt them tickling my ankles. They never knew I heard the wind, the leaping beat of the October night wind hunting through the hills at home. They never knew I heard the hound dogs, their voices rising and dying with the wind in the high back hills. I gave myself to it, the seeing and the feeling and the tasting. I knew I would conquer it when I went home for a little while; there, the ghost would become an unwanted reality which I would be glad enough to escape in a week or so.

I remember little of the ride home or of the walking through the crossroads village and up the hill. It was at the bridge over the creek that a strangeness overtook me, and I stopped and stood for a minute—wondering, puzzled by the sameness of the road and the path and the creek. The water was still, gathered in little pools, choked now and then with maple and poplar leaves. There were the same bright brown buckeyes on the ground, and the same cedars touched boughs over my head; and the odor was the same—cedar bough, leaves, water, and earth.

It was like that all through my stay at home. Bessie the cow had long since died, but her daughter had become another Bessie. Caesar had had a son to take his place, the same as Caesar, a gay black shepherd with brown spots over his eyes. When the first frost came, I walked about in the twilight and cut the cosmos and the marigolds to save them from the frost. I smelled the chrysanthemums, sharp and sweet like spice; and the flowers were the same as they had been during those other first frosts when I was a child, growing in the same places, the same flowers I might have said.

The days that fall were bright blue and gold, high skied with light warm winds out of the west. I was content walking in the woods with my mother and the dead Caesar's son at my heels. I gathered nuts, or sat silent for hours on the high sandstone cliff above the house, drowsing in the sun and staring at the hills. The nights were filled with wind and moonlight, and the sound of hound dogs out on the first fox hunts of the fall. Sometimes I lay and listened and watched the fire die by the hearth, but mostly I slept, a tired heavy slumber like that of a man worn from a long fight. There were no ghosts to haunt me, and if through the night I awakened and heard the wind beating like the wings of some great bird in the high back hills, I listened a time and fell asleep. I knew it was no ghost.

I thought sometimes of my work. I grew eager to go away. I would do thus and so when I went back. Nothing troubled me now, I was strong again. I could work harder than ever, give all my mind and my soul to the getting ahead.

The ghosts now seemed silly as fright over nightmarish dreams. But sometimes when I stood still in the woods and heard the plop of a falling hickory nut, or lay in the deep dead orchard grass and searched for the top of the sky until there was a glimmering in my eyes, I would grow afraid. I could not be certain of how it would be when I went away any more than a man lying down to sleep knows what he will dream. Sometimes I felt the power of the land over me, gently, but more terrifying for its gentleness, like the friendly handclasp of a powerful man who could, while he held my hand, crush it to pulp.

One night the terror of never forgetting was especially strong. I had walked with my mother to a corner of the front porch. As a child I had always followed her there, had stood with her while she looked overhead, then out—north, south, east, and west—to search out the sky and the hills, for not until she had read the next day's weather in the sky would she go to bed.

The moon that night was low in the west, streaks of it showing blood red between black pine trunks. When my mother looked west as she stood folding and unfolding her arms in her apron against the cold, she sighed and shook her head. "When th' leaves all come off, a body can see how they're thinnin' th' trees out on that hillside," she said.

"They?" I asked in some surprise.

It was her turn to be surprised. "Don't you recollect when I wrote—" she stopped and counted on her fingers, "three years it's been now—an' told you I'd make up my mind to sell off that lower forty acres so Lee could finish school."

"Oh," I said, and continued to look at the land where the trees grew, making bars for the moon.

"They're cuttin' down all th' trees," my mother went on, "some a th' poplars your father planted in that gullied spot by that little spring branch. I recollect th' day so well—he come in at dinner time, an' he said, 'Well, Millie, I've done a mornin's work that fifty years from now my children an' gran'children will bless me for.' An' he went on to tell me about all th' little yellow poplars he'd set." She sighed again and turned toward the door. "Look at it now," she said, "in a couple more years they'll have ever'thing off for crossties an' timber an' it'll start washin'."

I kept thinking of that lower forty acres. Because I liked to look out over the country, I had, since coming home, always walked in the higher woods and fields. Next day after our noon meal, I suggested to my mother that we go walking in the woods below the house. She didn't much want to go. "I hate it there," she said. "I never go into that strip a woods, but what it makes me mad, thinkin' how it used to be, an' how it could still be."

We walked a time, and I saw that what she had said was true. Most of the younger trees were gone, cut for firewood, others crippled and blighted by the careless cutting of larger trees. In spots the limestone rocks showed bare, like the white ribs of a skeleton. As we walked, my mother after her usual fashion stopped now and then to put a stone across the beginnings of a rivulet, lay a swath of dead cedar bough over a tiny young cedar to protect it from grazing cows. "I keep forgettin' it's not mine any more," she apologized now and then, until she saw that I also was doing as

I had used to do when I walked over my father's land . . . the same things she did.

When her breath came short as it often did now, we sat on a flat lime-stone rock under a cedar tree to rest. Soon, she talked again while I cracked nuts on the flat stone, going over the land bit by bit in her mind, knowing it as one knows the face of a lifetime acquaintance, seeing it as a child that could with a bit of help grow into usefulness and greatness, but now being ruined and wasted. "Recollect that bare, stick-weedy spot that faces due south? Well, when I had this piece I always meant to plant some black wal-nut trees there, but I never had th' time. I always thought, though, they'd ha' done fine there. An' all up an' down that gulch below our yard, I'd have some cedar trees or brush put to hold th' water from washin' so—."

"I think I'd fill gunny sacks with dirt and put in some sweet clover seed," I interrupted. "Remember we did that in the back north pasture when I was about twelve years old, and if—." I stopped and sat confused. My voice had sounded like my mother's voice and my father's a long time ago when he had talked of shaping his land.

My mother never noticed my silence. She talked again about the land and what she would do with it. I think sometimes I talked with her, but mostly I guess I was silent. I do remember thinking of things like the big crooked ash that ought to be cut so that some slender young poplars by it might be given a chance to grow, the dogwood and wild plum thickets in April after a rain, the muscadines blackening in the fall, and that the finest ladies' slippers and lamb's tongues of all grew on this particular bit of land.

My mother was the first to get up. The hillside was in shadow, and Bessie's bell was tinkling down the upper pasture before we had started home. Our talk of the land continued while we did the few barn chores together and on into the evening after supper. Cautiously, I asked her the price of the land and if it could be re-bought, and when she was certain that it could at a low figure—since most of its big trees were gone now—I tried to be unconcerned.

I reasoned carefully, coldly, all through the evening; the land would be a good investment; the trees would grow again; I could leave it in my mother's keeping and never trouble myself over it. I reasoned, too, that if I owned a bit of land, the ghost of the land that had haunted me through a year would lose its power over me. I could remember always that I owned land, had fenced and put away like linen folded in a chest all the things for which I had hungered in the city—if it had been hunger. Men never go hunting after the things they have, I reasoned.

I say I reasoned, but through the evening I was restless and uneasy— that is, when I remembered to reason. Mostly I talked with my mother and noticed only now and then that I was lost in plans for the land. Foolishly, in a moment's enthusiasm, I had hinted that I would like to buy it. "You've got land in your blood," she had said, and beamed on me and nodded her head.

I had said nothing to that; she was a simple woman who could hardly have understood that the only reason I bought land was to be rid of it. "It'll be like you had a child here or somethin'," she said after a time, "An' you'll be comin' home oftener to see about it—there'll be a sight you ought to have done," and she was gone again in a maze of plans.

It must have been midnight before we both noticed that the fire was no more than ashes on the hearth and that Caesar was whining to be put out for the night. We went to the front porch then to read the weather in the sky, but mostly we looked into the west across the strip of land I meant to buy. The moon had set but bands of its milky afterglow showed white between the trees. Tonight my mother did not sigh, but chuckled a little as she stood folding and unfolding her hands in her apron. "Aye, in fifteen or twenty years a body can hardly see the' moon for the' trees you'll have on that land."

I remember feeling nothing except a heady exultation, no regret at being bound by something stronger than ghosts. I wished it were day and I could make plans, go walking over my land again; the land I would own, something all my own from the center of the earth to the top of the sky.

<hr />

Sugar Tree Holler

Arnow's only epistolary story was probably written in Cincinnati in 1939, shortly
before or after her marriage to a writer for the Works Progress Administration.

Her husband, Harold Arnow, a former Chicago reporter, had homesteaded in
Alaska during the early 1930s. One of his favorite uncles was Michael Abel, a
Cincinnati artist. And the couple purchased land in Kentucky, where they moved
several months after their wedding.

———◦•◦———

*D*ear Cousin Sadie,
      They're going to investigate the WPA again, Federal Writers
and all. Can you beat it. And me with $140 saved,[1] and it took me
eleven months to save it, and I won't just draw it out and spend it for anything. I keep thinking of that land in Sugar Tree Holler; $5 dollars an acre,
and $200 dollars would buy forty acres, and the timber off of it would bring
$100 dollars, and if bad comes to worse I could come home and live with
Mama and have me a cabin built up there and rent it till I got ready to live
on it.

I am supposed to be writing an essay on the paleontology of the State,
but I've got to tell my troubles to somebody, and anyhow I don't know a
thing about paleontology, so I am going out to the University to talk to Dr.

Roark—recollect he's the man who wrote my geology essay—he is the nicest thing, but he's awful old. And anyhow even if I did know as much about paleontology as he does the office is so noisy I couldn't concentrate. Graft telephoned he wouldn't be in and all forty are talking at once; and that fat Lawton instead of keeping time talks louder than all the rest. But I am so full of trouble that it just spills out.

I told Abel—that new editor from Chicago I've been telling you about—I'm still wondering how he got on when I just happened to learn by something he let slip that he'd been in town only two weeks before he was certified and him from another State, I don't see how he managed, and now he's plenty worried too. I can tell by the look in his eyes; they are brown like Old Boss's, recollect that big Collie we had at home, the one that helped himself to a ham out of Emma Dodson's smoke house. Well, anyhow, Abel's eyes always make me think of Boss, they've got a lonesome look, and now he looks worried. I'll bet he has to support a mother and a lot of younger brothers and sisters back in Chicago, and maybe doesn't keep back enough money to eat on; his shoulders are like crowbars under his coat. But what I started out to say was that he's always asking me for dates—not that I would accept from a stranger like that—but all the same, we talk a lot, and I have told him about my plan of saving money for land all of my own so that I can be independent and not starve, and still try to write my animal stories for children—the one I wrote about the contrary calf came back—and how I could keep a cow and chickens and even have a garden if I didn't want to live off Mama. And he thinks it is a sensible plan.

And now there's no chance for any of that. I guess I'd better draw out my savings and go buy a fur coat or something; just anything so I won't have any money. Lawton passed the slips around this morning, and it asks a lot of questions, but the one worrying me is "Bank Account—." Then under it, it says "Other Accounts or Resources." It looks like they want to trip you into the penitentiary, for over on the back right at the bottom, it says something like this: "Any person proven guilty of intent to cheat"—that's not the word but I'm afraid to look and see how it actually goes for fear somebody will notice and think I am worried—but anyhow, it says that if you cheat the government you will be fined not more than $2000 nor sent to prison for more than a year.

They couldn't fine me more than the $140, but they might send me to prison for I don't think—from some of the remarks they make—that they like Kentuckians up here working on the WPA so well anyhow, but I had been up here over a year on that business course before I got certified. What would Mama—have you been up to see her lately and if you do don't say a word. She would be madder than when they wouldn't let her sell the quarter of an acre of tobacco she raised last summer—anyhow she'd just die, and when I think about the neighbors reading in the *Somerset Weekly News* that one of Mollie Hardwick's girls was sent to the federal penitentiary I get sick at my stomach. Oh, Sadie I don't know what to do. One minute I look at the back of the slip, in my mind I mean, and think one year or maybe longer in Atlanta, and they say they're awful mean to prisoners in big prisons, not a bit like our county jail. Then I think about that land in Sugar Tree Holler, all that pretty poplar and cedar and pine, and how sick I am of so much smoke and all these beer-drinking people—I wish I could learn to like beer—and I look at the front of the slip in my mind. It would be so easy to write "none," and keep my $140, and then I think about that gimlet-eyed woman that interviewed me when I got on. Oh, I forgot, there are two more parts to the investigation. After we fill out the slips, interviewers will come around and ask us questions, and then they will maybe visit where we live.

Then there's the F.B.I. You know I told you about them; something like the G-men only they work on the WPA people instead of just plain criminals, they say. There's a branch of them here in town, and nobody knows what they might be up to. Maybe they've already investigated all the WPA workers, and they know I have a Postal savings, and when that investigator comes, she'll know it, too, and she will ask me right out what about my $140. I never could lie to do any good. And what if I take it out right quick. That will show intent to deceive and that will be worse than

dinosaurs and elephants in this country several million years before Christ. The dinosaurs ate grass and were related to snakes and fishes and looked something like overgrown crocodiles. The elephants also ate grass but were not related to fishes. Before the mastodons and the dinosaurs lived, the country was covered with oceans and in the oceans swam—Lawton passed by, and I didn't want to take any chances of his looking over my shoulder. He didn't though. He was on his way to the pencil sharpener and stopped to ask Blakely—he's that man I was telling you about who has seven children, three of them born since WPA started and his wife that way again—if Blakely thought they'd check Christmas savings. It's February and Lawton has six dollars.

I wish to goodness you were here or somebody to tell me what to do. I think I'll write "None."

Well, I guess I'd better stop. It's so noisy that even Abel has quit trying to work and he does more than all the others put together, but when he can't work he comes around and asks me questions about Sugar Tree Holler, and lets hints out like food in these restaurants here is giving him indigestion—I let it slip once that I had a stove with an oven in my furnished room—and how he would enjoy nothing better than a home-cooked meal. I like him in a way—he's so tall and thin he makes me think of the men at home—but I can't make him out. He says he worked five years on a Chicago newspaper, and then was fired because he almost got them in a libel suit. And he tells such awful tales—regular Paul Bunyan yarns about how he spent three years in Alaska and killed moose and deer and bear and built log houses in the woods. And him a Chicago newspaperman. I'll bet he likes sugar in his cornbread and never saw a log cabin.

But I think if he asks me for a date tonight, I think I'll let him take me to a movie. Maybe he and the movie together would distract my mind, and I need distraction. Your loving cousin,

SUSIE HARDWICK.

*   *   *

Dear Cousin Sadie,

I thought you would like to know. I wrote, "None," and me with that $140. Now I wish I hadn't done it, but it's too late to do any good. If you have time, you'd maybe better go up to visit Mama, and read her tea leaves and find trouble in them so she'll sort of be prepared. For two cents, I'd take out my $140 and come home. But you know Mama. She shot the coat tails off that Fenimore Ghoulson when she thought he was trying to steal chickens and never batted an eye. Well, suppose I ran away home and they sent three or four F.B.I men after me. Soon's the dog barked and Mama saw them coming up the hill she'd call to know what it was they wanted the way she always does when strangers come, and when she found out they were after me, she'd turn the shotgun on them. Then we'd both be in Atlanta—for life—only Mama would go crazy quoting Benjamin Franklin. You know, he always said save your money.

Oh, yes, I was wrong about Abel. He's not a sissy. He did spend three years in Alaska. Last night—don't get notions, I'd never let any strange man or even a man I respect as much as I do him in my furnished room—Abel brought an album he'd had sent from home. We looked at it down at a little restaurant on the corner where we ate supper. There he was in the Alaska woods, all bearded and in boots looking like the men around home. One picture showed him with a moose he had killed, and another one showed him before a log cabin he had built. He trapped up there for three years after he got kicked out of college. "Then I got ambitious," he said, "and came back to Chicago and got a job on a newspaper."

He said he came down here because it was a smaller town and closer to some hills. I believed him, he has a lonesome look in his eyes—they are brown—and I guess he gets like me, hungry for some hills and some air that's not second hand. He lives in a furnished room the way I do, but it's smaller than mine without so much as a gas plate, and I have a stove with an oven. That only goes to show how dumb men are. Here, he is spending all his money to eat in restaurants and paying almost as much rent as I do, and me with a stove with an oven so I can bake biscuit or cornbread when I feel like it. But it's not much use to bake biscuit just for one.

Tell Mama when you see her—I've not had the heart to write her lately—that I'll send her five more dollars on the roof for the barn, but when she gets it to please hire somebody to put it on, and not go climbing up herself like when she roofed the smokehouse. But maybe you'd better not say that; she might get sort of bitter and complain the way she does sometimes that it's had enough to be a widow, but worse to have no boys in the family, and worse than that to have three son-in-laws that don't know barbed wire from lightning rods. I would like to see Mama have one good son-in-law; she deserves some

many shells are found in the limestone rocks of this region. They are the remains of the ancestors of the oysters and clams that were the first natives of this city, and whose characteristics may be seen today in the inhabitants of this city. There were also—well, the danger is past. I ought to have known better, for it's almost eleven o'clock and Graft, when he comes in, usually gets here in time to go out for lunch. I always thought he had it soft as a supervisor, but now I envy him more than ever. There's no investigation hanging over his head. He's non-certified which means he got the job on merit alone—but it would take a placer miner with a lot of patience to find the merit. Here he is head of a Writers' Project, and he never in his whole life wrote or published anything or worked for a publishing house, newspaper, or even an advertising company. Abel does all his work for him. But I should worry. I don't guess I'll have to bother with any supervisor much longer. They're sure to trip me up when they investigate.

I wish I knew when the investigators were coming. I know I'll faint when they walk through the door. Do you think I ought to draw out my postal savings? Then I could look her in the eye when I say, "None." But what if they ask how much cash I have on hand? I wish I could lie and never show it in my eyes. And then my ears turn red.

If it weren't for Abel, I'd go crazy. He talks about log cabins and helps take my mind off my troubles. But he has troubles, too. You see, he worked on this Chicago newspaper till last October, and the other day his father forwarded him a statement the paper had sent to his home address, and the statement said that the paper had forwarded the statement of his earnings to the Income Tax Bureau, and for the months he worked they were $2,243.43 and that will make him have to file an income tax return, and he is afraid the investigators will find out something about it, and he says they will not like him anyway for he is a lone man with no wife or children and they will think he does not need the money so much as men like Blakely who has seven children and his wife that way again; he could say he supports his mother but his old man—that's his slang for father, he uses the cutest slang—supports his mother and gets tax exemption for her, and his mother sells insurance in her spare time and makes money, too, so he can't find anybody to support. And he does not want to lose his job because he likes the work and the short hours for they give him time to work on his novel.

He likes to hear me tell him about Sugar Tree Holler, for he says he would like to have some land and trees all his own. Up in Alaska, it was government land and he just trapped over it; and his digestion bothers him too, he says the restaurants in this town are killing him, wrecking his digestion and he would give anything for a good home-cooked meal like his mother used to have.

But I'd better stop. It's almost lunch time and Abel wants us to walk by a hardware store so he can show me the kind of double-bitted ax he cut down trees with in Alaska. Your loving cousin,

SUSIE HARDWICK.

* * *

Dear Cousin Sadie,

Thanks for your encouraging note, but I was surprised to see you were so worried about me having dates with a strange newspaperman. He is a perfect gentleman, and smart, too. Last night when we ate supper together at the little restaurant on the corner, he told me he had been in Town only a week before he got a job as editor on the project, certified, at a dollar an hour and everything. I can see how he got the job for Graft's always on the lookout for somebody with brains enough for him to make a good showing in the State office, but I still can't see how he got certified with no pull, he's bound to have had brains to do it. Oh, I almost forgot to say what I started out to say in this note. The investigators are coming Monday, Feb. 27. I know I won't sleep any between now and then with that $140 hanging over my head. The F.B.I. may already be at work. I wish to goodness I had bought clothes and never saved it. But I'm in such a dither now that if I did draw it out I couldn't think of a thing I'd want to spend it for except that land in Sugar Tree Holler, and it isn't even surveyed, and anyhow a WPA worker is not supposed to have land. Maybe I can think of something to spend it for, and I will be able to write you a more cheerful letter. Right now I have to go out and stroll around town. Graft told me yesterday the State office was in a big hurry for the Paleontology Essay, so I have to make him think I am working on it. I went out to see that nice Dr. Roark at the University and he said he could write it quicker than he could tell me about it, and that he would have the added satisfaction of knowing it was right, so while he is working on it I can't do anything, but I have to make Graft think I am working, so I am going to sign out for research at the Public Library and stroll around town and see if there is anything I would like to buy with my $140. Your Loving Cousin,

SUSIE HARDWICK.

* * *

Dear Cousin Sadie,

I was glad to get your other letter. It's nice to know you've got friends in a time like this, and that you don't think I'm immoral or anything for keeping that $140 and writing "None." Oh, Sadie, if the Somerset Lumber Mills go under and you should lose your job keeping books, stay at home and live on poke shoots and rabbit and never come up here to hunt a job. You'd maybe land on WPA the way I did, and then you would maybe save a little money and then go crazy the way I am. Sometimes I think I'll quit right now, so they wouldn't inspect me, but what worries me is the F.B.I. may already know about my $140, and I have looked and looked all over town and can't find a thing I want to spend it for.

I got so worried I asked Graft about it, and he was real troubled. He'd hate to lose me he said, and went on and praised my work, and even showed me a letter from Dr. Latcher—he teaches English up at the State University and is Director of the Federal Writers of the State—and in the letter he had praised the Essay on Ethnic Groups of the State which I wrote for the Guide book. Of course, as Graft explained it, I hadn't been responsible for the finished product which was why his name instead of mine was on it, but he thought I had done a good job of research on it. I smiled and said, "Thank you, Dr. Graft," he has a doctor of philosophy degree in English you know, and I never let on that I knew it was just soft soap, and that I hadn't done any research on it, but went out to the University and got Dr. Banks—you know I told you about how lucky it was that Cousin Lucy Fairchild had been a secretary out at the University here and knew a lot of the people and took me out there to meet some of them and a lot of them were real nice for Dr. Banks and some of the others were from the South, too, and Dr. Roark who is doing my paleontology has traveled in Kentucky studying geology and while he was in Harlan County he spent three days with Cousin Jim Brack Hargis on Papa's side of the family and liked him a lot—but anyhow, they all like me and help me with the essays, and if they didn't, I don't know how Graft would manage, for Abel edits them and then they are better than ever, so that all Graft has to do is change the "buts" to "moreovers," put his name at the top and turn them over to his stenographers for final typing—and take the credit.

But I should worry with that $140 hanging over my head. Anyhow he told me I had better take my money out of postal savings, that maybe I would be safer that way, but I know I will lose it. I could give it to Mrs. Flagherty, my landlady to keep, but when you've worked eleven months to save $140 you are awful careful who you give it to, and I am a little leery of her; she drinks a lot of beer sometimes, and anyway I do not want her to lose her good opinion of me by learning that I have hoarded $140 against the law.

Anyhow I'm going to the post office and draw it out when I go to the Public Library for I have to go and find out what a brachiopod is—that nice old Dr. Roark wrote two pages about them for my paleontology essay, but forgot to say what they were. I do think that every Federal Writers' Project ought to have a dictionary, for every time I want to know what a word means I have to go to the library. I'll finish this when I get back, provided Graft is gone, and he usually is by two o'clock. I want to tell you about the date I had with Abel last night.

Yes, he's gone—a brachiopod was no bigger than an oyster and sometimes not as big—from the way Dr. Roark talked on about them, I had thought they were sea lions. Well. Sadie, I have my $140 in my purse, but it gives me an awful funny feeling, seven twenty dollar bills, and I am afraid I'll lose them every one. I think I'll ask Abel to keep it for me, only I would hate to bother him with the responsibility of my money when he has so many troubles of his own; his income tax returns, and nobody to support, and his indigestion.

But I never have said what I started out to say which is that Abel, besides being a good editor, is about the smartest person I ever met. Last night while we were eating supper I asked him right out how he got certified after coming from Chicago, and he told me. When he got in this town—he came because one of the papers here had offered him a job on the re-write desk—but when he got here and saw the set-up—that's his word, he uses wonderful slang—he decided not to take it. He was tired of newspaper work anyhow, and sick of never getting to work on his novel; he's writing a novel of Alaska and he gets wonderful rejection slips on stories, he let me read one from *Esquire,* but anyhow he wanted a job with short hours and he heard about the Federal Writers and he called Graft and asked for a job. Graft interviewed him and gave him the job—he needed a smart editor bad—provided he could get certified.

Well, Abel rented a room over in the West End—that's the poorest section of the city where all the case workers have such heavy loads they haven't time to investigate any but direct reliefers—and there he had some friends in Chicago, he has a lot of friends, write him a lot of letters to his address—and then in about a week he moved to a place in the same section but about five blocks away and cheaper than the first place; and then he had his friends write him a lot more letters to the second address, an awful lot of letters—then he took some rejection slips and letters he had, you know those sort of informal notes magazines send sometimes where they just say Dear So and So and leave off the address—well, he put an address on them—then he asked a colored woman who lived close if he could use her washing machine, she took in washing, and he run his letters through the wringer over and over and some he got a little dirty and some he smeared the postmark date with water or something, anyhow you couldn't read the year on any of them. Then he bought a book of rent receipts, and he looked around until he found an old tenement house they were tearing down, and then he gave a little colored boy a nickel to put a price and dates on all his rent receipts in the book, and then he put the rent receipts through the wringer, too, until they were old looking and smooth and dirty; then he took one of his shirts when it came back from the laundry and washed it in just cold water, of course, and put it on and his oldest trousers and wore them all day—and that day he didn't eat anything—he's thin anyway with big brown eyes, and that night he slept in his clothes and the next morning he got up real early, put on plenty of underwear and put his old shirt and his trousers back on, and took his letters and receipts and about two hundred pages of manuscript he had worked on back in Chicago and went down to the Employment Center without an overcoat. That's the first thing you have to do to be certified.

At the Employment Center, they filled out a card for him, and he begged them for just any kind of work. He would dig ditches he said. And the lady who talked to him was awful kind and concerned. But she cleared her throat and hemmed and hawed and looked him up and down. She smiled a little sadly, he said, and told him in a delicate way that he didn't look strong enough for ditch digging—just now, and he would need warm clothes and boots for such work and that he—well—offices demanded a certain standard of dress and well—here, she looked at the shirt he had washed himself, and there were tears in her eyes, he said.

Then she said, that is the interviewer, "Why don't you go over to the Elmendorf Building and see what they can do for you there?"

Abel asked her what was the Elmendorf Building.

"It's the place where you go to get certified for WPA or direct relief— that is food, rent money, or clothing," she said. Abel shook his head. "I want work," he said. "I can write, some day the world will know I can write," and he pulled out some of the old rejection slips with the right addresses on them and flung them on the table.

The interviewer studied the rejection slips and her eyes lit up, he said. "When you get certified you can maybe get a job on the Federal Writers," she told him. But Abel shook his head and looked sad. He picked up the rejection slips, and his novel manuscript and started away, "Thank you," he told the interviewer, "but I refuse to ask for charity. If you ever hear of a job let me know."

But the interviewer argued with him awhile. She called relief head-quarters, too, talked to the head of the works and I don't know how many case workers. Over the telephone she hinted that starvation had made him light minded—she hinted at a lot of things. She begged him again, and finally he agreed, but when he went he shook his head at her and told her he could never get certified.

I guess he was worried. Before he could get certified on WPA, he had to prove two things: that he had lived in the city a year or more and that he was ready to white-eye from starvation. But over in the Elmendorf Building, the case worker took one look at him and his shirt he had washed himself, and never asked if he had resources or anything. She asked him for his work record, and he sighed and flung the novel manuscript on her desk, too. "That is my work record for two years, two whole years," he said, "and nobody will touch it," and he pulled out the rejection slips and the letters with the right addresses and dropped them on her desk, too.

The case worker asked him, very gently, he said, for some proof that he had lived in the city for at least a year. Abel thought awhile and then he picked up his manuscript and his papers and his letters and started away, "I won't take up any more of your time," he said. "It is hopeless even if I starved," he said. "I've had to move twice in two weeks—no money for rent, and the place where I lived for a year was torn down." He said he didn't think there was a soul to vouch for him in the neighborhood, the poorest part of town, as he explained to her, and the people there either starved out and went to the jungles by the river or got a little money and moved on.

But the case worker begged him to wait, and didn't he have any rent receipts at all? He said he didn't think he had. Lately he'd been so hard up for paper that he'd written on everything, even poems on his rent receipts, and he never kept anything like that anyhow; but she insisted, the case worker I mean, and he looked through his pockets. He looked and looked and finally found a few, dirty and worn and scribbled over with bits of poetry—he writes the loveliest poetry—and notes on things he saw in the streets and dated more than a year ago.

The case worker glanced at the front of the receipts, and then she read some of his poetry on the back and there were almost tears in her eyes, and he got certified for WPA work. In three days he was working, and when he finished, telling me, I mean, I asked him if he didn't think he was terribly dishonest. And he said "no," that the premise of his plan—whatever he meant by that—was that WPA workers earned their money, and that he was working just about as hard, only shorter hours than he worked on the newspaper and making less money, and that he felt he earned every cent he got. And that's the truth. Since he got to be an editor, they send lots of copy down from the State office for Graft to revise and Abel does the work for him, and Abel says that as long as he earns his money he isn't dishonest.

But now he's worried. He says that a single man hasn't such a good chance now. They'll lay them off and give preference to the ones like Blakely with wives and lots of children, and he said he didn't blame them. He said he wished he had a wife so he wouldn't have to worry about his job. I told him why didn't he marry that feisty Hermaine who does his typing and is always making eyes at him and he won't give her a glance, and then if they didn't get along he could divorce her after they had lived together long enough for him to write his novel, and anyhow he could support a wife who could cook and look after him as cheap as he's supporting himself now, eating out all the time and sending even his socks to the laundry, not to speak of losing his socks—he lost one each of two pair last week— and ruining his digestion.

But all he did was look at me lonesome like and shake his head. "I don't want just any dame"—that's his slang for woman—"for my wife," he said, "for when I marry I want to marry like my old man, for keeps. Besides I don't guess she could cook."

I said I didn't guess she could either, and then we talked about the land around home and the trees, and how thrifty, hard- working people could manage if they wanted to. The restaurant was crowded and people kept smiling at us as we talked so we went outside. It was snowing and there we had the streets mostly to ourselves. We looked in show windows, and Abel took me by the same place where he showed me the double-bitted ax and showed me the kind of cross-cut saw he used in Alaska when he cut down trees, and a plane he would like to have.

And I told him about Old Bones, that cow I used to milk, recollect, and what a good hand in the garden I had been, and how when I was home we always had the earliest beans and the biggest dahlias of anybody in Wayne County.

He told me about trapping in Alaska and how he made all the furniture in the cabin he lived in, and about how he learned to make sourdough bread, and how to make porcupine hash, for one winter they didn't have much to eat but porcupine. He never seemed to mind that sometimes he was hungry then. "It was fun," he said. "I used to think about it when I had gone back to Chicago. Nights on the re-write desk, I'd want to cuss or cry. Here the reporters would be calling in news, people were fighting or dying or stealing or saving lives or making inventions or fighting fires or maybe just getting born, and what was I doing—writing about them, and not living at all.

And he looked lonesome there with the snow on his hat and his coat collar and never knowing there was snow on him while he looked through a plate glass window. We walked on to a house furnishing store and in one window there were iron pans and pots and kettles like Mama has, and I told him how when I had a cabin in the woods I would cook over the fireplace in winter days. Potatoes roasted in the ashes are better than any kind I know, and meat broiled on hickory coals is awfully good.

He looked so lonesome that I almost gave in when he begged me again to cook him a meal in my furnished room. He would buy the steak and all the other groceries, he said. I wish my landlady wasn't so full of funny notions.

It must be after three o'clock and I guess I've worked overtime again, but I don't mind for I have to have somebody to tell my troubles to, and you are the only one of all my relations that can keep her mouth shut. Burn this letter, so that you may never have to testify against me, but if you do have to, don't lie, for it's like Mama says, all our generations has always told the truth. Your loving cousin,

SUSIE HARDWICK.

* * *

Dear Cousin Sadie,

I hope this bad snowy weather hasn't made your cold worse, but I was awfully glad to know you like Abel a little better and that you think I ought not to have to go to the penitentiary, but I still can't think of anything to spend my money for and it is going to be the death of me. I am still carrying it in my purse, and yesterday—you know how I am about mislaying things—well, now I am rattle-braineder than ever, so when I went to wash my hands back at the drinking fountain I took my purse with me and left it there and forgot about it, and then nearly tore my desk apart looking for my purse when I found out it was missing. The whole office noticed. I bet that catty Hermaine who types things for me too—she's still trying to get Abel to invite her out and he won't give her a glance—is so jealous she'd tell in a minute if she knew. And now I bet they all suspect I have a lot of money in my purse the way I hunted around, but Hermaine's the only one, though, that would tell.

I'm afraid this letter won't make sense. Graft telephoned that he wouldn't be in, and with my purse and everything else and everybody making noise for that fat Lawton just waddles around and talks about what the investigators are going to do and Blakely's twins. Remember the man I told you about with the seven children and his wife that way again, well late yesterday morning his wife had twin boys and he was called from work. Lawton has a printed list of excuses, for absence that is. If a worker is absent for such and such a reason, he is allowed to make up the time like if he is sick or something; well, on the list there isn't any place for twins being born and Lawton has been talking with everybody in the office and calling the head timekeeper and trying to find out if Blakely can be allowed to make up his time. But it seems the rules don't say that he can, and I feel sorry for him; he is going around with a sort of surprised startled look in his eyes, and he is not like me classified as skilled and drawing 90 cents an hour, but he only gets less than 50 cents an hour because he is unskilled, and it seems a pity that people with as many children as he has, and all young at that, can't be skilled.

That was all bad enough and then a few minutes ago a man came with a briefcase and the most important look I ever saw. He whispered awhile with Lawton, and when people whisper like that, it makes me nervous. I thought maybe he was an F.B.I. whispering about the $140 I drew out of postal savings.

Everybody else in the office kept wondering what they were whispering about until Hermaine got the dust cloth out of the vault and went and dusted Lawton's desk real slow until she learned he was a notary public who had come to swear us in for being citizens of the United States. It gives me a funny feeling to swear anything, I never did, and to raise your right hand and swear you are a citizen of the United States seems strange somehow. Gramma would turn over in her grave, but maybe it will be another story I can hand down to my grandchildren the way she used to tell me hand-me-down tales of the ones that fought in the Revolution, and the Civil War. What gives me cold chills is that maybe somebody, not in our office, will swear allegiance and citizenship when they don't mean it. But then I am silly. I keep thinking of Abel. All morning I've been afraid to go up and speak to him for fear I would blush or something and all the stenographers would see. He must be having trouble with his copy; he just sits and stares out the window.

I wish I could do that instead of watching the people swear in out of the corners of my eyes. They are all giggling; and after the notary got through whispering with Lawton, they cracked jokes with each other, and it all doesn't seem right somehow. I wish it were . . .

They called my name, and I went up and lifted my hand and said yes when he had finished and signed my name to a slip of paper, and that was all there was to it. I wish the investigation would be as easy.

I know my ears are red now. Abel came around just now with my pale-ontology essay he is editing. We looked at it while we talked so none of the catty stenographers would catch on. He whispered to me that he had been thinking about my $140 and the investigation Monday, and that he thought he had found a safe way out for me and a good investment for my money, but before he could tell me about it he would have to come to my furnished room, that he couldn't explain it in a restaurant with a lot of people around or in the street by a store window.

I don't know what to do. I know it would be all right, but I would lose my reputation with Mrs. Flagherty. Sadie, I do wish you were here to chaperone us or something. I wish I could make up my mind, but anyway I think I'll sign out for research and go buy a steak just in case. Your loving cousin, SUSAN HARDWICK.

* * *

Dear Cousin Sadie,

Please excuse me if this letter is a little dizzy. I couldn't hardly wait to get down to the office this morning so I could write to you. I will try to begin at the beginning and make it clear.

My supper, for Abel I mean, was real good—he likes steak rare the way I do—and he bragged awfully on my biscuit and the blackberry jam I made while I was home last summer. It was kind of nice eating supper there with him. It was snowing, and outside in the alley the wind cried the way I've told you about, but it didn't make me so lonesome as it used to do.

After supper—I didn't want him to do it—but he helped me wash the dishes, and when we were all through and I was hanging up the dish towels I asked him right out what was his plan for me to escape the F.B.I. I had wondered about it all along, but somehow I didn't want to ask him. He'd acted sort of sober like and serious all evening. Well, he turned sort of red and picked up my Sears Roebuck catalogue and hunted until he found lumber and then sat down by the table. "You might not like my plan," he said, and kept looking at the catalogue.

"I'd like anything," I said, "that will keep me out of the penitentiary."

"This plan would do that," he said, and turned through my Sears Roebuck—you know I always keep one just to look at and plan—but I could see he wasn't thinking of what he looked at for he was reading the price of poultry wire and I don't guess he hardly knows a hen from a rooster.

"How?" I asked, and finished hanging up my dish cloth and came and sat down by him at the table. I looked at the bulletin on the mixing of concrete; before supper I had got out my government bulletins on building log houses and how to plan kitchens just to show him.

"Spend it on house furnishings," he said, and reached in his inside coat pocket and pulled out a billfold. "You were awful silly," he went on just as if he hadn't told me how to spend my money, "to put your cash in postal savings. Me, I'm my own bank," and he pulled a lot of bills out of his pocket book—tens and twenties and some fifties. I never saw so much money. He piled it all up on the table and then he stacked it off in four little piles. "This, $250, they gave me when they fired me; this, $100, I had saved before I left Chicago; this, $285, is what I got when I sold my coupe before I left; and this, $60, is what I've saved since I got on the project."

I just sat there and looked at it with my mouth open, and then I got up and pulled down the shade; nobody can see into the window of a third floor back, but I wasn't taking any chances on the F.B.I. "If I could work till June," he said, "by then it would be summer, and I could go to the hills, and I would maybe almost have my novel finished. I won't make much money on the first one, but I expect to live in the hills and keep on writing until I get a good one, but——," and he just sat and looked at me.

"You have enough money to buy a hundred acres of land in Sugar Tree Holler, and build a log house and buy a cow and get a start of chickens and maybe sheep," I told him, and something about his eyes made my heart feel funny under my ribs.

He shook his head. "I could build the cabin and make the furniture, but somebody would have to show me how to milk a cow and build chicken houses, and I can't cook, I mean I could never be a great writer on my own cooking."

"The government bulletins would teach you how to do all that," I said. He flipped his hair out of his eyes and sat and stared at the government bulletins. "They won't keep a man from getting lonesome," he said, "and, Hell, it's not just because I want to keep this job till June, but look," he said, and he moved his chair closer to mine—"if a woman saved $140 to buy house furnishings so she could set up housekeeping, they wouldn't say a word when she took it out of the bank. And if a young man just gets married—they wouldn't have the heart to take his job away from him, and then one of them would still have a job, and they could live on together on the man's salary until summer came and they could find a place in the hills where they want to settle and draw up their house plans and everything— and the woman could write her fairy stories and the man could write his novels and if they didn't make any money they'd still have a house and fuel and a cow and chickens and maybe a garden—and there wouldn't be any Graft to grab all the credit and no F.B.I. and—no smoke and the man wouldn't be always wasting his money the way he did when he was single in Chicago."

Something about his eyes made my throat hurt. I couldn't say anything, but I guess I nodded, for the next minute—Oh, Sadie, I don't want to write anymore. I'm too happy. Mama would like him for a son-in-law, but don't tell her yet—we'll come down when we come to pick out our land. My head is full of things running around and around. One minute I think that tomorrow when we go over the river, I always wanted to be married in Kentucky anyhow, I'll wear my blue suit with a white blouse and then I think I'll rush out and buy a new dress and wear it under my winter coat—but I don't know what I'll do—all I know is that I'll go over the river. Don't breathe a word of this; we don't want anybody in the office to know. I have two more days to work until the investigator comes, but let 10,000 investigators come and I won't mind; I saved some money and spent it for house furnishings for a three-room apartment. Abel knows of a lovely one right down in town and close to work with a private bath that we can get for $20 a month; it's a five-floor walkup, and going up all those steps will get us in good shape for the hills. Your loving cousin,

SUSIE HARDWICK.

*   *   *

Dear Cousin Sadie,

Yes, I got your special delivery letter telling me I was crazy to marry a man from Chicago when I didn't even know his parents and let alone his grandparents, but it's like Mama used to say we need new blood in the hills, and anyhow I was already Mrs. Abel when your letter came. It seems so funny to sit here in the office and look at him and think he is my husband, and nobody else in the office knows; and we have not given it away for I would be sort of embarrassed to let people know I married so quick with hardly any courting at all, but I am dying to tell somebody, and I wish I could take him down to Mama this minute, but it's like he says, we'd better wait till the roads are better and it is time to use next year's auto license. I forgot to tell you but we have a car.

the corals are well represented in this region, some of them are called horn corals and look a lot like a calf's horn, not quite so sharp as a Jersey's, but sharper than a Holstein's, and were made by small animals who lived in the warm seas about 400,000,000 years ago.

Sadie, I dare not write you another word today, for Graft came in early, and as he passed he looked over my shoulder, and now he is fidgeting around his desk and acting like he will come back again. He wants that paleontology essay, but after I finished it, Abel edited it and then we sent it out to the University for Dr. Roark to go over it again, but Abel says that if I am smart enough to get the whole town to do my work for me, I shouldn't work so hard in the office, and just two more days anyhow, but I think it is better to make Graft think I am doing something. The interviewers come tomorrow, and I will write you a long letter for the office will be in such an uproar nobody will notice anything. Blakely and Abel and myself are the only ones who are not scared. Your loving cousin,

MRS. MICHAEL ABEL (SUSIE HARDWICK).

* * *

Dear Cousin Sadie,

Well, they're here, one tall and stringy looking with sharp eyes and one of those new hats with a bunch of flowers on top, and the other one young and blonde in a fur coat and green kid shoes. I don't care which one I get for I will just tell them right out what I have done; and I am too busy to be bothered anyway. We moved last night after work, but never got straightened out like we should, for right in the middle of everything, we unpacked the Sears Roebuck Catalogue and the government bulletins and stopped and figured how much it would cost to build a log cabin with a stone foundation and a red cedar shingle roof. There are plenty of red cedar, do you remember, and flat limestone rocks in Sugar Tree Holler; and Mike, I'm so afraid I'll let slip and call him by his first name here, he made shingles— shakes they call them there—in Alaska and he could make a stone foundation, for you remember that schoolhouse over on Sinking Creek that the CCC[2] boys made out of limestone, well I know Mike could do anything that a CCC boy could do with a government bulletin to show him how.

I will write you more about the investigation tomorrow for then I will be through, and have plenty of time for writing letters. Right now I want to order some more government bulletins. I am all in a fidget anyhow for they have just called Mike's name and he has gone back in the corner where they have pulled away all the desks so the interviewers could be private. I do hope they don't ask him too much if he has any money and that they will be kind to him when they learn he's just gotten married. Me, I'm not a bit nervous for I know just how it will be. She will ask me, "Have you any savings?" Or maybe the F.B.I. have already investigated postal savings, and she will ask, "Why did you write "None" and then draw out a $140?"

And I will look her in the eye and say, "I saved that money to set up housekeeping and to buy a car."

And she will lift her eyebrows and say, "You are getting married?"

And I shall lift my eyebrows and look down my nose at her and say, I've been Mrs. Abel for three days, but I worked on out of kindness for Dr. Graft because I wanted to finish the essay on paleontology I have started, but after today—

Goodbye they called my name.

*   *   *

Dear Cousin Sadie,

Yes, I got your telegram asking me if I was in jail. I never heard of anything so silly, but I have been so busy I didn't have time to write you a letter. I knew that you would go looking in Mama's mailbox and [not] see a letter there from me, and be worried—but you mustn't tell her yet. I know she would like Abel for a son-in-law so much she would go bragging to all the neighbors, and we don't want it out yet for awhile. B

neither gold, nor silver, nor diamonds, but clay, yellow clay, white clay, blue clay, and clay that looks like just plain mud, but it is all valuable and has made this state rank away ahead in natural resources and first in the production of white hotelware, you know the kind they make mugs out of that they use in hamburger stands. Graft must be in early. I didn't think it was eleven o'clock, but he came and I wasn't going to take any chances of him looking over my shoulder. The State Office wants the essay on Natural Resources re-written so I took it out to Dr. White at the University, and he is working on it; he gave me lunch when I took it to him and was so nice that when I came home and told Abel about it, he was almost jealous.

Oh, Sadie, he is the best husband, our apartment isn't much to brag about for what can you expect for $20, but Mike weather-stripped the windows and did all kinds of things to make it comfortable, and adjusted all the burners so they wouldn't use so much gas, and he is wonderful, every day he brags on my cooking and likes his corn muffins without sugar and his digestion is already better, and every night he dries the dishes and brings home groceries for he says that it is only fair because I work just as many hours outside the home as he does, but when we get down to the hills and he is building the cabin and a chicken house and working on his novel and I have nothing to do but write fairy stories and cook for him, he will not dry the dishes for me then. He thinks I am wonderful, but come to think of it I guess you are kind of mixed up, for I think I told you in some other letters that I wouldn't be working. Well, I am.

They called my name, and the investigator, I got the thin stringy one, looked me up and down, then she looked that slip I had filled out up and down, and then she asked just like I knew she would, "And have you no savings of any kind?"

And I looked her in the eye and I said, "No," and then I said because I'd been dying to tell somebody and hadn't been able to tell anybody but Mrs. Flagherty, she went over the river with us to get married, so I said, "I did have $140 saved in postal savings, but I bought a car and furniture for a three-room apartment with it."

Her mouth fell open. "Child," she said, "how could you furnish an apartment and buy a car for $140?"

"It took a little looking around," I told her, "but there was a man with me who knows an awful lot about cars, and he found a Model A Ford in good condition only gone less than 60,000 miles, and it will go 22 miles to the gallon of gas, just the thing for a WPA worker to get out into the country with," I told her.

"You're very sensible," she said, "but how in the world did you furnish an apartment with what was left?"

And then I told her, because I had wanted to tell somebody so much all about how Abel and I tramped around that snowy Friday afternoon and Saturday. We bought a new mattress and springs from a man Mrs. Flagherty knew, he deals in job lots of slightly damaged furniture—our mattress, it's beautiful red satin with a $39.50 mark on a black silk label, and we got it for $15 dollars because somebody had ordered it made special and then didn't take it. Then I told her about how we bought everything else except a few dishes second hand for hardly anything at all, and how we went to the Salvation Army Store and the Goodwill Industries and a junk shop where we found a Rookwood vase, that's some fancy pottery they make here, for a quarter, and how we had $6.30 left over when we got through, and bought two of the best seats there were for the Ballet Russe.

She listened and listened, and now and then she asked questions, and when I finished she started telling me about her apartment some place in Mount Adams, that's a suburb here, that she painted all herself with a special shade of blue that she mixed herself. I'll always wonder how she mixed it, but when she was halfway through, the fat one in green shoes called to her in a sort of hissing way, "We're supposed to get through here by noon, so we can go on to the Historical Survey, and at your rate we will never get finished."

"That will be all, Miss Hardwick," she said sort of sudden like and getting sort of red.

And that was all. It wasn't until I was back at my desk and she was interviewing somebody else that I recollected I hadn't told her I was married. I'm still working, and we've figured out a budget so we can save one salary and live on the other one. Mike thinks that by the last of June, that's when everybody thinks WPA money will run out, we can have enough money for a 150 acres of land in Sugar Tree Holler, one cow, one sow hog, four sheep, twelve hens and a rooster, what tools we will need to build the house and maybe a mule, only he doesn't know anything about mules.

I'll write you more pretty soon, only now I am awful busy with not such time for letters. I brought my Sears Roebuck to work and while I am waiting for them to do my essays out at the University, I work on my kitchen plan and figure out how much it will all cost. Your happy cousin,

MRS. MIKE ABEL (SUSAN HARDWICK)

* * *

Dear Cousin Sadie,

Yes, I got your foolish letter, and I'm certainly not scared they'll put me in the penitentiary. Yes, there was a house-to-house investigation like you read about in the paper and married women with working husbands aren't supposed to be on WPA jobs. An investigator came to see Mike and me but not one of the ones that came to the office. She was a fat motherly sort of looking woman, but she didn't have much breath left by the time she climbed up to our fifth floor, so mostly she just beamed on us. Finally when she did get her breath, she kept calling me a little bride, and said I had courage and thrift and everything to start out with second-hand furniture and a WPA husband in a fifth floor walkup flat. Naturally, she didn't ask me my maiden name for how was she to know I was a WPA worker too?

Another investigator, not the same one, went to see Mrs. Flagherty, and Mrs. Flagherty told her, at least that is what she, Mrs. Flagherty, told me over the telephone that I lived there but was out, but she would be glad to show her my room, but it was in the attic on the fourth floor and the stairs were awful steep and high, so the investigator just looked up the stairs and said she didn't know it would do any good to walk up to my apartment when I wasn't in it. It was a good thing because Mrs. Flagherty's attic is just a store-all, and the investigator might have suspected something if she saw it. "I maybe lied a little," she said, that is Mrs. Flagherty said, when she called me over the telephone, "but them that try, I like to see get along," she said, and went on to tell me to keep letting my pay checks come to my old address, so nobody in the office would know. I could have kissed her. I think she liked Mike an awful lot, for she gave me four sheets and four pillow slips for a wedding present, and a blue handkerchief to carry for luck at my wedding. She said she was glad I was out of her furnished room and in a whole apartment with a good man like Mike. She had always worried about me, she said.

Oh, yes, I almost forgot, the next time any of the Pings come down from Sugar Tree Holler with a raft of logs, please ask them how much would 250 acres of land be. By June we'll save enough to buy that much, and the other day Mike was reading about reforestation and how much the government has given farmers to take care of their soil and plant trees, and so he thinks we should do that, too, so tell the Pings that if they have any washed out pastures or anything in Sugar Tree Holler you know where you can get a buyer, for Mike is writing to the county agent down there, I told him his name, to find out all about free benefits and money you can get for not planting crops, and the black walnut seedlings—we could have walnuts while the trees were getting big enough for timber—and other little trees they have to give away. So be sure and don't forget to ask the Pings about their land and tell them the buyer you know of is in a hurry to get it, for we would like to buy some of it now and start signing up for the free fertilizer and the seedlings. Oh, yes, and one more thing, do you know of a farm any place in the country that a man without any tools or anything could rent and get the farmer to stake him to fertilizer and such. You know this man Blakely I was telling you about, the one with the seven children and the twins, well, the investigators found out that he was working on the side and making about $10 dollars a week working at night as an extra waiter in a hamburger place. One of his neighbors told on him, and now he's out of a job, and I feel pretty sorry for

much sand and gravel in the rivers which is used for building purposes and road making, and a lot of clay that is used for tile and the tile is used to drain meadows and roof houses, except the same kind is not used for both things, but—well, he finally went on, but I'd better stop, he's still fiddling around his desk and not sitting down, and it's past eleven o'clock, almost time for lunch anyway.

Well, I'll be seeing you, Sadie, in another three or four weeks, for we're coming down to see about Sugar Tree Holler pretty soon, but before we come, I wonder if you could go up and see Mama and sort of read her tea leaves and see a fine son-in-law and a lot of happiness so as to sort of put her in an expectant frame of mind. And it's like I always said, Mama deserved at least one good son-in-law. Your happily married cousin,

MRS. MICHAEL ABEL (SUSAN HARDWICK)

MICHIGAN: THE 1940S & AFTER

King Devil's Bargain

The story was signed "H. Arnow," a pen name Arnow used to give her husband, Harold, credit for his contributions to the work.

Probably written in 1939 or the early 1940s, this unpublished story is from Arnow's novel *Hunter's Horn* (1949).

———◦◦◦———

*T*wilight was darkness in the valleys, and the Ballous were finishing supper when Jaw Buster Anderson's horn call came floating down from the ridge crest. Zing, the grizzled fox hound, ran to the road gate and whined, but Nunn sat still by the eating table with a wedge of molasses bread in one hand and a glass of buttermilk cold from the spring in the other, and listened, frowning.

The Keith horns from across the creek were soon answering Jaw Buster, and almost immediately after, there came a strange horn with an ugly tinny sound, blown it was plain by no practiced hand.

Milly stopped with a spoonful of green beans half way to Deb's open mouth, and looked through the kitchen door, "Why that's a comen from Rans Cramer's place, but Rans he ain't got no hound."

"Oh yes, he has," Nunn said in some disgust, and went on to tell between bites about that big hound pup the Sextons had, hardly nine

· 185 ·

months old and already as big as Zing; he was Zing's pup all right, looked just like him, and his mother was a brindly little bitch out of Ulie Lou Hargis, one of the best hounds that ever smelled a fox. Jaw Buster had wanted the pup bad; but the dirty Sextons wouldn't sell him to Jaw Buster. They owed him for hauling their cross ties; he'd offered them twenty dollars on the debt, but they'd sold to Rans for fifteen dollars cash. Wasn't that mean? "Rans don't know nothen about fox hunten an hounds," Nunn went on. "All he wants is to keep th pup three days an double his money on Jaw Buster. He come by th barn last night with th pup, a braggen his brags, an a sayen th pup ud make a better hound than Zing, an—."

"An be th one to git King Devil, Pop," Lee Roy interrupted.

"Sometimes I think nothen'ull git that danged fox," Nunn said, and listened again. Jaw Buster was blowing for Rans to bring his pup across the creek and up the hill, but Rans was holding out for the valley.

Zing loped through the door, ran up to Nunn and laid his nose on his elbow and whined, and when Nunn gave him no answer, he whined and nudged his arm. Nunn turned around and looked at him, "Listen, Zing, if you an Rans Cramer think I'm a goen to let you run yerself to death ever night jist fer some ole gray fox, an mostly so's Rans's pup can learn th ways a fox hunten, you're crazy—You've got to save yourself fer King Devil come late fall."

Zing whined at the word King Devil, and Lee Roy, the oldest boy, said eagerly, "Go, Pop, mebbe you'll git King Devil this very night."

Milly tried to catch Lee Roy's eye and shut him up; and failing, she gave Zing a sharp worried glance. He was livelier than he had been back in the hot weather, but he still didn't look any too well about the eyes. He'd nearly killed himself in the spring with long, heart-breaking chases after the big red fox that Nunn and the children called King Devil. Zing and every other hound in the country had chased him for going on five years and for all the good they'd done they might as well have chased the wind. Nunn hated him not only for his thieving ways with young lambs, chickens, and even suckling pigs, but for the endless, hopeless chases he led the hounds, wild races full of guile and trickery that had never led to a den.

Outside there was a talking back and forth of horns, and Zing ran back to the kitchen door and listened a moment, whirled and ran to the high shelf and stood with his paws on the wall under it, stretching up until his eyes were level with the shelf. He scolded the silent horn there with shrill sharp barks; then while he stood with his paws on the wall, he turned and looked over his shoulder at Nunn and barked like a quarrelsome old man cursing.

The children laughed and begged Nunn to get up and blow his horn and join the hunt; Nunn scolded the old hound good humoredly; only Milly was silent, glancing first at Nunn and then at Zing with a look of troubled uncertainty. Once she opened her mouth to speak, then closed it quickly. If she told Nunn about seeing King Devil up in John Whittaker's woods not two weeks back, he might get so mad with thinking that the fox dared come so close to his own land that he'd take Zing out and let him run himself to death; on the other hand, there was a chance that if Nunn knew King Devil had been in the country lately he would keep Zing home because he wasn't in good shape for a long race.

"Please, Pop, please," Lee Roy begged, and Zing sat on his haunches and whined with a high whine that seemed ready to break into a howl.

"Oh Hell," Nunn said, and got up and took the horn from the high shelf.

He stood in the kitchen door and blew, the long crying call of the yellowed, silver-banded[1] horn echoing and reechoing through the twilight. The others answered and it was at last agreed they should all come by Nunn's place. If the race looked any good, they would all climb up to the Pilot Rock to listen.

Nunn sat in the kitchen door with Deb on his lap and took his after supper chew of tobacco and lowed[2] there wouldn't be much of a race. The night was no good for hunting; an almost full moon, red stained with the autumn, was already showing above the pines at the head of the creek. Worse yet, there was a warm wind out of the southwest, and it would take a rare good hound to follow even the strongest and straightest of scents through the dry blowing leaves.

Rans Cramer came first, whistling as he walked the short cut path through Milly's upper garden. Ahead came his big young hound, frisking like a playful, friendly child. He ran to Nunn in the kitchen door, jumped on his knees, licked Deb's face, and then, his tail waving like a triumphant flag, frolicked into the kitchen. The eating table was not completely cleared of supper, and much to the delight of the children, Del—short for

Delano—leaped into the middle of it, and began eating wolfishly from a bowl of fried sweet potatoes rich with lard and honey.

Rans, running up behind, swore at the pup; the children screamed at Del to hurry up and help himself, and Nunn jumped up and jerked the bowl of fried sweet potatoes away, and roared at Milly, "What th Hell, Woman, a standen an letten him eat that stuff—he'll kill hissef a runnen full a that greasy grub."

Milly took her hands from the dishwater and wiped them on her apron. "Aw, Nunn, cain't he have somethen? He acts so hungry like," and she came over and stood with the others and studied the young hound in the dim yellow light from the lamp on the high shelf. She scratched the white patch on his throat, admired the shine of his brown chest in the lamplight, "He is a sight like Zing was when he was young. Recollect?"

And the old hound hearing his name spoken by Milly came from his listening post in the kitchen door and laid his nose on the table and studied his son with a lifting of his grizzled brows. And Del, after making certain there was no more food on the table, wagged his tail at Zing, barked a short greeting, and rubbed him with one paw like a playful kitten.

Zing twisted his head away and growled, and Rans cursed Del, and added, "They'll be a fighten in a minnit. Del he don't know how to act. I have to keep him chained up all th time."

"Why?" asked[3] Nunn who had been comparing the two hounds in silence.

"Th damn fool might go off an chase rabbits."

Nunn shook his head. It was too bad such a fool man had to have such a smart pup. "Leave him chase rabbits—if he will," he said after a moment. "If it ain't in him to leave ever thing fer fox scent when he finds it, you cain't put it in." He looked into Del's eyes, big and brown, full of something a man couldn't name; not sense exactly, more than sense, something Rans and a lot of men didn't have. A hound could have a deep chest and long strong springy legs and a cold nose, but if he didn't have that other thing he wasn't any good—and this pup, like Zing, had it.

"I wouldn't let him git wind a King Devil yit fer awhile," Nunn went on. "If he's real good he'd keep up close to Zing an Speed an run hissef to death, an if he's jist middlen he'll git so plum disheartened a tryen to unravel th scent he'll quit."

"If he quits, I'll kill him," Rans said.

Del looked up at Nunn and laughed at his owner's threats. His brown eyes were full of fun and a kind of joy as if he knew it was good to be young and full of life with a hundred good races ahead.

Nunn picked up one big but pinkish and uncalloused paw and squeezed it gently, "Rans he's so big, but he's sich a baby; he ain't through growen; why, he'll be bigger'n Zing; I don't think I'd let him run a tall; least not with fast hounds like Zing an Speed—mebbe not fore spring—treat him good, buy him some dog feed an you'll have a rare good hound," he advised, his dislike of Rans forgotten, his eyes kind and warm over Del.

Rans smiled slyly, "Mebbe he'll run so good I can double my money on him thout keepen him till spring—they's one wants him mighty bad. An anyhow he'll jist have a little fun tonight. I heared you say a comen through th garden th race couldn't last long."

Nunn shook his head, "Fox hunten ain't never fun to a serus-minded hound. An a body cain't never tell—King Devil might come out; he could ruin a pup like this, break his wind in one race er kill him even."

Rans laughed with a flashing of his big white teeth, "Nunn, you've tried so long to git King Devil an no luck you're a thinken he's bewitched. You're afeard this pup'ull git him an put Zing to shame."

"I wisht to God he could, but he won't," Nunn said.

Zing had left the group around the table and gone back to the door and resumed his listening, ears lifted, great eyes following the sounds that came to him from across the creek. Lister Tucker with his Sourvine and Jaw Buster Anderson with his Speed, the only two hounds in the country that could begin to match him in either wind or nose were coming over the hill. With them came Blare and Joe C. Keith, each with two worthless hounds, mostly mouth. They came on, the men walking down the post office path, the six hounds talking a little, now scattering, now together, sniffing, circling, hunting.

He glanced back at Nunn and whined impatiently for him to come on, but Nunn was smiling at some trick of Del's. A sound faint, but full of music, like a bow drawn once across the muted D string of a violin, came to him smothered like and low from John Whittaker's high growing poplar timber near the head of the creek.

He leaped through the door lifting his own clear bell-like voice in his hunting call. Sourvine was telling him he'd found fox scent, not a straight trail but scent that might be unraveled.

At Zing's call, Del lifted his head and looked through the open door. He stood a second on the table, the laughter gone from his eyes, a wonder coming there and then an eagerness. Nunn glanced over his shoulder at the empty door, then at Rans with a question in his face. He flung out his arm to grab the pup, but Rans's hand came between. Del shook his head like a child rousing from sleep, looked up into Rans's face, and realized he was unchained and that fox hounds were calling, and with a mighty bound that took him over the baby's head and half across the kitchen was gone out into the darkness.

He never noticed Milly running after him and crying, "Come back, Del, oh come back, Del."

In a moment his unformed, puppy's hunting cry was mingling with the others racing toward Sourvine's call, but Milly turning from the door was crying now to Rans, "Don't let him go. Please don't let him go."

And Rans laughed at Milly, "Hell, he's a fox hound. I tell you, you're all skeered to death he'll git King Devil."

Nunn and Rans and Lee Roy hurried outside, and Milly went back to the dishwashing. "He was a pretty pup," she said, "jist fer th world like Zing."

And Lucy asked, "Ain't he comen back, Mom?"

"I wouldn't lay money on it."

"Is it King Devil he's a chasen?"

"I recken so," she stared down into the dishwater remembering: big as a half-grown calf he had looked, his whole body red and glowing somehow like hickory embers; his eyes had been green fire when they looked at her; he had picked up John Whittaker's fat dominecker hen and vanished; he hadn't seemed to run or walk, just vanished like a proud red ghost; she'd known it was King Devil; many had seen him, but never his sign, and now it would be about like him to run on a windy witchery moonlight night like this.

Suse had stopped with a dish half dried and was studying her mother sharply, "You act like you knowed somethen, Mom."

And Milly took her hand from the dishwater and pushed her hair back with her wrist and tried hard to look like a woman who'd just been talking.

Outside, Nunn and Rans hurried up the hill toward the Pilot Rock, but stopped on the scrub pine hillside above the garden when the race crossed to Nunn's side of the creek and swung down the valley, going high into the hillsides, but still working down the creek course toward the river. Zing had reached Sourvine in time to unravel the scent, and as always he was a little in the lead with Sourvine right at his heels. Del came next, and Speed, who had got a late start, behind Del but gaining; strung out along behind were the four Keith hounds, all giving tongue as if the fox were right under their noses.

Rans was almost jumping up and down with delight at the performance of his pup—wind, nose, and tongue; he seemed to have them all; and Nunn had to admit that so far he was going good or better than Zing at his age.

Jaw Buster when he came with the others seemed to hold no ill feeling toward Rans for having bought the pup he wanted, but praised Del and said he would some day be a better hound than Zing. Rans tried to dicker with him, started with an asking price of thirty dollars, a bargain at that he said, and did not mention it was twice the price he had paid two days before. But Jaw Buster, who didn't like to talk about anything when a good race was on, never paid him much mind.

Blare Keith lowed[4] it was a gray fox Sourvine had surprised, and that in a little while they'd hole him or catch him even; he was going so fast, too hard pressed to take time out to backtrack or try in any way to throw the hounds off the scent.

But Lister thought he was a young, swift, red fox, out for a little fun, running for the joy of running; when he'd had enough he'd run back to the creek or onto a ridge where not even Zing could follow through the dry blowing leaves.

Nunn said nothing; the race was swift, but Zing wasn't close to the fox, or hadn't been when he last heard him. In the few minutes since the beginning of the race, the hounds had circled the hillside above his house, then above Rans's, turned high on the shoulder of Pilot Rock Hill above the mouth of the creek, and were now behind the Pilot Rock where they could not be heard.

Rans, who had hunted but little and then mostly when he was drunk, wanted to go up to the Pilot Rock where he could hear what was happening on the other side, but Lister argued that if it was a young strong red fox he'd be mighty apt to swing back this way; there was a gap in the ridge above Old John's place where there were no bluffs and pine woods all around so that the older hounds at least could hold the scent on the high ground, dry and windy as it was.

Minutes later Zing's voice came singing above the wind like a bugle as he raced hard down through John's pine woods. "Jesus God, they're a maken good time," Blare Keith said, and Rans said, "Be quiet," and strained on tip toe, mouth open, listening hard.

Sourvine's music and Speed's coarse wild bay came down through the moonlight, and an instant later Del's excited, happy yip. Blare slapped Rans on the back so hard he staggered, "He's gonna be a real hound, runnen like a fool," he cried.

And Rans shaking his shoulder after the slap said, "Gonna be, Hell, he is one. He'll have King Devil come Christmas."

Nunn smiled, "I been a gitten King Devil come Christmas ever year fer goen on six years."

Zing gave tongue again, no longer coming down the hill but swinging around, so high and close under the bluffs that he sounded far away instead of almost straight above. In spite of its faintness, Nunn thought he caught a kind of shrillness, a tinny sound that would come into Zing's voice when he got excited; he wasn't bad excited; the scent wasn't stinging his nose; he didn't give the broken almost breathless kind of call that told he was gathering himself for a kill. It was the scent itself that excited him. There was only one scent that would excite Zing.

Jaw Buster listened to his Speed, then shook his head slowly as if perplexed.

"God, that's a red fox, a youngen runnen like th wind," Blare said.

"Skeered," Rans said.

Lister smiled at Rans's ignorance, but was silent listening to his Sourvine, faint now like a ghost hound.

There was a little space of silence; the hounds were high up, running under the steep bluff on Nunn's side of the Pilot Rock. "Aimen to run around high, an not swing down toward th river," Rans said with some relief. The swift uphill climbing was bad for his untrained Del.

Jaw Buster took a sack of tobacco from his pocket, and pushed one big finger into its mouth for opening. Zing gave tongue close to the dead black gum that marked the upper corner of Nunn's land on the shoulder of Pilot Rock Hill. The hill led in an almost unbroken but ever steepening curve down to the river bluff. Speed was heard from next, then Sourvine and Del almost together, "Comen down," Nunn said, and bit off a chew of tobacco.

"Jesus God," Lister whispered, when his Sourvine with the others sounded half way down the hill, and added still in a whisper, "That bluff's a hundred feet high."

Jaw Buster was rigidly still, listening, his finger forgotten in the tobacco sack.

Lister said, "Lord, Lord," in a praying, not a cursing kind of tone when the four hounds bayed all at once, almost in a huddle they sounded, three fourths of the way down the hill.

With an abrupt jerky movement, Jaw Buster grabbed his horn from his belt and blew in a wild tuneless frenzy.

Rans whirled in surprise and began, "What th Hell, what—," but stopped when Lister began blowing as if through much sound he might escape death and destruction.

Blare Keith who only now understood what was happening began screaming at Rans, "Blow your horn, man; fer Christ's sake, blow that horn."

Nunn alone was calm, arms hanging straight by his sides as he stared through the moonlight, straining to understand the hounds. Old Speed, the coarse-mouthed one, sounded like a panther gone hoarse with howling at the moon. Even Sourvine, the sweetest singing hound in the country, broke the regular rhythm of his baying to bark in an excited, yipping, snarling way like he'd lost the scent.

The horns quieted, and Jaw Buster, sweat glistening on his forehead in the moonlight, started running toward the hounds but was brought up sharp by a steep walled gully that lay like a bottomless river in the black moon shadow. He cursed the gully once, then stopped and came to his senses for he heard Speed, plainly still well above the river bluff.

Lister's horn had quieted, too, but Blare and Joe C. were still urging Rans to blow his horn, and Rans stood puzzled, holding his horn as if it were some strange tool, the use of which he did not know.

Nunn in exasperation said, "Fer God's sake, everbody be quiet—I want to listen."

Zing bayed, a cautious old man's calling, still well up on the hillside, then Rans was jumping up and down and yelling, "Del's ahead a Zing. Del's ahead a Zing. They ain't lost th scent."

It was a happy, proud, gay Del, excited at leading them all on a hot fox trail, the scent suddenly so strong he laughed and cried that he would have the fox, low down he was, almost to the bluff edge, a hundred feet or more ahead of Zing.

"Man Oh Man," Rans cried, understanding nothing but that his hound was ahead, "Man oh Man, he's a leaden em all. What'll you give me fer him now, Jaw Buster? At thirty dollars he's a bargain."

Jaw Buster sighed a long, heavy sigh like a man bad disappointed but said nothing, and Nunn said to them all, "Be still."

Del gave tongue again, his puppy's cry was rising, carrying on into the promise of a full-grown hound's hunting call. Suddenly he was silent, and Zing near the bluff edge now was howling.

"What th Hell," Rans said, "Has—"

"Be still," Nunn said again, and listened hard.

Speed was calm again and baying, but Sourvine yipped and howled, and like Zing they were moving slowly and with caution. A gust of wind beat up the valley roaring in the pines and drowning all sound, but the hunters continued to stare through the ghostly dancing moon shadows as if through much staring they might hear. But no sound came but the wind sound, and after awhile Nunn turned away and looked at Rans. Jaw Buster and Lister and the Keiths looked at him, too. And Nunn said, "Well—."

"King Devil has shore done a pretty piece a business this night," Lister said.

"King Devil." Rans's eyes were like quartz pebbles in the moonlight. "You all knowed—why in th Hell didn't you say somethen."

"That's no way to talk," Nunn said in a low flat voice. "That pup had no business a runnen no how; an Zing, he never told me right away."

"To tell th truth, I wasn't certain till he headed fer th river bluff," Lister said.

"An once that pup was on King Devil's scent, you couldn't a called a him back no how, not with Gabriel's horn," Blare said.

Jaw Buster finished the opening of his tobacco sack, but stopped in the mid-rolling of a cigarette when Zing gave tongue again, his voice calm now but fainter as he rounded the curving river bluff.

"Zing an them others is all right," Nunn said reassuringly. "I figgered that if them three old uns had no better sense, why let em go to glory."

Jaw Buster shook his head, "I wasn't so certain," he said, and a note of sorrowful remembering crept into his voice, "He swung around high on a ridge exactly that away when he led my little Nannie Belle—an she was plenty smart—over Kelly's point—I'll allus recollect th way she looked, bloody souse meat like on them rocks below—like Del is now, I recken."

"Like Del," Rans said, forgetting even to curse.

Nunn grunted, "My God, man, didn't you hear th race?"

Blare spat out his chew of tobacco and squatted on his heels, the better to explain to the still unbelieving but open-mouthed Rans, "King Devil he's jist trotted along a taken his time down that steep hill. He walked clean to th bluff edge, a taken little short steps to make th scent strong, an most like right on th edge he's set down an reached over an patted th under side with his paws; then he turned sharp an walked on th very edge, so close that mostly th wind was a holden him up."

Nunn glanced at the moon, not an hour old in the sky. "We might as well go help hunt Del; King Devil's had his fun tonight an's headed now, I'd say, fer th Brush Creek country; he'll either lose his scent in th creek or on th ridges."

"Clean on yon side a th moon by now most like," Joe C. said.

Rans cursed the pup, "Fifteen dollars gone to glory," he said.

Jaw Buster sighed as they started down the hill, "I aimed to give you thirty an still he would a been a bargain; he was a pretty pup."

The Hunter

"The Hunter" appeared in *The Atlantic Monthly* 174 (November 1944): 79–84. Signed "H. Arnow," the story derived from Arnow's novel *Hunter's Horn*.

An editorial note explained, "H. Arnow is the pen name of a husband-and-wife collaboration, Harold and Harriette Arnow, who have their being as subsistence farmers in the Cumberland National Forest. 'We raise most of our food,' they write, 'sell a few cattle each year, sell a little timber now and then, sell a little coal—and sometimes when there is any time left over, we write.' This is their first story in the *Atlantic*."

⸺◦◦◦⸺

1.

Hour after hour the hounds, with Nunn Ballou's Zing in the lead, swung up and around Little Indian Creek over the strong hot trail that only King Devil could lay down. The men squatted in tense silence about a burned-out fire that nobody bothered to replenish—not even old Richmond, whose rheumatic bones ached in the cold. It was uncommon for the big red fox to run a straight race with no tricks and no foolery for so long. Maybe Zing was pressing him so hard he couldn't backtrack; for not once in the hours of the long running had the old dog boggled or fumbled or given anything except the angry but happy war cry he always gave when hot on the scent of King Devil.

All the men in the county were there, and others besides: Charlie Chitwood from the Gourd Neck in Wayne with one old worn-out hound that looked to be half cur, and Luther Crabtree from the other side of Cooper Creek with his two fine spotted July hounds, and Ernest Coffee who had come to the end of the gravel[1] in an almost new car with two hounds that he'd made his brags about before the race began, for he had paid one hundred dollars of coal-mining money for them last spring. But for hours now Ernest had said no more than Chitwood. His hounds were back somewhere with the others while Zing with Lister's Sourvine, a young hound with a deep wild voice like a cur dog baying at the moon, took the lead and held it.

Nunn squatted apart from the others with his back to a little pine tree and listened with that wild pounding hope in his heart that always came when King Devil ran—maybe this time Zing would catch him, and it would be the end. Zing gave tongue again, his bell-like cry rising up from near the head of Little Indian Creek and echoing and re-echoing out of the cliffs. Nunn could feel the anger and the eagerness in the call. King Devil would be close; Zing never gave tongue like that except when the scent was clear and hot. King Devil was an animal, flesh and blood and bone like Zing; press him hard enough and he could take no time for the devilish traps of back tracks and jumps and water runs he laid that would hold Zing up for minutes together while the red devil fox sat resting and laughing as he listened.

Zing's voice and Sourvine's voice grew fainter and fainter until they seemed no more than a note of the fitful December night wind that sometimes whistled and cried through the valleys below while it roared in the big timber of the higher hills or again sank into the faintest whispering in the stunted pines on the Pilot Rock. After a little space Nunn knew it was only the wind he heard. King Devil had taken the hard steep road up Caney Fork that ran west from Little Indian Creek, and Zing in the narrow gulch of Caney Fork could not be heard.

He heard the other hounds come up the creek, but they were the stragglers and did not count. He did not bother to unravel the tangle of sound and learn whose hounds were still in the race and whose had slunk home or gone possum hunting, but looked overhead at the sky, ragged with patches of stars and of cloud. The Big Dipper lay low in the northwest now, and when Zing first got scent of King Devil it had been well up in the sky, and now the bottommost stars of it would fall behind the hills before the race would end.

So many nights like this, going on six years now, since Zing first got scent of the big red fox and Nunn had made his brags about how soon he would have his hide. Night after night he had listened to Zing and watched the Big Dipper and the Little Dipper and the evening stars go down, and the morning stars rise and brighten and pale in the sky, and stared at the unblinking, unmoving North Star until he knew the patterns of the stars, at all hours of the night and in all seasons, as well as he knew the old fields and boundaries of his own land. Maybe this would be the last night. He was tired of the stars and the wind and the sitting in the dark—but the thought was old and familiar as the stars, and he got up and moved into the cluster of men.

"Don't be a-walken in your sleep an' a-fallen off, man," old Richmond warned.

"I know this cliff better'n my own bed," Nunn answered shortly.

Charlie Chitwood and Ernest Coffee were talking of going home. Charlie good-naturedly allowed his old Bogle had swum the Cumberland and was sound asleep at home in the kitchen and Rooshie would be up waiting for him with the poker and her quilting frames, for whenever he got drunk Bogle always went on home, but this was one night he was cold sober and away from Bogle. Ernest was plainly worried over his hundred-dollar dogs and wondered if they could be lost, though Lister told him he'd heard them start that car for going back to town. Richmond in some exasperation told them to go home or else shut up so a man could listen; he wanted to hear Zing come in.

But Nunn as always heard him first; to the other listeners it was only another noise of the wind, but Nunn knew and bowed his head and shut his eyes for better hearing. King Devil had skirted the sloping side of the ridge where the running was hard in the rocky sidehill ground, an old field grown thick with saw briars and sumac bush, and Zing's voice came faintly—too faintly for Nunn to understand much of what he said.

Maybe he was close—one leap, two leaps. The running through the briars and brush would be harder for the big, long-haired fox than for Zing. Maybe there, on Casseye Ridge, Zing would get him, now, this night, this very minute. He gripped his hands angrily, impatiently, as if he would tear away and destroy all the sounds between him and Zing's voice out there in the darkness: Lister's hoarse, excited breathing, the thin whisper of the wind, the river over the shoals, and far away a train blowing for a bridge across the Cumberland.

He stood so for a long while straining his ears, but when he heard Zing give tongue again he was on Kelly's Point at the end of Casseye Ridge, too far away and smothered by trees and rocks and wind to hear what he said—whether the scent lay hot like a fire in his nose or if King Devil was slipping ahead and the scent growing cold.

He squatted again and heard Lister cut a fresh chew of tobacco and old Richmond stomp his feet against the cold and Charlie resume one of his endless lying tales about how many cross ties he had cut down and hewn in one day. Nunn gave little heed to what went on about him, his ears remembering Zing's last call, and his mind working it over, trying to read it like writing half washed away by rain.

He and Lister sprang suddenly to their feet and stood listening, breath hushed, teeth clamped tight on tobacco, but Charlie was telling a ghost tale and noticed nothing, and by the time Lister had shut him up with a whispered curse, a gust of wind thundered up the valley and they could hear nothing more.

But Nunn squatted again, satisfied, smiling softly to himself in the dark. "Zing's a-pressen him hard tonight," he explained to Richmond, who couldn't hear so well. "They're a-comen straight down the ridge, a-taken that ole loggen road. An' when King Devil runs a road, he's in a hurry."

"They'll be a-comen down Richmond's road in full hearen pretty soon," Lister whispered excitedly. "I heared Sourvine not much behind Zing. An' man, oh man, they're a-pressen him hard."

2.

Even Charlie was silent now and listened with the others for the hounds to top the ridge. Nunn watched a little patch of ragged cloud come up behind the Gourd Neck, move on above Ann Liz's house on the hill above the river—watched it creep across one end of the Big Dipper and wondered if it would cover the North Star and how long it would take.

The North Star dimmed with the first touch of it, and the deep wild bay of a coarse-mouthed hound broke over the ridge crest across the valley, loud and clear as if it had been right on the rock. Nunn sprang to his feet and stood open-mouthed staring through the darkness toward the sound, and Chitwood called out: "Say, ain't that Sourvine? An' Nunn allus sayen that ole Zing can outrun any dog in the country. Where's Zing now?"

Nunn turned slowly, stiffly, suddenly tired with all the heat of the race gone from his body. "Zing, he's dead, you fool."

"Aw, Nunn," Lister comforted, not even listening to his Sourvine, who was giving tongue again. "Mebbe he jist hurt hisself; mebbe he got sick. Listen, mebbe we'll hear him."

"There ain't no rattlesnakes now, an' nothen could hurt him comen down a straight loggen road," Nunn spoke over his shoulder, for he was already moving through the darkness toward the first jump over the ledge that led to the path down the Pilot Rock. "I tell ye, man, he's dead. Ain't him an' Sourvine been runnen together for goen on three years, an' didn't they allus keep together with Zing allus a little in the lead?"

"But mebbe Sourvine got uncommon fast tonight." Lister came following behind, his talk loud but with no heartiness or belief in it.

Old Richmond was yelling for them to wait until they got a carbide lamp fixed; they'd break their fool necks in the dark. If a body did happen to miss the path by a foot on either side he would land on rocks a hundred feet below. But Nunn crammed his old felt hat into his pocket and sprang down with no more need of a light than King Devil himself. Lister and Ernest Coffee were at his heels and together they went down to the bottom of the valley, crossed the creek, and took the short cut through the woods to the ridge top where Nunn had last heard Zing. They walked swiftly, soundlessly, never groping or stumbling, though under the great hemlocks in the valley a man could not see his hands before his face. On top of the ridge along the road, the gloom was not so deep, but Nunn waited there and called back for the men with lights to come on.

"The last time I heared him he was jist about here," he explained. "An' then we heared Sourvine yon side of the schoolhouse, so I figger he's 'tween here an' yonder."

Charlie Chitwood and old Richmond turned their lamps on full blast and followed Nunn, but in the unaccustomed glare the night woods were unfamiliar to him and he kept stumbling and grasping at shadows, hurrying from first one side of the road to the other, only to find the bit of brownness he had thought was Zing a sandstone or a heap of water-soaked leaves or nothing at all.

It was Lister who found him lying in the middle of the old logging road. He lay on his side with his paws outspread as he lay at home by the hearth fire, and his mouth was open wide the way he opened it when he laughed with the children, but his wide-open eyes remained fixed and unwinking in the blue carbide light.

The men came up in silence and in silence squatted about him in a little circle and looked at him. "Funny," Lister said after a time. "He seemed well as could be, frisken around like a cur pup 'fore the race started."

"He was," Nunn said.

Chitwood glanced uneasily into the wall of darkness past the carbide light. "What killed him, then? A hound don't up an' die; an' nobody'ud pizen a hound."

"That danged fox run him to death," Nunn said. "I thought all the time Zing was a-pressen him so hard he couldn't take time for any of his devilish tricks, an' him with this head set all the time on runnen Zing to death. He knowed he was old."

Old Richmond, the farmer, shook his head and sighed: "Aye, he's a fox like any other fox; smarter than most, but not smart like a man."

"Whyn't ye kill him, then, Richmond, if you're smarter'n he is?" Chitwood asked. "An' he's all the time stealen your young lambs and chickens."

"Ain't I tried? Traps, hunten, watchen. Last spring that red devil carried off a lamb not a hundred feet from me, an' I never got a shot at him."

"Spotlight him with a carbide when he swings back this way like he's shore to do, an' ye'll get a shot at him," Ernest suggested, staring out into the darkness.

Lister glanced up at the stars. "Ye know, mebbe I'm crazy but lots a times I know he ain't a fox like other foxes. I recollect a tale my granmammy used to tell about a fox that changed itself into—" Somewhere in the woods a stick cracked. Lister jumped. For a moment all the men were silent. Then Lister suddenly, loudly asked: "How many times hev any of ye seen King Devil's sign, an' we been runnen him goen on six years?"

"Ye know nobody ain't never seen hit," Nunn answered shortly still gazing down at Zing. "But that ain't a-sayen he's a witch or some sinner's haint that cain't rest easy in his grave an' has to run over these hills. He's jist uncommon smart; he could be spotlighted same as a rabbit or a fish."

"He ain't no rabbit an' he ain't no fish," Charlie giggled. "But hit'd be right good pastime to see ye try. Ye're reckoned one of the best shots in the country, Nunn."

"Listen, man," Richmond spoke up eagerly as a boy. "If'n ye'll kill him this very night I'll give ye ten dollars. He'll kill five times that in lambs for me this comen spring."

3.

Nunn seemed not to have heard, and the others were silent while he stripped off his overall jumper and laid it over Zing. Lister looked down at the old dog and after a moment said with a little sigh: "He was the best foxhound, I reckon, that's ever been in these parts, an' 'thout him my Sourvine ain't worth a damn; he's the runnenest fool that ever was, but I allus knowed he used old Zing's nose. Now no hound'll ever unravel the scent and King Devil'll never be took."

Ernest took a chew of tobacco, then stopped with his mouth open, listening into the darkness. "He's still a-runnen. I hear Sourvine, an' I'm a-thinken of goen after my rifle an' gitten King Devil an' Richmond's money this very night. Reckon ye'd help me, Nunn."

Nunn rolled Zing into the jumper and buttoned it up. Charlie Chitwood tittered: "He ain't no man to be a-coveren up his face that-a-way."

"He was a danged sight more deserven of the name of man than many a one that walks on two legs," Nunn said. "He never lied to me or any man, nor swore, nor used his teeth on anything but a varmint I wanted him to kill. Many's the time I've seen him stand an' cry while the little young-ens, 'fore they's big enough to walk, ud pull his tongue—an' he never got drunk an' he never made his brags about how quick he'd ketch that red devil of a fox like I've done, an' anyhow hit's none of yer damned business if'n I lay ten-dollar gold pieces on his eyes an' bury him in a walnut coffin lined with wool and wrapped in silk."

"Aw, Nunn, nobody wants ye to leave him here for the buzzards. I'll help ye carry him home," Lister offered. "Ye're fergitten, I reckon, how ye helped me dig a grave for my little Bonnie that night she died a-chasen King Devil an' got bit by a rattlesnake I reckon hit was."

"I'll help, too, soon's I git my rifle out of the car," Ernest offered. "Reckon ye'd help me kill that fox, Nunn; I'll split the money with ye."

"Do ye honestly think a body could kill him by shooten?" Charlie Chitwood asked in a low, surprised voice.

"Mebbe he's jist part fox an' has got claws like a wildcat an' can climb a rocky bluff to his hole," somebody said, only half jokingly.

"Did ye ever think that mebbe—mebbe the scent stops an' somethen else a hound dog won't foller—or nothen a-tall begins?" Charlie asked, glancing uneasily at Ernest.

"Good Lord, but ye talk pure idjet," Nunn said, rising disgustedly to his feet. "Someday, sometime, somebody'll come along with a hound that'll press him so hard he cain't jump a bluff into the Cumberland or do whatever hit is he does do when he gits tired a-runnen. . . . Listen. Reckon Sourvin's chasen a haint; for all ye know, he's after Bill Weaver's haint back from hell an' a-tryen to find some liquor."

Old Richmond listened to the lone hound a moment, then shook his head reproachfully at Nunn. "When ye're as old as I am, man, ye won't be a-talken so easy an' off-like about hell an' them that's dead an' cain't help theirselves."

Nunn said nothin to the old man's reproach but continued to listen to Sourvine. "They're over in the Simp Jones Holler now, an' 'll be swingen back this-a-way 'fore mornen. I'd lay good money on hit; an' Charlie here can take his carbide an' find out if'n hit's a haint Sourvine's a-chasen."

"Not me," Chitwood spoke quick as lightning.

"Nunn," Richmond spoke with urgent earnestness. "Whyn't ye git a gun an' wait by the road an' help Ernest kill him? It ud be worth money to ever' farmer in the country to be rid of that red fox, an' you're about the best shot around."

Nunn shook his head. "I couldn't do it, old man. I've hunted him too long with a hound to spotlight him like he was no better'n a Jap or a rabbit."

"Aw, come on, Nunn, help me kill him. Look at the hounds he's killed. No hound'll ever git him," Ernest begged. "I'm afraid of bad luck by myself."

Lister turned wearily away from listening to his Sourvine. "Aw, go on, Nunn, spotlight him. Without Zing, we'll never git him."

Nunn felt the eyes of all the men upon him, but without answering he glanced overhead at the stars. About three o'clock it must be, and he was tired. Tomorrow while he walked miles rounding up his sheep and salting them, his usual Sunday job, he would be tired with his body crying for sleep, and he was tired of being sleepy, and tired of always hoping, and tired of remembering the brags he had made six years ago. He didn't even have a hound now, and no good pup in sight, and no money to buy one. He cleared his throat, but for a moment the words would not come, and when they did he spoke them to the stars: "Well, I'd try—but I'm not a-wanten to walk four miles home an' back for a gun."

"Ye're welcome to mine. A better shooten gun was never made, an' since we're jist a little piece from my place, I'll go git it into the bargain," Lister offered.

Nunn shook his head as if flies buzzed about his ears, and said nothing.

Chitwood shivered: "Hit could be that that fox could tear a man's throat, or make a gun shoot backwards."

Nunn's voice rose angrily. "Fool. He's flesh an' blood like any other fox. Give me that carbide an' a rifle, an' I'll kill him, spotlight an' bust him right between the eyes, jist as easy as killen a frog. He ain't Bill Weaver's ghost an' he ain't no haint, but I wish to the Lord I had a drink."

Chitwood pulled a pint Mason jar out of his overall bib. "I been a-saven this to git me back over the river, but ye're welcome. Hit's soghum whiskey, awful-tasten, but hit's got plenty of burn."

Nunn glanced at it, hardly more than a third full, but enough to warm a man's heart. He swallowed it all without taking his lips from the jar, while the others watched half jealously, half disapprovingly. "Don't go getten on one of your roaren sprees," old Richmond warned. "I'm getten old an' not used to sich."

"That wasn't enough to hurt a baby," Nunn answered and walked a few steps away and squatted with his back to a tree and waited for Lister and Ernest to come with the guns. He heard Sourvine give tongue—tired and worried he sounded—up toward the mouth of Brush Creek. King Devil was having his fun tonight letting that fool hound think he could catch him.

The Big Dipper turned lower toward the west, the wind died, and when Ernest and Lister came back frost was beginning to glitter on the withered leaves. No one talked of building a fire, for King Devil might see it. The men moved quietly about, stamping against the cold and talking in low voices like men at a funeral. Nunn continued to sit apart, looking sometimes at the stars, and now and again sighting down the barrel of Lister's rifle. It had a big buck sight, fine for hunting; shooting King Devil as he ran confused and befuddled into a sudden flash of blinding carbide light would be easy.

He heard Sourine loud and clear rounding the head of Nealy's Creek. King Devil had doubled and was on his way back. Nunn could not sit still but got up clutching the rifle in sweaty hands. Tonight he would make an end of that red-tailed witch, and then he, Nunnally Ballou, could be a man again, working his land and raising his family, instead of a piece of poor white trash getting drunk under the stars and cursing the coming of daylight because every bone in his body ached for sleep. Forget his loud brags and all the fine things he had said yonder so long ago when Zing first got scent of King Devil. He'd thought then it was a red fox he had to catch, not a red devil.

4.

Ernest touched him on the elbow and he jumped as from the touch of a ghost and swore for no reason at all. "How ye aimen to do hit, Nunn?" Ernest asked, too excited to notice that Nunn had called him a dirty name.

"Right between the eyes, God willen."

"I mean where ye a-goen to wait an' where'd I better stand? He's a-comen on fast."

Nunn considered a moment, and then without answering moved away through the darkness to the knot of men about the carbide lights who had long since left off their ghost tales and stood tense and silent listening, whispering when they talked at all. Nunn whispered too. King Devil could not have heard, but whispers went well with his tongue, for it lay dry and numb in his mouth, and he kept trying to work up a stream of tobacco juice and could not. He commanded them to fill the lamps with fresh carbide and more water, then directed Chitwood to give Ernest his lamp, while he took Richmond's for himself, miner's cap and all. He then had all lights put out, and with the others following, he went down the old logging road. Now and then he called to them in whispered curses to be silent, for Chitwood and the others, without lights, sounded like a herd of cattle crashing through the brush.

Sourvine gave tongue again, no farther away than the upper end of the ridge, and Nunn hurried, almost running toward what he was hunting for and found soon with no groping: a great moss-grown pine trunk, uprooted in some unremembered storm, thick enough so that a man on his knees could be hidden from anything on the other side.

In a high whisper he told Ernest to come on and get behind the log with him. He heard Sourvine again, no more than two miles away it seemed, straight up the ridge and already turned into the old logging road, and he cursed the hound in whispers for his noise. King Devil might come at any minute now, and if he was made of blood and bone like any other animal, he would, no matter how soundless his coming, make a noise that Nunn could hear.

He fumbled for a match and it seemed hours that his sweaty hands were fumbling to light it. The big brass inlaid buttons on his jumper, so good for striking matches, were with the jumper and Zing, and his belt buckle was too smooth. He grabbed Ernest and scratched the match on one of his jumper buttons, and it went out as he struck it.

"That's bad luck," Ernest whispered, staring down at the glowing but flameless match.

"Granny woman," Nunn said and struck another match, and lighted his lamp and Ernest's and listened for King Devil's coming. Faint it would be, like the Cumberland whispering on a rising tide or the noise of a copperhead coiling, but it would be a sound that he could hear.

They held their lights low behind the log, the flames so small they barely lived, and shielded by their hands and arms. "I'll give ye the first three shots," Nunn whispered, and his words sounded loud as Richmond's radio when the batteries were new, "an' if they stop him, Richmond's ten dollars is your'n. Me, I ain't a-wanten the money. An' lift your head an' shine the light when I say ready."

The carbide light in his miner's cap, encircled by his lifted arms, made a little world of brightness behind the log, and Nunn stared into it, listening. His stomach no longer lay heavy and dead like a cold anvil under his ribs, and he felt curiously lighthearted and happy. It would soon be over; King Devil would be dead and he could sleep easy in his bed like other men, not out staring at the stars, or sitting under a rock house for shelter from a cold, drizzly rain and listening, always listening and hoping and thinking.

Not twenty yards away a dry leaf rattled faintly, and Nunn whispered, "Ready," to Ernest, and both men turned their heads toward the sound and lifted their heads, turning their lights on full blast.

Nunn saw the green fire of two eyes—big as a man's eyes they looked to be, and somehow like a man's eyes they were, too. The eyes were looking past him, coming straight on, not turning away or blinking; blinded and scared, they seemed no more than a man's eyes in the lights. Ernest's bullets sang and he heard the pop-pop of Ernest's rifle; above him in the woods men were screaming: "Shoot, Nunn, you fool, shoot. Ernest ain't a-stoppen him. Shoot, dang hit, shoot."

He heard old Richmond's curses, and his mind, somehow loose and unhung like a feather floating from a striking hawk, thought that the old man ought to be turned out of church for such black talk, but mostly he thought that here was King Devil point-blank at the end of a loaded rifle and his eyes didn't look the way he had thought they would look; it wasn't a bit like shooting a rabbit or a skunk. Back when he'd worked in the company mines a coal car had broken loose from the engine and run backwards; he'd heard the man scream somewhere in the dark and he had gone with his miner's cap on his head like this and spotlighted the man's eyes—wide-open they were and they had looked like this for just a second and then they were not man's eyes, just something glittering like glass or ice or a bit of jack.

He automatically turned his head, keeping the oncoming eyes full in the glare of the light, expecting them to swerve aside or stop suddenly like a rabbit's eyes under the spotlight, and all the while he could hear the men behind him yelling and cursing him with black bitter oaths and Ernest's bullets still singing and the pops of the rifle that seemed minutes apart instead of seconds.

The popping stopped and Ernest was yelling: "If'n ye ain't gonna shoot, gimme that gun. This-un's empty."

Mechanically, like a man in his sleep, he rolled the gun over his forearm and handed it to Ernest, but even as he did so the eyes disappeared, like stars swallowed in a cloud. "He's jumped over the ridge or run behind a tree," Ernest yelled, and sprang over the log and ran toward the ridge side.

"Hey, ye'll break yer fool neck. They's a bluff there," Richmond called to Ernest, and his voice sounded old and tired and disgusted. "Ye cain't find him anyhow. Whyn't ye kill him, Nunn?"

Nunn sat motionless on a pine log, staring off into the darkness. "I wisht I had a drink," he said.

"Ye've had drink enough," Richmond told him. "Ye'd better be getten back to yer wife an' youngens."

"That little swaller's dead in me already," he answered and added softly, "Don't be getten mad at me, old man, an' don't be tellen me what to do. Nobody can tell me what to do. The good Lord in Heaven cain't tell me what to do, but I can tell ye what I'll do. I'll ketch that big red fox for ye, ketch him fair an' true with a foxhound. Hit went against my grain to shoot him—somehow—"

He got up and shook his fist over the ridge side. "I hope the good Lord in Heaven sends me to brile in hell for a million years if I ever stop chasen that fox 'fore I git him. I'll git him, if'n I have to sell ever' last thing I got to buy me a hound, an' sell ever' last chick to feed him. I'll chase him till I'm crippled an' blind an' bald an'—an'—"

Richmond turned away more in sorrow than anger. "Puts me in mind of the time his grandad got the call to preach. We was cutten pine logs to saw up for to build a side room on his house, an' that side room never got built till his oldest boy got up big enough to drive nails."

The Un-American Activities of Miss Prink

Marcella Arnow wrote on the untitled manuscript that she created this title for copyright reasons after her mother's death.

Probably written in Ann Arbor, Michigan, where the author lived from 1950 until her death in 1986, the story remains a working draft with blank spaces where some characters' names were to be added.

In a 1962 letter to Michigan activist Jo Goman, Arnow deplores the eroded civil liberties in this country. Her letters in the '60s indicate that she was an American Civil Liberties Union member who voted enthusiastically for Eugene McCarthy for President in 1968, and who deplored the actions of Senator Joseph McCarthy.

---

*D*id he mean everybody?

The voice had spoken out of turn, no lifted hand above it. Still, she nodded, smiling, seeing past it as she always did, the red dust of Virginia stirred by a breath of warm wind, the people crowding by the jail window, looking upward, listening, some frowning in disapproval, as Patrick McSnarty frowned now, others eager, drinking it in, believing, trying hard but not succeeding like those of the sober eyes.

"Yes, for every one—. . . [1]—For some of religious thought—you see, even then in Virginia when Washington was young—preachers of many sects such as we have today—Unitarian and Baptist—were jailed for preaching, but preached from the jail house gratings—Patrick Henry—and just as this pilgrim left England for religious freedom, so did many push west from over the Wilderness Road—and now I wonder."

Several hands waved among the class of forty-seven, and she turned toward the map—eager—thinking a little of all the other times—fifty at least for she had developed this unit in social studies must be twenty-five years ago—and twice a year in social studies with the 8B that until the war—and the children came in shifts—and kept coming in shifts in this factory workers' neighborhood.

And now the Wilderness Road[2] seemed fresher than ever, the children more eager—there were since the war more Southerners—hill children who had known and seen the white water and the smell of azaleas in bloom—and . . .

"Dey hadda go dis way on—dey couldn't get truda mountains no place . . ."

Fingers were snapping behind her and she turned to face the marble-like eyes, the smiling Jerry McSnarty, "Bud teacher, would Patrick Henry—would he ha stood still fuda Reds?"

"Reds."

He smiled at her. "Sure, yu know—du Communists like—yu know . . ." And his pleased glance went with no searching to Benton Skyros, two aisles over, six seats in front.

She looked into the blue eyes, but felt the black eyes on her face—thirsty—drinking from her as men drank from Patrick Henry—from preachers holding services through the jailhouse windows. "Communists," she said at last. "There were no communists then."

"Sure—sure, I know, but Patrick Henry, he u let um tell?"

"He wouldn't have agreed with them," she went on, conscious that even Junie Mae Branchcomb was still, her gum still, everybody still—as if they were grown people who'd read the papers for the past two weeks—had read how [a man, the father of one of their classmates,] had been called along with days and days of others before the unAmerican activities investigating committee. He had been called because an ex-cook had infiltrated and seen him at meetings in 1946—his picture had been [published] yesterday—a tired-looking man with somber eyes and he had said, "I refuse to testify on the grounds of self-incrimination."

Yesterday at lunch when the teachers ate their home-packed lunches in the sewing room, they had discussed it, remembering his children. Some like young Mrs. [Stanhope] had been critical. "Why didn't he tell the truth like a man," she had said, and now feeling the hungry eyes, Miss Prink was glad she had spoken out with a kind of authority that came partly from her years in the school and partly from a wide reading on such matters.

"Had he said he was not a Communist, they might have got him later for perjury—if he had admitted membership he would have had to testify against many others."

"Ugh," Miss Jameson had said. "Do you know in folk games none—not one—of the girls would dance with Jamie—it would have been all right—you know—the girls are often choosy but that horrible Junie May Branchcomb—nobody, of course, had chosen her—she grabbed him. 'It won't rub off,' she said. 'I ain't afeared.'" She sighed. "He looked so sick and pale."

"We must be kind to him in spite of . . ." Miss Prink had said with decision.

That was two days ago—the headlines had widened and blackened when yesterday a teacher from another school had been named by the ex-cook—and fired—nineteen years with no complaints and fired.

"But would Patrick Henry ha stood still an let them Commies tawk?"

"He wouldn't have agreed with them," she said, "but . . ." She drew a long breath—heard it—smiled to show she had not sighed into the silence—"but I don't think he would have been afraid to let them have their say. You see," she said, smiling now, "Patrick Henry had so much faith in our form of government—the government that was to be—that he wouldn't have minded the silly talk of a few Communists."

"Yu mean he would u wanted dem to tawk." The smile was unpleasant now.

"Oh, no—not wanted," she said. "But he wouldn't have been afraid."

The Wilderness Road was waiting and on this, the second day, she must always get Preacher Craig's company to the mountains where they had to leave their wagons for pack horses—and usually it was here she introduced Daniel Boone, the scout who had gone before.

Gradually thus the unit built around transportation would be complete—the Licking River went down from Boone's country close to Cincinnati—early water transportation—the German immigrants—the French —the trip this year promised well.

Once in the last war—a dark face with rotted teeth was waiting by her door. "Yu gotta cut out da 'Germans was good' stuff. I'm gonna git u FBI after you." And the face, lowering, sullen, turning away before she could explain, "always I try to teach here—it is so important here—that America owes her greatness to many nations and races—religions."

She had mentioned the matter to the former principal—. . . . old she was to weariness—working past her retirement because of the war. The principal had snapped, "Can't you remember the last war? The music teacher had to be careful—even 'Silent Night, Holy Night' was criticized . . ."

"And then remember it was no more war and leave the Germans—and speak well of the Russians because they were buying American-made machinery—creating jobs, as it were, for Americans in the Depression— just be careful."

Miss Prink had been glad—her special field of social studies was always centered on America—tried to remember troubles with the Germans in the first World War—but could not—and anyway, she'd been teaching straight history and geography then.

She never mentioned the matter of Patrick Henry to the new principal—he was young—so young—not an ex-teacher at all but a school administrator. She did think briefly of bringing it up at lunch—but. . . . forgot it until she reached the lunch room, a little late as always.

She couldn't remember her first awareness of their looking at her, silent, not eating, but she knew it was when she was unwrapping the Swiss cheese, domestic, on rye that young Mrs. Stanhope, Section B, third grade asked, "You knew her, didn't you?"

"Who?" she asked, unscrewing her thermos of Postum.[3]

"Mrs. Maki in Wheatley Elementary."

"Quite well," she said. "Wonderful teacher—she's developed a whole unit built around Father Gabriel . . ."

"Oh," said Mrs. Stanhope.

Miss Prink paused, the red cup of hot Postum halfway to her mouth, they—the five of them who brought their lunches—were staring at her so.

Miss [Bilky] in English—she'd looked at her that way before; no, it was the McSnarty boy on the Wilderness Road. Miss Duffy was asking, "Haven't you seen anything? *The Morning Bugle* or even last night's *Post.* It said she would be called."

"Called?"

Miss Pumphrey glanced at the door, fished down into her lap, then carefully flattening it, laid the front page of a Detroit paper on the table. "The children shouldn't know we're taking too much interest."

"Why?" Miss Prink asked, and then as Mrs. Shipley spun the paper round for her to see, she was still, the Postum in one hand, the lines in her forehead sharpening for the lines at the top were so big and so black each seemed more an exclamation than a letter spelling out the words, "REDS INFILTRATE PUBLIC SCHOOLS."

Under it, blown up and distorted, smooth, pretty, simpering was Mrs. Maki's picture, and by it were more black letters.

"It can't be true. She's such a good teacher," Miss Prink said, setting the Postum down at last, bending over the paper.

"Was, you mean," Miss Bilky said. "Of course, she'll be fired."

"But," Miss Prink said, "she must have taught at least twenty years—I taught her social studies, history it was then—must . . ."

"I wouldn't try to remember," Miss Payne said, looking at her too sharply.

"The Teachers' Association won't stand for it. I'm sure she's signed her loyalty pledge like—all the rest of us."

"But—well—commies sign pledges quicker than anybody—that is, they say after the pledges are signed," Miss [Bilky] said, and looked hard at her paper napkin tablecloth.

"But that girl can't be a—well, communist," Miss Prink said.

"She's attended proscribed meetings and she won't talk—that's enough to prove she's subversive."

"But they weren't proscribed when she attended. She told me once of marching in a protest parade—she was badly worried but she marched anyway."

"Oh," Miss O'Toole said, looking more interested. "What parade?"

"Something—two or three years ago. A young Negro boy was clubbed to death by police, you know."

"I wouldn't," Miss O'Toole said, reaching for the [paper].

"Mrs. Maki," Miss Prink went on, "took a lot of interest in bettering race relations and . . ."

"She would have done better," Mrs. Thompson said, finding Miss Prink's glance, fastening on it eagerly as if she had been searching a long while, "to have spent her time in going to church learning how to treat her fellow man instead of just treating him. Let's change the subject; it's only one teacher in all the thousands of us. No need to get excited."

"Who's excited?" Miss O'Toole said. "But it isn't just one," she added. "The paper says at least two hundred are suspect."

"There'll be a big murder or some minister will run a red light—you know and they won't be so short on headline stuff. And reds in the schools will be back page stuff."

"They won't fire her without proof," Miss Prink said, picking up her sandwich, laying it down again.

"Oh, but they—we will," Miss O'Toole said, giving the older woman a quick sharp look. "She could at least talk—clear herself, if she can be cleared."

Miss Prink looked toward Mrs. Sheridan, waited a moment for her to repeat what she had already said about rights and principles, but Mrs. Sheridan was busy pouring tomato soup from her red vacuum bottle and did not look up.

The wonder on Mrs. Maki who had taught 20 years, and was now fired on testimony of this ex-cook-waitress lay uneasily in the back of her mind through the afternoon. She kept backing away from the thing, trying to get a better look at it. People were innocent until proven guilty—but guilty of what and where was the proof?

The thought kept coming between her and the 3B's, working on early Detroit—building a city by a lake in the sand box, with two making a church for Father Gabriel.

The last class, then her homeroom in and out again—ordinarily she stayed late on Wednesdays till the janitor was leaving and worked on records and papers—but today she hurried, even rushing the studies a little—even the forever lagging Junie Mae who had come rushing back for forgotten homework in math. She wanted to telephone Mrs. Maki, reassure her, tell her she was certain the teachers' union would stand up for her. It must have been a terrible ordeal—after 20 years of teaching, no complaints on her work—even the paper had said that. She was welcome to the use of the telephone in the principal's office—but well—she would wait until she got home. Her father and Mr. Cramer from The Charleston would be deep in their chess game.

"Yu Miz Prink."

She turned, half startled, and saw the face glowering at her from the doorway.

"I'm Mary McSnarty," the voice went on, its owner a still bulky mass in the door, crisp curls of bright gold hair fringing a green scarf, too bright above a wrinkled red-cheeked face.

"Yes," she said, smiling her teacher's smile, moving toward the doorway.

"Don't grin at me," the woman said. "All I gotta say's yu gotta quit teaching mu kids that this guy—Patrick, Patruck—s'funny last name."

"Henry," Miss Prink said.

"Yu know, kids. Yu gotta quit teachen my kids that he'd u stood up fuda commies. You'se gotta learn u kids won't stand still fudu likes a youse—Communist." The word fell over her, hissing, spattering, somehow like a too wet snowball, and Mary McSnarty was disappearing down the hall.

Miss Prink was for a moment still, then started almost running after the sound of the steps, thumping down the stairs now.

"Aw, leave her be, teacher," Junie Mae said. "Nobody cain't never do nothen with that old son of a—that ole SOB—on account she all lies an tongue like her kids. You'd oughta hear th way they talk to Jimmy; gonna beat him up on account a his pop bean called in front a that American thing."

"UnAmerican," Miss Prink corrected automatically from long habit.

"You said it. That's right."

[Junie Mae] gave the slumped shoulders a reassuring pat as she sped out the door. "I gotta hurry. Them uns is aimen to be ganging up on Jimmy so's me and me brudder an u Shakovitch kids—why, we'll be there."

Miss Prink looked after her a moment, then turned back to her desk and began slowly, deliberately gathering up the papers.

Even though it meant hunting a place to park, she stopped on the way home and bought a Valentine—a pretty lacy thing. It had just occurred to her that Mrs. Maki, if home at all, would be too tired for a telephone conversation—Valentine's Day wasn't too far away—her homeroom was already planning the box—still it might be best to wait a day or so—people never sent Valentines early like Christmas cards.

She thought of the Valentine again the night the Teachers' Union met to vote whether or not to take action in the case of Mrs. Maki, discharged because she would not testify before the committee.

Important questions were usually decided by ballot, and when Mrs. Grinki, the president, called for a standing vote, Miss Prink already, unscrewing the top on her pen for long habit of doing the things she had planned to do, was standing.

There was an instant when she thought, looking about, that it was like in Church—she must go to church more often—when the minister asked the congregation to stand and sing or pray—there was always a moment's fluttering—women clearing their laps of hymnbooks and purses—only now it was very still—too still, like her room when Mrs. McSnarty and Junie Mae were gone—or even the lunchroom [when] they said they had read the paper.

She turned her head at last, looking about her. The next person standing was a young man—and he seemed far way. She straightened a little, conscious of twisting head and searching eyes—Miss O'Toole—past her a face flashed a smile—and she realized it was Mrs. Maki. She wished the other had not smiled—it looked, well, as if they were close friends.

Light burst about them. She blinked, realizing at last that the huddle of men in front she had taken for teachers were photographers.

Next morning, as she got her own breakfast, her father's breakfast, her lunch, his lunch, she glanced now and then at the paper, folded in half, but open enough that she could read the double headline, for the Teachers' Union must share with a man who had loved his divorced wife and so had killed.

"Teachers Favor Ouster of Subversive."

"Only fourteen teachers voted in favor of retaining the Communist to teach the overthrow of the government to our young children."

She realized as she poured her Postum into her thermos and watched the coddling of her father's egg that she was whispering. "We didn't vote for that." She, Mrs. Maki, was a good teacher—they said. You can't fire a person just—just for thinking—maybe she was just curious—maybe she really should send the Valentine.

She would explain to the teachers at noon why she had voted as she had—she'd taught freedom of speech—freedom close to 40 years—and could she deny freedom of thought?

She never did explain. The teachers never asked. There was, it seemed to her, a peculiar moment of silence, though of late, years when the sections had gone up to 35, 40, 45—two shifts, the teachers talked little—mostly they just sat, savoring silence.

Mrs. Clawson asked about her father. They lived in the same section of town and often they had exchanged car rides or even visits with an occasional trip together downtown. "He's fine," she said, "remarkably active for his years."

Miss O'Leary gave her a quick glance. "He must have married awfully young."

Miss Prink nodded, smiling even though Mrs. Dawson gave the other a quick silencing look—youth had gone, slipped away before she knew it to the 3B's down at the old Tomkinds School—she'd never been pretty—it was like she'd looked away and then back and retirement was close—something she could see and plan for.

"He's getting close to 80," she said. "Funny thing, he's never lost his love of people. He wants to move into the Charlestown—it's more like a hotel than an old man's home—but frightfully expensive."

"What isn't?" Mrs. Dawson said, and they were silent again until Miss O'Toole wanted to know if they'd read about the Craw Chuck Man.

They were silent, none saying they had read, and Miss O'Toole went on to tell of how the union had taken the nervy stand that no man unless he be an official should be fired because he was a Communist.

"But there's no proof he is a Communist," Miss Prink said, knowing after she had spoken that she should keep her silence, but going on, like one of the Wildcriess Road people in the middle of a swift river but unable to turn back. "And the last of that woman's testimony was for 1946 and . . ."

"I wouldn't call her 'that woman,'" Miss O'Toole said. "She's a great patriot, giving her time."

"She got paid for her espionage. And now she got paid $25 a day for her work as a witness. That's more than she was ever able to earn as a cook."

"You know a lot about her," Miss O'Toole said, giving her a sharp look.

"All Federal witnesses get that," Miss Prink said, sipping her Postum.

"Anyway, the men who have to work with that man threw him out yesterday. He bragged he'd come back today. I wonder if he did."

Miss Prink wondered through the afternoon—Jimmy was absent at the brief check-in of the homeroom—maybe he was only tardy.

At dismissal time, when her homeroom came trooping back again, she found herself staring at his empty seat and Mike Shenkey said, giggling, "Teacher's pet ain't here. Dey beat up his old man. He got tough wit um."

"Dey hadda fire his old man. He took a blackjack tu work wit him. S'againsa union rules—taken a weapon into du shop."

"He hadda right," Junie Mae said, her voice trembling as if underneath it there could be a cry.

"Commies ain't got no rights," Mike said.

Miss Prink opened her mouth, closed it firmly. "This is not a discussion period," she said.

"Didja know, Teacher, dey're gonna investigate u schools—clean out u Reds," Mike said, glancing briefly at her, then his pleased glance, going swiftly about the silent watching room. She knew, learning it slowly bit by bit, unconsciously through the years, that the fathers of some children, and the mothers, too, worked in Griggs plant, No. 4, where Jimmy's father worked. And some of these same fathers had no doubt helped throw him out, threatened him—and now they sat too silent and too watchful.

Mike who was often out of hand was repeating, "Didn't chas know dey're gonna investigate du teachers—send men all u way from Washington. T'row out u Reds—not jist u card-carrying communists but all u subversives."

"Row one may pass to the door," she said, realizing as she spoke it was almost a minute early—she heard the tramp of 4B's on the stairs.

She opened the door at last and stood in front of it and watched them down the hall. Mr. Banks, the principal, stood as was his custom watching them down the stairway, first holding them, the long line of them, waiting in the hall until section one of the 3B's had come up from the basement and cleared the main hall below.

The words of apology were there waiting when he stopped by the doorway. "I must have been in a hurry," she said. "It's my afternoon for the downtown library. There's a new book of sources, a lot of Christopher Gist's journal of his travels—it would enrich this unit on the Wilderness

Road, for Gist, you know, explored some of the same . . ." She saw he wasn't listening, though he looked at her with the polite smile—that made her think somehow of—well, a department store manager—so young, so well-dressed—she rubbed her forehead. It had gone so quickly—everything seemed old yesterday [when] the men teachers she knew had all been like Mr. Miles—ink-stained and chalky-fingered, their pants shiny—and their ties just something black to cover the shirt buttons. This man's coat was tweed, almost seemed like to his knees, and his tie—she mustn't look at it—he might think . . .

"Still on the Wilderness Road," he said.

She nodded, bright again. "We're studying pioneer life in Kentucky now. Almost ready for George Rogers Clark and his part in the Revolution."

"It must be a job," he said, "tying it altogether like that." He glanced about the room, crowded almost with the sand table, the work table, the posters, the pictures the children made, the bulletin board with clippings, pictures they had brought.

"It seems that Daniel Boone would be less work—and more suited to this age level," he said, and all at once he seemed to her, this neatly dressed young man with no smear of chalk or stain of ink about him, was critical, politely critical, the way teachers had been last night when she stood up.

She wished all at once she'd told him of Mrs. McSnarty—Mrs. McSnarty had been to him—that was it—and with times the way they were—he was trying to tell her—What was he trying to tell her?—to quit teaching Patrick Henry.

He was turning slowly about the room. "You get a wonderful pupil response," he said, studying the bulletin board now. "But with such a heavy teaching load—I'd simplify things—so much research for source materials—do you think children this age can grasp source materials?"

She nodded, trying not to look defiant. "Some of Daniel Boone's writings—well, like the letter in which—when he was old and tired—he asked for the job of improving the Wilderness Road—arouse much interest," she said. "And I remember . . ." But already he was turning away with the look she thought of a man who has not done all of what he planned to do.

She was glad she hadn't told him of how when she was a girl in the old Hancock school under Dr.———, the Indian, they always called him, she'd cried when the old man had recited Logan's speech—but that was all so long ago. Old Dr.———— could remember the Civil War; old she was and times had changed.

She was half way home before she remembered she should be driving to the library. She hesitated in the right turn lane until the man behind her tooted. She drove straight on; maybe she did work too hard—but she'd never somehow thought of it as work. The afternoon at the library, the evenings over papers, lesson plans, the array of cards of all colors, shapes and sizes. What else was there? her father—the lawn—church. She ought to go to church more often. She'd read the moving speech Supt. Morgan had made on God—good teachers had God in their lives.

She remembered she and the others had discussed his speech, and she had remarked aloud that she had wondered at times what Benjamin Franklin and Thomas Jefferson and Abraham Lincoln had thought of God, even George Washington when he was young.

Miss O'Toole had given her, well, the same look that time she brought *The Nation*—there'd been part of a book review she'd wanted to read, quoting three sentences. . . . She should have clipped it.

The mail had brought Valentines—two she saw were postmarked Korea, and suddenly she cried a little soundlessly sniffling; so many Valentines through so many wars—so many places—seemed only yesterday she'd had her first one from France. She'd been young enough for tears then— but years later she should have kept silent about the one she got from Spain—she'd cried so—but all that war on—his side had lost there—had won in Germany but—he was dead.

She should have sent more Valentines—it was too late now—even for Mrs. Maki. A shame to waste such a pretty Valentine—she took it out of its envelope—stared at it critically a moment—it wasn't too lacy and sweet for a boy—there would be a Valentine box in her homeroom. Jimmy, she thought, wouldn't get any; she'd write just his name, not her own for it would look strange for only one child to get a Valentine from his teacher. No, she'd print his name.

Jimmy, however, got more than one Valentine. She couldn't be certain, but she'd heard his name called six times. Some of the tightness, the coldness that had lain in her was gone. It was snowing past the windows, but inside her room it was brightly red and white with Valentines, red hearts of the children's drawings were bright on the blackboards, and the gay Valentines box, an enormous thing of white crepe, bright with pink hearts and the gold of radio paints, was empty.

The children crunched cinnamon hearts and bigger fatter hearts with greetings of "I love you" and "be my Valentine," her Valentine to all of them, and blushed and giggled over the greetings heaped on their desks. Even Junie Mae seemed softened, surprised, for she, quite new to the group, and among its many cliques and minor groupings, there had never seemed a place for her.

Miss Prink glanced quickly at the good sized pile in front of Jimmy, then down at her own desk, seeming no different from the other years when factory workers' children had money for Valentines—there were big envelopes with fancy things of lace, smaller ones with the hasty scribble of the child who'd just remembered teacher, chocolate hearts in gilded paper, two handkerchiefs decorated with pinch hearts. She, as always, opened them, the children crowding around to see, a few like McSnarty giggling in expectancy for as always there would be the comic ones—a teacher like in the comic strips with buck teeth and skinned back hair, and if they were not obscene, she always held them up for them to see, and shared in the laughter.

She unfolded a handkerchief, murmured "so beautiful," and glanced uneasily at Jimmy. He had opened one Valentine and sat now, staring down at it, stiff and still, his face red, his eyes bright with hurt and anger. Junie Mae leant above him frowning and Mike Pavlovitch was calling, "Let's see yer Valentines, Jimmy. Let's see." But Andy McSnarty jeered looking from Jimmy to her, "Let's see Teacher's first."

Miss Prink smiled at him, smiled and resolutely dove into the Valentines, found the neat and even McSnarty writing—for good penmanship was the pride of the McSnartys—and opened it. A homemade Valentine— a single sheet of drawing paper folded—inside a huge crimson heart and underneath, "This heart ain't half so red as yours."

She choked and hastily refolded it, though Jerry and other voices—a few girls now were calling, "Show us. You gotta show us."

Blindly she groped for a chocolate heart and held it up for them to see—there was a motto on it in curls of white frosting—and there was a moment's panic of wondering what the motto said.

It must have been all right for Catherine Schultz was giggling, nudging, "Boy, wait ull she sees mine."

The children were crowding round her now. She felt Michael Angelo's garlic-flavored breath, and Jimmy's, touched still with boiled beans and onions. Someone laughed and shoved another one under her hand. She saw that it was homemade, and reached past it, and smiling, fumbling, opened a lacy heart for them to see, but it seemed like all around her there were jeering cries, "Open this one, Teacher. Yu gotta show us whatcha got."

She glanced hopefully toward the door. Once when Jerry McSnarty threw a book at the young English teacher, the principal had happened by—maybe he would come now—they were making so much noise. The Indians screaming about Crawford with the hot coals pressed into his scalpless head.

She stiffened, and slowly her fingers numb, the paper crackling in the sudden silence, she opened the Valentine, large, the heart a sticky, vivid red, painted with fingerpaint, below it drops and splashes, only the printed words were black and clear. "We're going to shool that Commie bleeding heart right out of you."

She studied it a moment, spread as it was on her desk, then conscious of the heads crowding to see, she stepped backward, lifted it, and stood an instant still, the red dripping heart held in front of her.

There was silence broken at last by Jerry McSnarty's exultant giggle.

A short giggle, cut off by Junie Mae's resounding smack and her flat voiced, "You dirty, dirty bastard."

There had been a little flurry, but fortunately at least for the moment, Jerry had assumed the role of silent martyrdom, and had gone silently home, careful to let the blood stream down his lips and onto his clothing for Junie Mae's hand was large and tough and hard like the rest of her.

She thought of it now, as she turned into the narrow street of small homes close together. She should not let them see the Valentine in the first place and, above all, she should have marched Junie Mae to the principal for quick discipline—but she had done nothing.

Then, that is a moment later, her own Valentines had seemed a small matter. She'd somehow found, not hunting just finding among the other 44, Jimmy's face, saw his fist tighten above his thin heap of Valentines, and known that Jimmy's Valentines were like her own. She had folded her Valentines, laid them aside; the bell had rung, and the children gone to their cloak room.

They'd been strangely quiet after Junie Mae's slap—only Jerry's mumbling and groaning through the blood, making a slow seep down his chin, and above the shuffling feet, she'd heard the girlish whispers, hissing, curse like. "How come yu gotta send me a Valentine?—Gonna try tu make u other kids think we're buddies, huh. I ain't want nothen off u th likes a yu. See."

She looked up in time to see a blur of pinky whiteness strike Jimmy in the face and Catherine's yellow head gave a disdainful toss as she marched down the aisle.

She slowed, carefully, to 18 miles [per hour], shifted, glanced in her rear view mirror, swung out, then turned slowly into her drive. She mustn't think of all that—such little silly stupid things—that Valentine's Day was a year ago—almost.

Nobody remembered it. Mr. [Banks] had probably forgotten the dressing down he gave Junie Mae after Mrs. McSnarty came with Mike the next day—the lip only slightly swollen . . . "Mu kid's heart blood," but the shirt, the jacket, the sweater, ruined, "wit mu kid's heart's blood."

Miss Prink had, when called in, apologized for Junie Mae's outbreak and—she shivered—why think of it—the choking fear that followed her for days—suppose it got into the papers—the papers were forever eager for stories of poor discipline and teaching in the public schools. The story would have gone well with the headlines.

Two Hundred Reds in Public Schools—then smaller, much smaller, the story of how Stella Dodd, ex-communist, had come forward in Washington with testimony about the public schools across the land. Detroit was named along with other cities.

War and national politics, three sex murders, and the defections of a thrice-married minister had claimed the headlines through the fall. School officials had gone ahead with old plans for a bond issue to be put before the voters, of course, for badly needed buildings.

Miss Prink had thrown herself into that—well, not too actively—she attended a few meetings, and it was surprising the popular interest in public education. The press was, of course, unfriendly and one of the council men, who liked to boast that neither he nor any of his children had ever been inside a public school, got several front page stories by his charges of over much luxury in the building of schools, and in all the Letters to the

Editors columns there were the usual complaints by businessmen that their stenographers couldn't spell, by parents who wanted religion, morals, manners taught in the schools; the number charging socialistic tendencies and red infiltration had been no higher than usual, or so it had seemed to Miss Prink.

And she had for the past few months read the daily papers, more than usual. They kept some of the lonesomeness, not lonesomeness either—a teacher teaching eight groups of forty odd four times a week couldn't be lonesome—more like an emptiness.

She'd left out Patrick Henry and the Craigs—the Regulators—even the speech of Dragging Canoe—frontier thoughts she had called them for the frontier had thoughts as well as guns—the class periods, the days and the months had slid smoothly by—she switched off the ignition, sat a moment staring at the key—too smoothly somehow—of course, she only imagined it but seemed like Mr. [Banks] lingered more often in the hall by her door—she would glance up and through the glass she'd glimpse the shoulder of the well-cut tweed just turning away—the teachers talked less as they ate together—and there were fewer. Miss O'Toole and Mrs. Briggs went out for lunch most always now—and Mrs. Brown hadn't visited in a long while or suggested that they go out together to a play or a lecture or the symphony as in other years.

Mrs. Maki had written from another city—she had answered—should have answered.

She glanced once at the folded paper in the car seat, lifted her hand part way, dropped it and sat, staring straight in front of her.

She stared and tried to find pleasure in the rows of shelves, filled with labeled boxes and books and old lesson plans, as she had used to. Sometimes on rainy Saturdays she had used to come and file and sort her things, for in the boxes were all the Christmas cards, the Valentines, the foolish gifts, loud handkerchiefs, cheap perfumes, cheap glass and dinnerware—all cherished because they were the gifts of the children—so many small things and she could not use them all.

She glanced toward a box marked Valentines and looked away. Last year's Valentines were there—all of them—even the big red hearts. Tomorrow was Valentine's Day and what would she get—after this. She reached again for the paper. She was so tired—too tired to unfold it and read—she knew the headlines. Mrs. Dawson had wept suddenly in a great soundless outburst over them at noon, whispering, "Why? WHY?—Some—my own children might even think it could be me."

"Don't be silly," Miss O'Toole had said fiercely, and all day long the principal had tramped the halls, pausing at times to scrutinize some teacher's door as if asking, "Could it be she?"

She remembered the garage doors, not closed, and pulled the rope by which one could close the door without getting out of the car.

Then she looked down at the unfolded paper, the great headlines were like a black mist before her eyes, but she knew what they said. "Name twenty-eight schools harboring Reds."

She did not read the column, the upper part, but only the last part of the big print—"particularly was the Dewey School."

All afternoon she'd felt the children watching her, knowing she was the red. She was what the superintendent meant when, in a news release, he had complained that he as yet had been handed no list of subversives by any one of the four separate agencies he presumed was investigating Detroit's public schools—the state anti-subversive commission, the City Loyalty Commission, the unAmerican activities, the FBI, the American Legion, the Loyalty Review Board of the Teachers' Union, and the city police Red squad. None of these had as yet handed him a list. Oh, of course, the Board of Education checked on all possible subversives, reports of parents concerning the attitude and acts of some teachers—reports of other teachers.

That was it—she listed in her head the things she had done to arouse suspicion—the list seemed almost endless. Tomorrow there would be Valentines—maybe vandalism with COMMUNIST written on the wall.

Love?

This story was first published in *Twigs* 8 (Fall 1971): 1–15, a literary magazine issued by Pikeville College, in Pikeville, Kentucky.

*I*t seemed a sin to break that sprig of honeysuckle so fresh and pretty when she already had some in her hair. The flowers would wilt before she reached the Gospel Sing, but she'd still have the smell. Head lifted, reaching for a spray above the fence, her gaze went past the flowers into the sky. Her hands fell from the unbroken flower; only her head moved as her eyes followed the great circle of a hawk's flight.

High and far away, she knew him from any other bird. No other creature she'd ever seen was so at home in the sky, soaring through the high blue spaces without effort. Watching him made her feel proud as he, and like him free of all miseries down here on earth. He wasn't exactly free. He and his wife had to feed their young.

Early in the spring, the cow had wandered deep into the woods. It was while hunting the cow in the wild woods of the National Forest behind the house, she had first seen the hawk. He had not come in high, proud flight, but low with shrill, angry cries that told her better than words to be gone. She had walked on, not wanting to anger such a fine bird. His cries had continued; soon a second hawk cried out at her. She looked up; this one was smaller with a different voice, nor did it come so low, nor fly so widely. It had fluttered, more than circled around the broken out top of a tall maple. She'd tried to hide behind an oak to watch and try to see the nest she knew was high in the broken-topped maple. She'd learned there was no hiding from hawks and hurried away. Worried that she might have caused them to move their nest, for it had seemed too early for eggs, she'd gone back to that part of the woods a few weeks later. Afraid of upsetting them again, she had watched from the next hill over. By then the leaves were out, but after a long wait she'd seen flying low near the broken-topped maple the hawk she thought was the father.

She had by now seen him many times above the house and yard. Now and then she'd see him sitting high in an old hickory at the edge of the woods; and always he'd come when she was alone. His visits were her secrets. Oscar, her husband, liked to hunt. The wild ducks on the river or black birds in the corn were all one to his guns.

The hawk was now swinging lower, closer. She wanted to cry out: "Hawk, oh, Hawk, don't come any closer. My man's home. He'll shoot you down."

The hawk, as if he'd heard, circled higher, but his moving shadow was a telltale on the earth. Mostly he had come on cloudy days or in the very early morning while she was milking, shadowless as a ghost. Now, it was dew-dried late on a sunny day. He and his wife must have a hard go to find food for their young. She watched him become a speck and continued to watch until the speck disappeared in the sky.

He would be back. Oscar on the front porch shining his shoes would see its shadow. His guns were close. That would be the end of her hawk.

She must scare him, keep him from circling lower when he came back. Noise? What kind of noise could she make that wouldn't make Oscar suspicious? She drew a deep breath. Her mouth was dry. Her first notes were no better than a mouse's squeaks. She tried again, and let out loud and clear: "Rise fathers rise, let's go meet them in the skies, when we hear the trumpet sounding—." Oscar was yelling.

"Stead a wasten your breath an time on that old song, you'd better be getten your grub into the car. We don't want to keep Si waiten, an I'm about finished with my shoes."

She wished Oscar would call Mr. Silas Denton, "Mr. Denton." He was a friend of her parents; she'd known him since she was a little girl, and had never heard any one but Oscar call him Si. He'd been good enough to come out of his way to take them to the Gospel Sing in his car—and Oscar had kept him waiting while he shined his shoes.

She had already hurried into the kitchen; maybe they could get away before the hawk got back. She picked up the split basket of food she'd packed for dinner-on-the-ground between the morning and afternoon sings. It was so heavy she had to use both hands. She wished Oscar would come to carry it out; he could do it with one hand. She could carry the cake, the pickled beets, pickled peaches, and they'd be gone before the hawk got back. Oscar hadn't come, but at least he was opening the front screen door for her. No, it was Mr. Denton. He smiled at her.

She gave him back a wide happy smile. She was by now certain the hawk was safe. Oscar would have seen his shadow had he circled down again as he usually did. Mr. Denton carried the basket to the car parked in the shade. She helped him stow it so there'd be no spilling, then lingered a moment to look at the new car. She'd never ridden in such a fine car; the upholstery looked too fine to sit on. The nicest thing about it, though, was she could pretend to be looking through a window into the car while watching the sky on the other side. No hawk shadow.

She ran back for the rest of the food. She was crossing the porch when something gave her head such a quick, hard jerk, she almost fell on her back. She turned to see that spray of honeysuckle she'd put in her hair sailing over the porch. She didn't look as Oscar, but his angry voice followed her into the kitchen. "First, you want to wear your hair striggen over your shoulders like a damned whore. Next, it's flowers. Try to recollect you're a old married woman goen on twenty years old 'stead a bein fiesty as a— heifer in her first heat."

She gritted her teeth, and began to gather up her load. Oscar was having one of his Lord-of-the-Manor fits, showing off before Mr. Denton.

"Lulu's the same age as my oldest daughter. She wears her hair down. Most girls do." Mr. Denton sounded as if he didn't like Oscar's show too well.

"Not my wife," Oscar said.

She was glancing out the back door. No hawk. Quickly, she cradled the cake and other food in her arms at the same time taking care not to let anything touch the frosting on the cake. This time Mr. Denton didn't wait for her to reach the front door, but met her half way across the front room. She snatched up purse and hymnbook and hurried out to the porch. "This is all. I'm ready to go," she told Oscar.

Picking his teeth, he watched her until she'd helped Mr. Denton stow the food, then he called: "I've not seen any jug a buttermilk. You know how I like fresh-churned buttermilk, an I know you churned this mornen."

"It won't be cold," she said, not moving from the side of the car; when she looked up at Oscar on the porch, she could without being noticed lift her eyes still higher to see the sky. Empty; at least the part she could see.

"I said I wanted buttermilk. Damn it, get a move on."

She ran back into the kitchen and onto the porch. No hawk—yet. She must hurry. She'd have to put the buttermilk in a jug so it wouldn't spill all over the car—and she didn't have a funnel. First, she'd have to dip it out of the churn into her pitcher, and from the pitcher try to pour it into the jug. And where was the cork? She had everything lined up when Oscar yelled: "Get my gun, Lulu. I want to keep him spotted. Hurry."

Mr. Denton's voice was calm as a frozen river. "Biggest one I've ever seen. I wouldn't kill him, Oscar. He must be about th only one left in these parts."

Oscar's only answer was: "Get a move on, Lulu, with that gun."

She unfroze, ran to the side of the front room wall where he kept his guns, and took down the ancient no. 12 shotgun he hardly ever used.

Eyes on the hawk, he grabbed the gun from her, started to lift it to his shoulder, then with an oath flung it back at her. "You know damn well I can't kill a hawk with a shotgun. Get my rifle. It's getten away. Hurry."

Making time for the hawk, she bent to pick up the gun.

He turned on her cursing with God and Jesus. She dropped the gun and lifted her hands to her ears while her glance took in the hawk swinging high above the hill. She at last paid heed to her husband's curse-surrounded commands: "Go on. Git that rifle. He'll git away."

She ran back into the house. She knew which gun he wanted: that new deer hunting rifle with the telescope sight; he'd spent a mint for the outfit when she hadn't a decent shoe and no refrigerator. She took down the old single shot 22 and ran out.

This time he turned on her with the words she'd never heard before she married him. They'd puzzled her until she asked her mother what they meant. Her mother had been scandalized, worse than scandalized. She had wanted to know from whom her daughter had heard such talk. She had managed to keep from telling the truth without telling a great big lie. She didn't want her mother to know what kind of husband she had.

"Will you go bring my big new rifle. I could already a had him. Now, he's almost out a sight. But I'll get him."

Mr. Denton spoke up, sounded like he was wearing a too tight collar. "Let's get started. This is the Lord's Day. If you must kill th bird, leave it for some other day."

Oscar saw she had been listening. "Damn it, Lulu, bring me th gun I need. Hurry."

She skittered across the front room with no glance for the gun rack. In the kitchen she grabbed up a still shiny aluminum pan, then rushed onto the back porch. She might be able to scare the hawk if she could hold the pan so as to reflect the sunlight round and round him, but not in his eyes; that might blind or confuse him and make him go right above Oscar and his waiting gun. She heard Oscar's cursing command to hurry up with his deer rifle. "I can see him now. He's comen up th creek valley."

She couldn't see the valley from the back porch. She ran around the house corner, looked out and up. The hawk proud and free as ever was swinging out above the ridge in a high wide spiral that would in time bring him low above the barn. She screamed. "Don't kill him. Please don't."

She never heard the rifle, only saw the broken circle, the wing-flapping fight to stay in the air and get home to the tall, broken-topped maple. Each crooked wing beat carried him forward, but at the same time a bit lower.

She heard Oscar's cursing, and Mr. Denton's interruption: "You've nicked his wing. We'd better go find him then turn him over to the game warden—he must have his nest in the National Forest; or if he's too bad off put him out of his misery, but I think he's only nicked in one wing."

"Nicked, my eye. He's more than nicked. Good as dead. He'll either starve or a weasel will finish him off." He let out with a few oaths. "If my woman had a brought th right gun I'd a had him to stuff an hang on th wall."

"We ought to take time to hunt him up. I tell you he's just nicked. Might take him days to die."

"Who cares?" Oscar started cursing again.

His curses didn't hurt her any more. It was like Oscar's bullet had gone through her own body. She was doubled up in the grass, crossed arms clutching her breasts, head touching the ground. Of all the words she'd just heard, one stayed with her. "Nicked. Nicked." She whispered it over and over. She lifted her head. "Nicked?" Why, that meant the hawk could be mended, cured maybe.

She sprang up. If only she didn't have to leave home, she'd go hunt the bird as soon as Oscar was gone. She'd find him, mend his wing, and feed him. She'd doctored chickens lots of times; not long ago a hen with a broken leg. Oscar wouldn't let her stay home; he knew she'd been dying to go; he'd be suspicious if she changed her mind. Now, he was yelling at her to get his buttermilk and come on. She heard his feet on the porch steps. He was coming in to put his guns away.

She ran around the house corner and into the kitchen. He'd get his buttermilk all right. And as for having to leave the wounded hawk, her father always said, a body didn't really have to do anything but pay taxes and die.

The first thing she had to do was get that churn of buttermilk onto the kitchen table. The old-fashioned stone churn filled with milk and the butter she hadn't had time to take out and wash was heavier than she had thought. Her hands and arms were shaking by the time she had heaved it onto the kitchen table.

Oscar, outside on the porch now, again called for her to hurry. "I am," she answered, breathless.

She debated an instant. Better let him have his jugful. But he didn't deserve a drop. If it hadn't have been for his commanding buttermilk at the last minute, the hawk would still be cutting holes in the sky.

She took out a little gollop[1] of the freshly churned butter, smeared it over her palms, set the pitcher on the floor, then using both hands, tipped the churn until milk cascaded into the pitcher. Pitcher filled, she hung onto the tipped churn with one hand while with the other she struggled to get the pitcher, rather heavy now, onto the table.

The other butter-slippery hand was unable to get the churn back into an upright position. She stepped closer, let the churn tip still lower. Milk with gobs of butter poured over her dress, her hose, and into her shoes. She let out a good high scream. "Help me somebody, quick."

The men hurried in. Remembering his freshly shined shoes, Oscar stopped on the edge of the buttermilk sea with its islands of butter on the kitchen floor. Mr. Denton waded in and righted the churn, and set the pitcher on the table.

She was all ashake, scarcely able to thank Mr. Denton. "I was afraid that churn would fall an break," she explained.

"Why in hell didn't you leave it on th floor an dip it out?" Oscar wanted to know.

"You kept tellen me to be quick. I thought pouren would be th quickest." She turned to Mr. Denton looking as if he'd like to pat her on the shoulder as he would have one of his daughters. "Fillen a jug without a funnel is hard—an we've got no funnel."

Mr. Denton picked up the pitcher and filled the jug with a fairly steady hand.

She waited until the jug was filled and corked, then buried her face in her buttermilk-covered arms. She next got out some quite good sobs.

Oscar wanted to know what—ailed her.

She lifted her head. The buttermilk and flecks of butter that now smeared her face could pass for tears. "You'd cry, too, if you couldn't go to th Gospel Sing. I've been looken forward to it, practicen for months, an worked since before daylight this mornen to get my dinner ready.—It's not just that I like to sing, but I'd see all my family there, an everybody I used to know."

"Now, now, we can wait while you change your clothes. The little accident wasn't your fault. That big churn full of milk was too heavy for you to try to lift."

"I've got no other decent clothes," she answered, and buried her head again.

"You would have if you'd keep everthing clean an ironed," Oscar quarreled.

"I can't very well wash an iron something like shoes that I don't have," she answered. "These are ruined, the only Sunday shoes I've got. Papa bought em for me before I was married."

"Wash off th buttermilk. They'll do. You don't want to miss the singing," Mr. Denton insisted.

"Come on, Si. Our alto section can manage without her," Oscar said. He picked up the jug of buttermilk and strode to the door.

Mr. Denton did not turn away. "Change into something, anything," he begged. "Rinse out your dress—it'll dry in this hot sun just spread out in the car. We have to go pick up my wife and the children. We can plug in the electric iron and my wife or one of the girls can iron it dry in a jiffy."

"It's all greasy with butter," she said, face again on her folded arms; he was making her want to cry for real. It would be the nicest thing in the world if Oscar was the one talking that way, begging her to come, really wanting her to have a good time and be with him.

His voice came from the doorway. "Recollect to feed the sow an do th rest of the chores. I don't reckon I'll be back before mornen. I think Brother Dykes is preachen this evenin. I expect to have another long struggle on the mourners' bench tryen to git salvation."

"I don't think there are any plans for a night service," Mr. Denton said, no longer choked, but his voice dull-bladed like an old grubbing ax. "And," he continued, "if somebody does hold a short service, there'll be no call for converts. There never is this time of year when church members are busy with their crops, gardens, an cannin."

Poor Oscar, she thought, he'd need a lot of nights, an awful lot of nights on the mourners' bench; for now he was cursing again with Jesus, God, and a string of the words that had scandalized her mother—and Mr. Denton standing right there. Seemed there'd been a smear of buttermilk on the jug and he'd got some on his pants. He ended up by saying: "- - - -. Let's get goen. We'll be late."

Mr. Denton didn't move, but he did look at Oscar. "There're more ways than one to get salvation. Most begin at home to rid themselves of sinful habits such as swearen. There's many a man with no religion at all, able to curse for more than an hour without sayen th same oath twice, but not one oath do they ever let out under the house roof or any place else where there's women."

"I can't help it," Oscar said, face reddening. "But cussin is my only sinful habit." He walked out the door.

Mr. Denton looked as if he didn't agree. He turned and looked at her, shook his head. "We ought to stay and help you clean up this mess; but try to have a nice day in spite of it." He went out the kitchen door so as not to track buttermilk over the front room floor. She ran after him with a rag for him to wipe his shoes.

Men gone, she kicked off her shoes, and heedless of her buttermilk sodden clothes, soused half a bucket of water on the kitchen floor, and gave it a few swipes with the broom. The big cracks in the old floor of the lean-to kitchen that froze her in winter and made passways for copperheads in summer were handy now. She hurried with the work, storing in her mind the things she must take when she went to hunt the hawk. She knew she'd find it. But suppose it was up in a tall poplar or some other tree with no lower limbs to climb. Well, she'd manage somehow. She had a disinfectant, stuff for bandaging, but what could she use for splints in case a wing bone was broken?

Stripped, washed in cold water, and drying as she rushed about to collect the needed articles, she remembered with a smile what she had carried to the springhouse early this morning—the backs, wings, necks, and heads of the four young chickens she had fried for dinner-on-the-ground. This hawk loved chicken; twice, she'd watched him come down like an arrow shot out of the sky; but just when you'd thought he'd hit the ground, out would come his wings; a second later he was up in the sky with a fryer in his claws. She hated to see anything die, even the wild asters in the first hard killing frost. And it was her job to kill the frying chickens Oscar wanted for breakfast three or four times a week from the time the first hatching was barely big enough until the winter time when the roosters of the late hatching were getting tough. She figured the hawk with his two kills hadn't hurt the chicken any worse than she would have when its killing time came. In fact, he had saved her two hateful jobs.

Oscar had insisted she save the backs and other bony parts of this morning's chickens. He'd told her to boil them and make dumplings in the soup like his mother used to make real good. She figured the hawk needed the chicken worse than Oscar; and anyhow her dumplings always made him wish he was going fishing—sinkers were about all they were good for, he said.

She could tell him the hogs had got through the fence again and got into the springhouse and eaten all the chicken she'd saved for dumplings.

She'd mended the fence with brush and barb wire, but hadn't done a very good job.

Dressed in the old overalls she wore when hoeing in the corn, and ready for her trip except to get the chicken, she ran down the path to the cave they called the springhouse. She hurried across the wide-mouthed outer room, then bending and walking in water, for the passage was only wide enough for the spring branch, she went a few steps before reaching the always-cool inner cave. On sunny days light reflecting on the running water in the outer room made a quivering twilight here not too deep to work by.

She lifted the lid from the stone crock and began to take out pieces of chicken, dropping them into the little hoop-net Oscar used in fishing which she let lay in the water. She figured the running water would take away the smell of her hands; the hawk might not like the human smell.

She was getting down to the last pieces of chicken, when her quick hands were suddenly still above the crock.

Did she love the hawk better than Oscar? The hawk was made to catch varmints, rabbits, and chickens. Oscar had been made to kill hawks, varmints, rabbits, and fish. Could either the hawk or Oscar be blamed for what they did? No, there was a difference. The hawk had to kill or let himself and family die. Oscar didn't eat many of the things he killed, and he spent a lot of money on his guns for killing. He might in time get salvation, but that wouldn't keep him from killing what he didn't need to kill. The only sin he thought he had was cursing. What was sin anyhow?

She spoke the word aloud. The echo from the darkness beyond brought the word back to her; the question, not the answer.

She had promised in front of the preacher and a roomful of other people to love, honor, and obey Oscar. Was she sinning by making the buttermilk spill, and not bringing him the gun she knew he wanted? Wasn't all of that a great big lie? Lying was a sin. Breaking a vow was a sin. She'd never really lied to him until this morning. She'd just not told him things like the hawk getting the chickens. She'd always obeyed him until he'd asked her this morning to bring his gun. Did she love and honor him?

What was love? Oscar seemed to think it was just what two people did together in bed. She didn't mind the bed business unless she was awful tired. It was part of that obeying she'd always figured. At least part of love ought to mean doing good things for the one you loved. She'd given Oscar his buttermilk after she'd first thought she'd spill it all. That was love, wasn't it? She'd left some chicken backs and wings. She'd make him some dumplings. That was love, wasn't it? He made fun of her dumplings, but he always ate a lot of them.

Love? No answer. She hadn't noticed coming out of the cave, but here she was across the creek and hurrying through the trees on the hillside, the hawk's chicken held carefully away from her body.

Could a woman lie to and trick a man she loved?

Could love wear out like her Sunday shoes?

She hurried on to leave the question in the valley. Unanswered.

Interruptions to School at Home

Published in 1980 in the Louisville-based *Adena: A Journal of the History & Culture of the Ohio Valley*, Arnow explained that this story is part of "a long manuscript concerned with the lives of a rural, Confederate family who lived in south central Kentucky during The War."

This excerpt, set in 1861, comes from Chapter Four of *Belle*, the unpublished novel on which Arnow was working when she died in 1986.

⸻◦●◦⸻

*N*ext morning Belle felt school was going well in spite of her absentminded lapses of worried wonderings on William's plans[1] or the safety of the men in Dead Man's Cave.[2] Dave [Belle's twelve-year-old son] was less restless than usual; not once had he complained of having to be in school when he ought to be outside at work with the other men.

Robert, her prime pupil, had answered all questions in history, read in the fourth reader with never a stumble, and was now working his arithmetic problems. Allison [Belle's youngest child, a six-year-old daughter, nicknamed "Sissie"] had not once interrupted with foolish comments or questions.

Belle gave Zion[3] credit for most of their good behaviour; they didn't want to misbehave or show their ignorance before the help. She had learned from Victoria's answer to her question that Zion's arm was black and blue with bruises from the horse's teeth, but the place where the teeth had brought blood was beginning to heal; his arm was so sore he couldn't do much of any kind of work. Victoria had been pleased by Belle's second question.

"Yes'm, he's plenty able to come to your school. He needs schoolen bad for his writen—if you can call it that. His left arm is the one hurt so he can practice all mornen."

Belle soon discovered Zion remembered most of what he had learned in previous years and was reading even better, now in the sixth reader. His spelling and penmanship were poor as ever. She had no heart to fault him for not being able to spell past the third reader, though he was only a year younger than Dave. Runner and handyboy for both kitchen and still, Zion had little time left for study. Belle figured he must have run two or three thousand miles yearly for Victoria alone: back and forth to the spring-house, the cellar, the garden, the orchard, smokehouse. Then, he'd drive up the cows for Maggie's milking.

The room was quiet save for the click of pencils on slates. Belle dreaded the next lesson, Dave's recitation. No matter what, "Thanatopsis" or Hamlet's soliloquy, Dave would say it with never a wrong or skipped word. Trouble was, he never cared how he said it; sorrowful and joyful recitations were all one to him. The first thing she'd tried to teach him in McGuffey's Sixth Reader was the chapter on elocution. She might as well have been the wind for all the heed he'd paid her. Whatever he had learned at the subscription school he and the younger ones attended last year, it wasn't elocution.

She made up her mind that no matter how badly he recited today, she wouldn't try to correct him. Quarreling did no good, and he was doing much better in grammar. Yesterday, he had made few mistakes in parsing; at long last he recognized gerunds, no matter how they were used.

Time came for Dave to stand up and announce: "The Declaration of Independence written and signed by a band of rebels eighty-five years ago this past Fourth of July." Slate pencils stilled as Sissie and Robert listened to Dave who stared out a window behind Belle. He spoke clearly without running one sentence into another; his inflection never varied. He was just finishing—"That whenever any Form of Government becomes destructive of these ends, it is the Right of the People to alter or abolish it"—when Old Pop ran barking to the outside door. Seconds later Belle heard feet running over the porch.

Dave, his voice no longer a monotone, said: "Mom, Springpole Detty has come, runnen like the devil was after him."

Belle told Robert to go open the door, and tell Springpole to come in and sit quietly until Dave finished his recitation.

Springpole tiptoed in and sat down. He was breathing hard as if he had run fast and far. He seemed ready to burst with news, but sat on the edge of his chair in fidgety silence until Dave finished.

Belle was unable to make one comment on Dave's recital before Springpole burst out: "Oh, Miss Belle, I'm sure glad to see you all alive an not shot down dead by one a them three murderen rebels an a black man with seven horses. They're runnen wild around here."

Belle said nothing. She couldn't.

Springpole's tongue was a runaway horse with his teeth on the bit. "Lookout for the red-headed one. He shot the high sheriff when he come with a posse to put him in jail. They're jailen all the rebels. When you reckon they'll come to jail you, Miss Belle? Anyhow, the high sheriff come to that red-headed man's front door, kicked it open, and walked into the hall with a pistol in either hand. He saw the red-headed man in the back end of the hall with a rifle in his hands.

"The high sheriff fired off his pistols. He shot the rebel's wife down dead. I don't think he meant to do that. She caught his pistol bullets when she stepped out a room and into the hall. Then the red-headed man shot the high sheriff dead. The posse, just two or three men, started runnen around the house toward the back to trap the rebel. They wasn't half way there when shots started comen from the barn. They left to get a bigger posse. Then the red-headed man an two a his buddies got on their seven horses with his black man an went gallopen off." Springpole stopped to take a breath.

Dave was unimpressed. "That's mighty strange. Nobody around here has heard one word about our high sheriff bein shot."

"It wasn't our high sheriff, but one in a county away yonder, maybe in or close to the Bluegrass. I never heared the posse say when they lighted at granpa's place to eat themselves an rest an feed their horses, but they'd come a long way, had a real long ride. Their horses looked it. I'm tellen you the truth. I could swear it on a stack a Bibles forty feet high. An that posse knows they're around here someplace. People away off seen them three rebels with a black man on seven horses gallopen down the turnpike. They know them murderen rebels is somewhere around. While they was at granpa's place, a man—I didn't know him—come to tell he'd seen the whole outfit on the road to old man Higget's mill on Holy Creek.

"That posse left in a hurry after learnen how to git to the mill. I grabbed me a horse an follered them until I took a short cut. Pretty soon I seen old man Higget was flyen a strange flag. I reckon it was a rebel flag. That posse tore it down soon as they got there, told Higget he'd maybe have to go to jail for flyen a rebel flag in Kentucky.

"An law, you ought to a seen that posse hunten the rebels; same thing I reckon when they come down here. They looked all over the house, barns, an the mill. Then, when they couldn't find nobody, they lifted the dam gates an drained the mill pond; said the men could be hiden in the bulrushes around the edges of the mill pond. An, Lord, was old man Higget mad, an so was his old woman. But the posse didn't find nothen but two water moccasins. But they'll git em. I know they will, hunten all over, ready to shoot em down dead."

Dave had enough. "Springpole, you're scaren mom to death. Mom, them Yankees won't find nobody here."

Belle nodded. "It's enough to scare anybody." Let Dave and the others think she was scared of the Confederates or that the Union men would jail her and the children. Let them think anything as long as they didn't suspicion the truth. She feared for the lives of the men she had lead [sic] to Dead Man's Cave. Were they already gone or just leaving? They could have slept late. She must get to the cave; if they were still there, she could warn them to bide awhile and be quiet. She couldn't go now. Leaving school for the cave could lead some manhunter to the cave and men.

Springpole studied her face as he answered Dave. "Yes, Siree, I'd say she is scared, but you all ought to be, the way they're hunten down rebels to jail or drive out a the country."

Sissie tossed back her curls. "Jail's in the county town. I'd love to live in town for a change. Every day I'd wear my Sunday clothes."

"The way them Union men are hunten, somebody'ull end up in jail.

Do you know one a them Union men asked grandpa if he knowed of any caves round about where the men could hide." Springpole shifted his glance to Belle's face. "You know I didn't know granpa had ever been in that big hainted cave a yours until he told the men how when he was a boy the floor changed into a sinkhole an he would a died there if his brothers an some bigger boys with him hadn't got him out. They'd marked their way goen in, an when they got him out, they was all scared so bad, they turned around an went out."

Dave was showing more interest. "An suppose Dead Man's Cave was a good place to hide. A bunch of strange men runnen from the law wouldn't know about it, an if they did, they'd never find it with the cave-mouth clogged with vines and cedars."

Springpole nodded. "That's something like what Granpa told them men, an he told em that was the only big cave he knowed about, an if by some mischance the rebels had found it they'd never come out alive an whoever went in there hunten them wouldn't come out either. So, the Union men give up the notion."

Belle breathed again, and remembered she was supposed to be teaching. She said to Springpole, silent for the moment: "While you are here, we'd be glad to have you in school. I could loan you a slate or whatever you need."

"That would please Granma, that is if you're willen to have me part a the time. I'm spenden the winter with Granpa an Granma Detty, but I cain't allus git here on time. Like this mornen, Uncle Hoss didn't come home last night, an granma was so scared he was down drunk someplace, she sent Uncle Sweetfern to hunt him.—I reckon Uncle Sweetfern was sober enough.—Anyhow, I had to help with the barn work an help her with the cow an calf when she was milken, an fetch water and cookwood like I allus do."

"You come when you can, that will be all right." Belle tried to put a heartiness into her voice she didn't feel. She didn't want anybody, not even a child, talking of drunks and "drunkedness" around her children. Sissie, if around Springpole for even a few sessions of school, would start using his grammarless grammar and outlandish words. She couldn't revoke her invitation. Robert was inviting Springpole to come sit at the table with him and Dave.

She put a slate and slate pencil on the table, opened the PENMANSHIP GUIDE Sissie used, and told Springpole to write his real name at the top of the page, then copy the first two lines five times.

Springpole objected. "I'll have to use the name everybody knows me by. The name Pop give me when I was a baby is so awful I never let anybody know it so they won't laugh their head off an give me awful nicknames."

"You think we're all heathens to go laughen at a Bible name?" Sissie shrilled, angry. "I just know one a your names, Ananias. You ought to be ashamed to be afraid to use a good Bible name."

"It's a Bible name, but not a good one. You ought to know that Ananias give up the ghost because he lied to the Holy Ghost, an you're the one ought to be ashamed tellen a secret. I'll bet one a my sisters told you. She'll be about as bad off as the wife of Ananias when I git to her. Now, all the boys will be callen me *Annie*."

"It wasn't your sister told me. Anyhow, all the girls know part of your real name."

Springpole snorted. "Last year in that school was the meanest bunch of girls a body could find this side of hell. I'll bet you all talked about us while you was eating our roast pig last fall an the woods got—."

Dave spoke sharply with unusual loudness: "Boy, you're forgetten we're in school."

Belle, in spite of her curiosity about roast pig and what had happened in the woods was still more puzzled by Dave's sudden concern for good behaviour. She asked no questions; she had long since learned the one way to learn nothing of what the children considered their business was to question them. She now reminded the talkers they couldn't learn anything while talking and announced time for arithmetic.

She told Springpole that since she had given him no problems for today, he could write the multiplication tables through the sixes, sevens, eights and nines on the other side of his slate.

She next looked over the arithmetic side of Zion's slate, and soon realized the problems in multiplication and division she had given him were below his ability. She wrote a big 100, told him to erase his slate to be ready for the hard problem she would give him. Slate erased, she told him: "Write the size of a corn crib twenty feet long, ten feet wide, and ten feet high. The crib is filled with corn. How many gallons of whiskey will the crib full of corn make?"

He stared at nothing for a moment, then said: "That crib holds two thousand cubic feet. That makes 1600 bushels. Ma'am, do you want 100 proof whiskey?"

Belle nodded, ashamed she had forgotten to specify the proof.

Zion stared at nothing again before he looked at Belle and said: "Pop figures a bushel of corn with the right amount of malt makes about two and a quarter gallons of 100 proof whiskey so you'd have 3600 gallons out a that crib a corn."

She praised him for solving the problem, and in his head at that. She suggested he come to school regularly until his arm was healed and after that when he could be spared from work; when he left this morning he should take a slate and copy book so he could practice penmanship out of school.

He promised to work "real hard" on his writing, and he needed more help in arithmetic because "I don't know a thing about fractions."

Belle told him they'd study fractions tomorrow but did not tell him the problem he had just solved was filled with fractions. He was scared by the word without knowing what it meant.

She next asked Springpole to show her his slate work. He hesitated. "They's not much on it. I don't know the multiplication table."

No wonder Springpole hadn't wanted to show his slate; where a part of the multiplication tables should have been was a fair likeness of Old Pop; there were mostly legible copies of the sentence she had given him, but letters and words were missing. She asked Springpole to read what he had written.

He shook his head. "Readen writen is beyond me, an I don't know how to multiply high up."

Belle pointed to a letter as she asked him to name it.

"I cain't read my letters, but I can name them." He gave a quick recital of the alphabet.

She felt a rising anger at the world that let this child grow up unable to read or write or do the simplest of arithmetic. Why hadn't his parents and grandparents taught him at least his letters? She left the drawing of Old

Pop, erased the other side of the slate, and wrote the first six letters of the alphabet. She asked Springpole to repeat after her the names of the six letters. They named them together three times before Belle told him to copy the letters four times.

Belle glanced at the clock on the wall. Time was at a stand-still; close to three hours before she could go warn the men without arousing suspicion. School had to continue for another hour and a half, then she'd have to eat dinner, at least go through the motions, and after that she couldn't go rushing off.

"Mom, it's time for mine and Robert's recess." Sissie had also looked at the clock.

Belle had forgotten the break she gave the younger children. She nodded to Sissie, and asked Springpole if he wouldn't like to take a break from school.

"No'me, I'll stay an work on my letters. You've got a good school, not bad like some I've heared about. You know a batch a my cousins that lives close to the county town went to a school taught by a Yankee. He was an *ing*ing man, an he tried to make his scholars *ing* everything they said. Even outside when they was playen some runnen game like antiover, if that teacher heared one say 'runnen' or 'ketchen,' he'd tell them to say the word over agin with an *ing*. Aunt Sarie said that if God had meant for her children to use *ings*, he would have put it into their mouths. So she took em out of school."

Belle told him she taught grammar, but he was not to worry about *ings*. She thought of her troubled worries over *ings* during the first weeks in the Philadelphia school to which her father had sent her where she was a lonesome stranger in a foreign country with a queer language. However, she soon met other girls whose language she could understand, though two from the Deep South talked as if the letter *r* was not in the alphabet.

It was a girl from Georgia who made her feel the world around her was wrong and she was right. The Georgia girl wept often during the first few weeks and berated her parents for sending her to "a damn Yankee school." Her father would not let her attend the school she wanted; according to his angry daughter, he contended the school she wanted taught nothing but dancing, fancy sewing, and how to catch a husband. "An what's wrong with that?" the girl asked. "That's all I want or need to know, so what's the good of tryen to learn French, an I know my head wasn't made for that awful stuff they call algebra."

Belle did the algebra and French lessons for the girl, told her she was certain she'd find other girls from the South, and that during the winter months there were school dances to which a whole boys' academy came. She had—.

"Mom, here's that extra problem you give, gave me, said it might be too hard for me. Well, I got it."

Belle stared at the slate trying to remember the problem.

Dave's talk made it clear. "That problem cost me a lot of sleep an you two candles. About the hardest part was finden the size of the barn roof when all I had to go by was the length and width of the barn, and the height of the haymow at its highest part. That meant I had to take the width of the barn, square it, then square the height of the haymow, add em together and extract the square root; that was about as much trouble as layen on the shingles, but after I remembered the eaves, I came out with the number you said was correct."

Belle returned the slate. "I'm proud of you, Dave. You had to think to work that problem."

"It was a lot of trouble, but maybe someday I'll have to figure the shingles I'll need for a new barn a my own."

Springpole broke his long silence with a windy sigh. "Law, I wish I could do that kind a reckonin. You'd learn a lot more in this school, but wouldn't have so much fun as we had last year, like one a the boys slippen a handful a bombshell acorns into the hottest part a the fire. They'd soon pop loud as pistol shots, scare the girls to death, and scatter ashes all over."

Dave spoke with a piousness unusual for him. "School is for work, not fun."

"Law, Dave, a scholar ought to be able to have a little a both. I know you liked them good fox-an-hound runs that kept us out till dark sometime." Springpole explained to Belle: "Dave here an little Johnnie Wolfkill brung old newspapers frum home, an duren school we'd tear them up into little bitty pieces to use for scent. At dinnertime we'd cram down our grub in a hurry, and the first to finish an leave was the fox with his dinner bucket crammed full a scent. Dave was generally the fox because he was the fastest runner.

"An he sure led us on some races. He dropped plenty a scent, but he'd double back an run in creek water till we'd be forever unravelin his sign. Once, he led us clean down to Cumberland River droppen plenty a scent. An there by the river, we seen our little pieces a paper runnen down on that swift yaller water, too high an swift fer even Dave to swim. Some a the little youngens, they was wore out already in their wind an legs, began cryen, sayen Dave was dead and drownded.

"Robert, little as he was, didn't cry. He said his brother had too much sense to drown in Cumberland River. He'd dropped that scent somewhere upriver where he could find a outleanen sycamore to climb an drop scent from it. Well, it was comen on dark an the river fog was beginnen to rise, but we started upriver. We finally found scent, but no Dave. I was gitten afraid myself that he was drownded, and I didn't want to leave him dead there in the river. The little youngens was carryen on somethin awful, an some a the bigger boys was sayen we ought to turn back when I reckon Dave took pity on us. He called out to us from away up on a sycamore limb that hung over the river; if we'd looked up stead a down an out, we'd a seen him. It was hard to go back to the schoolhouse back packen them little youngens, but Dave helped.—I reckon we was lucky in a way; Dave wasn't drownded, luckier than when the girls et all our roast pig. That was a time."

"Springpole, why don't you go for recess with the others. Mom's not interested in such tales. Anyhow, you swore with the rest of us that you'd tell nobody." Dave's voice was more beseeching than commanding.

Belle's sympathy for Dave's distress struggled with her curiosity; a mother ought to know what went on in school, especially when her children gave evidence of having learned nothing. Springpole aroused her curiosity still more when he said:

"Better for me to tell a straight tale than have people believe the lies some a the girls told. Why, they claimed that roasted pig was stole; it was not. Nobody owned it. There was no kind a mark on it."

The schoolboys had argued over who among them was the best pistol shot. The only way to settle that was to have a shooting match, so Dave and another boy had turn by turn chosen all the other boys, and agreed that whichever side lost the match would catch and roast a pig for the other side to eat.

Next day, during noon recess, the boys had gone a long way into the woods, where their teacher, Old Baldy, couldn't hear them, to hold their shooting match with pistols they'd sneaked out from home. Dave's side won. Springpole and the boys on his side had to catch, kill, and roast a fair-sized pig that didn't have the owner's mark. They'd caught the pig the next day at noon recess and tied it up to wait till early next morning. They didn't have anything to scald it in, but somebody said it would be all right to shave it real close, and as many boys as could must sneak out razors. Next morning after the pig was killed, gutted and washed, the razors with some shaving soap did a real good job.

The sight and sound of Barstow roaring about the dullness of his razor one morning last fall came back to Belle. He'd declared the razor had been in great shape two days before, and continued to fume and quarrel when he had to stop trying to shave and strop his razor.

She glanced at Dave. Shoulders bowed over an open book, he was pretending to study. She could see nothing of his face except his sweat-beaded forehead. The room wasn't that hot, but Dave was. Maybe she should hush Springpole. She'd never heard of a child having been struck with apoplexy. Apoplexy or not, the boy was suffering for his sins, almost too much. She glanced at the clock; too early to send him to get Dixie and put her in the stable, give her a light feed of oats so that Belle could ride her to that far field as soon after dinner as she could sneak away. The poor boy would suffer more with uneasy wonderings on the rest of Springpole's tale if she told him to leave the room.

Springpole was still going strong, now nearing noon of the day for the roasted pig feast. Belle had lost part of the story, but learned through chance remarks that early, before school, boys on the losing side had dug a shallow pit, lined it with rocks and while others were cleaning the pig, they built a big fire in the pit to "heat it up." Pig ready, they had raked most of the fire out of the pit, put the pig in, covered it with rocks and earth, and built a great fire on top which, during recess, they had made even bigger.

Now, it was noon. The winners were not feasting on roast pig and the bread, pickles, and other fare they had sneaked out of cupboards. Winners and losers alike were fighting fire in the woods: "In Great-Granpa Detty's scrub timber, dry as a powder horn, an chock-full a sawbriers, dead leaves and other dry stuff that carried the flames like lightnin. We all fit that fire till we was ready to fall down an die. I don't reckon we ever would a got it out, if Uncle Sweetfern an Uncle Hoss hadn't come to help us. Nobody had a bite to eat an we was starving. Dave figured there'd be enough roast pig for the losers, too."

Fire out, the tired, hungry boys went to their expected feast. Instead of juicy roast pig, they found the girls giving the skin and bones they'd picked clean to the Detty dogs that had followed Springpole to school. Worst of all: "Them mean girls told us they'd tell we'd stole an cooked a fine pig so we'd all git a razor-strop thrashen at home, if we so much as pulled one hair on one girl's head or even bawled them out.

"Mostly it was Old Baldy's fault they got the pig. When he seen the smoke bilen up he told us boys to come with him an fight fire. He told the girls to stay away from the flames for fear their dresstails might ketch fire. He sent them to look over places to see if the fire was out. It had started from our pig-roasten fire; they must a smelled—."

Old Pop gave his company-is-here bark and ran to the hall door. Belle heard the sound of strange feet in the hall. Dave went to open the door. Springpole's eyes looked big as teacups as he whispered: "Oh, Lord, Miss Belle, the Union men have come to jail you."

Robert and Sissie, proud as peacocks, appeared in the doorway, each holding a hand of Deputy Sheriff Ramsey. They looked unusually small beside the tall, broad-shouldered deputy. Belle smiled at him as she would have smiled at any other family friend, told him she was glad to see him. She wondered if she were hiding her fear that he was on the hunt of three Confederates. He appeared to be in bad humor but wasn't wearing his pistols.

Dave brought over the largest chair in the room. Ramsey thanked him, then said to Belle: "Nothen would do Miss Betsy [Ramsey's wife] until I agreed to come down here an see if you are all right. Did the Union men hunters rough up your house, act mean, or cause you any kind a trouble? I heard they were comen here."

"Nobody here saw any Union men." Belle hoped nobody noticed the chokes in her voice.

"Why, they could have been here an nobody saw them. Recollect everybody was gone for a long time before supper." Dave, after a moment's thought, added: "But they, an nobody else, could hunt through somebody's home without first showen the owner their search warrant. That right, Mr. Ramsey?"

"That's pretty much what I told them after they walked in on Miss Betsy, scared her half to death. I told them the law let me or any other deputy or sheriff go into a home without a search warrant only when he was followen the trail of a suspected criminal with bloodhounds that led him, or me—I've done it—into somebody's home. And since I had neither seen nor heard their bloodhounds, show me their search warrant. They told me they were goen by martial law and didn't need a search warrant for any-body's home."

"An I reckon they hunted all through your house?"

Ramsey's face grew redder than his hair before he answered Dave. "No. I told them there was no need to search my house. As a peace officer my job was to apprehend any criminal or suspected criminal in my district. They left, but they had the gall to tell me, after describing them, that I could never take the red-headed one alive. So, if I come on them, bush-whack em all. Talk about the devil. I sleep better with the old gunshot wounds I've got and the bullet in me than I would with no bullet, no wounds but thinken on men I'd shot in the back; men an boys that died never knowen who killed them."

Springpole's eyes were uncommonly big as he said to Belle: "You don't know who was in your house while you was gone. That murderen man and his gang could a been here while you all was gone."

"So far as I know, the Union men haven't been able to murder any-body—yet," Ramsey told Springpole.

"I mean the Confederate that shot the high sheriff dead."

Deputy Ramsey's voice was unusually gruff as he asked: "Boy, suppose a man with a revolver in either hand come kicken open your front door, yellen your name, then fired two shots at you when you stepped into the back end of the hall, an a ball barely missed your wife. What would you do? Stand there and be shot?"

"Law, I heared the Union man killed the murderer's—I mean the rebel's wife. But it's a awful thing to kill a high sheriff when he's—."

Victoria came to the doorway. She was silent as she looked around the room for a place to put the tray she carried.

Dave took the bench from in front of the old parlor organ and set it by Ramsey's chair. Belle glanced at the tray: cup and saucer, spoons, napkin, cream and sugar, a plate of beaten biscuit and cheese, another of half-moon, dried apple pies, an empty water glass, and pitcher of water, another of whiskey.

Tray near Ramsey's right hand, Victoria said: "It's such dryen-out weather, I thought you might like somethen to drink an a bite to hold you till dinner."

Deputy Ramsey seemed pleased as he thanked her for the fare.

Victoria spoke in anger instead of pleasure. "You're more than welcome. I'm mighty glad to see you, Mr. Ramsey. Zion, when he came to tell me you'd come, said you'd been talken a mean men loose around here. Well, none of us has been murdered, but sneak thieves have been around the springhouse an my kitchen. I didn't tell Miss Belle, not wanten to worry her."

Victoria gone, Belle looked at Ramsey as he said: "Miss Belle, I don't think you'll have any more trouble with sneak thieves. If you do, I'll bring bloodhounds." He was pouring whiskey into the water glass, stopped when the glass was about half filled, considered a moment before pouring whiskey until the glass was better than two-thirds full. He sipped as he listened to Springpole.

"Don't worry, Miss Belle. It's awful to think how close you all was to them murderen rebels, but them Union men will git em, I know they'll git em fore they leave this part a the country."

Deputy Ramsey finished another long sip. "Springpole, I know you'll be disappointed, but the Union men have started home. They've decided the men they're hunten have never been in this part a the country."

Springpole's mouth fell open. "But, that man come to granpa's place to tell where he'd seen the murderer."

Whiskey glass half empty, the deputy, eating a pie, took his time answering: "From what I heard, he hadn't seen the men and horses; he told the men-hunters somebody had told him they'd been seen. The Union men are gone and to my mind the Confederate sympathizers were never in the neighborhood."

Belle had swallowed her guilt and no longer quailed at the thought of bloodhounds on her trail. She wanted to sing, dance, do anything but sit still. The three Confederates were safe in the place she'd led them to in Dead Man's Cave.

Notes

INTRODUCTION

1. Thomas A. Gullason, "The 'Lesser' Renaissance: The American Short Story in the 1920s," in *The American Short Story, 1900–1945: A Critical History,* ed. Philip Stevick (Boston: Twayne Publishers, 1984), 72.

2. Harriette Simpson Arnow, interview by John Douglass, 5 October 1982, for the Kentucky Writers Oral History Project.

3. Ibid.

4. Harriette Arnow, *What Berea Meant to Me* (circa 1952), 2.

5. Cora Lucas, "'A Dream . . . That's What I Came out For': A Recollection and Appreciation of Harriette Arnow," *Adena: A Journal of the History and Culture of the Ohio Valley* 1, no. 2 (Fall 1976): 128–29.

6. *Harriette Simpson Arnow,* videocassette directed by Herb E. Smith (Whitesburg, Ky.: Appalshop, 1987).

7. Nancy Carol Joyner, "Harriette Simpson Arnow," *Appalachian Journal* 14, no. 1 (Fall 1986): 53.

8. James G. Watson, "The American Short Story: 1930–1945," in *The American Short Story, 1900–1945. A Critical History,* ed. Philip Stevick (Boston: Twayne Publishers, 1984), 103–4.

9. Harriette Simpson Arnow to Harold Strauss, February 1938, Arnow Special Collection, Margaret I. King Library, University of Kentucky, Lexington.

10. Barbara L. Baer, "Harriette Arnow's Chronicles of Destruction," *The Nation* (January 1976): 117–20.

11. Watson, "American Short Story," 104.

12. Ibid., 109.

13. Ibid.

14. Ibid., 107.

15. Glenda Hobbs, "Starting Out in the Thirties: Harriette Arnow's Literary Genesis," in *Literature at the Barricades: The American Writer in the 1930s*, ed. Ralph F. Bogardus and Fred Hobson (Tuscaloosa: University of Alabama Press, 1982), 147.

16. David Bernstein to Harriette Simpson, 8 October 1935, Arnow Special Collection, Margaret I. King Library, University of Kentucky, Lexington.

17. Ibid.

18. Cleanth Brooks, letter to Harriette Simpson, 5 December 1935, Arnow Special Collection, Margaret I. King Library, University of Kentucky, Lexington.

19. It was reprinted in at least four anthologies: Cleanth Brooks, John Purser, and Robert Penn Warren's *Approaches to Literature* (1939, 1952); Brooks and Warren's *Anthology of Stories from the Southern Review* (1935); Albert Stewart's *Kentucky Writing: No. 4. Deep Summer* (1963); and Robert J. Higgs, Ambrose Manning, and Jim Wayne Miller's *Appalachia Inside Out* (1995).

20. Alex Kotlowitz, "At 75, Full Speed Ahead," *Detroit Free Press*, 4 December 1983, 24.

21. Hobbs, "Starting Out," 149.

22. John Flynn, "A Journey with Harriette Simpson Arnow," *Michigan Quarterly Review* 29, no. 2 (Spring 1990): 257–58.

23. Mary Rohrberger, "The Question of Regionalism: Limitation and Transcendence," in *The American Short Story, 1900–1945: A Critical History*, ed. Philip Stevick (Boston: Twayne Publishers, 1984), 148.

24. Quoted in Gullason, "The 'Lesser' Renaissance," 100.

25. Ray B. West, *The Short Story in America, 1900–1950* (Freeport, N.Y.: Books for Libraries Press, 1968), 116.

26. Haeja K. Chung, "Fictional Characters Come to Life: An Interview," in *Harriette Simpson Arnow: Critical Essays on Her Work* (East Lansing: Michigan State University Press, 1995), 280.

27. Watson, "American Short Story," 129.

28. Ibid., 126.

29. An unpublished typescript of "The Lamb Money" has "Chapter I" penciled on the first page. The story begins, "Nunnley Ballou rolled his quid of tobacco from one thin cheek to the other and read slowly, following each

word with a knotty brown finger, the printing on the can of dog food in his hand." Except for the spelling of Nunnely Ballew's name in the novel, the sentence exactly reproduces the opening of *Hunter's Horn.* The story is not reprinted in this collection because it so nearly matches the novel's first chapter.

"King Devil's Bargain" is a shorter version of Chapter Three of *Hunter's Horn,* which omits the opening paragraphs and the ending pages that appear in the novel.

30. Haeja K. Chung, "The Harbinger: Harriette Simpson Arnow's Short Fiction," in *Harriette Simpson Arnow: Critical Essays on Her Work* (East Lansing: Michigan State University Press, 1995), 101.

31. Harriette Arnow, "No Time for Fame," *Writer's Digest* 25, no. 2 (January 1945): 19.

WINKY CREEK'S NEW SONG

1. Arnow explains in *Old Burnside* that her first story was about a grand writing desk, full of cubbyholes, that could talk about what they held.

MARIGOLDS AND MULES

1. The published story reads, "Not one."
2. The published manuscript uses the present tense: "I look a long time."
3. "Aways" in published manuscript.
4. The published story uses "flash" for "flesh."

A MESS OF PORK

1. Arnow occasionally writes "post office" as one word.

KETCHUP-MAKING SATURDAY

1. Arnow also created characters named High Pockets and Delphine for her novel *Between the Flowers.*
2. Ketchup, unlike the popular red store-bought varieties, is a relish made from green tomatoes, onions, peppers, and other finely chopped vegetables and spices.

NO LADY

1. Her dark hair shone with red highlights.

BLESSED — BLESSED

1. The scripture verse is from the Beatitudes, Matthew 5:3–12.
2. A knitting term.

FRA LIPPI AND ME

1. In the orginal manuscript, Arnow often used dashes (—) instead of ellipses (. . .), though the ellipses in this story as it appeared in the *Georgia Review* clarify meaning, so we have retained them in this reprint.

FAILURE

1. A variety of grass.

SUGAR TREE HOLLER

1. Having savings during the Depression could make a worker ineligible for federal employment.
2. Civil Conservation Corps.

KING DEVIL'S BARGAIN

1. Arnow often omitted hyphens in compound adjectives such as this one; hyphens have been added to make reading easier.
2. Allowed.
3. Arnow placed the word "asked" at the end of the sentence.
4. Allowed, claimed, believed.

THE HUNTER

1. Arnow's working title for *Hunter's Horn* was "End of the Gravel," a reference to the setting of the rural Kentucky community of Little Smokey Creek which lay beyond the reach of state-maintained gravelled roads.

THE UN-AMERICAN ACTIVITIES OF MISS PRINK

1. Ellipses with four periods (. . . .) indicate where we have omitted words from Arnow's story because she left a blank space or an illegible phrase. We have used three periods (. . .) to indicate the ellipses Arnow herself placed in this story.
2. The American pioneer route through the Shenandoah Valley of Virginia to Fort Watauga in East Tennessee. Following the route of buffalo and Native

Americans, Daniel Boone blazed the trail, extending it through the Cumberland Gap. After the American Revolution, it became the primary route for westward migration.

3. A drink like coffee. In the manuscript, (Sanka) appears after Postum, apparently a reminder that she might want to substitute a more recognizable beverage, though she used Postum throughout the story.

LOVE?

1. Dollop.

INTERRUPTIONS TO SCHOOL AT HOME

1. Belle's sixteen-year-old son William plans to join the Confederate cavalry.
2. In the chapter preceding this excerpt, Belle has helped three Confederate soldiers to hide in a cave on her property.
3. Zion is the youngest son of Victoria, a slave whose mother had been part of Belle's mother's dowry. Throughout the manuscript, Belle refers to slaves as "the help."

Works Cited

Arnow, Harriette Simpson, interview by John Douglass, 5 October 1982. Kentucky Writers Oral History Project, Ann Arbor, Michigan.

———. Letter to Harold Strauss, February 1938. Arnow Special Collection, Margaret I. King Library, University of Kentucky, Lexington.

———. "No Time for Fame." *Writer's Digest* 25, no. 2 (January 1945): 11–19.

———. *Old Burnside.* Lexington: University Press of Kentucky, 1976.

———. "Some Musings on the Nature of History." Clarence M. Burton Memorial Lecture. Kalamazoo: Historical Society of Michigan Publications, 1968.

———. *What Berea Meant to Me* (circa 1952).

Baer, Barbara L. "Harriette Arnow's Chronicles of Destruction." *The Nation* (January 1976): 117–20.

Bernstein, David. Letter to Harriette Simpson, 8 October 1935. Arnow Special Collection, Margaret I. King Library, University of Kentucky, Lexington.

Brooks, Cleanth. Letter to Harriette Simpson, 5 December 1935. Arnow Special Collection, Margaret I. King Library, University of Kentucky, Lexington.

Chung, Haeja K. "Fictional Characters Come to Life: An Interview." In *Harriette Simpson Arnow: Critical Essays on Her Work.* East Lansing: Michigan State University Press, 1995, 263–80.

———. "The Harbinger: Harriette Simpson Arnow's Short Fiction." In *Harriette Simpson Arnow: Critical Essays on Her Work.* East Lansing: Michigan State University Press, 1995, 101–15.

Flynn, John. "A Journey with Harriette Simpson Arnow." *Michigan Quarterly Review* 29, no. 2 (Spring 1990): 241–60.

Gullason, Thomas A. "The 'Lesser' Renaissance: The American Short Story in the 1920s." In *The American Short Story, 1900–1945: A Critical History*, ed. Philip Stevick. Boston: Twayne Publishers, 1984, 71–102.

Harriette Simpson Arnow. Videocassette, directed by Herb E. Smith. Whitesburg, Ky.: Appalshop, 1987.

Hobbs, Glenda. "Starting Out in the Thirties: Harriette Arnow's Literary Genesis." In *Literature at the Barricades: The American Writer in the 1930's*, eds. Ralph F. Bogardus and Fred Hobson. Tuscaloosa: University of Alabama Press, 1982, 44–61.

Joyner, Nancy Carol. "Harriette Simpson Arnow." *Appalachian Journal* 14, no. 1 (Fall 1986): 52–55.

Kotlowitz, Alex. "At 75, Full Speed Ahead." *Detroit Free Press*, 4 December 1983, 14–15, 18, 22, 26, 28.

Lucas, Cora. "'A Dream . . . That's What I Came out For': A Recollection and Appreciation of Harriette Arnow." *Adena: A Journal of the History and Culture of the Ohio Valley* 1, no. 2 (Fall 1976): 126-36.

Miller, Danny. "A MELUS Interview: Harriette Arnow." *MELUS [Multi-Ethnic Literature of the United States]* 9, no. 2 (Summer 1982): 83–97.

———. "Harriette and Harold Arnow in Cincinnati: 1934–1939." In *Harriette Simpson Arnow: Critical Essays on Her Work*, ed. Haeja K. Chung. East Lansing: Michigan State University Press, 1995, 33–43.

Rohrberger, Mary. "The Question of Regionalism: Limitation and Transcendence." In *The American Short Story, 1900–1945: A Critical History*, ed. Philip Stevick. Boston: Twayne, 1984, 147–82.

Watson, James G. "The American Short Story: 1930–1945." In *The American Short Story, 1900–1945: A Critical History*, ed. Philip Stevick. Boston: Twayne, 1984, 103–46.

West, Ray B. *The Short Story in America, 1900–1950.* Freeport, N.Y.: Books for Libraries Press, 1968.

Acknowledgments

WE THANK MARCELLA J. ARNOW AND THOMAS L. ARNOW for their permission to create a collection of their mother's short stories and the MSU Press for its continued commitment to scholarship on Harriette Arnow. We especially appreciate the editorial contributions made by the acquisition editor, Martha Bates, at the Press.

This collection of Arnow's short stories also owes much to the Appalachian Center in Berea College, which provided a fellowship for Haeja K. Chung to travel to Kentucky to conduct research and photocopy Arnow's stories; to the Margaret I. King Special Collection at the University of Kentucky Libraries in Lexington; to the Appalachian College Association Mellon Faculty/Student Fellowship that supported Sandra L. Ballard's research; to the Carson-Newman College English Department students and staff, Angela Ellis Roberts, Amy Hartman, and Kara Pack, who patiently typed the stories; and to Appalachian State University students Katherine Duffala Vinesett, Erin Casto, and Aaron Davis, who assisted with the proofreading.

Michigan State University Press is committed to preserving ancient forests and natural resources. We have elected to print this title on New Leaf EcoBook 100, which is 100% recycled (100% post-consumer waste) and processed chlorine free. As a result of our paper choice, Michigan State University Press has saved the following natural resources*:

19	Trees (40 feet in height)
7,942	Gallons of Water
3,194	Kilowatt-hours of Electricity
875	Pounds of Solid Waste
1,720	Pounds of Greenhouse Gases

Both Michigan State University Press and our printer, Thompson-Shore, Inc., are members of the Green Press Initiative—a nonprofit program dedicated to supporting book publishers, authors, and suppliers in maximizing their use of fiber that is not sourced from ancient or endangered forests. For more information about the Green Press Initiative and the use of recycled paper in book publishing, please visit *www.greenpressinitiative.org.*

*Environmental benefits were calculated based on research provided by Conservatree and Californians Against Waste.